THE BLACK MOUNTAIN PACK

THE COMPLETE DUET: SHIFT AND HOWL

LANA SKY

SHIFT

THE BLACK MOUNTAIN PACK BOOK 1

Shift

Shift By Lana Sky

Copyright © 2022 by Lana Sky
All rights reserved.

No part of this publication may be reproduced, distributed, or transmitted in any form or by any means, including photocopying, recording, or other electronic or mechanical methods, without the prior written permission of the author.

This is a work of fiction. Names, characters, businesses, places, events and incidents are either the products of the author's imagination or used in a fictitious manner. Any resemblance to actual persons, living or dead, or actual events is purely coincidental.

Cover Design and Interior Formatting by Charity Chimni
Editing by Charity Chimni

ACKNOWLEDGMENTS

Thanks so much to everyone who supported this draft along the way, including the many beta readers who provided encouragement! Please keep in mind that this story includes dark, graphic, and explicit content matter that may not be suitable for readers under the age of 18—or for readers who are uncomfortable with the following subject matter: age-gap relationships, explicit sex, mentions of abuse, and graphic depictions of violence.

1

*L*oren Connors faced the world beyond the battered screen door with the same hope she had every morning since moving in ten months ago. Was it too much to ask if today could be…

A little less shitty?

As always, the optimism didn't last. Seconds into her trek to the bus stop, a familiar dread ran down her spine, heralding a truth that seemed as inevitable as the rain promised by the purple clouds swirling above. Today would be just like the rest—another shitstorm she'd have to trudge through in a worn pair of sneakers.

The shoes were a sticking point, weighing on her mind with every step. Last night, she'd hoped to convince her father to buy new ones. A pair of boots, perhaps? It was the least he could do. Considering that she'd destroyed her sneakers performing the job that should have been his—delivering newspapers to their outlying part of town.

She planned to spring the request on him last night after dinner, when he was well into his second beer. Winter was approaching fast, and the bottoms of her *Kicks* were already reinforced with more duct tape than the original soles.

To be fair, the attempt almost succeeded. She cooked dinner like usual and even managed to stay out of his way afterward.

But then…

She got too close. Close enough for him to smell *it* on her—the intoxicating scent of fresh air and horses. Instantly, he knew she had been *there*.

Game over.

Instead of new shoes, that bit of disobedience earned her a blow to the chest that still ached beneath her sweater. Her sole consolation was that he didn't hit her in the face, where the resulting bruise would signal that all was not well within the crumbling walls of the Connors' household.

Devising excuses to explain the multiple injuries had become a game of sorts during the few months she lived with him. Today she'd need a reason to skip gym, where the thin T-shirt wouldn't be enough to disguise this newest injury.

Her period, maybe? Or had she used that excuse last week? Lost in thought, she didn't notice a hot pink sports car pulling up alongside her until one of the occupants called out.

"Hey, Connors." The driver, a beautiful blond by the name of Naomi, cackled maliciously. "Need a ride?"

Loren didn't bother replying. Like a turtle recoiling in its shell, she had her own tricks to avoid detection—keep walking and mentally count the steps remaining between her and the bus stop.

One. Two. Three.

"Naomi," a minion stage-whispered from the convertible's back seat. "You know she's like, *mute*."

Loren felt her lips quirk into a faint smile. As far as the student body at New Walsh Academy was concerned, she had spoken all of ten words since she'd moved there. Namely to teachers, and never without vigorous prompting on their part.

The rumored consensus was she was cripplingly shy, or a little "touched." Mute. The real explanation was a lot simpler. It was so much easier to live a lie in silence. There was a selfish motivation, too. If she *hadn't* clammed up all those years ago, the sound of her own screaming might have driven her insane. Still, she should have had enough sense to hide her emotions this time—her smile was too wide, and Naomi's green eyes cut to her maliciously.

"You think this is funny?" The tires of that expensive sports car squealed as Naomi slammed her foot on the brake. "I think I prefer your dumb blank stare to that shitty little smirk."

"Hey…" The second minion spoke up. "Naomi, I don't want to be late again—"

The blond shrugged off the protest. "Just a second."

With her head held high, she climbed from the driver's seat to block Loren's path.

"You think you're so much better than us, Connors?" she demanded, hands on her perfectly slender hips. "Ever since you moved here, you've been a stuck-up little bitch, walking around with your nose in the air. Hello? I'm talking to you—"

Loren barely heard her. She was too busy eyeing the girl's beautiful pair of faux-kidskin boots. Obviously, she didn't have to beg *her* father for new shoes.

"Hey!" A pair of manicured fingers appeared beneath her nose, snapping impatiently. "I'm talking to you, Connors. Do. You. Think you're better than us?"

Naomi gestured to her so-called friends, who all seemed like bleached-blond copies.

Loren shook her head and kept walking.

Five.

Six.

Seven—

"Not so fast."

A hand latched onto her forearm, wrenching her around. She staggered to find her balance, and a sharp pain lanced through the sole of her foot. *Oh no.* Some of the duct tape must have worn through.

Distracted, she missed the manicured hand swiping at her face. *Wham!* The blow dislodged her woolen cap, and her hair fell loose, tangling around her shoulders.

"Did you hear me?" Naomi demanded. "Or are you *deaf*, too?"

Blank, Loren scolded herself, fighting to smother her shock. *Be empty. Make your face a mask—that's it. Never let them in. Never let them see.*

Once she regained control of her breathing, she stooped for her hat. The second her fingers contacted the wool, the heel of a thigh-high white boot descended to crush them.

Loren gasped before she could reel it in.

Mistake, a part of her scolded. *Big mistake.*

"So, she *does* speak!" Naomi cackled with glee and snatched for her forearm next.

Dragged to her feet, Loren lost her grip on her bag, spilling books and materials over the sidewalk. "No! Don't!" she croaked, this time consciously.

Unbothered, Naomi stooped for her bag and rifled through it.

"Oh, what?" she taunted. "Don't want us to see what the little mouse is always hiding?"

She overturned the bag, dumping out the contents.

Loren winced as her homework scattered on the wind, but nothing tugged at her heart more than the plastic baggie full of carrots that landed in the street. Or the apple that dented against the damp ground.

"Is that her lunch?" Someone giggled from the car's back seat.

No. Most of the time, she went hungry, though some days Mona, the lunch lady, tossed her a banana from the lunch line if she looked pathetic enough.

The carrots, carefully rescued from the back of the fridge among the many cases of beer, had been a gift meant for the only friends she had. And Naomi gleefully stomped them into mush without a second thought.

"Guess you'll just have to go without, hun," a blond from the convertible suggested.

Don't cry, Loren told herself, blinking against that warning sting prickling the backs of her eyes. Still, her heart lurched as Naomi turned her attention to the discarded apple.

"Stop!" The plea broke loose, hoarse and broken. She raced forward, but Naomi kicked the apple out of her reach.

"Hold the bitch back," Naomi demanded, and, like well-trained dogs, her two minions scrambled from the back seat to do her bidding.

One snatched a chunk of Loren's hair and used it as a leash to keep her restrained, while the other kicked the fruit into the street.

"Aw, look," the culprit taunted. "She looks like she's going to cry."

Loren tried to keep the tears at bay but failed. Unbidden, they coated her cheeks in bursts of warmth. Sorrow wasn't the source —just guilt and rage. It had been so *hard* to scavenge those meager offerings. If her father knew that she had stolen the carrots, he'd…

Kill her.

"Aww, lighten up, Connors," Naomi urged cheerfully. "It's not like any guy will give you the time of day, even if you went on a diet."

They all laughed, but Loren flinched, subconsciously huddling tighter within the confines of her sweater. Attention from anyone was the last thing she wanted.

The only plus side to having little money to spend on clothes was that the few things she *did* own were nondescript and shapeless. The perfect armor to go unnoticed. The sweater she wore now was four sizes too big and hung to her knees, perfectly obscuring the pair of black leggings that had cost fifty cents at *Goodwill*.

"Ah, look, Naomi," the second minion remarked on a laugh. "She's blushing."

"Maybe she already has a boyfriend?" the girl clutching her hair wondered with a playful yank.

"As *if*," Naomi countered. "Who would date a freak like her? I wouldn't walk around so high and mighty if I came from a shithole like little Loren here. My dad knows the police chief from Ridgerton."

Loren flinched at the name. It was a town a few hours north, and the focal point of most of her nightmares.

"I heard them talking about a case that occurred under my father's friend's jurisdiction. A certain case involving a woman who killed herself one day, leaving her daughter to be shipped off to an uncle who lived in town. From the outside looking in, everything had appeared okay at first. Until neighbors started hearing the screaming at night—"

No. Fear gripped Loren's lungs, painfully squeezing out whatever air they contained. *No.* She *wouldn't* go back there. Not to that house, or that room—*God,* not that room. Not to the stifling scent of cheap cologne, or the darkness, and pain…

"Naomi…" Minion number one took a step back. "This isn't funny. Knock it off."

"Why?" the blond demanded. "I was just getting to the *best* part. Apparently, this Uncle *Bart*—"

"Stop!" The other minion was shouting now, disobeying the unspoken cardinal rule of being one of Naomi's "friends."

Like sheep, Loren thought around a hysterical snicker. Naomi liked her friends like a shepherd liked his sheep. But Uncle Bart hadn't liked it when she talked back, either.

He didn't like it at all.

"No," Naomi hissed.

Then she crouched before Loren so that they were nose to nose.

"They say a neighbor finally called a cop one night," she continued. "Apparently, the girl wouldn't speak. She just went to school one day and *stopped talking.* Clammed up. When they searched that house, the things they found there... Some on the force still talk about it to this day."

Loren knew damn well what they had found. A room. One so small it seemed more like a closet. In fact, it *was* a closet. Clothes had been kept there—sometimes, lying there at night, she could almost smell the mothballs.

Of course, what had caught everyone's attention had probably been the chains. Long, they had stretched from a man-made post drilled into the wall. The perfect length for her to use the bathroom at night whenever her cell happened to be unlocked.

"The conditions were so bad that they relocated the girl to a different city rather than find a foster family in Ridgerton. With a father who hadn't even wanted her in the first place." Naomi's voice was cold. Like the detached voice of a narrator on the evening news.

And the girl, whose name has not been released, was removed from the home. Rescued...

Only not really.

"*Still* think you're better than me, Connors?" Naomi snarled. "Still think that, huh?"

"Naomi! We're leaving," Minions one and two announced, backing away as swiftly as their nice shoes could carry them. "We can *walk* to school."

"Fine. Leave then," Naomi snapped. "But don't think this changes anything. You're *nothing,* Loren Connors."

But that was the whole point. She *was* nothing—hell, she strived to be nothing.

"But, hey," Naomi added with a cruel smile of mocking perfection. "Like mother like daughter—"

Snap!

It was something internal. Some intangible muscle right *there* in the pit of her stomach that cracked at the comparison. Like daughter, like…

Mother.

Her mother had been beautiful, happy, young, carefree—before life and sorrow beat her down. Loaded her with pain that she couldn't bear. Couldn't escape, except for one way out…

In the pit of her soul, Loren knew that she wasn't like her mother.

She wasn't brave.

She was weak. Too weak to fight. Too weak to die.

Until now.

Her vision went red. *Insanity,* Loren thought. She had just gone insane.

Lost her damn mind.

She once read in a book that one of the signs of schizophrenia was alternate perceptions of reality. You saw things that weren't there. Heard things…

But Loren doubted that description included launching yourself at your enemy with your hands drawn like claws.

And, she was pretty confident that when most people succumbed to schizophrenia, they didn't growl. They didn't bare their teeth like fangs and…snarl.

At least, for the first time in her life, as she raked her nails along the perfect skin of Naomi Tanner's face, the blood on her fingers wasn't her own.

2

L oren!

Loren Connors!

Someone was calling her name—though the ringing in her ears could be another symptom of insanity. She'd already hit the trifecta of potential red flags. Hearing voices. Losing control of her limbs. Feeling so much rage, she could *explode*.

For the first time in her life, Loren Connors didn't want to hide. She wanted to…

Kill. The impulse wasn't coherent—more like a writhing mass of urges, she felt all at once. A need to draw blood, attack…bite? Experimentally, she snapped at the air. Oh hell, yeah, she wanted to bite, but something firmer. Her teeth ached with a sudden need that had her glancing down, through a haze of red.

She wanted flesh…

"LOREN CONNORS!" The bellowed shout resonated like a gut punch.

As her vision cleared, several realizations confronted her at once. The foremost being that she was straddling Naomi Tanner. Not only that, but…

God, she had both hands around the girl's slender throat—so tightly Naomi's green eyes bulged from their sockets.

And blood splattered her chin. In tiny rivulets, it stemmed from three violet marks streaked across the side of Naomi's fashionably tanned cheek.

Oh no, Loren thought, horrified. *Did I do that?*

"Get the fuck off me!" Naomi lashed out. With the strength that came from years of training as the head cheerleader, the blond easily shoved her off. Not before giving her a kick to the stomach as a parting gift.

But, Loren was forced to realize that *she*—a girl with barely enough muscle on her wiry frame to fill a teaspoon—had knocked Naomi down in the first place.

And choked her.

Wide-eyed, Loren gaped at her own hands. They couldn't belong to her, not mousy Loren Connors. Someone else. *Something* else.

"Oh, I am so pressing charges, you stupid bitch!"

"That's enough, Ms. Tanner." The voice was too deep to belong to one of the minions. Or a woman. It was masculine, richer than any baritone she'd ever heard.

"Did you see what she fucking did? Well, aren't you going to *do* something?"

It was only then that Loren noticed the man nearby, standing behind the open door of a police squad car. He was tall, imposingly so, with stern features and piercing gray eyes. Eyes that bore into hers as he spoke a command solely directed her way.

"Get back." To her ears, it sounded like a stern suggestion, but inside her head…

It was an order.

Heart pounding, Loren scrambled backward until she sat fully in the mud, a good five feet from Naomi.

"God! She scratched me!" the blond shrieked, cupping the side of her face. "Should I go to the hospital? Get a damn rabies shot or something?"

"I'm sure you'll be fine, Ms. Tanner," the officer replied. Once again, his tone resonated with double-meaning. Less concerned and more…mocking? "Though, if you want, I can call ahead to the hospital to let them know you'll be coming in."

"Thanks," the blond muttered as she flashed Loren a glare that could melt steel. Then she entered her car and took off.

The officer waited until that pink vehicle finally turned the corner before returning his attention to Loren. Tense with anticipation, she braced for a scolding.

Care to explain? It was what her father said when she did something wrong. Before she could respond, he always followed up the question with a blow. A kick. A punch.

Instead, the officer inspected her with an intensity presumably reserved for only the most dangerous criminals. He started with her head, roving his gaze down her body, almost as if searching for something. *For any weakness,* a part of her suspected.

"You could be in a lot of trouble, Ms. Connors," he said finally. His voice was no less booming, reducing her to a cowering puddle. It wasn't only his tone causing such a reaction.

From her position on the ground, he seemed massive, undeniably handsome—but in her world, beauty meant danger.

He had a face that could have been chiseled from stone, with stern cheekbones, pink lips, and a smattering of black stubble along his jaw—a jaw currently set in a firm line.

"Especially if Naomi Tanner does decide to press those charges," he continued. "Her father is the head of the city council."

Loren felt her bottom lip tremble. Then, hot and fast, more tears spilled down her cheeks. All she could do was brace her blood-stained fingers against the muddy earth and try to keep her composure.

Sobbing would help nothing. Neither would begging, but both impulses were all she seemed capable of at the moment.

"I'm sorry," she rasped. "I'm so sorry. I didn't mean—I mean I…I didn't…I just." She was rambling. After years without carrying on a full conversation, even forming a coherent sentence took effort. "I'm sorry. I'm sorry. I'm sorry—"

"Here."

In the space of a second, the officer cleared the distance between them, holding her backpack by its filthy strap. He was trying to be helpful; she could tell that much. He had no idea that the sight of him, towering above, reminded her of someone else.

"I'm sorry!" She threw herself face-forward into the icy muck, hands over her head to ward off the blow she knew was coming. Instead of the threat of physical violence, the only sound she heard was…

Thunk. Peeking through a fringe of hair, she realized the noise was that of her math book being dropped into her bag by the officer. He did the same with her scattered pencils and notebook. Then he extended a calloused hand in her direction.

"Can you stand up?" Once again, what sounded like a harmless question resonated in her bones far differently.

Stand up. Her limbs lurched into motion before her brain processed the action. As she inspected herself from the neck down, she couldn't suppress a groan at the sight of her clothes. Her tights were caked in mud. So was the bottom of her sweater.

If she went to school like this, they'd send her home. Or worse, call her father. Either prospect was so terrifying she didn't hear the officer speak until he shouted.

"Loren, did you hear me?"

She jumped, too shaken to wonder just how he knew her name. Though…as she eyed the planes of that strong face, she realized that she knew *him.*

Officer McGoven. *That asshole McGoven,* according to her father. The very same officer who came by whenever he and his drinking buddies got too rowdy and alarmed the neighbors.

He had never seen *her,* of course. She would watch him through her bedroom window and wonder how one man could possess so much patience.

Never once did he raise his voice, even when her father and his cohorts would threaten violence. He seemed unshakable, someone worthy to carry a badge—a rare quality in her opinion.

From far away, she'd gotten a good idea of his bulk, but up close, he was downright intimidating. She'd never met anyone with eyes like his. They gleamed silver in contrast to his dark hair, which looked slicked back as if by a lazy hand. Tanned skin the exact shade of pure honey softened the effect somewhat, keeping him from seeming frightening. Just stern. She wondered at his heritage—Native American, mixed with a bit of European to explain the eye color?

It was the same guess she figured most people made whenever they looked at her, with her dark hair, pale skin, and wide hazel eyes.

"If you would like to get a change of clothes, I can give you a ride to school," he offered. "It looks like you missed the bus."

Oh no. Loren realized it must have passed by during the scuffle with Naomi, and her heart sank. His offer aside, walking was her only choice. She loathed deceiving an officer, but she rationalized it the way she always did—lying wasn't a sin if survival was on the line.

"I...I don't have any clean clothes," she told him. "And it's laundry day. I'll be fine on my own." As the words left her mouth, the man gave her an odd look that made her stomach flip. Like he knew she was lying. Regardless, for once in her life, she couldn't seem to shut up. "Our washing machine is broken, too. My father hasn't gone to the laundry mat yet. I'll be fine once I get to school—"

"You should wash up," he repeated. His voice was so strange, seeping into her brain and battling the logical part of her that resisted. *You should listen,* a part of her urged. *It's fine. Go with him...*

"F-forgot my key," she lied again.

He cocked his head. Then he returned to his patrol car, still holding her backpack hostage. "Get in. My place isn't far from here. You can wash up there, and I'll have you at school before the bell rings."

Loren tried to keep the panic from her voice—she was all out of lies. "R-Really, I'm fine."

"I insist." His tone left no room for argument. "Get in."

Like a puppet on a string, she lurched forward. Step by tortured step, she approached his vehicle.

"You can sit up front," McGoven suggested. Already, he had climbed into the driver's seat and leaned over to push the passenger-side door open.

Aware of her filthy appearance, Loren perched herself on the seat's very edge.

"Sorry," she whispered in anticipation of causing a stain on the spotless upholstery. "I…I can clean it."

Officer McGoven didn't say a word—but Loren didn't miss just how tightly he gripped the steering wheel.

He's going to turn you in, a part of her insisted. *They'll see the bruises. They'll call Youth Services.*

Or, no, they wouldn't. She was already eighteen, aged out of the system. If they thought that her father wasn't a fit guardian, they'd place her in a shelter. Or out on the street. Alone.

The thought spurred her to keep talking, desperate to find an excuse that would stick. Most people never tried this hard—her silence always scared them off.

"I'm fine, honestly. I don't know what happened. Please, I'll apologize to Naomi. I don't mind walking, either. It's not that far."

Officer McGoven said nothing, purely focused on driving.

In defeat, she stared fearfully from the window, bracing for the moment they would pull up to the police station. Instead, he abruptly turned down a dirt road that led into a swath of country surrounding the town like an insulating blanket.

He headed north, leaving the town proper, and Loren's pulse quickened. She knew these wide-open fields only a stone's throw from her father's backyard. She also knew the area was quiet and mostly deserted. A "no one around to hear you scream" type of wilderness. Warily, she eyed Officer McGoven with a different perspective.

What if he wasn't as honorable and upstanding a citizen as she thought?

"I can't let you go to school looking like that," he explained as if sensing her fear. His tone was sufficiently gentle, nothing like the coarse bellow he used before. "And I would be entertaining truancy if I allowed you to skip. Let me do my good deed for the day, just this once."

Is that all you want to do? Loren might have asked that if she were the brave, bold sort of person used to questioning police officers. Someone who might be terrified of the fate that could await her out in the middle of nowhere, with only the wind to snatch away her screams.

As it was, she just felt…

Tired. Dodging her father's fists took most of her energy these days. The threat of being murdered didn't even faze her anymore. At least she wouldn't have to go home and hide her soiled clothes.

It might have helped if he resembled the monsters she was used to. Dejectedly, she observed him more closely, convinced the honorable spiel was just an act. What secrets lurked behind those gray eyes?

Or, perhaps, in plain sight—he had a tattoo on his neck, barely visible from beneath a fringe of black hair and the collar of his jacket. Tendrils of indigo ink were all she could make out. A harmless design?

Or something nefarious?

The interior of his car didn't allude to any ulterior motives he might have. Every inch was spotless, devoid of even an air freshener as decoration.

She was so lost in her observations she barely noticed when the squad car came to a stop before a pale blue farmhouse.

A house she knew all too well.

"This…t-this is the old Baker farm," she croaked, bolting upright. The property was directly behind her father's house, past the woods and a shallow stream. All in all, a ten-minute walk with time to spare if she ran the whole way.

The white barn near the west field was where she spent the most time these days. Achingly aware of the loss of the apple and carrots, she felt her hands clench at the air.

Then a chilling thought took hold.

Why on earth would he bring her all the way out here?

3

*T*he sound of the driver-side door opening startled Loren so badly she jumped.

"You okay?" Officer McGoven asked. He already stood before her, his expression blank.

"Y-Yes," she croaked, unhooking her seatbelt.

"Come inside. You can get cleaned up, and then I'll drive you to school." He headed up the pathway leading toward the house. Helpless, Loren found herself scrambling out of the squad car after him.

"Y-You live here?" she asked in a small voice.

In this house, resting in the center of the old Baker farm—*her* paradise. She spent so much time in the barn just a few paces away, that it never occurred to her someone might own the property. Not just anyone, but an officer of the law. At least, now she knew why her father had always forbidden her from this place.

A creaking sound jarred Loren back to awareness. Officer McGoven had climbed the front steps of the house and eyed her from the porch while holding open a battered screen door.

"Come on."

She hesitated, wrestling with the building panic within her. The fact that he lived *here* of all places was an even bigger reason to avoid him. The smart thing to do would be to run and take her chances getting to school on foot.

Nothing was worth angering her father again—not with her new shoes on the line.

She even took a step toward the woods before the logical part of her brain kicked in. Sure, she could leave, but then *what?* Spend the rest of her life avoiding the police officer who just so happened to live in her backyard?

After all, he still had her backpack.

Left with no choice, she mounted the steps leading to a large wraparound porch that encircled the house on three sides. Genuine awe diminished some of her fear. She had always admired the sturdy, old-fashioned home. On her visits, she made sure to catch a glimpse of it from the barn at least once. It was the polar opposite of her father's dreary brown ranch-style house.

Up close, the old estate was far more impressive despite the peeling white paint and vines creeping as high as the upper stories. Would the interior look as decrepit and wild? Before the unease could steal her nerve, she gripped the handle of the front door and peered inside.

The second she glimpsed the foyer of the house, her guard dropped further. She had envisioned some plain furniture. Maybe a television and a beer-stained recliner, like the one her father owned.

Not a wide, open floor plan decorated in alternating shades of brown and emerald green. Both hues evoked the earthy, secluded feelings of the forest, and Loren could almost taste the scent of pine. Intrigued, she ventured deeper inside and found Officer McGovern in an open kitchen, rummaging through cupboards.

Past him was a spacious den, with a bookshelf along the far wall, stocked with countless leather volumes. The walls were a soothing shade of gray, and the wood floors gleamed beneath a fresh coating of wax. Ironically, there wasn't a TV in sight, though one could probably entertain themselves by gazing out at the view, showcased by a large bay window.

It was breathtaking. Jealously, she imagined McGoven sitting here with a cup of tea, gazing out fondly over the west fields, and the stream…

And the barn.

Her cheeks seared at the sight of it, clearly visible from this very spot. No wonder he knew her name. He probably sat here every day, watching her trespass onto his property.

Which brought up a bigger question? How did she miss the police cruiser parked around back? Though, to be fair, the front of the house faced east, and she had always snuck up directly behind the barn.

Not that the excuse would exactly matter once she was on trial facing criminal charges.

"The bathroom is straight back, down the hall." She flinched as Officer McGoven's voice came from the doorway. His tone wasn't angry, like someone gloating over her crimes against him might be. Merely impatient. "You don't want to be late. I promised to get you to school before the bell rings."

"O-Okay."

Off the living room was a hallway leading to a small bathroom. Closing the door behind her, Loren faced the mirror, steeling herself against what she might find.

A wild-haired, she-devil? Or perhaps the freak Naomi accused her of being?

Instead, a ghost watched her with mournful hazel eyes. Only a vibrant smear of blood gave the pale creature any definition against the white walls. Her chin was bleeding. Ironically, the injury was the only eye-catching thing about her. Lifeless brown hair tumbled down her shoulders, streaked with mud. Her sweater hung on her frame, making her resemble a child playing dress-up in their father's clothes.

Sighing, Loren hobbled to the sink and splashed some cool water onto her face, scrubbing away most of the blood. The motion brought attention to her fingers—the nails of which were encrusted in ruby-colored crud. With a shudder, she shoved her hands beneath the faucet and watched as reddish water circled the drain. Finished, she wet a paper towel and went to work on erasing as much of the mud from her sweater as she could. The tights were a total loss, soaked through.

Ten minutes later, she emerged, looking no less scrappy than before.

At least, Officer McGoven seemed to have found whatever he'd been looking for. Two sandwiches lay spread out before him. *Tuna,* Loren sensed with an appreciative sniff.

Not only that, but two shiny apples sat on the counter, complete with a stick of cheddar cheese. Hope swelled in her chest. It was more than she'd eaten last night. Hell, more than she ate most nights.

As if sensing the direction her thoughts had taken, McGoven cocked his head her way. "I take it that was *your* lunch smeared all over the sidewalk?"

Loren didn't know what to say.

"Here." To her immense shock, McGoven swept the food into a brown paper bag and offered it to her. "Is this enough to replace it?"

She nodded, too grateful to refuse. "T-thanks." Even as the word left her mouth, a sense of dread rushed to replace it.

These days, people rarely did anything without expecting something in return. *What would he want?* She snuck a glimpse of that unreadable face through a fringe of her hair.

There were only a few things someone like her could give him.

Suddenly, he frowned. "Wait—"

Loren nearly dropped the food as he opened a drawer. When he pulled out a knife, her heart sank.

Fearlessly, he brandished the blade and brought it down right over the middle of the second tuna sandwich. Taking one half for himself, he tossed the knife in the sink and nodded toward the remaining slice. "One for the road."

Loren stared at it for all of two seconds, before snatching the food as if afraid he might take it from her. Without hesitation, she crammed the entire thing into her mouth. She chewed so quickly the taste barely registered in her mind, but it was *good*—she knew that much.

And, she knew that he was watching her.

Rather than question, he quietly left the house.

Loren rushed after him, clutching the brown paper bag to her chest like a king's ransom of gold. Once again, Officer McGoven opened the car door for her, but he didn't speak.

She could have been invisible if it weren't for the fact that he silently cranked up the heat the second she began to shiver in her damp sweater. It was a cold, dreary day, even for fall, and the threat of rain seemed inevitable.

Loren just hoped that the storm held until she made it home. Tracking mud into the house was a surefire way to rile her father —if he wasn't already aware of the drama before school.

Luckily, the streets and plain buildings of New Walsh passed in a blur. Far too soon, she found herself staring at a sign reading New Walsh Academy.

As far as Loren was concerned, it could have read *hell on earth*.

To be fair, school itself wasn't all bad. She got decent grades, and there were a few subjects she liked—but the Naomi Tanners of the world excelled at spoiling even a glimmer of happiness. Ever since the day Loren dared to set foot inside New Walsh Academy, the blond had been there nipping at her heels with increasing viciousness. Judging from the mess this morning, it was only a matter of time before Naomi got her expelled.

Today might not have been that day, though—a certain pink car wasn't in the parking lot.

"Here we are, right on time," Officer McGoven remarked as he parked near the path leading to the front of the main building.

"T-Thank you," she whispered, gathering her belongings.

"I don't want to see you in this position again, Ms. Connors. If you don't mind me saying it. You recognize me, don't you?"

He angled his face her way, allowing the daylight to illuminate every sculpted plane. Her breath caught, her belly on fire with an emotion she couldn't name. The look in his eyes diminished the awe somewhat—he was disappointed.

"Yes," she admitted.

"I don't want to have the same relationship with you that I do with your father. Do you understand?"

Loren hung her head in shame. The double-meaning lurking within his tone was perfectly clear—*I don't want to see you in this position again…like him.*

"I understand." On that note, she gathered her things and scrambled out of the car. Protocol dictated she turn tail and run, but lingering gratitude made her look back. "T-Thank you," she stammered. "Thanks."

With a curt nod, McGoven leaned over to close the passenger-side door—but not before two last parting words slipped out to greet her. "Take care."

Loren watched him drive all the way to the end of the street, where he made a left and became lost in the bustle of traffic. The second he disappeared, she turned on her heel, skirted around the school building, and headed straight for the woods.

_____

$\mathcal{A}$ torrent of rain fell the moment she set foot beneath the trees, but the thrill of freedom displaced any fear she might feel. Nothing compared to this—the slick earth beneath her feet and the cooling rain on her skin. Every falling drop caressed her as if in welcome, urging her further from the hostile New Walsh Academy.

She didn't belong there, in sterile hallways and suffocating classrooms.

This was her true playground, the forest. It and the Baker farm were the only places she felt safe these days. The open spaces contained no bullies waiting to attack, and the twisted branches above had no mysteries to hide.

There was simply nature. Invitingly, forebodingly, terrifyingly _natural._ Rarely did the environment fall out of step with that beautiful, terrible rhythm, and Loren appreciated the monotony. Biology was one of her favorite subjects merely for its focus on this wilder part of the world and the creatures who inhabited it. One creature, in particular, drew her interest the most—_Canis_ *lupus.* Their social dynamics seemed so at odds with the moniker some attached to people like her. Lone wolves who shunned most interactions. Real wolves were fascinating predators, killing purely out of need, with the same instinctive desire, she possessed to breathe.

They didn't relish violence the way humans could.

Though, what's your excuse? a part of her sniped, conjuring the image of her straddling Naomi Tanner.

Loren shook her head to clear it as she ran even faster. She hadn't meant to hurt Naomi. Had she? Her fingers twitched as if to betray that hope.

She hadn't wanted to *hurt* Naomi. No, she wanted to destroy her.

Bite, scratch, tear. Make her suffer.

And you wonder why you don't have any friends, a part of her hissed. *You're a freak. Someone sick enough to fantasize about biting schoolyard bullies.* Though, if *anyone* deserved the brunt of her sudden viciousness, Naomi wasn't at the top of the list.

Her father might be.

Don't think about that. Loren pushed every thought from her mind, as the rain came down harder, soaking through her sweater. Thunder rumbled ominously in the distance as if warning her to take cover. In her peripheral vision, her father's house appeared and vanished.

When she finally came to a stop, chest heaving, she stood before a white barn, where the pungent stench of animals persisted despite the rain. Warily, she clutched her now soggy brown paper bag to her chest and hesitated. It was stupid to come here, especially now that she knew who owned it.

But…

Much like the wolves she studied, she couldn't forsake her duty to her pack. Even if said "pack" members weren't exactly her species. They loved her all the same, and a little food every now and again was the least she could give in return.

She saved the apple especially for Bunny—the old nag loved fresh fruit—and Esther would appreciate anything, even if it wasn't her beloved carrots. They were her friends. Or the closest things in the world she could apply the term to.

Therefore, trespassing on a police officer's private property was entirely worth the risk.

That didn't mean she wouldn't be careful, though. Cautiously, she peeked around the edge of the barn, toward the farmhouse, which seemed no less intimidating from far away. The driveway wasn't visible from here, but something told her that Officer McGoven had to be out on patrol, or whatever it was police officers did during the day.

Besides, she had taken a shortcut through the woods; he couldn't have gotten there so fast by car. Not with traffic to contend with. When he did return, she'd surely see him long before he saw her.

Five minutes, she told herself, as she entered the barn. As always, the main door was unlocked. Why hadn't that ever bothered her before?

She always assumed that someone came by to care for the horses, though the place seemed abandoned most days. There was a hole in the barn's far wall that had yet to be repaired, and this time of year, the drafty air seeped inside. Loren's teeth chattered, but her lips formed a rare smile as a triangular head appeared above the door to greet her with more compassion than she'd ever felt from a human.

"Hey, honey," she murmured, stroking the mare's gray muzzle. "I've got a treat for you, Bunny girl."

Bunny tossed her massive head as Loren presented one of the apples.

Nearby, on the wall above a line of saddle racks hung a set of tools that must have been used to repair the worn leather. From the selection, Loren took a knife and sliced the fruit into quarters, smiling as the others caught a whiff of the scent and demanded their treats with impatient nickers.

"I'll save some for you," she promised Esther as she gave two slivers of apple to Bunny. "You too," she called to Xavier, the quiet mustang in the corner stall who hadn't warmed up to her yet.

As the storm raged on outside, Loren lost herself in the busywork of giving everyone their fair share.

The horses were the one saving grace she discovered while living in New Walsh. In the early days after moving in with her father, she spent most of her time wandering the massive property behind his house.

The presence of so much empty land set New Walsh apart from the busier town of Ridgerton. It was quieter, too, with plenty of open space that invited exploration. One day, she strayed too far north and found a small white barn, where, just outside in the neighboring field, grazed three beautiful horses.

It didn't matter that Bunny, the old palomino, had a swayback and was far too brittle to be of much use. Or that Esther, the gentle mare with a glorious chestnut mane, had a long, jagged scar marring her left flank—animal attack, Loren assumed.

Xavier, with his ink-black coat and proud posture, was the only one of the three who truly seemed valuable. Too valuable, maybe, to spend his days cooped up in a small barn with two nags. But he was skittish. Loren could barely pet him, though he seemed to have no trouble snatching bits of apple from her hands.

Once the horses were fed, Loren curled up in the corner of the barn and waited for the rain to pass, telling herself that she'd make it home in time to intercept any call from the school about her absence. The storm was too dangerous to risk venturing out in, anyway. Heavy droplets of rain pattered off the roof of the barn like the frantic beating of a drum.

Winter's coming, she thought wistfully. *I wonder when it will start to snow?*

Would the barn finally be locked then? The prospect sent a pang through her chest. Winter was the time of predators, and there were stories of wild animals circling the outskirts of New Walsh. Primarily wolves, and the occasional bear. Other farmers in the area reported missing or injured animals every now again, and the morbid stories dominated the news.

But she had never heard of anything happening around the old Baker property. Looking back, she had been drawn to this place, despite plenty of other farms in the area—always creeping back to watch the animals graze, until she felt bold enough to view them up close.

Stupidly, she asked her father about the strange property so close to his—a question which earned her bruises that lasted for weeks after.

But it had been okay, a part of her reasoned with a cold sense of detachment; school hadn't started yet, so there had been no one to hide the injuries from. It was funny how her life had switched course. From *wanting* to be hidden to *having* to hide.

Even now. She didn't know how long she sat, listening to the drone of the rain play against the old wood. It could have been hours before her body felt too heavy—when the shelter of the barn and the soft murmurs of the animals lulled her into a drowsy state.

Her eyelids became heavy, drooping despite her best attempts to stay alert. It had been days since she'd slept through the night, and exhaustion tempted her to do the most dangerous thing she could in that moment.

She fell asleep.

5

Dangerous.

She's…dangerous…dangerous…

"She's dangerous—" The deep voice startled Loren awake.

Alarmed, she wrenched her eyes open, blinking against a harsh light. A wave of instinctive fear inspired her first coherent thought.

Was it morning already?

Her father would be angry if she didn't deliver the newspapers on time. Though, if she were lucky, last night's tally of beer might have left him too hungover to get out of bed. Though, she couldn't quite remember just how many beers he'd had. Or what she made for dinner. Or…

Ever leaving the old Baker farm.

Oh no! She bolted upright, finding the source of the light—a nearby table lamp. That was the first clue she wasn't in the barn. She wasn't home either. Instead of her father's moldy, second-

45

hand furniture, she rested on a pristine leather couch. Draped over her legs was a woolen blanket too luxuriously thick to belong in the Connor household.

That wasn't all, she realized amid growing dread. It was dark beyond a nearby window, way past nightfall. Her father would be furious—but his wrath took a back seat to the present danger.

A familiar voice resonated through her body, but it definitely didn't belong to Fred Connors. "I didn't sign up for this. If you don't come up with a solution, I will—no, I don't give a damn about protocol. *Listen to me!*"

Loren obeyed, bracing her hands protectively over her face. As she eyed the room fearfully beyond her fingers, she realized the speaker's anger wasn't directed at her. He wasn't even in sight, but in another room close by, where his voice echoed off the walls.

"I agreed to watch *Connors*," he continued. "Not his damn daughter! She was supposed to be human. Well, guess what? She attacked another girl today. I practically had to drag her away. No. Thank God she didn't change, but she had blood all over her damn hands. If she's human, I'm the Queen of fucking England."

He paused, and Loren swore she heard a faint mumble as if someone was shouting at him, though from far away. A phone, maybe?

"You know damn well what I mean," Officer McGoven replied, just as heatedly. "Don't put this on me. She's just a kid. Hell, she probably doesn't even know what she is, but I don't want to be responsible for her. That isn't my place. She needs guidance. She needs... Are you even listening to me?"

He paused again, and fragments of his tirade ran ceaselessly through Loren's brain. *Responsible. For her.*

Could he be referring to Naomi? Though, it didn't matter. She had more important things to worry about, and she shifted her weight, freeing herself from the blanket. Heart pounding, she searched for her backpack next. How in the hell had she slept for so long?

Even so, it wasn't long enough to combat months of living with her father. She winced as the full effects of sleep deprivation seemed to strike all at once. She felt dizzy. Her throat ached. Her head throbbed, and the bottom of her chin stung as she swiped the hair from her face and tried to focus.

Think!

"No, I'm not going to calm down," Officer McGoven shouted, derailing her fragile train of thought. His increasing agitation triggered a tendril of alarm that ran down her spine. His voice was too deep—more guttural than her father's at his most furious. "Get the damn pack to take her in, then. Isn't that what you do? Protect your own? Invite the outcasts into your loving, *welcoming* family? She needs more than sentiments and meaningless platitudes, Sonia. She needs help! Oh fuck, come here and see for yourself, then! Well, *do* something."

Loren lurched to her feet, swaying to find her balance. Confused, she eyed her trembling legs as if they didn't belong to her. In this moment...they didn't seem to. It was like they moved on autopilot, driven by two words. *Do something.* In fact, every nerve in her body prickled as if waiting for another command. *His.*

But why?

"I didn't ask for this," he said a fraction softer, and some of the uncanny tension in her muscles eased up. "She's not my damn problem. She's not some burden to unload like baggage. You have a duty to her, the same as I do. Oh, of course, you must beg your precious Alpha first. Call me back with his decision, then. Fuck!"

Presumably, he hung up the phone, but heavy footsteps alluded to him pacing. With every passing second, his anger only seemed to increase, smoldering like wildfire. Loren suspected at least some of it was directed her way.

Though, she didn't plan to stick around long enough to find out. The front door was visible from here, but her knees buckled as she staggered toward it, suddenly too weak to support her own weight. It seemed to take ages to reach the front door, but the second she did, the back of her neck prickled with awareness.

"Wait."

Just like that, she froze as if rooted to the spot. Heavy footsteps advanced from behind her, preceded by a scent that puzzled her the second she breathed it in—pine?

"I'll drive you home," McGoven continued, sounding paces behind her now. "I need to speak to your father, anyway."

Loren's blood ran cold. Helpless, she turned to find him standing in the kitchen doorway. He had shed his jacket, revealing a black T-shirt with short sleeves that bared his forearms. She swallowed hard at the sight. He had more muscle than anyone she'd ever seen in person.

"You brought me here," she croaked. Though it might have been far worse if he carried her home and her father witnessed. Still, she couldn't fathom why he hadn't. "Why? I'll be late. I need to get back."

He raised an eyebrow as if surprised by her line of questioning. "You seemed exhausted. I hope you don't mind, but I thought you might prefer somewhere warmer than the barn." The explanation seemed rehearsed, disguising his real reason for bringing her here.

Though she could have been paranoid. Rather than gratitude, a helpless jumble of words spilled from her throat the second she opened her mouth. "I can't...I...why did you let me sleep? Why didn't you wake me up? God, he's going to—" She had enough sense to break off before finishing that sentence. "I have to go home."

A task easier said than done—she couldn't move, not even as terror welled like bile in her throat. Her own body wouldn't obey the frantic commands her mind issued.

"I have to go home," she croaked as if saying it out loud would somehow make her limbs move.

"I know." McGoven's expression didn't betray a hint of emotion. "You don't need to be afraid. I will drive you home."

"No!" Frantically, Loren shook her head. "Please. I need to go *now*."

A strange note colored her voice. Like she was asking permission, but in a sense, it felt like she was. Something inside her seemed hung on his every word—compelled by them.

She couldn't move unless he told her it was okay.

"It's storming out," he replied in an even tone. Gone was the volatile anger he displayed on the phone call. "You'll catch your death if you walk home, and I'm not going to allow that to happen. You can wait for me out in the car. Go."

Finally, she could move again, and she practically ran from the front door. The porch steps were already slick, but she descended them swiftly—but that was as far as her autonomy extended. She fully intended to run past the driveway and make a break for the woods, but she approached the squad car instead. A persistent mantra dominated her thoughts, impossible to ignore. *Wait for him in the car.* But why?

The further she ventured from the house, and the man inside it, the more confusing her obedience seemed.

What's wrong with me?

It wasn't like she wanted to listen. Maybe there was just something broken inside of her that *liked* being at someone else's whim?

No, she thought as her hand reached for the passenger-side door. Without Officer McGoven in sight, the thought seemed stronger than before, resonating in her mind.

No. She couldn't stay. Her father would kill her.

Wait for him. Wait for him in the car.

"*NO!*" Stumbling, Loren took another step—only this time toward the looming fields she could barely make out in the dark. *No,* she thought frantically as she took another step. And then, another. And another.

It was hard. Like wading through thick cement poured up to her ankles. Painful even, as if a part of her hated leaving. *He told us to wait,* it cried mournfully. *We need to wait for him in the car.*

Sheer willpower pushed her to ignore it. A few more steps, and she was paces from the trees separating the farm from her father's neighborhood.

Just a little more, she urged her aching limbs, as if distance were the cure to the strange compulsion. Maybe it was. The farther she got from that house, the freer each step felt until…

Snap!

Like a breaking leash, the strange hold over her shattered, and Loren took off for the woods like a bat out of hell. She couldn't stop running. The need to move felt instinctive, and she had learned a long time ago to trust her intuition above all else. It told her to leave. *Now.* Before he found out, because if he did—

A shout rang out like a rumble of thunder, and she realized it was too late.

"LOREN!"

She winced and stumbled over her own feet. It was as if an invisible hook sank into her chest, pulling her back. *Dragging* her back.

No, she couldn't go back. *She couldn't!* Fear was a buffer, smothering everything but the need to escape. *Run!* Desperate, she raced toward the stream and blindly waded through the shallow end. The chill stole the air from her lungs, cutting her down to the very bone. Her shoes were a mess, the duct tape long since torn off, but the discomfort didn't faze her.

Couldn't faze her. If she stopped for even a second, all hell would break loose. She could feel it in the air—dangerous tension.

Luckily, she made it to the sleepy neighborhood beyond Baker farm without incident. Even so, she was shaking by the time she reached her father's backyard. She could barely mount the porch steps and wrestle open the door.

She didn't even make it over the threshold before she was struck in the face by an unseen force. *Wham!*

As pain seared through her cheek, Loren went limp like a rag doll, guarding her face with her hands. Tense with anticipation, she braced for the next hit. The next kick. The angrily growled "Care to explain?"

Instead, only the cool kiss of rainwater greeted her as the door creaked lazily on its hinges. When she finally peeked through her fingers, the porch light revealed her attacker—the handle of a broom that had fallen by her feet. Otherwise, the kitchen was empty, utterly dark.

With a sigh of relief, she crept inside, hoping the noise didn't wake her father. There was no sign of him downstairs, at least. The television was off, as were all the lights. The sole illumination came from a flickering red indicator on the answering machine.

The deceptively innocent device presented a new wealth of danger. Who could it be? Naomi Tanner's furious parents, demanding retribution for their daughter's injuries? The school calling to report her absence?

Feeling sick, Loren pressed the play button before fear could steal her nerve.

"Girl," the message began, rough with static. "Don't wait up. I've got some business to take care of over in Weller."

Click. End of story.

She played the message two more times before it finally sank in. Her father was gone, and the relief nearly knocked her over. She was safe for now…but for how long?

Unwilling to test her luck, she hobbled up the stairs to her room. After stripping off her soaked, filthy clothing, she ran the shower until the stall filled with steam, and she lost herself beneath the rush of hot water.

As inevitable as the sun rising and setting, she knew that this brief reprieve wouldn't last.

Regardless, she enjoyed the peace for as long as she could.

"—The hell do you want?" The shout snapped Loren from a painful, dreamless sleep. Alarmed, she tried to make sense of the shadows blanketing her room.

Her father wasn't in view, though she certainly recognized his voice. Her bedroom door was still closed. He was in the house, but further away. Downstairs? The slam of the front door cemented that suspicion.

He wasn't alone.

Whoever replied to him spoke so softly only a few words caught her ears. "Here...about Loren..."

Shit! At the sound of her name, she shrugged off her cheap comforter and braced her feet against the floor. She knew of only one man with a voice that deep. What did she intend to do about it, though? The only available course of action was to listen.

"What about her?" Her father's voice was a hostile hiss in comparison. It was obvious he had been drinking.

"Not here to fight." McGoven's words were even harder to distinguish. Loren could only clearly make out two more—*her* and *pack*.

"The hell I will," her father grumbled, sounding insulted at the mere idea of…whatever they were talking about. "She doesn't need those bastards. A lot of good they've done you. Big shot William-fucking-McGoven. Hell, they shun you, and you still do their dirty work like a lost pup. It must be lonely out here without a bitch to keep you company. Is that why you're sniffin' around my girl?"

Officer McGoven's reply came in a series of guttural notes. "*Don't test me.*"

"The girl doesn't need *them*," her father insisted.

Was he referring to long-lost family? She had already had enough of estranged relatives. Like, *Uncle Bart,* who still haunted her nightmares.

"You don't get to make that decision," Officer McGoven said, sounding louder than before. "Especially if she's—"

"She's not. If she's any daughter of mine, she *wouldn't* be. Though you know that better than anyone, don't you, *Bill?* You fucking pure-bloods and your rules."

Bill. The oddly harmless name stuck in Loren's mind. *Bill McGoven.* The man would unintentionally get her killed if he mentioned her skipping school or falling asleep in his barn.

"Rules don't determine our ways—biology does. Even a mongrel like you can sense what she is. You know what could happen to her if you keep her secluded," McGoven said, in a tone decisively more somber. "She'll become isolated. Demented. You wouldn't want that."

"You don't know what the hell I want, Bill. Now, get the hell out of my house! I'm of half a mind to call that precious Alpha of yours. You aren't supposed to speak to me directly. Just report on my every move like a good dog—"

"Goodnight, Mr. Connors."

The sound of retreating footsteps echoed amid the slam of the screen door. Loren scrambled to the window in time to catch sight of a dark figure striding from the house to an awaiting patrol car. Right when he reached the driver's-side door, he looked up, and she swore his gaze fixated directly on her.

She jumped back as more footsteps broke the silence, only these were louder, inside the house, mounting the stairs.

A second later, her bedroom door flew open to crash against the wall. Dingy, orange light from the hall lamp illuminated dark hair, matched by two narrowed eyes set in a face that didn't seem capable of holding a smile.

"Girl," her father snarled. The whites of his eyes were bloodshot —he was most definitely drunk. "Care to explain why that fucking bastard McGoven just came over here asking about you?"

Loren could barely squeak in her own defense. "I-I don't know."

"You don't know?" He lumbered forward, his hands in fists. Compared to McGoven's bulk, he appeared scrawny, swallowed by his stained T-shirt. Loren cowered anyway.

She used to wonder why he never took her in after her mother's death, despite being listed on her birth certificate. He never visited, never called. The first time she met him had been the very day social services dropped her off after a failed placement with a distant relative. Not long after that, Loren realized the grim truth —Fred Connors wanted nothing to do with her. In fact, they looked nothing alike. His hair was sandy blond, and their eyes were shaped differently. They may have had the same, wide, oval face, but so did her mother.

"You didn't talk to him?" Her father's tone was dangerous, daring her to slip up.

Careful, Loren thought. "He stopped me on the way to school," she began in a tentative whisper. When that didn't seem to spark a rage, she continued. "He spoke to me—"

"And what did you say?"

"N-nothing—I mean," she croaked. "I-I was polite, but I didn't say anything. I told him to leave me alone. I swear."

He appeared to mull her answer over in silence. Finally, he turned, bracing one of his fists against the door.

"The next time he tries to speak to you, you tell him to go to hell, understood? He's a fucking pervert. Probably heard down at the station how much money I get for you from that bitch's insurance. That's what he's after."

Loren winced, but he was already stumbling down the hall to his own bedroom. He slammed the door after him, but she didn't dare move a muscle.

Neither did she have the nerve to close her bedroom door, or even creep into the hallway to switch off the light he'd left on. She stayed frozen until morning, when the dull light of dawn entered her window in a silent reprieve.

It was Saturday.

"Lazy day" her mother used to call it, a weekly holiday they would spend in pajamas, eating cereal, and watching cartoons.

Those days were long gone. Loren didn't even realize it was the weekend until she hastened downstairs for the bag her father kept the papers in, only to discover that it wasn't there.

Saturday was the only day of the week he delivered the newspapers himself. Mainly, Loren knew, because he used the time to collect on his gambling tab from a man who lived across town.

A good thing, too, she thought once she returned to her room and fished her battered shoes from the corner. They were beyond salvageable. Mud and rainwater had dissolved the remaining duct tape, and both soles held on by only a thread.

Who knew how she'd get to school on Monday. Or how on earth she was going to find the money for new shoes.

Don't slip up this time, she told herself. *Ask again. Get him in a good mood.*

With that goal in mind, she busied herself with the many chores her father demanded she complete. As always, the living room was a landmine of empty beer cans and scattered TV dinners. She cleared those first, only to discover a bigger mess waiting for her in the kitchen.

She tracked mud in last night. Either her father had been too drunk to notice, or he just didn't care. Regardless, she'd been spared at least one beating for the day.

It took an hour of scrubbing to get the floor remotely clean, and then another run with the mop to erase all traces of muck. Once the house was decent enough, she curled up on the couch and savored what little peace remained until her father returned.

While Saturdays weren't exactly "lazy" anymore, they were still one of the rare moments she had the house to herself. Usually, she'd spend it at the old Baker farm.

Bunny might get to stretch her legs today, she thought while glancing out the window to see a faintly cloudless sky. The old nag loved being in the pasture.

Xavier, too, she assumed with a smile. The stallion needed plenty of exercise to stay happy. She was so lost in the thought that she didn't hear the first knock on the door.

But the second rap sent her scrambling from the couch. Her initial fear was her father had locked himself out. He'd blame her if she kept him waiting too long.

Heart pounding, she raced to the door, but—as if held back by some force she couldn't comprehend—her hand froze over the knob. *Pine.* Her nostrils flared, catching the strange scent in the air.

A scent that didn't belong here. At that exact moment, a stern voice seeped through the wooden barrier, impossible to resist.

"Loren. Please open the door."

She jumped back, slamming her hip on the couch. Amid her smothered gasp, McGoven's voice rang out clearly.

"I just want to talk. You can let me in."

No, a part of her warned, even as her body disobeyed. Robotic steps carried her forward and, despite her panic, her fingers deftly undid the lock. The door opened from the outside, revealing the man dominating the doorway.

His voice sounded calm, but he looked angry. His eyes were narrowed, glowing in the pale daylight.

Loren swallowed hard as a potential explanation for his visit came to mind. Had Naomi decided to catch her unguarded on the weekend? She braced herself for the moment he'd slap her in handcuffs. Surprisingly, all he seemed inclined to do was watch her.

Silently.

Being ogled by strangers was par for the course as the new girl in town, but his scrutiny felt different. Probing. Penetrating. His gaze seemed to pierce her clothing, weighing every inch of her beneath. How did she measure up?

As a disappointment, apparently. The worn lines around his mouth deepened by the second, exaggerating his frown.

Fortunately for her, what he thought didn't matter. His presence alone could get her punished.

"You can't be here," she blurted, scanning the sidewalk behind him as if her father might appear at any moment. "Please. I—"

"May I come inside?"

The request threw her off. It wasn't *really* a request, though. His low tone proclaimed something else that spurred her limbs into motion. *Let me in. Now.*

"I can't," Loren insisted. As the words left her mouth, she jerked aside to let him pass anyway.

"Thank you," he said, and he almost sounded genuine.

She didn't want him here—and he knew it. He seemed as out of place in their cramped living room as a wolf in the middle of a sheep's pen. He was too close—even though a good ten feet of space separated them, and she had her back pressed against the wall.

"M-my father isn't home," she said in a small voice. "You shouldn't talk to me without—"

"Naomi Tanner decided not to press charges." Officer McGoven's baritone cut over her easily. "I don't think you want your father to know that. Do you?"

Loren could only shake her head, flinching as those gray eyes found her again. She felt minuscule beneath his scrutiny. Like a child shriveling beneath a police officer's perusal all over again.

They had all seemed the same back in those days, a bunch of featureless faces topped by a dark uniform. Only he wasn't wearing his now. Instead, a green polo revealed his muscular forearms, and a simple pair of jeans were tucked into his leather boots.

The boots held Loren's attention. They looked firm. Sturdy. If only she could manage to talk her father into buying her a pair like that. Though if Naomi had her thrown in jail, she might never wear shoes again.

"D-do you know why?" she asked, focusing on the topic at hand. "Why she didn't press the c-charges?"

McGoven shrugged. "She decided it may not have been in her best interest."

In other words, he convinced her not to. Was Naomi susceptible to his commanding voice like she was?

"She won't be bothering you again," he added as if to confirm that unspoken suspicion.

"T-thank you," she stammered, but a gnawing sense of paranoia ate at her gratitude. *What did he want in return?* Nobody did anything for free.

Sure enough, he met her probing stare with one of his own. "Loren, I need to ask you something."

"Y-yes?"

He seemed to hesitate, taking time to inspect the modest living room furniture—a stained couch and musty recliner. His gaze lingered, appearing to note everything down to the dust in the corners—but Loren still sensed the second his focus returned to her.

"What do you know about your father?"

She frowned. "Not much." Only that his name was Fred Connors, and after her mother died, his house was the only place she had left to go. "But he is my father, and I...love him."

Everyone else accepted that generic answer. It might have been true to some extent. After all, this home was better than the last one.

Rather than satisfied, McGoven looked... Uneasy. His probing stare intensified, demanding the truth she was too chicken to say.

He's a monster—not in the literal sense. She didn't know why it seemed essential to make that distinction. Sure, he might not have had claws or fangs or bulging yellow eyes, but real-life monsters were always the worst. Just ask the average serial killer, who seemed more frightening than the story of *Little Red Riding Hood* any day.

Give her a real monster, complete with fur and a spine-tingling growl, and Loren knew she could hold her own. Somehow. Her father, on the other hand? He was a far more formidable threat.

And if he knew she had a man in his house, he'd kill her. The thought consumed her, and she barely heard what Officer McGoven said next.

"What about your family?" he pressed. "What do you know about them? I heard your mother wasn't from around here—"

"My mother's dead," Loren replied before she realized what he probably meant. Other family. Grandmothers. Grandfathers. Cousins.

"My mom was all I had," she added. "I-I mean *besides* my dad."

Officer McGoven didn't seem to like that, and Loren swallowed at the emotion that contorted his expression too quickly to name. Anger?

"Have you ever heard of Black Mountain?" he asked.

"No." She wasn't too familiar with the area around New Walsh. Up until a few months ago, her entire existence had consisted of the small town of Ridgerton.

"You haven't. What about any mention of a territory up North? Friends of his?"

"He doesn't have friends," she replied. "Outside of his gambling buddies, anyway."

And if he did, he certainly hadn't introduced them to her.

"I'm sorry," she blurted as McGoven's eyes flashed. Anger was definitely the emotion she failed to name before. For whatever reason, he seemed determined to disguise it from her. He turned away, but his posture was too tense. Furious. "Fucking bastard," he snarled under his breath.

Her? Or her father? At the thought of him, her entire body went cold.

"My dad will be back soon," she lied. "He won't like it if you're here. He won't—"

"I'm leaving."

He was in the doorway before she could blink, but the fluidity of his movements sparked a grudging appreciation. Despite all that muscle, he moved with easy grace, like a dancer.

But he hesitated. "Oh, before I forget. You left your bag last night." Sure enough, he had it slung over one shoulder. She didn't know how she had missed it before.

Maybe because her eyes never left his face for longer than a few short seconds? Her fingers shook as she reached for the bag. From the weight, she could tell all the necessary materials were inside it.

"Thank you," she murmured, staring down at the floor. There was only one place he could have found it—his barn.

How could she have been so stupid? Forget Naomi; would *he* pursue charges?

No, something told her, even before she saw the decidedly un-angry gleam in his eye. He would just extend his visit and abuse her gratitude to ask more questions. "What happened yesterday?"

Her mood shifted from hopeful to ashamed. "I'm sorry. I shouldn't have skipped school. I just—"

"No, not that," he said over her. "Naomi. I called the school, and they sent me your file. You've never gotten detention, let alone into a fight. You have straight As. Honors courses. Not even a warning."

Her file. Could he do that? Apparently so. His uncanny authority must work even on school officials. But why the interest in her?

"She must have done something to provoke you, Loren. You drew blood." He didn't sound accusatory. Just curious. "What happened?"

"She..." Loren bit her tongue.

The truth wouldn't matter to him—it never did. People like Naomi, with their money and influence, would always win over people like her. If McGoven was looking for a reason to avoid pressing charges, he wouldn't find it here.

Though, to be fair, he didn't seem to care about this in his capacity as a police officer. His interest went beyond duty. It was like he was hunting for something. An answer he wanted her to give.

"What happened?" he demanded, his eyes flashing.

"Nothing! I mean, she said—"

"I don't care what she did. What did you *feel?*"

"Angry," Loren admitted. Her cheeks flamed. It was such a childish response.

"That wasn't it," McGoven pressed, unsatisfied. "What else? When you knew you'd drawn blood? What did you feel then?"

"I..." Her true emotions were too insane to verbalize. She felt anger in the core of her very being. A fury that still raged even now. It demanded more than an apology from Naomi to soothe it. It wanted retribution.

Blood.

"Did she hurt you?" McGoven was closer, his voice impossible to resist. That strange scent of pine she smelled whenever he was near, it wasn't the forest. It was him. His very being seemed infused with the essence of the earth.

But she didn't feel the same calm she felt while out in the woods. Her belly flipped, her toes curling. Whatever this feeling was, it made her pulse race. It felt...bad. Uncontrollable.

"Loren?" he prodded. "Is Naomi the one who hurt you?"

She shook her head, struggling to keep up with the conversation. Every word he uttered made her feel dizzy. "I'm fine—"

"Your left hip is bruised." He spoke with such conviction she blushed.

Then, she looked down, irrationally convinced she must have answered the door naked. But she wasn't. Her thick sweater should have disguised every ache on her body. Unless he searched her while she'd been unconscious…

"I-I don't know what you're talking about," she croaked, crossing her arms over her torso. The thought of him eyeing her body made her feel violated, but she couldn't shake the feeling that he would never do that.

There had to be another explanation. Like…he just knew.

At her denial, his eyes narrowed. With a sweep of his gaze, he homed in on her chest.

"There is a bruise on your left hip," he reiterated with unnerving confidence. "Two… Maybe three days old. Another fresh injury is on your chest. On your left forearm is an older mark. Your right shoulder, too. Left upper back. Left lower back. There are more, but they span weeks—"

Suddenly he surged forward, and there was nowhere to run but to press herself against the wall.

"Were these all caused by Naomi Tanner?" He raised his voice only a fraction, but she cowered as if he shouted. The muscles of his neck were corded, his face dangerously close to hers. "Answer me!"

"I-I don't…" Panic wiped her mind blank. Had her father been right about him after all? No…

Rather than fixate on her mouth, or a part of her a pervert might be interested in, he just…

Inhaled. Over and over, his nostrils flared with increasingly rapid intakes of air. Whatever he smelled made him swallow, and a sound rumbled in his throat a heartbeat later, too deep to form audible words. No, it was something that a part of Loren hesitantly attempted to name. A growl?

"How do you know?" she asked, barely able to form the words. "How?"

"You know I can smell them—" He snapped his teeth shut, and a muscle in his jaw twitched. He seemed to realize how it sounded —he could *smell* a bruise.

Loren knew she misheard him. "W-What?"

Suddenly, he was across the room, heading for the door. "Don't worry about it. I was wrong. Have a good day, Ms. Connors. I… I think it's a good idea if you stay away from my property from now on."

Loren nodded, still shaken. Somehow, the loss of her haven mattered more than his strange interrogation. Did he know about her previous trips?

His face gave nothing away. With one last raking glance, he left the house entirely, slamming the door in his wake.

Creeping to the window, she noticed that he entered a green pickup truck instead of the squad car.

In a matter of minutes, he was gone.

7

The rest of the day passed in a blur. In the absence of McGoven she felt oddly calm. With every passing second, his strange behavior became a distant memory. She could barely remember exactly what he'd said—but she didn't dare question it.

Instead, she threw herself into busywork, desperate for a distraction. As a result, she cleaned the house—twice—and watched a staticky program on the television. Afterward, she did her homework, and when five-o-clock neared, she started dinner.

The evening came and went, with no sign of her father. After another hour passed, Loren left his plate in the fridge and crept into bed.

I'll just wait, she told herself. She wouldn't fall asleep. As soon as he came home, she'd ask about the shoes.

What felt like mere seconds later, she wrenched her eyes open as a monstrous sound shattered the quiet. It was her bedroom door flying open and striking the wall. Before she could react, a brutal force seized her arm and yanked her into the hall. The stench of stale beer gave away the intruder's identity. Her father.

He was shouting incoherently, hauling her toward the staircase. Loren reached for the banister, but a shove to her back robbed her of balance. The air rushed past in a whoosh as she struck the topmost steps. Then another. Another.

Tuck. The instinctive voice had saved her too many times to count, so she threw her hands up to guard her face as her body tumbled like a ragdoll. It felt like an eternity before her descent came to an abrupt stop. Blinking, she found herself in the living room, tasting blood on her tongue and instinctively clutching at her left side. God, she hurt.

Ignore it, that inner voice told her. *You can cry later. All that matters is staying alive.*

Because she was in danger. Her father stood over her, still raging. His voice echoed off the walls, but she could only hear the blood rushing through her ears. From the way his lips moved, she could piece together the gist of his tirade—*care to explain...*

Something.

Her mind raced, parsing through which event could have enraged him.

Naomi? School?

"Did you hear me, girl?"

She saw his leg fly out, delivering a blow to her side. The rush of pain seemed to snap the sense back into her, and she could clearly understand what he snarled next. "Care to explain why you had that asshole McGoven in my house?"

McGoven. Paralyzing fear raced down her spine. How did he know? She cleaned the house twice. Every trace of Officer McGoven had been scraped, wiped, and vacuumed away.

"Well?" her father bellowed. His next kick caught her ribs. Long-honed practice was the only thing that held in the scream.

"Huh, you little bitch? Answer me!"

"He wouldn't leave," she croaked, gasping for air. "I'm sorry—"

"What did he say to you? What did *you* say to *him*?"

Loren shook her head. "N-Nothing—"

"He had to want something." Her father glanced her over with disgust, settling on the high collar of her nightgown. "He thought you were one of those pompous little bitches. What lies did he feed you, huh? That he could take you away to paradise? And what the fuck did you give him, you little slut?"

When he reached for her, Loren flinched, breaking that protective, blank shell. Like a shark sensing blood, he caught wind of her fear. It made him bolder. Louder. Angrier.

"Huh?" He snatched her sleeve, wrenching her unceremoniously to her feet. "What did you do, you little slut?"

"N-Nothing," Loren stammered. "He j-just asked about us," she added, voice tight with pain. "He asked if I had any other family—"

It was the wrong thing to say.

Wham! She barely saw him form a fist before it collided with the side of her face. Sparks danced before her eyes as the world swayed beneath her feet. The next slap caught the other side of her face, sending her into the wall.

"And I'm sure you told him everything, didn't you," her father snarled. "Didn't you?"

For the first time in years, Loren forgot all about being a turtle and making herself a small target.

She ran.

The kitchen was her only refuge, though deep down, she knew it was pointless to hide. She was boxing herself in and merely prolonging the inevitable. It didn't matter. The need to move was instinctive, too urgent to ignore. *Run!*

"Where the hell are you going?" He was paces behind, taking his time as if confident she wouldn't make it far.

Run, Loren thought frantically. With no other option, she raced for the back door.

This time was different. She could taste it—sense it, right down to the inevitable stench of death on her own skin. He had hit her in the face, without bothering to worry about bruises. He had kicked her without concerning himself with how loudly she might scream.

He was angry. Angrier than she had ever seen him before, and when she fumbled with the lock on the screen door, he caught her by the waist.

As if she weighed nothing, he threw her aside into the counter.

Thwack!

Wincing, she caught herself on the kitchen sink and scrambled upright. By the time she regained her balance, her father was closing in with the eerie, predatory grace of a wolf. It was as if the rage had a calming effect on him.

He was enjoying this. Even the look in his eyes was different. Sharper. Colder. Meaner.

Run!

Loren jerked on her feet, unsure of what to do. If she resisted, he'd only hit her again. Hit her harder. Kill her…

Stop! That calm, commanding voice returned, snapping her limbs into action. *Focus!*

Trembling, she wrenched open the nearest drawer. There, ready for the taking, was a knife—the same one her father ate his steak with. God, she couldn't really use it… Could she?

She *had* to.

"What the hell are you going to do with that, girl?" her father demanded as she gripped the brittle handle.

It felt so damn heavy. She could barely lift it, though the metal was that cheap, synthetic kind and not real steel. *Hold it,* the shadowy part of her hissed, and she didn't dare hesitate.

"Lo-ren," her father sing-songed. She rarely heard him say her name, let alone like this. Playfully. Hungrily…

"Huh, girl?" he demanded with a cold laugh. "What you gonna do with that?"

Use it? She had never intentionally hurt someone. Ever. *Liar,* a part of her hissed. *You hurt Naomi, and you enjoyed every damn bit of it…*

"Stop!" Loren didn't know if the plea was directed at herself, or the man still advancing at a lazy, casual pace. "P-please. Just leave me alone."

"You've been a bad girl, Lo-ren," he growled. "*Very* bad. Just what did you say to that damn McGoven to get him sniffing around you, huh? Just what did you give him, girl?"

He lashed out for the neckline of her nightgown and yanked. With a violent *rrrriiiipp,* the cotton tore down to her navel, revealing pale, bruised skin.

Shame flooded her cheeks as she scrambled to shield what she could with her free hand. "P-please stop—"

"You let him take you, you little slut?" her father shouted over her. "You let him have you? Mark you? I bet the bastard would love a little bitch like you. Just as easy a slut as your damn mother."

NO! Loren didn't know what happened. She saw him reach for her and her own grip tightened over the knife, lifting it…

But it was like something else took over, guiding the blade in a wide arch.

"Son of a bitch!" Howling with rage, her father stumbled back, clutching his arm to his chest. A sharp scent tinged the air—one she recognized with a shudder. Blood. "You cut me!"

There wasn't time for fear. Loren took her shot and lurched for the back door, wrenching it open. It was raining hard. The torrent churned the earth into a slippery soup that coated her bare feet as she jumped off the porch and raced for the woods.

"Loren!" His voice rang out behind her, punctuated by a harsh laugh. *Where ya going, Lo-ren? You can't run from me…*

But she tried. Panting for air, she navigated the darkened woods while her thin nightgown bunched up around her legs. The soles of her feet ached. She couldn't see anything but looming, endless black.

But she could hear him well enough. "Where ya running to, darlin'?" The drunken endearment seemed to come from every direction at once. Far away. Too close.

Inside her head.

"Darlin,' Darlin'… Where you going, Darlin'? Don't you know I'll always find you?"

Noises crashed through the underbrush just paces behind her.

"H-help!" Forsaking stealth, she screamed. "H-help…me. Help me…help!"

It was too late.

A flicker of movement from the corner of her eye was her only warning before she went sprawling, thrown by an impenetrable force. Boneless, she tumbled down a hill, landing in a heap near the bubbling path of the stream. Sometime during the fall, her nightgown tore completely, hanging open as she scrambled to her knees.

A desperate hope grappled with the building terror. Somehow, she made it all the way to the Baker farm. She was close enough to view the barn through the trees.

But would anyone hear her?

Sucking in a breath, she put her effort into making sure someone would. "Help me! Please—"

"Get back here, you little bitch." Her father's voice reached her in advance of his heavy footsteps. He took his time, seeming to leisurely pick his way through the underbrush.

You're dead, a part of Loren whispered. *Dead, dead, dead.*

But she still had the knife in her hand. Her knuckles whitened over the handle, not that it would help one damn bit.

"You think you can run from me?" Her father posed the question casually as he appeared at the top of the hill. "You think that I would just let you *leave*? So you can take all that fucking money for yourself?"

No, Loren thought sadly. She had always known how this story would end. One final chapter concluded with violence.

"You deserve this, don't you?" He came clearly within view, his arms at his sides, lips quirked into a cold smile. "Say it."

He waited for her to nod. Give up. Acquiesce. She always did, submitting to being a punching bag.

But this time… She just eyed the night sky, unconcerned by the raindrops speckling her face. If this night was to be her last, then she might as well go out with her dignity intact.

Be blank…empty. Don't let them see…

"I asked you a question, Loren." He crouched and snatched her chin, forcing her to meet his gaze. "You deserve this, don't you?"

She said nothing, too exhausted to play along.

Fresh anger distorted his features to an alarming degree. His eyes seemed to glow, his jaw lengthened. Those yellowed teeth even seemed sharper…

She was hallucinating. She had to be.

"You deserved this." As he spoke, his tone deepened, becoming more guttural. "Say it, you little bitch!"

He raised his fist but reached for her throat instead. Using the grip to pin her down, he turned his attention to the skin bared by the torn halves of her nightgown.

Loren froze. He never touched her. Not like this.

"You didn't wait long to let that ass, McGoven, have you, did you?" He breathed harshly. "How long have you been fucking him, huh?"

Loren frantically shook her head, squeezing her eyes shut, trying to breathe. *No.*

"If I had known what a little slut you were, I would have used you to pay off my damn debts, rather than work my ass off—"

His hand trailed to the strap of her bra, tugging, and that was the last thing she remembered.

Gggggrrrrrrrrrrllllllll.

The growl shattered through everything. Even the earth seemed to ripple with the force of it. It could have been a roll of thunder, but as the thought crossed her mind, some part of Loren snickered—*Ha-ha, you wish.*

"Fuck!" Whatever it was, the sound startled her father. He withdrew from her, scanning the forest frantically. "The asshole wouldn't dare." His voice quivered. He was afraid.

Of what?

"I'll deal with you on my own damn property. Come on—" He reached for her again, and a part of Loren knew that it was her only chance.

The knife was still in her hand, but she had no conscious control of her limbs. With an eerie sense of calm, she felt that impulsive force take hold of her again. Her arm moved, bringing the knife into something firm that grunted at the blow.

And then suddenly...the knife was gone, ripped right out of her hands.

When she stood, the only thing she was aware of was the falling rain on her skin.

Keep moving, Loren, that calm voice commanded. *Just keep moving. Just move. Don't stop.*

She didn't make it far.

After a few steps, she stumbled and went down face first. By reflex, her eyes flew open, and everything fell into focus. She saw the silvery rain that pelted her outstretched fingers…mingling with a darker, more vibrant color.

Red.

"No!" The wail ripped from her throat. Helpless, she curled up in a ball, knowing the truth in her gut even though she never turned her head to look. She couldn't look.

She didn't know how long she huddled there, screaming out wordless howls as the rain died down to a whisper. But she knew the exact moment when *he* came.

By then, the rain died down to barely a cool mist as if to herald his arrival. Even nature didn't dare to challenge him.

He approached her slowly and watched her for what felt like an eternity. His presence alone penetrated deeper than even physical touch. *I'm here,* he seemed to convey without saying a word. *It's alright.*

Weakly, Loren turned toward him. Though she couldn't make out any of his features, she had no doubt who the man above her was.

And as concerned as he seemed to be, one fact would tarnish any pity he might have felt toward her.

"He's dead," she croaked, watching those silver eyes flash in response. "I…I-I killed him."

8

*W*ait here.

He didn't say so out loud. He didn't have to. One look conveyed the order and more. *Wait for me.*

Though, it wasn't like she had any place left to go…

She lay there, freezing, as the horror of what she'd done set in.

Murderer! You killed him.

It didn't matter that he seemed intent on killing *her.* Though, she never confirmed it for herself. Maybe she'd only injured him? *He could still be alive…*

"Shit." The gruff curse came from nearby—McGoven. He didn't sound like a man confronted with a still-living victim. No, he sounded horrified.

Dejectedly, Loren stood and stumbled toward the stream, driven by an impulse to put as much space between herself and anyone else. She was a monster. The icy water felt like a slap against her

83

bared toes, but as the water reached her calves, she sank to her knees and attempted to…what?

Gather her senses? She didn't have any damn sense *left*.

Nothing but the overwhelming horror of what she'd done. *I killed him.* Not only that, but she had shown up practically on an officer's doorstep, complete with the body, murder weapon, and all.

McGoven would drag her to the precinct before the blood on her hands even dried. She would spend the rest of her life behind bars—and how damn ironic was that?

Out of all the monsters who'd done her wrong, *she* would be the one punished in the end. There was only one way out…

Slowly, Loren eased herself forward, and the Autumn chill biting into her skin faded away. The scent of the rain-drenched forest, marred by the metallic odor of blood, drifted into oblivion. *Bye-bye* went the sounds of approaching footsteps.

She just sank beneath the ice-cold water of the stream and let it drown out everything else. The frigid temperature knocked her sideways, even as she allowed her body to go limp, submerging her head completely.

What the hell are you doing? a part of her cried as her lungs screamed for air. *Are you insane?*

Probably.

But she was so damn tired…

"What are you doing?" The shout accompanied a harsh grip that dragged her back from the water, pulling her higher up on the stream's bank until she landed on her back in the mud.

Breathless, all she could do was stare into endless silver.

Officer McGoven stood over her, though he looked far from an officer now. He must have been in bed. His hair hung loose instead of slicked back—as if he'd run the whole way there, through the wind and rain. Though, that wasn't all Loren realized as her eyes tiredly glanced him over. He was…

Naked.

Completely. He wasn't even wearing shoes.

Thick, sinewy muscle coiled under every single inch of golden skin. Sculpted limbs branched from the broad expanse of his chest, down…to where Loren attempted to keep her gaze from traveling.

It did anyway, catching sight of a dark trail of black hair leading from his navel down to… Mercifully, there wasn't enough light to see where. Faint moonlight pierced the cloud cover, glinting off the rest of him. Each strip of muscle stood out in definition. The man resembled a carved statue more than a living, breathing being. Every inch of him seemed rock solid.

Lethal. *Dangerous*, a part of Loren whispered. Though on second glance, he wasn't entirely perfect. Scars speckled nearly every inch of his body, adorning the brawn. They were thin, jagged lines, glimmering like streaks of silver. Ten. Twenty. More. Too many to count. Was he whipped? Either that or fed to tigers—the only animal Loren could think of capable of leaving such brutal marks. Even her own many scrapes and bruises paled in comparison.

"Loren."

She flinched at the sound of her name, feeling her heart pound in her chest as if his voice alone zapped some life back into it.

Though what was the point of living? Every thrum of her pulse echoed as if to drive home how worthless her existence had become.

Loren, Loren, Loren.

Loren Connors, that girl who killed her father. Stabbed him in cold blood—though the newspapers would probably come up with some way to lay on the drama, by mentioning years of suspected abuse. Her tormented past.

"Traumatized girl murders father in the woods."

"Loren."

She blinked to find him closer than before, crouched on one gloriously bare knee.

"Look at me." He spoke slowly as if in the space of a few minutes, she had reverted to a child. "What happened?"

Helpless, she shook her head. She couldn't say it.

"Loren—"

"No, no, no..." Her voice was so shrill. She sounded hysterical. Crazed. Some poor little girl in the middle of a nightmare that needed to be woken up. "No, no, no, no—"

"Loren." He didn't have to raise his voice. She *felt* rather than heard her name come from his lips. The sound encased her, blocking out everything else but *him.* "Look at me."

She did, and the sight of those gray eyes filled with concern set everything over the edge. He would have to take her soon. Shove her in the back of that squad car and drive her into town, where strange looks and whispers would follow her for the rest of her life.

You know, Loren Connors—that crazy girl, who...

"Loren, breathe!"

She was hyperventilating. Her breaths wheezed. She felt dizzy...

Look at me!

The command erupted inside her skull, too authoritative to deny. When she raised her head, gray eyes held her captive more securely than any handcuffs.

"Loren... Shit!" His eyes cut down to her front. Judging from the cool breeze tickling her chest, her nightgown was completely in tatters.

"Damn it." The curses flowed from him, one right after the other, matching the anger that had him reaching for her breast. She didn't have the strength to panic. His warmth leeched into her skin—he was so damn hot. Like a furnace, throwing off heat.

Even his fingertips felt like hot pokers on her skin. She flinched at the contact—had she escaped one nightmare only to jump right into another? But no...he only grabbed for the torn edges of the gown and held them closed.

He noticed her reaction, and his grimace made her feel guilty for shying away.

"Did he...fuck!" He turned, glaring into the trees as if he couldn't even *look* at her and pose the question. When he spoke again, his voice was barely audible. "Did he *hurt* you?"

Loren shook her head, sensing that he wasn't referring to the bruises forming all over her body.

He remained silent for so long that Loren almost wondered if he had turned to stone right before her eyes. A living, breathing statue. Slowly, he faced her again, but his expression made her heart sink.

A grim frown warned that, whatever he'd decided, it wouldn't be good... Not for her.

She tried to move, stand, run away—*anything,* but his presence was like an invisible weight, holding her down. Keeping her in place. At least until he gave her *permission* to move.

"Loren, listen to me. This was an accident—"

"Please..." She didn't want him to paint a bright shade over the stark, grim truth. "I'm a monster."

"No," he said in a tone she felt down to her toes. "You aren't. But, if you let me...I can take it away. I can *take* the pain away."

She blinked.

Then she waited for the laugh. The cruel smile to tell her that it was all some sick joke. Neither came, and after a few seconds, panic set in.

He was serious.

"I can take it all." His tone all but promised there was a catch. "I can *help* you...but you have to trust me."

Trust?

Loren glanced down at her hands, painted red with her own father's blood. There was nothing left *to* trust. She was a monster. A freak...

"Just let me die," she whispered, cutting her gaze longingly to the lethal waters of the stream.

"I can *help* you!" The offer was a growl, whispered heatedly into her skin. "It won't be easy. You won't like it...but I can help you."

He can help, that calm, familiar voice whispered tiredly from the back of her mind. *We can trust him. Just let him…*

In the end, she didn't have much of a choice. When he lunged, pinning her with his full weight, the decision was made.

She couldn't even scream.

9

She was drifting, floating aimlessly from one cloud of delirium to the next. She had no clue where she was, but she wasn't alone. At some point, bits of conversation reached her like static through a faulty radio connection.

Had to.

The only way.

I couldn't leave her.

"The pack wouldn't take her in. It was the only way."

All at once, the world stopped spinning, and Loren fell unceremoniously back to earth. She was on a bed with a mattress softer than any she could remember sleeping on before. The air smelled safe, rich like the forest. She couldn't see—it was too dark—but she could sense other people nearby.

Two people.

"Did you call them when you found her?" a gentle voice prodded. Someone female? "Did you *ask*?"

"No—" this voice was gruffer. *Definitely male.* Familiar, too. A name didn't come to mind instantly, just a breathtaking face set with silver eyes. "But the other day, you all didn't seem to give a damn about her anyway."

"Don't lump me in with them, Bill. I told you that it wasn't my choice."

"There is always a choice!" Anger penetrated his voice in guttural notes, and Loren shivered. Though, for the first time in her life, it wasn't out of fear.

Discomfort? She didn't like that he, whoever *he* was, was angry. It made *her* feel something that could have been anger as well. Her pulse raced, surging through her limbs as if electrified.

"She looks so young," the first speaker remarked. "Are you sure she's even old enough to—"

"Birth records claim she's eighteen," the man replied. Loren could tell from his inflection that he was uneasy. "But… She claimed that the bastard hadn't touched her tonight—I don't think he did. But she was covered in bruises. Her memories are like a fucking nightmare. I can't—"

"Oh, no. That poor girl."

Poor girl, Loren agreed amid a rush of sympathy. Whoever they were talking about, she seemed to deserve the pity.

"But you can't really keep her *here*," the woman added. "You said she doesn't even know the truth. What makes you think that she'll—"

"I'll handle it," the man replied. *Case closed.*

"Alright. But at least let me talk to Lukka again. Obviously, she's one of *us* if…if she's mated to you. He has no choice but to take responsibility. She needs a *pack.* She needs to be around her own kind. Even he will have to understand that."

Mated. The word seemed to convey several meanings at once. Bound, tied, linked. Connected.

Chained.

"Talk to the bastard," the man didn't seem to care either way. "Let him take her off my hands—*I don't want this.*"

"Then why get involved?" the woman asked. "Why mate her at all? I hate to play the devil's advocate, Bill."

"Who's playing? You are an advisor to Lukka, after all—"

"I'm not here to fight; I'm here to help," the woman insisted. "And, playing devil's advocate, one might think that you didn't have to get involved at all. She's lived as a human. Human laws could dictate her future now."

"So she can attack an inmate next? Rip out someone's throat while in shackles? I thought your precious Alpha valued discretion above all."

"It could have been better for her in the long run. Better than being plunged into a dynamic she doesn't understand."

A gruff laugh boomed like thunder. "Forget human laws. Why not try her by ours? Committing patricide should be enough to make her the next fucking Alpha. It worked for Lukka—"

"Bill, please!" The woman sounded pained. "You know I can't hear you speak ill of him. Besides, I'm not blaming you. You had no choice. I believe that. I just want to make sure you can defend this against the barrage of criticism we both know is coming. So... Can you?"

There was a long silence, and Loren imagined them both straining to compile a logical response. It took minutes before the man cleared his throat.

"Sonia, I couldn't leave her like that," he began haltingly. "She tried to *drown* herself in the fucking stream. You should have seen her. Smelled her. She was covered in blood, terrified. Only God knows how long he's been terrorizing her before this. She had no one. You know how it feels to be cut off. Alone. I warned that asshole Connors what could happen if he didn't take her to the damn pack—"

That *asshole Connors*. Some nameless girl wasn't the subject of this debate, but *her*. Which meant the man dominating this conversation could only be…

"What's going to happen to her, Bill?" The woman seemed to hesitate. "The police, will they—"

"I've handled it," McGoven snapped. "They think the bastard got what was coming to him. He had more gambling debts than we could keep track of. He even put his fucking house up for collateral. It was only a matter of time before one of his enemies came to collect. As for the girl, Loren will stay with me until… Until I decide what to do next."

"It's funny, Bill," the woman remarked after another brief silence. "You always swore that you wouldn't take another mate—"

"She isn't my mate," he countered coldly. "She is my problem until I figure out a better solution."

"I mean in general," the woman said. Her voice was softer. Wistful. "For so many years, you seemed set on your hermit ways, shunning everyone who tried to prove you wrong—"

"Who would want me?" he argued just as softly. "You might have a short memory, Sonia, but everyone else *doesn't*. Offering me pity isn't the same damn thing as accepting a murderer with open arms."

"You always swore that you were done with pack life," the woman continued as if he'd never spoken. "Only now, it's as if it just fell into your lap, regardless of whether you wanted it or not. Some might say you did this purposefully, though. With a mate, you could form your own pack. Challenge Lukka directly—"

"That isn't funny," the man growled. "I called you here because you're the only one in that place I trust. So do your duty as my friend and as an emissary. Call Lukka. Convince him to come. The sooner he can take her off my hands, the better—"

"Bill," the woman scolded, still utilizing that gentle tone. "No pun intended, but she's not just some puppy you can pawn off."

"Don't be cute. This isn't funny, and you know better than anyone that she'll be better off without me—"

"Look, I'm honored that you still trust me after everything we've been through," the woman insisted. "But I don't have the influence you seem to think I do. What could I possibly say?"

"You wanted to play devil's advocate? Well, here's the truth—I don't want her here longer than necessary. Despite what *they* might think, I don't want a fucking mate, and I'm asking Lukka to do the job he wanted so damn badly and fix this."

"I understand," the woman replied. "But that poor girl..."

Wasn't that the irony of it all? Loren thought drowsily. Every person who so-called "rescued" her, never wanted her in the first place.

*I*t was morning.

Her father would be angry if she didn't get up soon. After all, the papers wouldn't deliver themselves. Then there were her chores to contend with. Wallowing in bed wouldn't make those looming problems disappear, either.

Hurry up, Loren told herself. With a sigh, she rolled over and attempted to peel her eyes open. *You can still make it if you hurry.*

Once she finally caught sight of her surroundings, delivering papers was the last thing on her mind. She wasn't in her room. This wasn't even her house.

The walls weren't covered in peeling gray paint. Instead, dark wooden paneling encircled a room large enough to contain both her father's living room *and* kitchen.

The blue curtains shielding the window weren't stained. In fact, the window itself was massive, stretching almost the entire length of the wall, beyond the foot of the bed. A large, *spacious* bed, covered in a blue comforter, and a gray blanket draped over Loren specifically.

Because her nightgown was gone. So were her bra and underwear. She didn't even have on socks.

The foreign room, the bed, the nakedness—Loren figured they should have affected her, but the only coherent thought to flood her mind was the same word in a soothing mantra.

Safe. This place was safe. This room was safe. This house was safe. The feeling seemed ingrained in the very foundation, more obvious than if someone had erected a sign proclaiming, "Nothing can hurt you here."

When she tentatively placed her feet on the floor, she wasn't afraid. But something was off. The pain was still *there*—her entire body ached—but it was as if it were held at bay by an invisible wall.

She could sense it lurking just beyond that boundary, but it couldn't touch her. Nothing could. Just peace. It permeated the air like perfume, smothering any trace of fear before it could rise. And boy, she should have been afraid the moment she stood—wrapped within the blanket—and crept into a hallway that seemed way *too* familiar.

The stairs led directly into an open kitchen overlooking a modest living room. She could see a white barn from here, visible through a large bay window.

The smells of cooking food drew her notice, and she padded toward the kitchen, following the scent. Someone sat at the center island, watching her approach.

Despite the strange calm, Loren knew instantly that she didn't recognize this woman. She was beautiful, whoever she was, with curling dark hair and large blue eyes set in a delicate face that instantly conjured images of a porcelain doll.

"Hello," she said warmly, fingering the rim of a steaming cup of tea. "You must be Loren. I'm Sonia, and I think we really need to talk."

$\mathcal{H}$e smelled her everywhere. Her scent permeated his bed, his house. Even the fields were impregnated with it.

She didn't smell like most women did, or even *wanted* to. Loren Connors reeked of a strange mixture of horse, fresh air, and the faintest hint of cleaning supplies, as if all those things had become a part of her. Ingrained.

After last night, he could add *blood* to that list. Rage ripped through him, mingled with regret. He should have never let her go back there. Any idiot could see how terrified she was of Connors. Hell, she reeked of fear.

His only comfort was that he didn't spend enough time around the bastard to truly know him. His job was to keep his distance, watch, and report. Before Loren's arrival, he avoided that damn house unless necessary—though he still wound up being called out at least once a month while on duty. Fred Connors was the sort of man who didn't need lycan instincts to cause trouble—his alcoholism and inclination toward violence were more than enough. Nothing about the man screamed suitable placement for a minor. Bill hadn't even known about the man's supposed daughter until the day she appeared.

Loren Connors had thrown a wrench into his life long before he chose to intervene. There was something about her, an intangible quality that people like Naomi Tanner and Fred Connors were drawn to. A part of him sensed it, too. *Easy bait*, her aura proclaimed. Weak, broken spirit, won't bite back. She was the mortal personification of a mouse, always hoping that a hawk wasn't watching.

Though, the proverbial hawk in this equation was *always* watching her.

He could recall the exact moment she first set foot on his land. He had been gathering firewood when her scent hit him with the strength of a punch to the chest. Struck dumb, he stood there *counting* the milieu of flavors composing that foreign, feminine aroma.

Animal musk, stream water, *Mr. Clean.*

It amazed him still that his first instinct hadn't been to hunt down whoever dared to trespass onto his property. Had it been her damn father, he wouldn't have hesitated, but her…

Instead, he waited, puzzled by how her presence melded into the environment like it belonged there. This was *her* land, that wild aroma told him. He was just living on it. Instant attraction had been only natural—or so he told himself. As much as it disgusted him to admit, he'd felt a pull then and there—the primal urge to claim a lone female wolf who dared to venture so close.

Until he saw her and realized his mistake. That frail waif of a girl was no lycan. She couldn't be.

The second time she came, he intentionally left those horses out, curious how she would react to them. How they would react to her. From a distance she could never fathom, he observed her approach. When she saw them…

It was *because* of those animals that he believed she was human. They let her go near them. Touch them—a courtesy they never tolerated from him, despite the years he owned the property. It was instinct. To them, he reeked of a predator's scent. The dark one had even tried kicking him once, but they never showed the same fear toward Loren Connors.

If she really were lupine, he couldn't explain the exception—not logically, anyway. At least her visits gave the animals some social interaction. Sure, they let him put food in the stable and bring them out to pasture, but that was it.

Once, he considered hiring human stable hands, but humans were instinctively nosy, and he relished his privacy. Fortunately, Loren kept to the barn, never venturing any further than that.

He was *convinced* she was human…

Witnessing her on top of the Tanner girl was enough to challenge that belief. So much for being a mouse. With barely any provocation, the prey sprouted claws on the spot. Growled. Got its first taste of battle-worn blood.

And *liked* it too—he recognized that hungry look in her eyes. Instinct had awoken, transforming her from hunted to hunter. It was a good thing that he stopped her—otherwise, who knew what she would have done?

Though, if he were honest with himself…he *shouldn't* have stopped her at all. It wasn't their way. Were they in the pack, protocol would dictate she assert herself and scratch out her place in the pecking order.

If only that asshole Connors had taken her to the pack when he had the chance. Their laws would have forbidden them from refusing her. Lukka, that arrogant prick, would have had to listen.

However, as long as there was any doubt, they could ignore her existence entirely.

In retrospect, Bill figured he should have taken her his damn self. His only comfort was purely selfish—Fred Connors couldn't possibly be her father. That low-level bastard couldn't sire a lycan.

But therein lay the drama. Which one of those pricks in the pack had fathered the girl and then abandoned her without a second thought?

Ironically, there wasn't a law for punishing that action. To be fair, there was no need. Children ensured a legacy, and most men acknowledged their bastards, if only to guarantee their bloodline lived on. It was primal instinct rather than honor. Loren's sire either didn't know of her existence, or he was as much of an anomaly as she was. Though, for now…

No other family mattered. She was *his*.

From now, until he released her, she could never go anywhere he didn't allow, or do anything he didn't give explicit permission for. A part of her would always be connected to him. Like in this very moment, when he sensed she was awake.

A possessive urge to protect her flooded his veins, strengthening by the second. *Mine.* It went beyond logic. Emotions. Morals.

Still, disgust mingled with the newfound bond. As much as he tried to rationalize it to Sonia, he didn't *want* this. Not since Emma—though this time it was different. So different, the contrasts blew his damn mind.

Emma had wanted him. They had shared their thoughts and emotions through their link, almost greedily. With Loren, the connection to her was completely sealed off—*for her own good,* he told himself. The only parts of her he allowed himself to access were her emotions. Her pain. Her fear. Those damn dark memories—he prevented her from feeling any of it. It was the least he could do.

Until Lukka…

Damn, he just hoped the bastard came soon.

He couldn't keep her here—even though her scent already seemed like a permanent part of the atmosphere…

11

"**H**ave a seat," Sonia told Loren, gesturing to an empty stool. "Would you like anything to eat?"

There seemed to be plenty. Loren sniffed, sensing eggs, bacon, and pancakes. All things she hadn't eaten in years. Cautiously, she crept over to the stool, holding the blanket to her body so tightly that her hands shook.

The food wasn't the only aroma flooding the house. That familiar scent of pine lingered in the air…on her *skin*. It was everywhere.

"Something wrong?" Sonia asked, noticing her uneasy expression.

"T-This is Officer McGoven's house," Loren croaked while attempting to mount the barstool without losing her grip over her covering. "How did I… How did I get here?"

Sonia's warm smile remained frozen in place. "I'm a friend of Bill's," she began, ignoring the question. "I want you to know that you are safe here. Don't worry about anything else. Did you sleep okay?"

She paused as if waiting for a reply.

Loren couldn't think of one.

"I'm here visiting for a few days," Sonia went on, still smiling. "So, how do you feel?"

Loren thought it over. "Strange," she whispered after a long minute.

Something wasn't...*right.*

Much like Sonia insisted, she felt safe—when she shouldn't have. She'd woken up in a stranger's bed, for one. A stranger who just so happened to be an officer of the law. Now, here she was, talking to an even stranger woman in said officer's kitchen over an offer of breakfast.

And why on earth was she naked? Why did scrapes and bruises seem to cover every inch of the skin that wasn't shielded beneath the protection of the blanket? Strangest of all, why didn't she seem worried about spending the night in a man's house, while her father...

Fear stabbed through her chest, shattering that invisible barrier. *Her father.*

"I'll make you some tea." Sonia shot to her feet. "And how about some eggs?"

Before Loren could reply, she retrieved a pan from the stove and scraped a heaping pile of food onto a plate. Minutes later, Loren found herself served with a full meal, complete with two strips of bacon.

"Eat up," Sonia urged, reclaiming a stool. "You must be starving."

Loren felt way too uneasy to be hungry—though, Sonia seemed to possess the same unspoken authority McGoven did. A fork was already in her hand, and she shoveled a helping of eggs into her mouth before she could help it.

She chewed woodenly, inspecting the large kitchen all the while. A few things stuck out to her. The fridge was devoid of any decoration or random clutter—even her father kept a magnet from one of his favorite beer companies on the front of theirs.

Moving on, the sink was spotless. The center island was clear, save for her plate and Sonia's tea. Even the countertops didn't hold anything of significance other than a potted plant and a coffee maker.

No empty beer bottles, crushed soda cans, or the remnants of a late-night poker party. It reminded Loren of one of those fancy show kitchens in a magazine. Perfect, but oddly uninviting. *Unlived* in.

"Your food's getting cold."

At the prompt, Loren choked down another mouthful of eggs, but as she swallowed, Sonia's cheerful expression faded.

"Loren, how much do you remember? About last night?" Anxiety colored her voice. She was worried.

"Last night?" Loren set her fork aside and mulled over the question. She remembered sleeping in her own bed...only to be awoken by—

Suddenly, she gripped the counter, trembling from head to toe.

"Are you alright?"

Loren shook her head, fighting to suck in air. *Remember.* Once the memories started, it was like watching a train wreck—she couldn't look away.

She had been dragged out of bed by her father. Thrown down the stairs.

Beaten.

Her father chased her into the kitchen, she grabbed a knife, and…

That was where her recollections ended like a movie cut short. The rest was blank. Empty.

Erased?

But he's dead, a part of her whispered. She knew that much.

"I think… I'm an orphan." Her voice sounded flat. Empty. The despair she would have imagined feeling was absent. It could have been a normal day.

No. The thought prickled at the back of her mind like an unreachable itch. *Think! This is wrong.*

"Loren…" Sonia suddenly reached across the table and grasped her hand. "I'm so sorry about your father. They think it was a robbery gone wrong, or at least that's what Bill told me."

A robbery. The only hole in that theory was that her father didn't have anything worth stealing, let alone killing him for. Though, she could just be in denial.

His death meant that she was truly alone. An orphan at eighteen.

"Bill thinks that it's better if you stay here," Sonia added. "At least, for now—"

"Why?" Loren blurted. She should have been in a shelter. Or, perhaps, the interrogation room of the police station. After all, she'd been in this position before…

"He was the one who found you. In the woods." Sonia eyed the wall behind Loren's head as she spoke—anywhere but her face. "He thinks that maybe the person who killed your father attacked you too. It might have been revenge over his gambling debts. You'll be safer here. He's cleared it with the station and the school as well. Everyone agrees this is the best situation."

Loren mulled over that in silence—but it didn't make sense. In fact, *none* of what Sonia had said made sense. The so-called mysterious murderer. Her being found wandering the woods in the middle of the night alone...

Before she could think too hard on it, the front door opened.

Pine. The scent rode a gust of cool air, more pungent than ever— preceding the exact moment a dark-haired figure entered the foyer. He paused, stomping mud and rainwater from his boots. He wore a thick navy windbreaker and jeans that alluded to the cold temperature outside. It must have been raining too, because his hair dripped as he slicked a hand through it. Only then did he finally glance in her direction…

And the world made sense again.

Sonia said something, her pink lips moving, but Loren couldn't hear her. She lurched to her feet, clutching the blanket. It was an impulse as unavoidable as a heartbeat. Instinctive—*Get up. He's here.*

And all along, something within her had craved him from the second she awoke. It had been waiting for him. His presence was an anchor against any doubt. She could feel the calm taking hold as his eyes flitted over her.

But then he turned away, addressing Sonia. "See if these will do."

For the first time, Loren noticed the duffle he carried over to the counter. As he set it down, Sonia withdrew its contents, mainly clothing. Not only that...

They were hers. *Her* ratty sweater still encrusted with mud. Her oversized T-shirt. Her one pair of jeans, and two long, shapeless sundresses. The only things missing were her white nightgown and her shoes.

"This is it?" Sonia sighed at the meager collection. "Are you sure?"

Officer McGoven followed her gaze and nodded. "Everything else was his."

"This will have to do for now, but you *have* to get her some new clothes. If you need the money, I can give you a few hundred—"

"I don't need your charity, Sonia." McGoven's eyes narrowed, and Loren felt an answering emotion ignite within her. Irritation. He was right. They didn't need charity. They just needed...

Him. She needed him to look at her.

"It's not charity," Sonia insisted, while folding the clothing strewn on the countertop. "After all, if Lukka does accept her, I'm sure you'll be compensated."

"Compensated." McGoven scoffed and began to pace, eyeing the floor. "That is if he doesn't conjure some old law out of thin air that declares this a crime."

Loren held her breath as he passed by her position, but he never looked up.

Please, a part of her whined. She twitched on her heels, possessed with the desire. *Look at me. Look at me.*

"Oh, Bill." Sonia sighed and placed a hand on his shoulder. "Don't be—"

"Look at me!" The voice sounded like Loren's—but louder than she would ever dare to speak. In unison, McGoven and Sonia turned to see her standing there in her thin blanket.

Sonia gasped, but Loren ignored her. Nothing mattered but those gray eyes. Finally, they met her gaze, and her heart raced, her tongue went dry, even her palms started to sweat.

This is it, a part of her murmured excitedly. *Look at me. Acknowledge me…*

"This will have to do, for now," he grumbled, returning his attention to the woman at the counter. "I'll take her out tomorrow. Though, I don't know what the hell I'm going to do about her school."

"Maybe just get her assignments?" Sonia pitched, but her eyes darted warily in Loren's direction. She hadn't missed the outburst. Both she and McGoven seemed to be deliberately ignoring it. "At least for the first week—"

"But do you think that'll—"

"Why…why can't I go to school?" *Bad girl, Loren,* she thought as both sets of eyes turned to her again. Only Sonia's lingered for longer than a second.

"It's not safe," McGoven replied, eyeing the window.

Not safe, that persistent voice in her head echoed. But no. That wasn't all.

"Why?" she asked.

His head seemed to swivel in slow motion. Like lasers, his eyes went to hers, penetrating with a single, searching stare.

She'd gotten her wish. She made *him* look at her.

But he didn't seem to like what he saw. Not one bit.

12

He took her in vertically, starting with her wild, tangled hair, before moving down to her battered face, her throat, and finally, the bits of her visible from beneath the blanket.

He drew the observation out to the last second. Stalling. *Please,* that voice in her pleaded. She waited for those gray eyes to lock with hers. Waited for him to say something—anything. But there was no spark of recognition. No expression, whatsoever, played over that handsome face.

And it hurt. It physically *hurt* to be denied…something. A look. Reassurance. Her heart panged, her stomach in knots.

Please…

He cleared his throat and turned to the window again, inspecting the gray sky with unusual interest.

"You've been through a lot, Loren," Sonia said to fill the awkward silence. "It might be better if you just rest for a few days."

Was that what he wanted? Loren couldn't take her eyes off him.

He was ignoring her. She could tell—but that silver gaze flitted her way every few seconds as if he couldn't help it. He took stock of her in pieces. Her trembling frame. Her *eye* especially, which throbbed whenever she blinked.

Abruptly, he turned back to Sonia. *Do something,* that gaze demanded, almost helplessly.

"Loren," Sonia's voice was suddenly strained. "Why don't you get dressed?"

She fished a garment at random from the pile on the counter. "This is lovely," she exclaimed with more enthusiasm than necessary, holding up the straps of a pink paisley sundress. "Why don't you wear it today? Here—" She returned the dress to the duffle and handed it to Loren before she had the chance to reply. "Do you need me to show you where the bathroom is?"

Loren shook her head only to belatedly realize that the offer had been a not-so-subtle cue to leave.

Now.

Stiffly, she retreated into the living room, still gripping the blanket, but she couldn't stop herself from glancing at *him* one last time.

He stood nearly the entire length of the kitchen away, his back to her, as if a spot on the wall was far more interesting than she was.

You're being ridiculous, she tried to scold herself as she turned into the hallway. *You're a half-naked freak standing in the middle of his house.*

But still…

Why won't he look at me? The thought chased her into the bathroom, where she shut the door and faced her reflection with a heavy sense of dread.

Her appearance could explain his reluctance. She looked awful. Her hair was a mess, her face swollen and battered. An ugly mark stretched along the length of her jaw, contrasting with the pallor of her skin.

Just as alarming was a twin bruise encircling her throat…

She turned away from the mirror in favor of inspecting the clothes. They weren't all the duffle contained. There was also a toothbrush, hairbrush, comb, and underwear—all hers. There was only one way Officer McGoven could have gotten them, but the thought of him prowling through her father's empty house made her shiver. At least she didn't have to wear the blanket any longer.

She washed up on autopilot, pulling the dress on after. It was long enough to disguise the worst of the bruising, though the thin straps left her arms bare. Ignoring the sight, she focused on her hair.

A part of her just wanted to coil the mess in a bun and be done with it—but that would mean no protective covering to hide behind. Though, McGoven seemed to have no problem probing beneath her protective measures. In the end, she settled for dragging a brush through the worst of the kinks and then braided it, like her mother used to, all those years ago.

Once finished, she felt weirdly exposed. A turtle without its shell. Before she could change her mind, she entered the hall, leaving the blanket—folded neatly—and duffle behind.

Sonia and Officer McGoven seemed to be in the middle of an intense conversation, huddled together near the center island.

"What are you going to do?" Sonia asked in a hushed whisper.

McGoven shrugged and braced his hands against the counter. "Have you called Lukka yet?"

"Y-Yes, but…"

"But what?"

"He says it will be at least a week before he can come to see her. Even then, he made no guarantees that he would accept her into the—"

"Fuck!" McGoven slammed a fist onto the counter, and Loren felt an answering twinge through her chest. It was as if she were a mirror, reflecting whatever he felt. Now? More than rage plagued him. Fear?

"What the hell is he so busy doing that he has to wait a whole week?"

"He's the Alpha Bill," Sonia said softly. "If he says he's busy, then he's busy. Besides…as cruel as it sounds, she's not one of his—at least not yet. He has no responsibility to her. Why should he hurry?"

"Because I don't *want* her, that's why." McGoven groaned in frustration, cradling his face in his hands. "What the hell am I supposed to do with her for an entire damn week? It's hard enough smoothing over that mess with her father. Sooner or later, the wrong people will start asking the right questions."

"Help her," Sonia suggested. "Protect her. Keep her safe. I know this is a lot to ask of you, but she doesn't have anyone else. Look at me, Bill."

He did, and something inside Loren lurched. It was the same envy she'd felt while Naomi pranced around in her fancy boots— but times a million. Poisonous jealousy. *No,* that voice within her cried. *He shouldn't look at her. Not her. Me!*

Her jaw ached with the restraint it took to remain silent. This was insane. She had no right to be upset.

Then, Sonia placed her hand on his shoulder, and her mind went blank. *NO!* The protest ripped through her skull. Her body—as if Sonia simply touching him went against the fabric of her entire being.

Her lips parted with the impulse to voice just one word. Scream it. *Mine—*

"Loren, are you okay?" Sonia had both hands against the counter now, her head cocked with concern.

No, she wasn't. Heart pounding, Loren darted past the kitchen for the front door. Outside, the cold air felt like a slap, but it didn't help to knock any sense into her. She couldn't erase the sight of them from her mind.

He can look at her, a part of her cruelly whispered. *He seems to have no problem touching her—it's you he can't stand.*

He said so himself. *What am I supposed to do with her for a whole week?*

Apparently, he was waiting for this *Lukka* to come for her. To take her where?

She had no idea. But wasn't that how the game of her life seemed to be played? People just came and shuffled her from one place to the other, and she never had any say.

Well, I do now.

Gritting her teeth, she descended the porch steps while the wind tore at her braid and her bare feet sank into fresh mud. The slight discomfort wasn't enough to make her turn back.

Where could she possibly go, anyway?

Run, that familiar instinct urged. *Just run away. No one will miss you…*

It wasn't like she had any ties to New Walsh. Her father was dead. That crappy ranch house at the end of the street was empty.

She had nothing left. Except…

Her feet carried her forward without any input from her brain. Almost on autopilot, she reached her destination—the barn.

She was freezing by the time she muscled open the door and pushed her way inside. Once enclosed by the familiar four walls, she felt safe. It was with an almost dream-like calm that she went over to the saddle rack and grabbed a set of tack at random, then headed for the back stall.

Bunny and Esther greeted her warmly, but Loren only had eyes for Xavier. Out of the three, he was the only one fit enough to ride and, as if knowing her intention, he didn't shy away for the first time in months as she opened his stall.

She had never ridden a horse before, though she seemed to instinctively know how to clip the reins onto his halter and lead him fearlessly to a nearby bench that made for the perfect makeshift mounting block.

A strange sense of urgency drove her on—*Hurry, hurry, hurry. Can't let him see.*

Though what did it matter?

Officer McGoven didn't seem to give a damn about her. The loss of his animal was the least he could suffer in exchange for having her out of his hair once and for all.

Determined, she hiked up her dress and braced one foot on the bench while swinging the other over Xavier's ebony back. Once she sat, fully mounted, that rebellious sense of determination faltered.

What now? She had no clue. On the other hand, Xavier seemed to know exactly what *he* wanted. When the horse bolted into motion, Loren just held on.

Experimentally, she tugged the reins to one side, and Xavier followed, storming through the gate and down the muddy path. She felt her eyes drawn to the house, watching anxiously for any sign of movement.

Would they notice her?

Even if they had, she was already out of view. Xavier flew across the earth, apparently eager to stretch his legs. When Loren squeezed her thighs, he seemed to have no trouble going faster. She had only a second's warning to grip his mane before he broke into a gallop over the hill.

She hung on and tried to breathe. For the moment, nothing else mattered but the icy chill of the wind bearing down her back. Who knew where she'd end up?

Anywhere was better than where she wasn't wanted.

The ride seemed to last an eternity, but it could have only been a few minutes later that they neared the edge of the Baker farm boundary—and that was when the horse lost it.

Suddenly, he reared, kicking up mud and earth in a stinging spray. A frantic whinny rippled from his massive chest, sending a chill down Loren's spine.

Her first thought was that something had spooked him, and she patted his flank, murmuring soothing words. She tried twisting the reins in another direction, but once again, he shied back. And then again, when she tried another direction. It was as if an invisible wall prevented him from crossing the property boundary.

"Come on, boy," Loren urged. She shifted, intending to dismount and lead him on foot.

The second she moved, all hell broke loose.

Xavier reared again, bellowing a high-pitched cry that would haunt her nightmares. Loud, terrified—panicked. Dislodged completely, she fell from the animal's back. No, it felt more like an invisible hand caught her collar and yanked her down *hard*. She braced for the fall, but when she finally collided with a firm surface, there was no pain.

Just noise. *Thunder?* No, this sound went even *deeper*, rumbling beneath her skin. Words? Yes, but it was a long, dizzying minute before she could make out any clearly.

"What the hell is wrong with you? Are you *insane?*"

Probably, Loren realized as her nostrils flared, catching the scent of pine. She wasn't on the ground after all, but in someone's arms.

14

"**A**re you alright?" her rescuer demanded, his eyes a chilling silver. He crouched, manipulating her onto her knees before him. "Are you hurt? Are you injured? ANSWER ME!"

He was shaking her, Loren realized. *Physically* shaking her. Her head lolled back and forth as he wrenched on her shoulders.

"Can you speak? Loren!"

"I-I'm fine," she managed to choke out.

Abruptly, he let her go and stood, hissing in relief. Her response seemed to console him, but marginally. He was still angry, but above all else, he looked…worried?

"Do you have any idea how dangerous they can be? Fuck, you could have been—" He broke off abruptly and turned toward the west end of the field. In an ebony blur, Xavier bolted as if the devil himself were at his heels.

You could have been… A vivid imagination allowed Loren to fill in the blanks. She could have broken her neck or been crushed beneath a flurry of racing hooves. In fact, the only reason she hadn't been hurt at all, was because of him. McGoven. Though, how had he caught up to her in the first place?

Silent, she took in his wind-swept hair and heaving chest. Both pointed to one insane conclusion. Had he run after a galloping horse on foot?

"I'm sorry," she blurted. Fear for Xavier especially made her sick with guilt. "I'm sorry."

"Shut up." He didn't yell, but her mouth snapped shut instantly.

Then she winced. Her lower jaw was on fire. *Swollen,* she remembered, though the cause was hazy. A punch? Gingerly, she traced her bottom lip, only to freeze the second she contacted the tender flesh.

He was watching her. Worriedly, his gaze traced the planes of her face, and he was on his knees in a heartbeat. One of his hands reached for her, but visibly hesitated, before brushing her bruised cheek.

Every muscle in her body tensed at his touch. Not out of fear, but he was warm. So warm. A foreign emotion bubbled in the pit of her stomach. Greed maybe? His heat traveled hungrily through her skin, inciting an urge that had her aching to move closer. Become engulfed in that furnace-like warmth.

The look in his eyes stopped her, though—something told her that if she *did* touch him, he wouldn't hesitate to bat her hand away.

I don't want this! The memory of the declaration was almost as painful as what he said next, "Don't you *ever* do this again. Ever. In fact, don't ever leave this property without my permission. Do you understand?"

Her heart sank beneath the weight of the order. *Never again.* She nodded, but he was already on his feet, his focus beyond her.

"I need to find the horse. Come with me." He took off, and she followed robotically, cutting across the field.

Xavier had carried her farther than she'd realized, and it seemed to take an eternity to return to the heart of the property. McGoven remained silent during the entire trek, but his tense posture spoke for him. *I'm angry. Don't you ever do this again. You could have been killed!*

She was shivering by the time they reached the farmhouse—not only because she walked barefoot in a sundress. Dread was another reason her teeth chattered. She knew that look in his eye. One way or another, she would pay for this little stunt.

But is there any room left? she wondered, glancing at her fresh bruises. It didn't really matter. When they mounted the front porch, Loren tensed in anticipation of a blow.

But—even though he seemed just as angry—the only move McGoven made was to sidestep Sonia, who rushed to greet them.

"Is she okay?" the woman asked breathlessly. "Bill? Is she okay?"

He didn't answer. With single-minded focus, he stalked off in the direction Xavier had taken off in. Simmering fury battered off him in waves, cutting through the icy mist.

"Ugh, *Men.*" Sonia clucked her tongue and rolled her eyes. "So damn dramatic. You okay? Bill nearly had a heart attack when we saw that you'd gone off on that horse." She bit her lower lip at the memory. "They can be a little wild, as I'm sure you've found out. To be frank, I'm surprised he hasn't sold them yet. Keeping them here has probably caused them more stress than anything. Not to mention the expense. I guess it's out of loyalty. The rogue who used to live here kept them for so long—" She broke off, shooting Loren a worried glance. "Oh dear, you still look a little shaken. Your hair is a mess. Let me—" She attempted to finger a lock of wayward hair, but Loren nearly tripped off the bottommost porch step in her haste to back away.

While Sonia might not hurt her, she couldn't say the same for everyone on the property. Fearfully, she eyed the direction Officer McGoven had marched off in, only to find that he'd vanished from view.

"I'm going to have to give him a little *talking to* about proper ways to express our anger," Sonia muttered ominously. "Come on inside. I've made some chamomile tea. Oh, you're feet! Let's clean you off first."

Loren waited while Sonia ran inside to fetch a towel. Once clean, she retreated to the couch, and Sonia reappeared armed with a steaming mug of tea. As Loren took a sip, she eyed the window, just in time to witness a dark shape streaking across the west field.

Xavier. But something else was hot on his heels. Or make that *someone,* who easily herded the animal straight into the barn. Still holding the stable door, the figure turned as if seeking *her* out through the distance.

"Oh! Loren!" Sonia was staring at her, wide-eyed. "You're bleeding."

Sure enough, she had unintentionally bitten her bottom lip. Warm beads of blood dribbled down her chin, but she barely felt the sting.

"Wait here," Sonia said, before racing down a hallway. "I'll grab the first aid kit!"

Loren remained on the couch, tucking her knees beneath her chin. That inevitable ache in her gut that always preceded one of her father's rages plagued her ceaselessly. That "shit's about to hit the fan" feeling.

When she heard the sound of approaching footsteps, she tensed, but it was only Sonia sitting beside her with a white case on her lap.

"This might hurt a little," the woman warned as she fished out a length of gauze. "But we don't want it to get infected—"

"I'll do it."

Both women turned to the doorway, where officer McGoven stood as if he'd been there all along. The only signs that gave him away were mud-caked boots and tousled hair. The scent of fresh air diluted his unique smell, and Loren couldn't help how her nostrils flared. He smelled wilder than ever.

Ours, the voice within her purred as if thrilled by his disheveled appearance. His clothing clung to every straining bit of muscle, damp with sweat.

"Are you sure, Bill?" Sonia clutched the med kit to her chest. "I can—"

"No." He stepped forward, his voice ringing with authority. "I'll do it."

Sonia shrugged and retreated to a corner while Officer McGoven continued to approach. As he came close enough to touch, Loren cleared her throat.

"W-Wait." She didn't know what made her speak up. Maybe guilt. "X-Xavier? Is he alright?"

"Is who alright?" Sonia asked. McGoven frowned, equally confused.

No wonder. Loren's cheeks flamed as she realized her mistake. Esther, Bunny, and Xavier were names *she* had given the horses. Unlike the portrayals of stables on television, Officer McGoven didn't have his animals' names on the doors to their stalls, so she named each one based on its personality.

Esther, for her big, soulful eyes. Bunny, for those droopy white ears, and Xavier, who seemed too regal to be called anything else. It had never really entered her mind that their *real* owner might have called them something else.

"The horse," she croaked, forcing herself to meet that piercing gaze. "Is h-he alright?"

Officer McGoven gave her the strangest look. "No."

Loren's heart sank. "Oh, God…I'm so sorry—"

"He's spooked," Officer McGoven explained matter-of-factly. "He's winded…but he'll live."

"Oh." Relief nearly barreled Loren over. Xavier was okay.

"See?" Sonia began tentatively. "You were worried for nothing. Bill, it's fine. I can fix her up. You don't have to—"

"I'll do it." He shifted to deliberately block Sonia's path.

With a sigh, Sonia turned to the kitchen. "I'll just make more tea."

Nervous energy filled the air as she left. She seemed like the type who needed to keep busy, feeding everyone, or soothing emotions during a crisis. The natural-born mom.

Officer McGoven, however, eyed the first-aid kit as if he had no clue what to do with it.

"Hold it for me," he ordered after a moment.

Loren scooted to the very end of the couch and wrestled the kit onto her lap. Seeming to change his mind, he took it from her, and she had nothing better to do with her hands than fidget with the hem of her dress.

It felt thinner than tissue paper as he sank to one knee before her. His scent flooded her lungs, intoxicating. Powerful. The first aid kit resembled a toy box in his large hands, flimsy and fragile.

"What were you thinking?" He posed the question so softly she barely heard him. "You could have been killed."

"I just thought…" That somehow, stealing his horse would be okay in the long run if it got her off his property. "I'm sorry. I thought… It would be better if I left."

His frown gave her the excuse to stop talking. He lowered his head, propping the kit on his knee. "Do you even know the first damn thing about riding a horse?" he asked.

"No."

He made a deep sound in the back of his throat. *Interesting.* "Do you realize that the horse you took is a full-grown stallion who could have *thrown* you the second he wanted to?"

She had known that much, at least. "Y-yes."

"*And—*" Officer McGoven continued. "Do you realize those horses will never leave *my* property unless I give—" Abruptly, he changed the topic. "Open your mouth. You're still bleeding."

He gave her no warning, and she tried not to flinch as one of those massive hands cradled her chin. If only he felt as dangerous as he looked. Despite the muscles coiling beneath his skin, his gentleness was a shock. He barely touched her at all, just softly eased her head back so that he could dab at her bottom lip with a bit of antiseptic liquid smeared over the cotton ball.

Their eyes met, and Loren expected anger. Hatred. Rage. What she found in his gaze only confused her. Fear? Genuine fear that didn't seem to ease until he wiped away most of the blood and set the first aid kit aside.

Rather than withdraw, he remained crouched. Then, much like Sonia had tried to, he tucked a loose piece of hair behind her ear.

She didn't recoil—she couldn't. It was like her body became magnetic, drawn to his touch. Her toes *curled,* and an unfamiliar emotion flooded her belly. Another time she might have flinched at the sensation, but she was paralyzed.

It felt…nice having him there. Right.

Ours, that voice murmured, louder and more insistent. *Ours. Mine. His.*

She felt as though she could endure his touch for eternity. Longer, even.

Though nothing in the world could have prepared her for the moment he leaned forward and pressed his mouth against her jaw.

15

*H*e didn't kiss her. Instead, his lips ghosted over what had to be the only unmarked sliver of skin she had left.

Panic stirred at the back of her mind, but something in his movements made her relax. He wasn't brutal or rough. Just… patient. He angled his face, but carefully, ensuring his skin contacted hers. As a result, his breath basted her skin, lessening some of the discomfort in the bruised areas. It was strange. His mouth nudged a tender bruise on her cheek next. Rather than pain, she felt…

Better.

It was as if his touch was magic—but he didn't stop there. His lips blazed a trail along her entire jaw. Her nose. Her swollen upper lip. When he finally stilled, his mouth hovered inches from hers.

His nearness made her dizzy, but though her heart pounded, she wasn't afraid. Not even as she felt his fingers untangle the remains of her braid to cup the back of her skull. Like lightning, a million thoughts jolted through her all at once—*stupid* thoughts.

The main one being that he couldn't mean to... He couldn't possibly *kiss* her. Her lip was busted, and he didn't even *know* her. Not to mention the fact that he had to at least be in his mid-twenties, several years older than her.

None of that, however, mattered more than the simple fact that he *couldn't* kiss her because...

"I'm making cookies!"

The excited proclamation came from the kitchen, and Loren recoiled against the couch while Officer McGoven stood, crossing his arms.

"What the hell did you just say?" he bellowed.

"Cookies," Sonia cheerfully reiterated, poking her head through the doorway. "I found some stuff in your cupboards."

"Sonia..." McGoven rolled his eyes, but, overall, his expression revealed none of the shock Loren felt. As if it were the most natural thing in the world to press his mouth against a stranger's face and walk away with no explanation.

She wasn't so unaffected. Boys her own age were an enigma, and men... In her experience, their touch only inspired terror, nothing more—until now. Her cheek tingled, but not like the slaps she was used to enduring. In fact, her face felt better overall. Numb instead of throbbing.

On second thought, McGoven's unshaken demeanor seemed to be an act he put on for her benefit. His eyes kept darting to the window—the woods. While he'd safely wrangled Xavier, something had him worried. Suddenly, he cocked his head as if picking up a noise.

Loren strained her ears but heard nothing. A heartbeat later, McGoven was storming across the room.

"You came alone?" Belatedly, Loren realized he was speaking to Sonia.

"Yes." The woman barely looked up from the contents of a bowl she was stirring. "Why?"

"Nothing—" His frown deepened, and he eyed the window more intently. Did he see something? Suddenly, he lunged for the doorway. "Stay here. I'm heading out."

He was at the front door before Loren could blink.

Sonia didn't seem worried. "Kay," she called back. "I'll save you some cookies."

McGoven only grunted in acknowledgment before leaving, letting the door slam behind him. Alone, Loren crept into the kitchen. Without his cold mystery as a contrast, Sonia flitted across the space with childlike energy that betrayed her youth. She couldn't be any older than her early twenties.

"I hope you like sweets?" she asked once she caught Loren staring. "I think they'll have to be sugar, though. He doesn't seem to have any chocolate chips. He always was a health nut. You know, he used to eat tuna by the can every day. What a freak of nature—" Beaming, she looked at Loren only to realize that she wasn't in on the joke. "Oh… Well, let's just say where we come from, beef is the most common thing on the menu, cooked rare, if at all."

Her father must have been from the same place. Steak seemed to be all he ever ate—unless beer counted as a meal item. The thought unnerved her for some reason, tugging at a memory on the periphery of her consciousness. Why couldn't she remember?

"Where are you from?" she asked absently. Now that she thought about it, McGoven didn't seem like the other citizens of New Walsh. He wasn't stuck-up like Naomi Tanner, or hostile to outsiders like her father.

"Somewhere far from here," Sonia said warily. "Bill and I grew up together. In a place called Black Mountain. Ever hear of it?"

Loren shook her head.

"Really?" Sonia's eyes widened, but she disguised her surprise behind a tinkling laugh. "Well, it's beautiful, but not exactly a haven of culture. Tuna fish is about the most exotic thing on our menu. Though, luckily, we do love our cookies. Wanna give me a hand?"

"S-sure."

Beaming, Sonia tossed her a small glass bowl and three eggs. "I love to bake," she chirped, still stirring her mixture. "It gives me something to do with my hands. Though, I probably *should* go and check on Bill."

Loren followed her gaze out of the window above the sink. Visible against the backdrop of the forest was the hulking shape of Officer McGoven. He wasn't heading for his truck, or even the squad car—both of which were parked in the driveway alongside a blue car she assumed was Sonia's.

Instead, he marched toward the woods with a determination that made Loren suspect he wasn't going for a lighthearted stroll. No. She could...feel his unease. It flavored the air like smoke, warning of impending danger.

Did he sense something out there? she wondered, creeping closer to the window. The same something that had spooked Xavier?

She opened her mouth to ask, only to be presented with a bowl of tan-colored gunk. "Wanna add the eggs?" Sonia asked.

Woodenly, Loren added all three to the mixture. As Sonia stirred, she glanced at the window again. Already, McGoven had vanished.

"Don't worry about him. He'll be back. Bill is…" Sonia sighed, following her gaze. "Well, he can seem grumpy at times. Perhaps a bit cold. Don't take it personally. He's been through a lot, and let's just say he isn't used to carrying on a full conversation."

"What happened?"

Sonia eyed her sharply. Her tongue flitted across her lips, and Loren suspected she was weighing whether or not to tell her this piece of McGoven's past. But suddenly…a part of her needed to know—craved anything that could lessen his mystery.

"Please," she croaked.

"Well, he had a… *Wife*. A wife once, but she died. It was awful —" Pain constricted Sonia's features, and she leaned against the counter for stability. "Bill changed after that. He left home and took over this farm. It's been five years, and this is the first time I've seen him."

Five years. A wife. Those new bits of information seemed to devastate that newly woken inner voice in Loren's mind. *We didn't know…*

"I'm surprised to find that he's kept this place in good shape at least," Sonia said, forcing a smile. "Old Josiah, the man who used to own this place—well, he wasn't fond of visitors for a start. I only came here once in those days, but I think Bill has done his best to update the interior."

"Josiah?" Loren hadn't heard that name before.

"Josiah Baker. He was a…friend of Bill's father, more like an uncle to him than anything. After he died, Bill took over the farm and all its little eccentricities. Josiah was never happy at the compound, under our laws. The second he left, I think he bought those horses merely to prove a point. At his core, he saw himself as human. Nothing else. Um, I mean, as a cowboy at heart," Sonia added in a rush. Her cheeks were faintly pink, but she huddled over the sink, hiding her face. "Anyway, Bill's lived here ever since."

With another sigh, she inspected the empty driveway and shrugged. "Well, I suppose we should get these in the oven."

Without mentioning McGoven, Loren set about obeying any task Sonia sent her way until the cookies were cooling on the counter.

Every now and again, her gaze drifted to the window, as those remnants of his past played on her mind. He had a wife once. Someone he loved.

Someone she knew she could never compare to—not that it mattered. To McGoven, she was a burden.

Nothing more.

16

---

*H*e didn't return. At least not before nightfall. By then, Sonia hustled her off to bed with a yawn, promising to wake her in the morning.

Once again, Loren found herself in that strange room, on an unfamiliar mattress, helplessly eyeing the ceiling. The gray blanket from before was gone.

But she could still smell him. This was *his* room; it had to be—but that wasn't the realization that made her breath catch. No, it was the fact that he had shared this bed with her at least once. Her body just *knew*, even if she couldn't remember. Had it been the other night?

She tried to picture him there, that bulk lying beside her, not too close—but close enough to feel that warmth. Her traitorous body tensed, longing to feel it again. Without the presence of someone else, this room was too big. Too cold. The mattress creaked with every movement, and as crazy as it seemed, it didn't feel *natural* lying on his bed without him.

Hit your head a little hard, when you fell off that horse? she wondered, annoyed, turning on her side.

She couldn't sleep, though she wasn't sure how much time passed before the front door finally slammed open.

He was back. His presence filled the entire house, relieving some of the tension she hadn't been aware of until then. That inner voice murmured excitedly. *He's here. Ours.* Anticipation flooded her veins with a sudden need to see him. She had to. The urge felt as vital as breathing.

But he never came upstairs. Instead, those heavy footsteps retreated toward the living room, and Loren could guess his final destination with a pang of despair.

The couch.

She didn't know where Sonia was, but at the thought of him near her… Loren bit down on her already tender lip.

You don't know him, a part of her argued. *He's a police officer, and he doesn't even know you!*

None of the excuses could penetrate that stubborn inner voice insisting the opposite. He belonged *there.* The only reason he *wasn't* was because of *her.*

The thought followed her into a dreamless sleep, where a barrage of nightmares awaited. She was running. Running, racing, falling. No matter where she went, she couldn't find peace. Safety. Monsters lurked on every corner, and she just wasn't fast enough…

"Loren."

She jolted awake, heart in her throat, as the remnants of the dream washed over her like ice water. Gradually, the darkness faded, and she was shaking beneath the covers.

Safe, a part of her insisted firmly. Then a familiar scent flooded her lungs, calming her racing heartbeat.

"Get dressed."

She whirled to find someone watching her from the doorway. McGoven, fully dressed in his navy windbreaker and black slacks. His eyes were sharp, betraying none of the exhaustion she felt after waiting up for him.

Safe, that voice insisted again. As long as he was there, nothing in the world could touch her.

"Sonia made breakfast, but I'll—" He turned away, and the rest of his words were grumbled, barely audible. "I'll be out in the truck. Come join me when you're done."

Breakfast? Sure enough, it was morning already. Bright light spilled in through the curtains shielding the window, illuminating the plain surroundings. Already she could tell it would be another rainy, overcast day.

At least now she didn't have to face it *naked.* Per Sonia's suggestion, she had gone to bed wearing her oversized T-shirt. At least until "Bill" could find her something else.

Rather than new clothing, someone had placed her duffle at the foot of the bed. After a quick appraisal of the contents, she chose her muddy sweater and jeans and headed for the bathroom with her toothbrush in tow. The one upstairs was larger than the one below. In it, she dressed quickly, and stumbled downstairs minutes later.

"Morning," Sonia called tiredly from the kitchen. Compared with yesterday, she looked less chirpy and more…exhausted. Had she waited for McGoven all night, too? Without saying as much, she yawned and gestured toward a steaming plate of bacon and eggs sitting on the center island.

"I made breakfast. Eat, and take your time. I'll make sure he waits."

Aware of McGoven's warning, Loren snatched a piece of toast from the spread and gobbled it greedily. Then, she rushed out the front door before Sonia could call her back. Her heart pounded as she raced down the porch steps and bounded the length of the driveway.

That green pickup idled near the road leading from the farm. When she finally clambered inside, Officer McGoven inspected her, an eyebrow raised.

"You could have eaten breakfast," he said. "I would have waited."

Loren shook her head. "I'm okay."

She was starving. Despite eating some of Sonia's cookies last night and a dinner of spaghetti, she could have easily devoured that plate of eggs and then some. Part of it was just greed. She wasn't used to having so much food on demand. Though, the thought of him waiting on her was *worse* than hunger.

Officer McGoven shrugged and drove into town without any comment. Gazing from the window, Loren tried to smother her curiosity. Soon, the anxiety turned into downright panic the closer they came to the heart of New Walsh.

This was it. He was taking her to the police station. There, she would be questioned about her father's so-called murder, and everything would start to unravel. There was no way around it. Things didn't add up with the whole "murder/robbery" story— who knew what the police officers thought?

She was on edge, nearly rising from the seat the moment the car came to a stop—to bolt or just run inside the station herself? She had no idea. Fearfully, she faced the window, only to discover the elegant façade of New Walsh Academy, not the station.

It was that twilight hour right before the doors opened. The calm before the storm. Loren had no idea what he could possibly expect to do here so early. She didn't even have her backpack.

But, obviously, explaining wasn't his strong suit.

"Come on," Officer McGoven commanded as he exited the truck first.

Loren moved to follow him only to realize, the moment her bare foot hit the pavement, that she was completely barefoot. When she didn't appear beside him, he turned to see why, eyes darting directly to her filthy feet.

"You forgot your damn shoes," he began in a hiss.

Loren shook her head. "No, I…"

There weren't any "shoes" left to wear. Her *Kicks* had all but disintegrated and weren't even among the things he retrieved from her house. He flinched, and she could imagine him running over the contents of her bedroom in his mind—*Were those pathetic sneakers the only ones she had?*

"Never mind." He turned abruptly, waving her off. "Wait here."

Sick with worry, Loren watched him enter the school. Though he wasn't in uniform, he looked no less intimidating in slacks and a windbreaker—an odd outfit considering how cold it was. Loren was freezing in her thick sweater.

She huddled on the front seat, feeling like a kenneled puppy.

He was inside a long time. Already, the trickle of students heading into the school was starting to pick up. It felt strange to not be a part of the morning rush. Even stranger to be sitting in a police officer's truck.

When he finally exited the school building, she sat bolt upright, tense with anticipation. His expression alone revealed nothing. He wasn't smiling or frowning. With no explanation whatsoever, he wrenched open the door on her end and dumped a pile of books onto her lap.

"Sign it," he demanded, nodding to a document resting on top of the pile.

Loren took the pen he offered and complied, scanning the document as she did so. It seemed to mention something about termination—withdrawing from academic activity.

Before she could read more, Officer McGoven snatched the page and shoved it into his pocket. Then he returned to the driver's seat, started the engine, and peeled out of the quickly filling parking lot.

"From now on, you'll do your assignments on your own," he explained while turning onto the main street. "Someone will drop off the work and turn it in for you. This way, you won't fall behind. At least until…"

He seemed to deliberately keep himself from saying more, but Loren had a grim idea of what words filled in the blanks.

Until Lukka comes for you.

Dazed, she eyed the textbooks on her lap. They were for all the subjects she was taking, along with a few notebooks from her locker.

She didn't dare ask any questions, not that Officer McGoven seemed inclined to tell her anything else. Silently, he drove through the heart of town, finally parking along the busiest street. Here, various stores sold everything from clothing to ice cream.

"What size are you?" he asked gruffly.

Loren blinked, but her hesitation only earned her an impatient scoff.

"Your *shoe* size. What shoe size are you?"

Confused, she inspected her bare feet. She had always just grabbed a pair that fit, without ever worrying about that little number on the bottom.

When she shook her head, Officer McGoven palmed one of her knees without warning. Shock paralyzed her as he lifted her leg, cupping her bare foot in the center of his palm. He seemed to weigh it, inspecting the shape. Satisfied with whatever he'd observed, he released her and left the truck, slamming the door behind him.

Loren waited, wondering what on earth he could possibly need with her shoe size. When he finally emerged from a nearby store, she saw the box first. Big and beautiful, it consumed her attention as McGoven approached and shoved it unceremoniously onto her lap.

"Try them on."

Without even explaining what "them" was, he headed toward the driver's seat.

Loren had an idea, though... Her fingers shook in anticipation as she wrestled the lid off and set it aside.

A mixture of shock and awe left her dizzy. She couldn't even speak. "Them" was a pair of boots. Sturdy hiking boots, to be exact. Naomi Tanner wouldn't be caught dead wearing a similar style, but Loren thought they were the most beautiful things she'd ever laid eyes upon.

"Try them on," McGoven insisted, his voice slightly less gruff. "They should be snug but not too tight."

Heart in her throat, she removed each boot gingerly. Someone had shoved a pair of novelty socks in each one, both decorated with ribbons and trees for Christmas. She pulled them on first, then the boots lacing them tightly. Marveling at the feel, she gave her foot an experimental kick.

"How do they feel?"

"P-Perfect," she stammered. "Thank you…but I can't—I can't possibly pay for these."

He gave her an exasperated look and started the truck as if he needed the distraction to compile a response. In the end, he grated four words through his teeth, "Don't worry about it."

They didn't speak all the way back to the farmhouse. The second he parked, Officer McGoven grabbed her stuff and mounted the porch where Sonia stood in the doorway to greet him.

Loren took her time, relishing the feel of her new boots.

"Nice," Sonia said appreciatively as she mounted the porch steps —but Loren could read the unease written over her face.

"What's wrong?" McGoven demanded.

Sighing, Sonia led the way inside and marched directly into the kitchen, where she fished a cookie from the plate on the counter.

"Lukka's called me back," she announced before taking a bite.

Loren sensed the words meant more than the obvious. McGoven's furious snarl proved it.

"What?" he shouted. "What the *hell* do you mean?"

"I'm sorry." Sonia's blue eyes darted everywhere around the kitchen but his face. "He called me back," she said once she swallowed. "He says that 'I'm needed' though he won't say for what. It doesn't matter. I can't refuse a direct order. I have to leave. Tonight."

17

"You can't leave." Angrily, McGoven formed a fist, and Loren half-expected him to smash it into the wall. He flattened his palm against the countertop instead with an almost helpless groan. "Sonia, I *need* you here—"

"I know," Sonia said softly. "But, it's not like I can refuse him. He'll see it as a challenge—especially if it's to stay with *you*. Besides, if we piss him off now, he might never come and see her. We can't take that risk."

Loren froze as they both turned in her direction.

Sonia looked miserable, but the man beside her… He looked crazed. Desperate. His eyes were molten silver, his throat cording with tension.

"What the hell am I supposed to do without you?" He sounded like a child pleading not to be abandoned.

"The same thing you've *been* doing," Sonia said gently. "This could turn out to be a good thing, for all of us. While I'm there, I can speak to Lukka directly. Now that I've met Loren, I can vouch for her. You… You were right, Bill." Her tone conveyed a double meaning.

"Yeah," McGoven hissed. "I'm sure he'll love to hear you say that. He'll roll out the fucking red carpet!"

"I'm sorry." Suddenly, Sonia stood on tiptoe and pressed her lips to his cheek.

Loren dug her nails into her palms. The intimate expression startled her—not because of the warmth in it, but because she wanted…

She wanted to march over there and drag Sonia away, by her *hair*. Shout, kick, scream—better yet, order her to never touch him again like that.

She didn't know why, but she couldn't ignore the building anger. It clawed through her chest like a living creature. It *hurt*.

Just as quickly, Sonia withdrew from him, and the unwarranted anger diminished slightly. "I'm leaving tonight," she said. "You'll be okay. I know you will. But I'll call—"

"Don't bother," Officer McGoven said ominously. "You have a point. There, you can convince the asshole to see her in person. If he hasn't sent his spies already."

Sonia raised an eyebrow. "What are you talking about?"

McGoven tossed Loren a cautious glance. Then he squared his jaw and said, "You saw how that horse bolted the other day? I thought it was because of the territory markers, but when I checked the perimeter, I caught a scent."

"What?" Sonia's eyes widened. "Another rogue?"

"No. They were too careful—much like a scout. I didn't recognize their scent, but I know your Lukka has been building his ranks, letting in plenty of outsiders to swell his numbers. All that talk about loyalty. You thought I didn't know?"

Sonia's cheeks flamed. "Bill, it isn't my place to—"

"I'm not asking for your political opinion, Sonia. I'm asking this —why the hell would your precious Alpha send a scout on the heels of a trusted advisor?"

A hard gleam sharpened Sonia's gaze. In an instant, the girlish charm vanished, and she looked on par with McGoven as far as maturity went. Just as shrewd and just as angry. "Maybe Lukka didn't give me exact permission to come," she said cagily. "I may have left on my own."

"You?" McGoven crossed his arms. "Go against your precious Alpha? What is this world coming to?"

"Don't mock me," Sonia snapped. "You called me, so I came. If he forbade me outright, I wouldn't be here."

"Or he let you come here as a distraction. Then he sent a guard dog after you to scout my property and report back," McGoven said darkly. "What the hell is he playing at?"

"You know what he's like."

"Oh, yes." McGoven's eyes flashed the color of steel. "I know exactly what he's like. That's what I'm worried about."

Sonia choked out an exasperated sigh. "*You* are the one who left us, remember? Lukka has done his best to keep order. You want so badly for him to fail, but he hasn't. We're doing fine under him, and I won't deny that because of your…history. I'm sorry if that upsets you."

"That's not what I meant," McGoven said softly. "I just want to know you're safe."

"*We* are."

"And… Is Kyle still his second?"

Loren stiffened. Irritation prickled her skin suddenly, white-hot. It didn't stem from her—just him. His face may be blank, but the guttural way he uttered that name left nothing to the imagination as to how McGoven felt about this man. Kyle.

Pure, unadulterated hatred.

"H-Huh?" Panic flitted across Sonia's features before she smothered it behind a cheerful smile. "Enough pack gossip. Don't worry. Please. It will only be a few days until Lukka comes himself. You'll be fine. Both of you. As for what you sensed… I'm sure it was just a scout, making sure I arrived safely."

"Even so, his scout most likely picked up her scent. Then, all of a sudden, your Alpha calls you back. Why?"

Sonia stammered. "Um…."

Loren didn't miss the way they both glanced at *her*. The tight-lipped expression could only be described as…wary. Whatever the source of their unspoken tension was, it had to do solely with her.

"I'll sort this mess out," Sonia insisted. "I promise."

This time, she didn't sound as optimistic.

18

OUTSIDE NEW WALSH

"He smelled me," the dark-haired youth murmured excitedly, bouncing on the passenger's seat. "I *know* he did, though I think he was more worried about that horse, but I saw her—"

"You did?" Kyle cocked his head, his interest piqued. "Well, what did she look like?"

The boy, barely nineteen, shrugged. "I couldn't get a good look. She's pretty, though. Tall and skinny. Lukka might want her, after all—"

"Get your head out of your cock, kid," Kyle scolded. "What about her *eyes?* What did her damn eyes look like?"

That detail might reveal who her real father was, at least.

The kid paused. Judging from how long it took him to process the damn question, Kyle's suspicions were confirmed—he was a fucking idiot.

Figures. When it came to reconnaissance, he always got saddled with the bottom of the barrel. At least, this latest fool—his name was Micha, or something like that—could shift at will, and he was fast. You *had* to be to outrun Bill McGoven on his own damn property.

"Green. I think," Micha announced. "Though, I wasn't really looking at her *eyes,* if you know what I mean—"

"I don't," Kyle snapped. "Now shut the fuck up. I need to think."

He palmed the steering wheel, eyeing the deserted road they were parked alongside. McGoven's property was over an hour away, but he could still sense the bastard. He just hoped McGoven had noticed him in return. Wouldn't that make for an interesting reunion?

"Why hasn't Lukka taken her in?" the boy asked, fidgeting in the passenger seat. While skilled physically, he was apparently too stupid to heed a direct order. "He takes in outsiders all the time. He took me in—"

"Because we aren't a damn halfway house," Kyle replied. "And you and the others *earn* your keep."

Besides, the scrawny rogues were nothing more than cannon fodder—though Kyle didn't mention that. He also didn't mention that the girl in question was as good as dead. Lukka had made that clear. The Alpha may hide behind the fact that no law stipulated he *had* to take the girl in, but that was just a cop-out. Whatever helped him sleep at night.

The truth was the girl was mated to Bill McGoven. For that alone, she had signed her own death warrant. This was personal. It didn't matter that the asshole claimed he'd had no other choice or whatever bullshit that bitch Sonia had spewed to justify the action.

He was in *exile*—forbidden from ever partaking in pack life. Lo' and behold, taking a mate was a *major* fucking part of pack life.

Kyle hadn't even taken one yet, and he was well past the age when his wolf called out for a mate of his own.

But hey, he could wait. By jumping the gun without permission, McGoven had gone too far. If losing the girl was what it took to make him realize the gravity of the situation, then so be it. The last time Kyle had checked, rogues in exile couldn't fucking take any woman they wanted.

And obviously, his little female wasn't just *any* old woman. Why else would he keep her so close? Days after their joining, and he barely let her off his property.

The fucker was hiding something, which was why Kyle was here in the first place, hours from pack territory in the middle of bum-fucking nowhere. Lukka was too much of a pussy to do his own dirty work.

Kyle was used to it. Even before he took over, Lukka preferred using his brains over brute force. Not like the great and powerful Bill McGoven—the same man everyone assumed would be the future Alpha once upon a time. As it turned out, *Lukka* claimed that mantle, and only the Alpha could decide who was worth saving or not.

This poor little mated female *wasn't,* and Kyle would see to it personally. Though…it wasn't like he could just stroll onto that farm and drive a stake through her chest himself.

Not with McGoven and the Carlisle woman there. Micha might have been fast, but Kyle doubted the pup could hold his own against a full-grown wolf like McGoven. Even that little bitch, Sonia, could put up a good fight if she wanted to.

Besides, they had to play nice. For political reasons, of course. After all, it wouldn't look good on Lukka's part to be responsible for the murder of a young girl just because he happened to hate the bastard who claimed her.

Yep, they had to play by specific rules, make it look like an accident. Kyle already had a few devious ideas in mind, but it wasn't like he could put any into practice without narrowing down the playing field by at least *one* hostile wolf.

Right on cue, his cell phone buzzed at his hip.

"Go," he told the runt beside him. "Scout for a mile. Make sure the coast is clear."

"Okay!" Micha bounded from the truck without a backward glance, and Kyle brought the phone to his ear.

"Yes," he grumbled the second he sensed the runt beyond earshot.

"The Carlisle girl's out." Lukka's voice crackled from the other end of a bad connection. "She'll leave tonight. Tomorrow, you move in."

"Excellent," Kyle said around a cold smile. "I'm bored babysitting."

"But you know the drill," Lukka snapped. "Be clean about it. I don't want this in any way traced back to me."

Yeah, yeah. Mentally, Kyle rolled his eyes. That was Lukka. Sure, he could *order* a murder easy enough, but when it came to the grisly details, he blanched. Though, how hard could killing one girl be? Hell, even McGoven seemed to want her off his hands. In a sick way, they were doing the bastard a favor.

"Don't make her suffer," the Alpha added.

As if he really gave a shit.

If McGoven had *really* wanted her, Kyle figured he would have been ordered to string the girl up by her toes and make the asshole watch him kill her. It wouldn't have been the first time Lukka had him get "creative" to prove a point to a rival.

Still.

"It'll be neat and clean, Lukka," Kyle promised. "Your little problem will be wiped away, and McGoven will once again be solely at your beck and call."

It was a win-win for everyone, really.

Except for the girl, of course. She got the short stick in the end. But in a twisted game of power and revenge, someone had to be the pawn.

19

*L*oren bolted awake, a scream poised in her throat. *It was dark. So dark. She couldn't see anything—couldn't see him—but she knew he wasn't there. She had been searching and searching, but he was never there…*

"You're alright." The stern voice encased her in an eerie sense of calm. Instantly, her fear vanished.

Safe…

"It's alright. You're dreaming," that same someone told her, their voice gentle and deep. Something brushed the top of her head. It took a second to identify it, but her heart fluttered once she did —warm fingers stroking through her hair. "You're alright."

Shivering, Loren glanced up. Her first thought was that it was the moon she saw, glowing through the oppressive dark. Make that *two*, both filling her with peace, while that familiar voice vibrated down her spine.

"It's alright," he repeated. "I'm here."

The words conveyed more than comfort. They were a promise. A vow.

I'm here.

Loren felt her eyes drift shut, her body heavy. A second later, she was asleep, so deeply it was as if she'd never woken up at all.

oren was shivering. Once she opened her eyes, she realized why—she was curled into a ball, on top of the covers.

Icy daylight streamed in through the gap in the curtains, falling over her like a spotlight. When she finally found the strength to move, she fully expected to find someone right beside her.

Instead, there was nothing on the blue comforter but her own puddle of drool.

Puzzled, she stumbled into the bathroom to brush her teeth. Then, she got dressed, this time in the other sundress. The dull, brown cotton hung down to her toes, giving her *some* protection from the cold.

But not enough to erase the building dread that she was alone. The bottom floor of the house seemed just as deserted. For the first time in two days, there was no aroma of cooking breakfast. No cheerful Sonia to greet her with a plate and a smile.

The only things waiting for her on the center island were exactly two pieces of toast and a note. *Be back soon. Stay here, Bill.*

Bill. Loren shivered as her fingers traced the firm, steady handwriting. A glance out the window revealed the driveway was empty, save for the green pickup. He took the patrol car today, though she wondered where he could have gone so early, when the sun had barely risen.

Puzzled, she downed the toast in a few bites and padded into the living room, feeling as out of place as a mouse smack dab in the middle of the cat's den.

What should she do? The only likely option seemed to be to start on the massive pile of schoolwork the school assigned her.

Some of it was stuff they had already covered, though the new material didn't seem that hard. Loren finished it all in no time—way too soon to fill the hours of empty space that stretched on and on…

By the time lunch rolled around, she made herself a peanut butter sandwich, feeling guilty with every single bite. He didn't seem to be keeping her prisoner—at least not the whips, chains, and forced starvation version. Of course, he meant for her to feed herself while he was gone… Right?

Not that it mattered. By late afternoon, he hadn't returned.

Loren sat in the kitchen, drumming her fingers against the center island. Waiting. When she heard a sudden knock on the door, she raced for the foyer. It was only then that a part of her realized he wouldn't have to knock to get inside his own house.

As she hesitated, whoever stood on the other end opened the door without an invitation.

"Well, well, well." The husky purr accompanied the familiar green eyes that took her in with one calculating sweep. Definitely *not* Bill McGoven. "I was wondering what kind of loser would take both Advanced Microbiology *and* Calculus."

"N-Naomi?" Loren blinked as if just doing so would transform the hostile blond into someone else.

No such luck.

"The one and only," the blond snapped, pushing her way inside. "You gonna invite me in, or do I have to freeze my ass off?"

"T-This isn't my house," Loren stammered. Judging from the pile of paperwork she held, she figured that *Naomi* was the person the school assigned to deliver her work.

"I know," Naomi said, glancing around the spacious entryway with a sniff. "*Yours* is all covered in that caution tape shit. What the fuck did you *do?*"

Loren flinched. It had to be all over the news by now that her father was dead.

"You must have done something pretty bad for a *police officer* to take you in," Naomi added suspiciously, fingering a lock of blond hair.

Apparently, the fact that Officer McGoven lived on the Baker farm wasn't much of a secret.

"So, where do you want to be tutored?" the blond demanded, crossing her arms over the front of a sleek, designer sweater. She looked as bitchy and perfect as always—minus the large, square bandage stuck to the left side of her cheek.

How did she explain that to her minions? Loren wondered. *Plastic surgery?*

"I don't need a tutor," was all she could think to say.

Naomi shrugged. "Tough shit. It comes with the territory. They want to make sure that you 'understand the material' before attempting it on your own." She even utilized air quotes.

Loren bit her lip against a groan. First, she woke up naked in a stranger's bed to learn her father was dead. Now the girl she'd attacked was here to teach her calculus?

What next?

"I guess this will do," Naomi sighed, traipsing into the living room uninvited.

To Loren's immense shock, she took a seat on the couch and proceeded to open a workbook.

No threats. No veiled efforts to insinuate that she might press charges. No references to the scratches hidden by that bandage. It was as if she truly didn't care about the incident at all.

Or, that inner voice whispered. *Someone made her forget.*

"Time's ticking," she snapped when Loren didn't move. "I have a hair appointment in an hour."

"Why are you here?"

From what little Loren knew of the homeschooling system at New Walsh Academy, students *volunteered* to deliver the work. Call it skepticism, but she doubted that Naomi would do so out of the goodness of her heart.

"You're in advanced courses," the girl said as if it were obvious. "Surprise, surprise, *I'm* the only one qualified to tutor you—"

Loren raised an eyebrow. She vaguely remembered something about Naomi taking AP courses, but she had always just assumed that the blond had bought her way in or something.

"There are other students," she countered.

"I'm the only one with a *car,*" Naomi added, flashing a cocky smile. "Now, can we get this over with?"

Loren claimed an armchair, unsure of what to expect. Submitting to this "tutoring," seemed more like a convict being tortured slowly before execution.

But, to her immense surprise, being tutored by Naomi Tanner wasn't *all* bad.

The girl was rude, snippy, and impatient, but she managed to make the math make sense at least, describing the complicated equations in a way that even the teacher, Mr. Hollings, couldn't.

But she wasn't nice about it.

Within an hour, they finished the last assignment. Not a second later, Naomi gathered up the work, plus what Loren had already done beforehand.

"Same time tomorrow," she said with a heavy sigh as if their session had been the most excruciating way to pass the time possible.

"Okay."

Loren watched her head for the door without so much as a parting jibe at her expense. Before she could open it, someone else did. A dark figure appeared in the doorway, draped in shadow.

He's here, a part of Loren murmured excitedly. Those silver eyes sought her out as she lurched to her feet, and her heart swelled. *Yes,* that inner voice murmured happily. *Ours.*

Abruptly, he turned to Naomi. "Ms. Tanner. This is a surprise."

"H-Hey, Officer McGoven," the blond stammered, swaying slightly on her feet as if his presence had shifted the universe. "I was just leaving."

Officer McGoven nodded, easing aside so that she could stumble past. "Tell your father hello for me." He was polite—at least until the door shut behind her.

When he turned to Loren, his gaze was questioning. "Why was Naomi Tanner in my house?"

"*She's* who the school sent over with my schoolwork," Loren said softly, barely believing it herself.

"Really?" That eyebrow shot all the way up. "I can call and have it changed if you want."

"No." Loren shook her head. Doing so would only give Naomi some sick sense of satisfaction. "I can handle her."

If anything, that reply made him *more* skeptical. The intensity in his stare seemed to skewer her, right through skin and bone down to the pit of her soul. "That's what I'm worried about."

With that, he headed for the kitchen.

Loren followed him, noticing how the muscles of his back strained the fabric of his blue windbreaker. The sight did something to her. Made her belly flip and parts of her body heat. Her cheeks. Her throat. Between her legs…

The last sensation alarmed her. Her face flamed, but she couldn't tear her gaze away. He was in uniform today, explaining away the all-day absence. A sudden concern sent a chill through her entire body, cooling the reaction he'd inspired.

Was he assigned to her father's case? She should have asked, but all she could focus on was how he still smelled inexplicably like fresh pine. Nature. The wild. She breathed deep, letting the scent travel through her stomach, right down to her toes. Gradually, that heat returned, growing hotter.

"Did you eat?"

She blushed as his gaze focused on her and shook her head. "No."

"Here." He turned to the fridge and withdrew a carton of what looked like tuna salad and a loaf of bread. Silently, he compiled two sandwiches, eventually handing one to her.

Sonia's words came back to her. *A health nut.* If tuna could give a man that much muscle, she wondered why everyone didn't hoard the stuff.

"Something funny?" McGoven asked. His voice was soft, not accusatory.

Loren realized her lip was quirked. "N-No," she said, taking the sandwich.

She ate it perched on the end of a stool, while he leaned against a nearby counter. Together they just…

Watched each other, like two wild animals sizing up one another for the first time.

Comically, Loren couldn't help but picture two stray dogs—a husky facing down a ratty little Shih Tzu. Who would sniff who first? Of course, *he* was the one to finally break the tension, tossing her a question after he swallowed his last bite of bread.

"You let Naomi in. You could have told her to go to hell. Why?"

Loren lifted her shoulder in a shrug. She didn't dare admit the truth. *Because I thought she was you.*

Instead, she improvised. "Because she's not worth it."

She had bigger fish to fry—starting with the confusing jumble her life had become.

Officer McGoven seemed to mull her answer over in silence. *Interesting,* she pictured him musing as he scratched the dark stubble along his chin.

"What's between you two, anyway?"

"I don't know," Loren admitted truthfully. She shifted on her stool, propping her elbow against the island's surface. "She just never liked me, I guess."

Though, how pathetic did that sound when said out loud? Frowning, she tried to explain it, that crazy, unwarranted hostility. "Naomi… She… Well, she…"

"What?" Officer McGoven demanded. His tone alone warned he wouldn't let her off so easy. *Don't put a happy face on it. Don't dress it up.*

The truth.

"She's a bitch," Loren blurted, surprising herself. "From the day I came here, she's had it out for me. I don't know why, but I can handle her."

The corner of his mouth twitched into an amused grin.

And the world stopped spinning. It blew her mind how something so simple could utterly transform him. Instantly, those eyes were less intimidating—more dove-gray than silver. His lips glistened, a welcoming pink.

Her own lips parted and closed. She felt dizzy. Hot. Then… confused. Shouldn't he be scolding her?

"Where I come from, you're expected to fight back when boxed into a corner," he said cryptically. Was that his way of signaling that he approved of what she did? If so, why had he been so angry that day? Furious.

"Black Mountain," she blurted, focusing on the most harmless piece of his statement. "Sonia said that's where you're from?"

The words barely left her mouth before she realized she miscalculated. This subject was a landmine. He sucked in a breath, his shoulders tensing. "Sonia…" He seemed to groan. Then he shook his head and met her gaze directly. "Something like that. Did she tell you anything else?"

Loren cringed, hating the thought of getting Sonia in trouble. She wanted to deny it—but she couldn't. "Yes," she gasped as if the confession were being ripped from her. "She told me you had a wife."

"A wife." His lips fell into a hard line. "Something like that."

Her heart twitched, hating the confirmation. He loved someone once. And yet, she wanted to know more. Needed to. "What was she like?"

Someone beautiful, she suspected. Full-figured and blond, with enough charm to reach a man as guarded as he was.

"She was… Emma." His voice turned hoarse, and Loren felt a pang in her chest. Pain?

"Your mother," he said, turning the tables. "What was she like?"

It was her turn to flinch, struck by the agony of memories. Words were never her forte, and even now, they failed to convey just who her mother was. "She was nice," she said haltingly. "Funny. I loved her."

"I'm sure she was," McGoven said. His words didn't ring hollow like the empty condolences she was used to enduring. It was as if he knew exactly how she felt and was acknowledging that in the most genuine of ways.

She tentatively met his gaze again, and she wasn't sure how much time passed before he cleared his throat.

"I'll be busy all day tomorrow," he said, tactfully changing the subject. "You can take the bed again tonight. I'll take the couch."

The bed, Loren thought with a shiver. A bed he just confirmed was *his*.

"I could take the c-couch—" The look he sent her way rendered her silent. *The hell you will,* his narrowed gaze conveyed.

"It's fine," he said tightly. "You need the sleep."

Apparently, chivalry *wasn't* all dead in the McGoven house.

"Don't wait up. I have something to take care of tonight," he added.

And they were right back to square one.

Loren fidgeted, trying to think of some way to undo the damage she'd done. Suddenly, a buzzing ringtone sliced the tension.

Never taking his eyes off her, Officer McGoven reached into his pocket for his cell phone.

"Hello," he grunted, pressing the device to his ear. He listened for a moment, and then all at once, his entire face changed, his brows furrowing. "Sonia? Slow down—"

A knock on the door gave Loren the distraction she needed to distance herself from what was obviously a private conversation. With her luck, Naomi had forgotten something.

"Sonia! Slow down!" She heard Officer McGoven bellow from behind her. "What are you saying?"

As Loren approached the door, the knocking slowed to a lazy rapping.

Tap, tap, tap.

Definitely Naomi—unless there was more than one person out there, who believed the world was full of peons whose duty it was to wait solely on them.

Sighing, she pulled the door open. "Did you forget something?" She began—only it wasn't *Naomi* standing there, drenched in the aftermath of another rainstorm.

This visitor was a man.

That was all Loren was sure of before a hand clamped down over her wrist, wrenching her toward the stairs. In that split second, a massive shape rushed to block her from view, swallowing the space of the doorway.

"What the fuck are you doing here?" Officer McGoven's voice was guttural, ripping from his chest like the roar of an engine. Or a growl.

With him blocking the door, Loren couldn't see how the visitor reacted to the hostility, but when they spoke, their voice didn't hold any hint of fear.

"Is that any way to greet an emissary?" His tone was equally low and slightly mocking, but overall business-like. Stern. "I come here on behalf of Lukka. For *her*. As you requested."

20

"No!" McGoven surged, forcing the newcomer onto the porch. "*You* aren't taking her anywhere. Get the fuck off my land, or I swear to God, I'll send you to your Alpha in pieces."

Loren trembled. Obviously, this man was not Lukka—but he and McGoven weren't strangers. A subtle tension radiated between them. Hate? Something far deeper than mere aggression. She felt it in her bones, and that inner voice growled. *Enemy!*

"If Lukka wants her, then *he* can come for her," Officer McGoven continued. Strangely, there was no real anger in his voice. His point was perfectly clear.

The other man's reply came muffled. "He's a busy man. It might take him a whole month to find the time to travel all the way out here just to see one little pup—"

"That's his *duty*," Officer McGoven snarled. "He should have been here the second I called—"

"His duty is to protect his *own*," the stranger replied, just as harshly. "She isn't one of his—at least not yet. He doesn't owe a damn thing to her or to *you*."

The words seemed to land like a well-placed jab. McGoven flinched back—enough for Loren to finally view the figure standing before him in a puddle of cool moonlight.

He was tall, with bright red hair cropped tightly to his scalp and brown eyes that reminded her of a hawk's. They glowed the same way, visible even through the dark. Predatory.

"But, of course," he continued emotionlessly, "Lukka would never allow a stray to wander loose without pack ties. That's where I come in."

"Oh, really?" McGoven didn't even try to hide his skepticism. "And let me guess; you're here to welcome her with open fucking arms into your loving family?"

"Something like that." The stranger's eyes glowed with a mischievous light. "If Lukka can't come for her, then I'll just have to take *her* to *him*."

"Hell no." McGoven took a step, wordlessly forcing the stranger further from the doorway. "If Lukka wants her, he has to come and get her his damn self—"

"But that could take months," the other man countered. "How easy do you think this will be by then? How attached to you will she be in a few weeks? A whole month? Do you really want to play around with that kind of bond?"

A bond? The term confused Loren, but McGoven's shoulders slumped, and he looked back. His tormented expression said it all —*no.* Whatever this "bond" was, he didn't seem to want it at all.

"Why can't he come for her?" he demanded, turning back to the newcomer. "An asshole like you can't fill in for him for a few damn hours?"

The man's mouth curled into an icy smile. "Lukka doesn't work via substitutes. He is the Alpha; his word is the law. Do you think people can just 'go without' the law for a couple of hours?"

"Fuck," McGoven growled. He sounded torn, as if he were being wrenched in two completely different directions. "But why *you*? Why couldn't anyone else—"

"Who else could Lukka trust with something *so important* as transporting a stray female? Sonia Carlisle? She has other duties which don't concern acting as a liaison between her Alpha and a rogue. No. From now on, you deal only with me. I am his Beta, after all."

Beta. Loren didn't recognize the word, but the man's tone implied that it was something important. Too important for Officer McGoven to argue against.

But he didn't have to accept it, either. "Fuck." His gruff tone revealed more frustration than if he'd smashed his fist into the wall. Or the newcomer's face. "I'm guessing they won't let me take her myself? I'd prefer that to this."

"You're in exile. You stray within even a mile of pack territory, and you know the consequences."

Loren didn't like the way this conversation was headed. All of it —as everything had these past few days—seemed to center around taking her away. This strange man wanted to, but Officer McGoven…

"Fuck," he repeated.

All at once, the entryway seemed smaller as he backed inside, body hovering between the doorway and her position on the steps.

"There isn't any other way?"

"Of course, there isn't." The strange man cautiously took a step over the threshold—but the act seemed more monumental than that. A visual representation of how the tides of this silent battle were turning. With a shrug, he tapped his wrist, though Loren saw that he wasn't wearing a watch. "Time is ticking."

McGoven sighed. Then he turned to face her. His eyes went to her chest, avoiding her gaze. "Get your stuff."

Those three simple words sliced through her like knives.

"W-What?" *No,* a part of her pathetically whined. "No," she whispered out loud, surprising herself. This was *wrong*—her entire body trembled against it.

"Loren." His tone left no room for argument. "Go upstairs and get your stuff. Now."

He turned back to the stranger who watched them both with an unreadable expression, and Loren stumbled up the first few steps. *No.* The thought screamed through every nerve and muscle. She couldn't leave him. Her stomach lurched at the prospect, her throat dry.

Finally, she hesitated on the top step. "I-I don't—"

"GET YOUR STUFF!"

She tore into the hall, driven purely by his anger. Like an invisible hand, it pushed on her spine, forcing her into the bedroom to grab her duffle and shove her clothes inside of it. When she returned downstairs, Officer McGoven was in the kitchen—as far away from her as physically possible.

It was the stranger who stood to greet her at the bottom, his lips contorted into a mirthless smile. Whatever silent argument had waged between them, McGoven had soundly lost.

"I'm Kyle," he said. "You must be Loren—"

He reached out to help her down the bottom step, but she jerked back without thinking. *No!* The desperation wasn't solely hers. She could sense it, and her gaze was drawn to the kitchen where McGoven stood in the doorway, his jaw clenched.

Low, his voice resonated through the very walls to reach them. "You don't have to touch her." It wasn't a suggestion.

Wisely, Kyle stood back, holding his hand limply in the air. "You're right," he said, shoving the offending hand into his pocket. "That's *Lukka's* job."

His tone was intentionally cutting—insinuating something...

But what?

Officer McGoven's tight frown gave nothing away, but he shifted, keeping his focus on the man's visible hand.

"We should go," Kyle suggested, inclining his head toward the partially open front door.

Through the crack in the doorjamb, Loren could tell it was raining with a vengeance, reducing everything beyond the porch to a shapeless blur.

"If we leave now, we might be able to make it into the territory before midnight," Kyle added.

Six hours from now, according to the clock built into the coffee maker.

"Whatever," McGoven hissed. "Go now."

Kyle took a step and paused. Chuckling, he nodded to Loren. "I think you might have to tell *her* twice."

Loren flinched as a pair of gray eyes swiveled her way. His lips parted, and she braced for the sound of his voice. "Loren—"

"No!" The word tore from her throat. "No," she repeated, rocking on the balls of her feet. A rush of adrenaline fueled the disobedience. He was wrong—she couldn't go. Every muscle in her body told her to stay here. With him.

"*Please.* I d-don't want to go."

The man, Kyle, gave her an odd look—but he wasn't her focus. Just McGoven.

His upper lip pulled back from his teeth as if it pained him to deny her. And it did. She could feel it. "Go with him. It'll be okay. You'll be safe." His tone was gentler, though unflinchingly firm. *Shoo.*

"No," Loren whispered. Being abandoned by her mother, and rejected by her father had hurt, but this…

The pain tore at her. Tore *through* her.

She didn't even know him, but the thought of leaving made her entire body shake.

"Loren, *go!*"

She couldn't refuse. Robotically, she went to drag her new shoes from where they rested by the door and put them on.

Kyle watched her. "This won't last for very long," he said. "Once Lukka accepts her." It wasn't reassurance. It was a threat.

One McGoven reacted to visibly—he flinched. "He better." He raised his voice to carry across the entire room. "And if he *doesn't?*"

Kyle shrugged. "Then someone else will. You've done your good deed for the week. Don't worry, I won't bring her back."

Loren didn't miss the finality in his tone. *She won't be coming back...ever.*

"You won't make it back by midnight if you don't leave now," McGoven warned.

After the previous hostility, his tone was eerily casual. Even Kyle seemed shocked by the change, though he shrugged again. "Fine. Come on," he called to her.

Utterly numb, she took a step after him.

"Wait." A rush of air was her only warning before something heavy fell over her shoulders. Confused, she looked down to find a familiar blue windbreaker draped over her dress. It was so long that the hem reached her knees.

"It's freezing out," a gruff voice told her by way of explanation.

"She won't be able to wear that on Lukka's territory," Kyle warned, eyeing the jacket as though it were a snake. "You know the law."

"Sure I do." McGoven stood back, but Loren didn't miss how he adjusted her jacket until the very last second, ensuring it fell closed over her front. "She can take it off at the gate."

An angry flush crept over Kyle's angular jaw, but he didn't argue. Despite whatever power this Lukka person wielded, for now, McGoven had the upper hand.

Once she left the safety of the farm, what then?

"We need to go," Kyle insisted, jerking his head sharply toward the door.

Officer McGoven returned to the kitchen without a word—but Loren could read his body language. His shoulders were hunched as if her mere presence was an annoyance. *Go,* he told her without having to say it. *Get out. I don't want you here.*

No, no, no, that inner voice cried. *This is wrong. Wrong!*

"Come on." Kyle's voice was a knife, cutting through the panic in her mind.

It wasn't exactly like she could argue. After his command, her throat seemed clenched shut around any words that might go against what McGoven told her. *Go.*

Stiffly, she moved forward, huddled beneath the windbreaker. Near the threshold of the doorway, she paused, half-expecting…

Nothing. No command to stay. No goodbye, either.

The only sound at all was the muffled pitter-patter of rain as she stumbled into the darkness after Kyle.

21

*K*yle led her to a truck left idling in the driveway behind McGoven's.

He hadn't come alone. Someone sat in the passenger's seat, a dark-haired boy who lurched from the cabin to greet her, his green eyes flashing.

"This is her?" he asked excitedly. He was tall but slender and lean with an energy that made Loren envision an overworked puppy. "Wow. Up close, she looks even bett—"

Kyle nudged him firmly in his side. "Get in the truck," he snapped. His gaze was firmly fixed on Loren, almost as if daring her to run back to the house like every muscle in her body commanded her to do.

Slowly, she entered the truck instead, climbing in between the two front seats to sit on the back bench. Without a word, Kyle took the wheel, and the boy bounded into the passenger's seat.

"He just let her go?" he chirped, his attention on the house. "He really just let her go? With *you?* He really didn't want her? Wow, he must be—"

"Micha, shut up," Kyle commanded.

The youth clammed up instantly, still bouncing on his seat.

Loren swallowed as the truck lurched into motion, kicking up mud in a violent spray. Helpless, her gaze drifted through the rear windshield, noting the dark figure standing impassively in the kitchen window.

No, a part of her whined. The dread became a physical ache in her chest as the truck hurtled around a corner. Suddenly her pulse surged. She couldn't breathe. *I can't leave...*

"Hi!"

She blinked, staring directly into a pair of massive green eyes.

"I'm Micha," the chirpy voice belonged to the younger figure who twisted around to face her from over the headrest of his seat. "You're Loren."

"Y-Yes," she stammered, wondering just how he knew her name. Though, maybe she should have been wondering about a lot of things?

Like why Officer McGoven let her go with two strangers? Or why he seemed so determined to send her away in the first place? Why take her in, if all he wanted was to pawn her off on someone else?

Lukka.

"So—" The playful tone drew her attention back to Micha. "Why didn't McGoven want you?"

"Micha!" Kyle's tone deepened, not that Micha had the sense to look ashamed. His stare was persistent, demanding an answer.

Why didn't he want me?

"I...he found me wandering in the woods. He took me in, though; it was just for a little while." *Lies.* When said out loud, the explanation didn't make sense. What kind of person took in a teenage girl whose father had just been murdered? Not to mention...why hadn't he brought her to the police station—at least for questioning?

An interview?

To claim her father's body?

He hadn't even asked her about funeral arrangements. Overnight, McGoven had taken control of her life with little effort. Already, she was being shipped off to only God knew where, on his say-so, and...

You're just okay with that? a part of her wondered. Strangely enough, she *was*.

She didn't know why. Whenever she tried to question it, the same old thought would play through her mind like a bad song stuck on rewind—"Officer McGoven said..."

His words seemed ingrained in her mind, her very soul.

I don't want this.

Lukka can have her.

Loren go!

"You'll love Black Mountain," Micha gushed, once again intruding into her thoughts. "It's big. There's lots of space to run around, though I haven't lived there long—" He lifted his thin shoulder in a shrug. "When Lukka found me, I was little more than a stray myself. The Alpha of my old pack was a total—"

"Alpha?" The word dislodged some long-forgotten memory. McGoven had said it—though as if it were something comical. A mockery. "What's an Alpha?"

Micha gaped at her. Then, he looked at Kyle, who only curtly shook his head—*no.*

"Oh!" Those big green eyes got even wider. "You mean she really doesn't—" He seemed to stop himself from saying any more. Instead, he fidgeted in his seat, his dark curls bouncing against his scalp. "Oh, wow!"

Her apparent ignorance only seemed to increase Micha's interest in her. He didn't speak, but he never turned around, observing her intently as though she were some curiosity on display. "Wow," he'd murmur every now and again.

Loren felt uneasy. She wanted to demand they tell her something, but an instinctive part of her knew that Kyle would just shrug her off. He was impatient, glaring at the road, gripping the wheel tightly.

But, when Micha had mentioned the word Alpha, even he had shuddered.

Through the fog and rain, Loren couldn't make out much of where they were headed. All she knew was that Kyle skirted through the back of New Walsh, toward the country roads and just kept driving north.

Black Mountain, Micha said. The place where McGoven and Sonia had grown up.

"Is it cold there?" she found herself asking, barely audible over the staticky radio currently broadcasting show tunes. "This Black Mountain?"

"Oh yeah!" Micha turned back around, this time sticking his head between the two front seats. "I think so. I never really noticed before."

Loren raised an eyebrow at that. What kind of person lived on a mountain and didn't notice the obvious difference in the weather?

Obviously, Micha was not the brightest tool in the toolbox. But he seemed nice—which put him a cut above everyone Loren knew. He also apparently loved to talk. So, she decided to take the risk and draw out as much information from him as she possibly could.

"What's there?" she asked. Sonia hadn't given her much of a description of the place. "A town? A city?"

The questions earned her another impish grin and an incredulous look. "The territory," he said, as if that explained everything.

"Is there a school?" Loren wondered, thinking of the massive pile of work sitting on the end of Officer McGoven's couch. She only had a few months left, but already, after a few missed days, graduation seemed light-years away.

Micha nodded. "Of course! And a post office, and a town hall and all that boring stuff. But there's so much land. Lukka has more territory in this area than anyone else in the region. Well, maybe except for the Eislander pack—"

"Lukka?" Loren seized on the mention of the name and ran with it. "Who is he? The mayor?"

Obviously, he wielded some amount of clout. She recalled how Sonia had defended him to Bill—even when it seemed like she didn't exactly want to.

"Who is Lukka?" Micha's dark eyebrows shot right up into his dense tangle of hair. "He's the Alpha."

There was that word again. Micha didn't seem to notice her reaction.

"He controls Black Mountain—the entire pack," he went on. "He's probably the youngest Alpha in a century to dominate so much territory. He succeeded his father, who is a legend. Lukas Grehmaine. I'm sure you've heard of him, right? My mom told me stories when I was a pup about how he rebelled against his Alpha and forged his own territory. I heard rumors growing up, too, in a territory miles from here. About Lukas and his prodigy, Bill—"

"Bill?" Loren practically lunged out of her seat. "A prodigy?"

"Yeah," Micha said, frowning. "It's crazy how things worked out. That's why we had to come here. If you leave the pack, you leave our ways—all of them. He isn't allowed to hunt, or even marry. Especially not take a mate—"

"That's enough." Kyle reached and deliberately flicked the radio dial until the sounds of wavering country music filled the cabin.

With an apologetic frown, Micha shifted in his seat, and Loren couldn't silence a hiss of disappointment. At least for now, she wouldn't get anything else out of him.

What she had learned just confused her further. Prodigy. Pack. Mate? She didn't understand. Putting it from her mind, for now, she settled for staring from the window, trying to remember every detail of the landscape whizzing by.

The next few hours passed in utter silence. Micha had drifted off, resting his head against the window. Kyle just drove without so much as an attempt at conversation.

A part of Loren wanted to risk his ire just to ask *something*. More about Lukka, maybe?

She inhaled deeply to gather the nerve, but then her thoughts derailed entirely. *Pine.* That pure scent carried with it the wild aroma of the forest, faint musk, and the fresh flavor of the wind that whipped through the trees…

Wham!

She must have drifted off—somehow—because the next thing she knew, her body was being flung forward through the gap in the seats.

Quick thinking from Micha was the only thing that saved her from a bloody nose—his thin arm shot out, slowing down the momentum.

"What the hell?" he murmured sleepily. "What's going on?"

Loren was in awe of how quickly he'd reacted while half-asleep, and even more impressed once she realized why they'd stopped. The truck was stuck in a ditch. Hissing, Kyle jammed his foot on the gas, only to send mud churning from the wheels.

"Fuck. Something ran me off the road—"

"What?" Instantly, Micha's whole demeanor changed. He sat up straighter, and his eyes took on a sharper gleam. "Kyle, do you know where we *are?*"

"You think I'm a fucking idiot?"

Obviously, the thick forests and rolling hills that lined the road weren't this mysterious Black Mountain.

Not even close. As Kyle's gaze darted to the windows, even Loren could tell that he was uneasy. Micha was downright panicked.

"This is *Eislander* territory," he croaked. His nostrils flared as if the air inside the truck held a repulsive scent.

"The outskirts," Kyle admitted, wrenching the key from the ignition. "The usual road was blocked, so I thought we could take a shortcut."

From his defensive demeanor, Eislander territory didn't seem like an ideal place to be stranded in.

"Call Lukka!" Micha's voice was an octave higher. "He'll have to send Greg or Tom to come and—"

"No reception. The truck's transmission is shot," Kyle snapped, wrenching open his door. With fluid ease, he jumped down to land ankle-deep in the mud. "It's not far. One of us will have to head to the Michaelsons'. They could help."

"I'll do it." Micha was out in a flash. Literally. Loren barely saw him lope around the truck; he moved so fast.

"Take this." Kyle tossed him the cell phone and pointed to a thicket of trees. "Head north. Call Lukka the moment you get to the closest cell tower."

"Okay!" With that, Micha took off.

"As for you, girl. Get out of the truck." Kyle's voice reached her, as authoritative as a whip.

Loren scrambled out—but she had to admit that it wasn't because of that same instant pull she felt whenever Officer McGoven gave her a direct order. This time, her thoughts controlled the compulsion. If they were in danger, she needed to get her bearings. It helped that she instinctively felt better the moment her boots hit the muddied earth, and the fresh scent of wind filled her nose.

It had stopped raining, though the wind had taken on an icy edge this far north.

"I need to scout around," Kyle told her. He scanned the surrounding forests, as if at any moment an enemy might spring from the shadows. "You stay here—"

"By myself?" Loren couldn't help the apprehension in her voice. "I could come with you."

"No," Kyle snapped. "*You're* going to stay by the damn truck. I won't be long."

Before she could protest, he headed in the direction opposite Micha. And she was shocked to find that he was just as fast. Obviously, wherever they were from, the men knew how to keep fit.

In addition to abandoning people on the side of the road.

She tried to tell herself that he would come back. It was the middle of the night—even if this Eislander place wasn't friendly, who would notice three people stranded on the road this late?

They would, something told her, without elaborating on just who "they" were. Or what. *This is wrong,* that same instinct warned. *Be ready.*

On impulse, she climbed into the truck and pulled open the glove compartment. Her father always kept a knife in his, *just in case,* though he never explained in case of what.

Kyle didn't have anything like that in his. All she found was a small flashlight hanging from a keychain. The pale light barely cut through the shadows—not that Loren exactly needed it.

The moonlight piercing the thinning clouds was more than enough to see by, illuminating the road. Even the slight flicker of the branches swaying in the wind held an unusual clarity.

She couldn't hear anything. But something… Something deep down told her that the apparent calm meant nothing. The silence. The quiet—they were merely on the surface.

Something else stirred underneath, way too careful to make any noise. Hiding. Lurking, watching her through the trees—and it was hungry. Maybe not in the literal sense, but…

She wasn't quite that surprised when two men appeared in the middle of the road. They were too tall—not Micha or Kyle. They didn't seem like the type to offer roadside assistance, either.

Careful, that instinctive voice warned. *Easy. Watch…*

They stood there for a long while, just taking her in. Loren was almost willing to write them off as only two bystanders who'd happened by for a nighttime stroll. Until they moved forward, eerily in sync. Until she saw their *eyes*, glowing through the shadows.

Until they chuckled, as if they knew damn well she was there.

And that she was alone.

"Hey, little girl," one called, his voice a husky rasp that seeped into the truck. "You lost?"

"All alone out here, cutie?" the other one wondered though Loren could tell that he didn't seem very concerned. "Don't worry, we *like* to make friends."

Her first thought was to lock the doors and barricade herself in— but something held her back. That inner voice. *No. You'll just make yourself an easy target. Run!* Without questioning the impulse, she bolted from the driver's side and took off in the direction Micha had.

Kyle had told him to run north—there had to be something close by.

"Aw, baby!" one of the men called out. "Don't run away!"

Another joined in, "We don't have to do this the hard way!"

Run, run, run! Loren allowed the frantic thoughts to drown out the sounds of anything else.

She could see headlights, spilling through the trees—but the two men were in between her and the road. She could sense them behind her, picking their way lazily through the gnarled branches.

Laughing.

*L*oren forced herself to keep moving, sucking in painful breaths with every step. But while Micha and Kyle had speed on their side, she didn't.

Her foot caught on the edge of a root a few paces in, and she tripped, tumbling down into the mud near the base of a small field. Tall grasses cast wavering shadows, shrouding the two other figures already in the center. Waiting for her.

She had walked right into a trap. The fact was all but proven as mocking laughter reached her ears. Heart heavy, she turned as the other men approached from the direction of the road.

"We brought some friends, honey," one of them crooned. "We'll be real nice. Don't be afraid."

Run! Loren lurched to her feet, wincing as pain shot through her ankle. Ignoring it, she stumbled in a random direction. Almost instantly, someone was there to block her path.

"Easy, baby," the man purred as she stumbled back, the heel of her boot catching over the grass. "Don't hurt yourself, now. We don't bite—"

"Hard," another man finished for him, chuckling. "For you, I think we'll make an exception, though. That pretty milk-white skin looks so soft."

There were rumbles of agreement. A few even whispered suggestions as to just how her "milky" skin would feel—sick, twisted things, that would haunt her nightmares.

If she lived long enough to sleep another night.

Heart racing, she turned on her heel—only to have someone block her path again. And the next direction she tried.

And the next...

They were too fast, treating her like a living volleyball in some sick four-person game. Smirking, they surrounded her from all sides, closing in with the eerie grace of a pack of hunting wolves.

"So pretty," one of them murmured. "Such a shame."

"I don't think this little baby's *all* innocent, though," pitched in the man nearest to her, his bright eyes haunting in the darkness. "I can smell a man on her. Her mate, maybe?"

There was a chorus of "oh nos" and several mocking chuckles.

"I guess he'll just have to share," another figure suggested.

All at once, they moved closer, forcing her into the center of a makeshift ring.

No. That shadowy, calm voice was back—but different. Louder. Intense. There was an edge to it that Loren knew hers never had. *Don't let them get close.*

Go!

She chose two of the men at random and darted in between them. She barely made it a yard, before someone yanked her back —hard—by a fistful of hair.

"Aww, boys!" They chuckled, shoving her to the center of their circle. "This one's shy."

"Don't worry, honey," a man with blond hair crooned with false sweetness. "It won't hurt for very long. I promise, you might even like it…"

He reached for her, and Loren's entire body vibrated with adrenaline.

Fight!

She didn't think—only reacted. Her hand swung out, catching the bastard on his jaw. Instantly, she knew she'd drawn blood.

She could smell it, coppery and fresh. Inside her, something rumbled, like hunger—but different. A need.

"Bitch!"

Another man swung at her, striking her mouth. Stars exploded across her vision—but rather than fall back in the face of the pain, Loren lunged into the blow, opening and closing her mouth on the thickness of a finger.

Howling, the man tried to pull back, but she only bit down harder, feeling flesh and muscle give beneath her teeth.

"Shit!"

An oppressive flavor exploded on her tongue—*blood,* that inner voice smugly supplied. She could see the dark liquid dripping from his fingers. There wasn't time to be horrified. She had already pivoted—before her mind comprehended the motion—evading the remaining two men.

Had they been like her father and numbed by alcohol, she might have had a shot. As it was, the first of the two caught her easily, hooking his arm around her waist like a crowbar.

"The little bitch wants to play," he grumbled, the words vibrating down her spine. A cruel hand ruffled through her hair, snagging at her scalp, and forcing her chin into the air. "Let's teach her a little lesson about proper manners on the playground—"

Just what those "lessons" were? They never elaborated.

The next thing she knew, she was being shoved face down into the moist earth, with someone's unforgiving hand clenched around the back of her neck.

No! That shadowy part of her howled, filling her body with rage. *Fight! You need to fight!*

She kicked her legs. Lashed out with her hands, snagging skin and clothes beneath her nails. When struggling didn't loosen the restraining grip, she screamed. Piercing, long and sharp, the sound rang out through the clearing, droning on until a firm knee rammed into the small of her back.

She went silent with a moan, gritting her teeth and digging her hands into the mud, as a lazy hand wrenched up the skirt of her dress.

She wouldn't scream again, she told herself—she wouldn't give them the satisfaction. She clenched her jaw so tightly she thought she heard the bones crack. Her heart raced with panic.

She wouldn't scream...

The resolve lasted until she felt a clumsy hand rub her inner thigh. Then, she broke, mouth opening for a cry that instantly became swallowed up by the sound of something else.

Loud, it rumbled out over the weeds like thunder—but it wasn't. No. It was a *growl*—that was her only thought before something heavy slammed into her from behind, knocking the breath from her chest.

Wham!

She winced at the sound of crunching bone—only to realize that it hadn't come from her body. From above her came a harsh shout, cut short.

Oh, God. That growl came again. Deeper this time—triumphant. With her face against the ground, Loren couldn't breathe— couldn't see. Her lungs screamed for air. Until, all at once, the pressure holding her down eased, and she could finally lift her head.

"Oh, shit! It's a rogue!"

The shout was the last coherent statement she heard. The men scattered, darting in various directions, fleeing a presence that Loren could sense was directly behind her.

Before she could turn, the entire world shifted. A shadow seemed to fly across the earth, as dark and huge as if a cloud had drifted over the moon overhead.

Only it wasn't a formless shape. Unbelievably massive, it darted toward the closest of the running men—long, lean, and undeniable in what it really was. The man she'd bitten couldn't outrun it, and with a howl of pain, he went down, swallowed by shadow.

For the space of a second, Loren allowed herself to stare. Allowed herself to become awed by the ebony limbs, rippling with sinewy muscle as the creature turned from the fallen man to stare her dead in the eye.

Blood dripped from its mouth, sharp claws ripping at the earth as it tensed to lunge.

Finally, Loren ran. She couldn't see. Darkness encased her—that massive shadow rushing toward her, so huge it blotted out the light of the moon.

Loren, wait!

The plea, whispered around the edges of her mind, startled her so badly that she stumbled and fell. An ominous ripping sound came from her dress as she landed hard on one knee.

Don't look, a frantic part of her urged. *Don't look, don't look! It'll kill you too!*

That shadowy part of her was stronger. *Turn around,* it urged. *Face it. Face him.* Body shaking, she braced her hands over the cool earth and looked back.

The beast loomed only a few yards away from her. Not a man, though something just as large, crouched on four lean legs. It was a wolf, one three times the size of any she'd seen at the zoo.

A thick pelt of black fur covered it from head to toe—except for a crisscrossed jumble of silvery lines that marred the flesh of its chest. A deep rumble seemed to hum in the back of its throat. Another growl—but this time lower.

Reassuring.

And its eyes… They were familiar. A glowing silver, they stared unflinchingly from a triangular head, holding her captive as it took a slow pace in her direction.

Loren tensed, falling back with a gasp as the creature shifted. Its entire body seemed to ripple, like a disturbed reflection over water. That muscled body wavered, shrunk, and compacted into a leaner shape hunched over the earth. As Loren watched, that coating of dark hair receded, revealing tanned skin bulging with coiled muscle underneath.

The only thing the beast shared with the man that appeared in its place was a pair of piercing, silver eyes.

Officer McGoven didn't speak.

Not even as he stood, unabashedly naked.

$\mathcal{H}$e held her gaze for so long Loren felt numb when he finally turned away. Tussled and wild, his hair hung down his shoulders as he inclined his head without a word. *Come on.*

Shakily, Loren crept after him, wincing every time her ankle hit the ground. She felt nothing. No fear. No relief. It was as if an invisible hand held the emotions at bay, even as she spotted the still shape of a dead man lying only a few feet away.

McGoven didn't acknowledge the grisly sight. He merely slowed his pace so she could catch up. It was only when she winced, biting down hard on her bottom lip, that he turned to face her at all. Dangerously dark, his eyes went to her ankle, narrowing the moment she swayed on her feet.

A flash of silver was her only warning before he lunged. The next instant, she found herself swung into his arms, cheek coming to rest against the hardness of his chest.

She felt too stunned for shock. He was warm and cool at the same time. A light sheen of sweat, mixed with rainwater, clung to his skin. He smelled too. Like earth, mud, and everything dangerous and wild in between. Long and lean, his legs carried her through the trees as if he knew the way by heart.

This felt familiar, being carried in his arms, held against bare skin. The blood on his chin, however, wasn't.

He didn't speak. Not even a word of comfort to reassure her that what she'd just seen him do wasn't humanly possible.

What could she say? *Oh, by the way, you're not a beast, are you?*

There was no way around it. No explanation fit other than the obvious...

He was the wolf. Where the beast had been seconds prior, Officer McGoven had appeared. He even moved like one, weaving through the wilderness with an easy grace. It didn't help any that the logical part of her couldn't rectify why he wasn't wearing clothes.

I just saw someone murdered right in front of me, she thought—almost calmly while her heart hammered in her chest. *Two people,* she mentally corrected. *Ripped apart by the man carrying me in his arms.*

She figured she *should* have been terrified. But the only thought to cross her mind, as Officer McGoven darted in between the trees, was that he had to be freezing.

She was—even winded and breathless beneath his windbreaker, or what was left of it. A hole pierced the sleeve; it must have torn when one of the men grabbed her. Irrational guilt made her heart sink. Though, the state of his jacket seemed to be the furthest thing from McGoven's mind at the moment.

In no time at all, they reached the dark stretch of empty road—further up from where Kyle had hit the ditch. Parked in the center of the highway was a different truck. A darker, familiar one reeking of pine. Once McGoven settled her on the passenger's seat, he moved to close the door.

"Stay here," he commanded. Then he reached over her to wrench open the glove compartment. Unlike Kyle's, *his* held something a little more useful than a cheap flashlight—a gun, glinting lethally in the moonlight.

"Stay inside," he reiterated gruffly. "Lock the doors. If anyone comes close who isn't me, use it."

He shoved the weapon onto her lap and turned, loping easily up the road. He was back before Loren had the chance to feel uneasy. What seemed like seconds later, he appeared by the driver's side, wrenching open the door the moment she unlocked it.

More blood dripped down his leg but, rather than pain, a satisfied gleam glinted in his eyes. Something told Loren that the other two men hadn't made it very far.

Without saying as much, McGoven pulled on a pair of sweatpants snatched from the back bench and climbed into the driver's seat barefoot. It was only when he jammed his foot on the gas and drove straight down the winding road that some of the tension coiled in his muscles finally eased.

Some of it.

"Where is Kyle?" The question seemed deliberately spoken as if it had taken every bit of energy he had in him just to keep from shouting. Yelling. Breaking glass.

Loren shook her head. "I don't know. H-he and Micha left to—"

"*They left you alone?*"

She recoiled against her seat, eyeing him fearfully. When he spoke again, his tone was a fraction softer. "Did they?"

She nodded, and he swore, smashing a fist into the steering wheel. His jaw was clenched so tightly that a muscle in his cheek jerked. It was only when he attempted to ask another question that she understood the source of his anger. "Did those bastards in the clearing…did they—"

She shook her head, and he sighed. He didn't say anything after that, not that he had to. His body language spoke for him loud and clear.

She had never seen anyone so furious. Not her father. Not even McGoven himself when she took off on his horse. Loren was afraid that he might rip the steering wheel from the socket if he happened to turn it hard enough.

"How…how did you find me?" Her throat ached. She wasn't sure what made her speak at all. It probably wasn't a good idea. Her stomach lurched as he swiveled his head toward her, eyes like molten silver.

"I followed you," he said.

Oh. He made it sound so natural. *I followed you. I breathed. I blinked.* The next second, his gaze was back on the road, and overwhelmed, Loren slumped into her seat.

"I wanted to make sure," he added, through clenched teeth. "But I never thought that asshole would be stupid enough to cut through *Eislander* territory. What the hell was he thinking?"

Loren didn't have an answer right away. With shaking fingers, she gingerly lifted the gun from her lap and returned it to the glove compartment. Only then could she recall what Kyle himself had said.

"He said that a road was blocked—"

"Bullshit!" McGoven's voice bordered on a growl. "There is a protocol you follow. You don't trespass without permission. Not here. He should *know* better. And to leave you alone? To let them touch you—" He inhaled raggedly and became rigid. A heartbeat later, he had all the windows down to let in the freezing night air. "Four men. I could sense their intentions. All of them. Those sick bastards."

Loren swallowed hard, suddenly cold. He could tell that via smell? Though, this wasn't the first time. He once claimed to know the number of bruises on her body from their scent alone.

She wanted to ask him, make him talk. Something warned her not to. For the first time, that plaintive inner voice was muted around him. *He's angry,* it whispered. *Wait.*

Angry was an understatement. He glowered, his teeth bared. The muscles in his legs bulged as he slammed on the gas until the gauge on the dashboard ticked closer and closer toward the maximum. It wasn't until they were on the highway, far from the dark woods, that he finally slowed to a speed closer to the legal limit.

It was nearly eleven, she realized, glancing at the dash—almost five hours after she left with Kyle. That dangerous stretch of Eislander territory must have been close to Black Mountain, which explained why Micha seemed to have no problem running off on foot.

Was it just on two? a part of her wondered. Apparently, the men around here seemed to shift into four-legged animals at will. She inspected McGoven from the corner of her eye, watching the muscles of his shoulders ripple as he drove. Or, maybe they just did that constantly? Roiling with tension.

Some subconscious part of her knew that she should have been afraid. It flinched in fear as she pictured that same body, hunched in the middle of the field, dripping blood. But locked inside the cabin of the truck with him, breathing in that wild scent of pine…

She just couldn't find the energy. Though, she might as well conserve her strength for when he left her for good. They had to be close to Black Mountain by now—she was sure of it. Tense with anticipation, she stared from the window, straining to catch a glimpse of her new home.

An hour later, and she started to note familiar landmarks she'd already glimpsed on the ride with Kyle. Rather than north, McGoven was heading straight toward New Walsh.

With every mile gained, the air became thinner, flooded with pine. Her body lost that crippling anxiety, and her head began to loll with every motion of the vehicle.

Sleep overwhelmed her before she knew it, and a firm hand on her shoulder startled her awake what felt like seconds later.

"Loren—"

Drowsily, she blinked and found Officer McGoven watching her, with one foot out of the truck. "We're home," he said.

Home.

Obviously, he was referring to his property alone, but still. In that moment, *home* seemed like the proper designation for the big house before her, bathed in the pale light of dawn. She inhaled, greedily sucking in the familiar scent of wind, mud, and horses. *Safe.*

"Can you walk?"

McGoven was watching her. He kept his distance, but his eyes were on her ankle. Something told her that if she lost her balance, he'd catch her before she could even hit the ground.

Experimentally, she took a step. "I think it's okay," she said. The pain was sharp, but not unbearable. She'd felt worse. "I can walk on it."

Officer McGoven headed straight for the house without acknowledgment. He didn't look as angry as he had in the truck, but Loren wasn't fooled. The rage simmered within him, ready to boil over at the slightest provocation.

Like, when he turned and saw her weakly limping up the porch steps. His lips curled back from his teeth, and Loren half-expected him to shout. Yell. Smash his curled fists into something.

All he did was nod curtly toward her feet.

"The boots." His voice rang with authority. "Take them off."

Without questioning it, Loren sat on the worn wood of the porch and complied. Her feet ached after being confined for so long, but watching her toes, still in their Christmas-themed socks, flex against the floor, she wondered why he made the request at all.

Even more so when he jerked his head curtly to her body. "The jacket, take it off."

His voice sent a tremor through her body. It was deeper, impossible to resist. Robotically, she dragged the thin material from her shoulders. When she held the jacket out to him, he motioned for her to drop it. Now. He was stiff, his weight balanced on his toes, his eyes blazing as they raked over her battered, dirt-streaked frame.

Was he angry about the damage done to his windbreaker? No. He didn't even look at the clothing. Just her. A few specific things drew his attention—namely, the dried blood she could feel encrusted over her chin, and the long rip in her dress exposing her thigh.

He swayed when he saw that, and his eyes almost appeared to turn...black—but what upset him most of all, was whatever he sensed when he leaned forward and inhaled the air above her body.

"That dress. Take it off—"

"W-What?" Loren stiffened, crossing her arms over her chest. The brown cotton was filthy and matted with mud around the hem, but it still covered her for the most part. Not to mention, her other clothes were in Kyle's truck.

None of those concerns seemed to matter to Officer McGoven.

His gaze was as stormy as the rain clouds swelling overhead. His nostrils flared, and whatever he smelled had him crouching on the balls of his feet, practically lunging away.

"Loren, *please*," he choked out the words, fighting to keep his voice steady. For her benefit. He really wanted to bellow. Growl. She could feel the same urge nipping at her thoughts, foreign and overwhelming. "Take. It. *Off!*"

His anger scared her, but there was a desperate, pleading edge to his tone that had her reaching for the hem of her dress. Modesty didn't matter in the face of his pain. In jerky, unsteady motions, she wrestled the garment over her head and tossed it aside.

Cheeks flaming, she huddled down, drawing her knees up to her chin, and tried to ignore the fact that she was outside, in the freezing cold, wearing only her bra and underwear. The nakedness exposed her to more than just the frigid temperature. He could see her. All of her.

There was nothing left to hide the scars. Nothing to shield the bruises on her arms and legs. Her father wasn't the only monster to mark her, and the evidence was painfully fresh. A streaky trail of mud painted her inner thigh, along with tiny scratches left by groping fingers…

He seemed to notice them at the same time she did. The guttural sound that tore from his throat had Loren cringing back so violently she almost fell off the porch.

"Fuck." With that, he wrenched open the screen door so hard it slammed against the wall. "Get in."

Loren limped inside, flinching as she passed him. For a rare instant, his eyes weren't on her, but scanning the horizon of trees along the property. After only a moment, he slammed the front door shut behind them both, leaving her clothes out on the porch.

"The bathroom." He led the way, unconcerned as she struggled to keep up.

Once there, he herded her inside the narrow room and turned on the shower at full blast. Loren stood by awkwardly as he snatched a towel from a shelf by the door, and fished a bottle of body wash from underneath the sink. He handed her both items and inclined his head toward the rushing water.

She hesitated. Did he really expect her to shower with him standing there?

As if reading her mind, something that could have been guilt contorted his expression, displacing the rage. Silently, he moved to stand just outside the door with his back to her—but that was all the privacy he seemed willing to give. His body language said it all—*I'm not leaving you.*

Strangely enough, a part of her wanted him there. His presence helped her face the mud and blood that washed off her without screaming. Without seizing up in fear at the memory of an unfamiliar hand inching up her leg. Imbued with the scent of pine, she washed up in minutes and blindly reached out for the towel.

"No." Officer McGoven still stood near the door, but the man seemed to have eyes in the back of his head. "Again," was all he said.

Loren lathered up in even more body wash. The second she started to rinse, another bellowed command came from the doorway. "Again."

She shampooed her hair twice.

"Again."

Another rinse. Another. It felt like ages before she felt clean enough—and at least three more passes of lather before Officer McGoven seemed satisfied. A part of her almost instinctively knew when she could finally shut the shower off and shimmy nervously into her towel.

The second she was fully covered, a dark T-shirt appeared before her, thrown by an unseen hand. After making sure his back was to her, she dropped the towel and wrenched the garment over her head.

A glance in the mirror revealed a logo for the New Walsh police department stamped across the front of the gray cotton. It smelled like him—overwhelmingly. As if this was the very shirt he'd worn while tailing Kyle's truck, dripping with furious sweat. The mental image stole her breath.

Unfortunately, the ensemble didn't improve her appearance any. She looked a mess. Her hair hung limply over her shoulders. She wasn't wearing a bra, and the shirt's thin material clung to her in all the wrong places.

And he noticed. A glance out the corner of her eye revealed him watching her unashamedly.

Strangely… She didn't feel the same crippling impulse to hide she felt around everyone else. The sight of him inspired jealousy instead. Even streaked with dirt, and with blood seeping through the leg of his sweatpants, *he* still managed to look brave. Invincible. Strong enough to face a group of four men head-on without flinching.

"I'm sorry." Guilt instantly transformed him, making him look less fierce, and those eyes a little less silver. Nervously, he ran a hand through his hair, ruffling it into a messy tangle. "I shouldn't have yelled, but I couldn't bear to smell *them* on you."

The heat in his tone shocked her—or maybe it was the subtle possession lying beneath it? *I couldn't bear to smell them on you.* Was that why he kept his distance and made her shower until her fingers ached?

Hell yes, that dark gleam in his eye claimed. Not only that, but… she could tell from the way his fingers twitched at his sides that he wasn't satisfied with just wiping the strangers' scents away. No, he wanted to replace them. Needed to.

With his touch. His scent. The impulse was so strong Loren's knees buckled, and she gripped the counter. If she didn't, she might go to him. Demand he do…something. Anything.

That uncomfortable, prickling heat was back, building beneath her skin. Her chest. Between her legs. *Only him,* a part of her whispered, pleased. *Only he can touch me.*

Overwhelmed, Loren sat on the lid of the toilet, wrapping her arms around her chest. Where the hell had that come from? Obviously, she had hit her head during the attack. She even felt along her swollen bottom lip, hoping the pain might snap some sense into her.

"I'll kill him—" Officer McGoven stood by the sink, glaring at the mirror. He wet a rag and tackled his legs and arms haphazardly before washing his hands beneath the faucet. Afterward, he remained there, in between her and the door. Massive, his body blocked her in, but for whatever reason, she wasn't alarmed.

"Kyle, that son of a bitch, will pay for this," he growled as the last droplets of water dripped from him. "He should have *never* left you alone. Not there."

But he *let her go in the first place*, a tiny voice inside her argued. If he hadn't followed her…

"Did you kill them?" Again, Loren didn't know what made her speak at all. She couldn't even look at him and stared down at her knees instead.

He didn't answer, but the look in his eye—once she found the strength to peek at him—said without words what he wouldn't.

"Loren, there is something you need to understand." He reached for her, and Loren jerked back.

Not out of fear, she told herself—for some reason, she couldn't bring herself to truly fear him—but…

The heat in his gaze startled her. No one ever looked at her like that. Ever. It was so much more than just anger or fear. No. Protectiveness? An emotion that drove him to kill.

"Loren…" Awkwardly, he held his hand in the air, inches from her face. "I would never hurt you. You know that, don't you?"

Something made her nod before her mind had even processed the words. He wasn't like her father or the men from the woods.

She knew that.

"They hurt you to get to me," he said. "They knew what you are… What you mean to me. If I didn't… They would have never stopped. Do you understand that?"

Tentatively, he reached for her again, coiling his fingers around her wrist. The air left her lungs. His touch traveled through every inch of her body, hot and electric. Through bone. Flesh. Muscle. Her mind whirled with the sensation, and she almost missed the moment he tugged, easily pulling her to her feet.

And into his chest.

$\mathcal{K}$yle leaned against the wall of an alley an hour outside of Eislander territory, next to a crummy pay phone, and waited.

It was showtime. He had already mastered his "sad face" and had his sob story together. *They forced us off the road. The girl ran. There were too many of them. When I found her, she...*

He just hoped no one expected any more from him than that. Already, he'd spent too much damn effort making sure that this plan went off without a hitch. It hadn't been easy. The thought of staging something so close to Eislander territory, still made a shiver run down his spine. It was risky, but more than worth the danger in the end.

The girl was dead, and nothing could be traced back to him. *At least now McGoven no longer has the mating bond to worry about,* he thought around a chuckle.

It had probably been broken even before the girl had died. After all, the cheap bastards he'd hired to do the deed had only asked for one thing in addition to the money he'd paid them.

Any other day, he might have felt guilty. The poor female's last moments couldn't have been fun.

But who the hell cared? Lukka got his subtle revenge, and McGoven was back to being the brooding mate-less outlaw.

Win-win.

All Kyle had left to do was pat himself on the back for a job well done. *Piece of cake.*

Only when midnight rolled around without any word, his shoulders started to tense. By the time dawn approached, still without a peep, he had become downright panicked. His palms began to sweat. His already rapid heartbeat kicked it up a notch. He knew he was in deep shit even before the phone finally *did* ring.

"You fucked up."

The voice didn't belong to one of the seedy bastards he'd hired to kill Loren Connors. The power in it could only be conveyed by an Alpha.

"You hear me, Kyle?" Lukka snarled. "You. Fucked. Up."

"What the hell happened?" Kyle countered, feeling somewhat defensive even though he already knew *something* had gone wrong. The bastards never called to receive their second half of the payment, and there could only be one explanation.

Lukka growled. "I had my men scout the perimeter—"

For show, of course. Once Micha showed up, claiming attack by the Eislanders, Lukka would have had to put on his big boy Alpha panties and at least *pretend* to take the threat seriously.

"—only, they caught a whiff of McGoven in the area."

"What?" An uncharacteristic tendril of fear pierced through Kyle before he could help it.

No wonder the bastard let them go so easily. He'd expected a bigger fight, and assumed McGoven had been desperate to have the girl off his hands—but no. The damn rogue had followed them, and Kyle had been too confident to notice.

It was a ballsy move. Kyle might have been impressed—until he remembered that McGoven was a snake. If only he showed the same vigilance reserved for Loren Connors toward all his mates.

Emma might still be alive, in that case.

"I had the security footage pulled around that damn town where he lives," Lukka went on.

Mentally, Kyle had to chuckle at that. While the man might not have had the guts to pull off his own dirty work, he didn't seem to mind using the power that came with being the Alpha of one of the most powerful packs in the area.

Go figure.

"He was with the girl. She's still *alive*," the Alpha added, stating the obvious. "And he'll know that you tried to kill her."

"Why do you figure that?" Kyle asked, though more to stall than anything else.

Fuck. McGoven may have turned his back on pack life, but some instincts couldn't be forgotten—ignored. The mating bond went way deeper than any other connection. It outlasted mother, father, brother, friend, sister. Kyle could only compare it to what he'd felt for his twin—an instinctive pull, as though she were his other half. A piece of his soul.

Such a deep, lupine tie couldn't be forged on a whim. Seeing his mate in danger would have sent McGoven into a rage that Kyle shuddered to imagine. A fierce, primal need to protect at all costs.

He just wondered vaguely if there was anything left of the mercenary bastards that could be traced back to him. Though, his failure would mean more than a few dead contacts in the long run. McGoven would never release the girl now. And the longer the man remained bonded to a mate, the more dangerous he would become.

To be fair, revenge might have explained McGoven's tenacity, at least partly. The animosity between him and Kyle went beyond hatred.

It was personal; Kyle could admit that. Why pretend? If poor Bill McGoven lost his mate for a second time, then—and only *then*— would he feel a fraction of the pain Kyle felt every fucking day. Until that moment, there could be no truce. No forgiveness. Not even an "order from the Alpha" could make him play nice.

"Did you hear me? McGoven will be out for blood," Lukka went on, sounding all "I hope you're happy"-like.

Kyle laughed. "No, he won't."

He covered his tracks too well. The men he'd hired weren't from Lukka's pack or the Eislander territory. They were shady, greedy little rogues who should have been honored to die as pawns.

Having McGoven fuck things up definitely put a snag in his plan, but he could be flexible. After all, the best revenge always came with a plan B.

"I'll handle it," he said.

"Before or after McGoven comes for your throat?"

"He won't get the chance," Kyle countered, confident of the fact.

As far as anyone knew, they had gotten stranded on Eislander territory. If anything, McGoven would just assume that *they* were the ones who attacked her.

In fact…

"You just sit tight, Lukka." Kyle grinned as a new plan unfurled in his mind. Sure, it involved a little murder and some finagling on his part—but he had always been creative.

"Be a good Alpha and offer your condolences. You can even throw McGoven a pity party if you want and lower his guard. Just leave the rest to me."

His heat engulfed her, and despite everything she'd been through, Loren relented to the embrace. Eagerly. *Too* eagerly.

She couldn't get enough of him—of his heat, his scent. She needed him closer. Her body went limp as her chin settled against the hard line of his shoulder. Nose buried against his flesh, she inhaled, and the rush of his scent in her lungs was… Incomparable. Her belly flipped. The pressure between her legs was a constant ache—but it didn't feel wrong. Nothing to be ashamed of. Her reaction just meant…

He is mine.

Surprisingly, he allowed the embrace, but with restraint. He was careful, like one wrong move, and she might break. With utmost care, he ran his fingers through her hair, parting the wet tresses along her scalp while avoiding the area still throbbing from being pulled.

This is wrong, a part of her whispered. He was a stranger—and they were both half-naked. But she was so cold, and to be fair, he only seemed willing to *hold* her, nothing more. His warm breath ghosted the side of her cheek, alluding to the fact that his mouth was a respectful distance from hers.

Still, she didn't stiffen when his hands slid from their neutral positioning on her ribcage down to her waist. Before fear could even enter her mind, she felt his fingertips brush over his intended destination—the bruise left behind after one of the men had crouched on her back.

The memory made her shiver. If he hadn't…

She didn't even want to think about what might have happened —but he was. His nostrils flared, and she recalled something from what felt like an eternity ago.

"My bruises." She struggled to form a coherent question. "Can you really… Smell them?"

"Yes," he said heatedly. "Every one, just as easily as fresh blood. There is a slight difference, but our senses can pick up even the smallest injury."

"You saved my life," she choked out. Acknowledging that felt too important not to voice out loud. She needed to say more. "If you weren't there… Thank you."

He didn't answer. Instead, he cocked his head to bring his jaw against the crook of her shoulder. Loren exhaled sharply, her spine rigid with anticipation. She could sense his lips, a hairsbreadth from her flesh—but no closer. A ragged inhalation betrayed his intention—to breathe in her scent.

"I should have never let you go with that bastard."

Not, *I should have never let you go at all,* a part of her remarked— but it was close enough.

With a shaky breath, Loren copied him, losing herself in the heavy scent of pine.

She had forgotten what this felt like. Physical contact. Even a hug. Her body hummed, as if his nearness revitalized parts of her that had grown rusted with disuse. She hadn't experienced a similar embrace since her mother had been alive. Though McGoven was certainly taller than she had been. And wider, and stronger…

The muscles in his forearms alone were thicker than her own, but he utilized that strength with a gentleness that made her head spin. Even as he maneuvered her against the wall.

He moved too quickly to resist. Within seconds, both of his hands palmed the wall on either side of her, forming a cage of flesh and bone. Another soft intake of air was her only warning as he lowered his head, this time inhaling along the flesh at her throat.

In tendrils of whisper-soft warmth, she felt two fingers trail the length of her shoulder—so gentle, she barely even felt it. But she certainly felt him press the side of his face against her swollen, aching cheek.

He was still breathing, but shallowly, in and out. With every exhalation, his cheek collided with hers. Gently at first, then more firmly. Loren tensed for pain. Instead, a warm tingle washed over her entire being.

Her eyes widened with recognition. It was the same sensation she felt after she'd fallen off Xavier. This time, he concentrated the contact along the worst of the bruising while angling the rest of his body away from hers with what seemed to be a deliberate effort.

By the time he pulled back to observe her with that piercing stare, she couldn't feel anything at all.

"Better?" he asked.

She could only nod.

"Good—" Even the sound of his voice made her dizzy. Breathless, she slumped back against the wall. "I think you should go to bed."

She shook her head. "But…what—"

"I'll explain everything," he said over her. "Once you wake up. But now…" He trailed a finger down the side of her jaw, brushing back a damp tendril of hair. "You need sleep."

The words seemed to set something off inside of her. An intense exhaustion she hadn't even been aware of until then.

Go to sleep.

A part of her wasn't sure whether she made it to the stairs before her mind drifted into black.

*L*oren choked on the verge of a scream.

There were shadows everywhere—hunting her…chasing her through the trees.

She couldn't see—it was so damn cold—but they were gaining. She could tell that much. Their snarls rode the air, and the harsh snap of biting teeth nipped at her ankles. Any minute, they would catch her, and she was too exhausted to fight anymore—

"I'm here." The gruff voice shattered the nightmare, ripping her from the icy darkness of the forest, and leaving her curled up and warm on a bed.

Trembling, she inhaled the scent of pine and knew instantly that she was in McGoven's bed. Only she wasn't alone. Her companion's presence was unmistakable. They were big, with a muscular arm thrown lazily over her waist, holding her tight. However, when she attempted to look back, the comforting grip became a restraint.

"You're alright." That voice was a soothing rumble that echoed like the thunder sounding beyond the window, where a mid-afternoon rain came down in heavy sheets. "I'm here. You were only dreaming."

Drowsily, she allowed her eyes to drift shut, surrendering once again to the darkness. And all the while, that deep tone egged her on, as dexterous fingers stroked through her hair. "You were only dreaming…"

*L*oren woke up to the sound of a car door slamming shut.

Dazed, she rolled over, almost surprised to find that there was no one beside her. The red sheets had been draped neatly over her, tucked in along the edges of the mattress. There wasn't even the indent of another body.

With a sigh, she crept to the edge of the bed, shook out her hair, and…

Realized that all she wore was a man's oversized T-shirt—and very little else. Not to mention, her body ached all over, and the back of her head felt as if someone had taken a baseball bat to it. She traced her bottom lip with a trembling finger, shocked when the tip came away red with blood.

What in the world happened?

It was only when she tried to stand up, gasping as her ankle throbbed, that she remembered everything that happened in the woods.

Kyle, Micha…and Officer McGoven.

While not in this room, he was still in the house. She could sense *him* in the same way she felt her own heartbeat playing through her chest. *He's down below*, something told her. *Waiting.*

Her body trembled as she padded into the hallway and down the stairs. The instant she made contact with the first floor, a pair of gray eyes sought her out from the direction of the kitchen.

He stood at the center island, dressed in another pair of sweats… and very little else. In a rare display, his chest was bare, and every scar glimmered like silver in the waning daylight. As he pivoted on his heels, she snuck a glimpse of his naked back, and her breath caught. The man was a maze of flesh and silvery scars. And ink. For the first time, the tattoo on his neck was clearly visible— a simplistic design consisting of four lines, stretching down between his shoulder blades. Their deliberate placement brought to mind more violent imagery—claw marks.

Surprisingly, that wasn't the most shocking observation to catch Loren's eye. The fact that he watched her while holding a half-eaten tuna sandwich to his mouth was. In contrast to the man who took on four men to save her, it was a comical scene. Until his eyes met hers, as stern as ever.

"Naomi came by," he said, before taking a bite. "I had her leave your work. I thought you'd appreciate a reprieve from her for a day at least."

That explained the slamming car door. Sure enough, glancing out of the window, Loren caught sight of a pink car speeding down the road. It had to be late, if school had already let out—meaning she had slept all day.

"Thanks."

She stood awkwardly on the bottom step for at least another full minute, before she finally found the courage to enter the kitchen. He finished his sandwich while she approached. Then he stood aside to reveal a second, untouched sandwich on a paper plate.

"Have a seat—" He inclined his head toward an empty stool and placed the food in front of it.

Loren complied and began to eat. As soon as she took a bite, he placed a hand on the counter inches from hers.

"What are you thinking?"

The question threw her off, and she choked on a bite of tuna. He had to get her a cup of water, and she gulped it down, desperate to compile a coherent reply. What *was* she thinking? Her eyes trailed over that stern jaw, following the line of it up and across his face.

"You were the wolf." The words came out stronger than she would have thought. Steady.

But she had caught him off guard. Almost too quickly to track, he raised an eyebrow before his expression smoothed into a blank mask. He watched her for so long, she could sense the darkness thickening outside until it was fully nightfall.

Finally, he nodded. "I was."

He said it without any emotion, almost as if daring her *not* to believe him. And the funny thing was...

She did.

"How?"

How. Not, *You're crazy.*

This is insane.

I'm calling the police.

She didn't run from the room. Even stranger, was that the admission wasn't surprising in the least. All along, she'd sensed that he was different—from the moment she first stepped foot in this very house, in fact.

"It's in my blood," Officer McGoven said after a while, leaning against the opposite counter. "We call it lupine instinct." The careful phrasing implied something. Something…dark.

"Like a disease?" She didn't know what made her use that word. *A disease that makes you sprout hair and grow fangs?* Nervously, she crammed another chunk of sandwich into her mouth.

Officer McGoven didn't seem to take offense. "More like hereditary," he said. "An inherited trait. The beast you saw is a part of me, and I am a part of it. Think of us as two halves of the same coin."

Oh, Loren thought somewhat breathlessly. He must have rehearsed this speech, putting it into terms she'd understand. Though, most people inherited just their eye color from their parents. Apparently, *he* had inherited the ability to change into a beast at will.

"It's not how it sounds," McGoven added. He crossed his arms and frowned as if trying to come up with the right words. The awkwardness betrayed just how little he was used to holding an actual conversation. "It's *instinct,*" he settled on finally. "I'm not a monster, or a mindless animal. Even in my other form, I am still me."

Loren trailed her gaze over his chest, across the scars, up to that thatch of dark, curling hair. Hair, the exact shade of a certain snarling wolf.

"So, you're a werewolf?" Her voice came out small, as she tried to recall what little she knew from horror movies.

Did he bray at the moon? Howl? Get fleas?

He flinched. "We prefer the term *lupine*. Lycan. Wolf-man—anything but *that*. And—" He paused deliberately, preparing her for another bombshell. "You are as well."

"I'm what?" Loren blurted stupidly before she realized what he really meant—one of *them*—lupine. She shook her head. "I'm not."

The only things she had inherited from her parents seemed to be an awful streak of bad luck, an inability to communicate with others, and a panache for making life difficult for those around her. Besides, one would think that if she *did* possess the ability to change into a wolf, she would have discovered it by now.

"You *are*." He met her gaze and held it, silently begging her to listen. "You must have inherited it from your father. That is how lupine blood is passed down. I'm guessing your mother was a human, but—"

"No," Loren said. "My father wasn't a werewolf."

Fred Connors had been a violent alcoholic, but he never sprouted claws.

"Fred Connors was not your father, Loren," McGoven said cautiously. "He couldn't be. Not if—"

"I'm not a wolf. I'm not—" She wracked her brain for the right word. Brave? Strong? Lethal? "Like *you*," she settled on helplessly.

"You are lupine, Loren. You *are*. I can sense it on you. Even now. You know I followed you out to that clearing, but you don't understand how. By your scent. I could feel every step you took—"

"S-stop." She dropped her sandwich onto the plate and scooted from the counter. Her heart was pounding, head throbbing, and, for once, the reaction had nothing to do with fear.

"Thank you," she stammered. "You've been so nice to me, b-but I'm not—I can't do this. I'm sorry."

He's crazy, a part of her thought as she scrambled for the front door. He had done more for her than anyone else—but he was obviously off his rocker. He had to be. Especially if he thought she was anything other than a messed-up teenager with nowhere left to go.

He didn't storm after her or stop her from leaving. The front door was unlocked, and the frosty night air hit her like a whip as she stumbled out onto the porch. After descending the steps, she hit the ground running and didn't stop, hair flying out behind her— though a part of her wailed in annoyance when she reached the one place that wasn't far from him.

The second she entered the barn, Bunny and Esther's heads appeared over the doors of their stalls in greeting. Xavier kept his distance, though, hidden firmly in the shadows.

Clumsily, Loren pulled open the door to the nearest stall and slipped inside, pressing herself against the farthest corner.

It didn't take him long to find her. Like a shadow, he appeared near the door, massive enough to block the entire exit. If she hadn't sensed him already, the horses' reactions would have alerted her—all three stomped their hooves, breathing heavily.

"Loren." His voice reached her easily above the clamor. "It's freezing out. Come back inside."

Loren felt like a child, fighting the urge to stick her fingers in her ears and chant, "Na na na na, I can't hear you."

"Loren. We need to talk—" He must have taken a step, because Bunny balked, and Esther shrieked, the whites of her massive eyes flickering.

Instantly, he retreated to the doorway, but he didn't leave. "Come here." He dropped the politeness. It was an order, one that had her flinching in his direction before she could help it.

Why is that? a part of her wondered helplessly. No one else had ever affected her with so much as a few simple words. Even when she obeyed her father, it had always been out of fear, but with him…

It was as if a part of her *needed* to obey, even as she dug her heels into the straw-strewn floor and gritted her teeth.

"Loren," he insisted, his tone deeper. "Get out of the barn."

Resisting him was like trying to hold her breath. After so long, her muscles ached, and every inch of her screamed with the need to give in. *Go!*

Gasping, she took a stumbling step toward the mouth of the stall, and then another… She could clearly see him now. He stood just beyond the doorway, eyes blazing against the darkened sky.

"Come here."

The words yanked her forward another few steps. *I have to,* a part of her insisted. *I have to listen to him.*

But why? All he did was confuse her even more. She was a turtle, content in its shell—and he was the eagle, trying to peck her out of it, all the while claiming that she really wasn't what she'd spent her whole life believing she was.

Regardless of her unease, her body continued toward him—but when he reached for her arm, something inside Loren snapped.

No! She lunged, taking off in the opposite direction, and his grasping hand caught only air. Any triumph she felt didn't last long. She could sense him on her heels, but he wasn't clumsy like the men from the clearing.

Her entire being shuddered with his presence. His scent cloyed in her throat, and she knew that, no matter how fast she ran, she'd never be able to escape him. Though, there was a tiny piece of her that really didn't *want* to…

Panting, she made it to the west field and took off randomly for the trees. *A little more,* she urged as her limbs started to burn. *Just a little more.*

She didn't even see him coming.

Wham!

She went down sprawling, trapped beneath a heavy force that pinned her to the ground.

No, she thought, fighting back the dark memory that threatened to overwhelm her—*darkness, groping hands, harsh pants. She would never get away!*

"No, no, no, no—"

"You're alive!"

The chirpy tone threw her off so badly that she blinked, forgetting all about the icy fear that crept up to swallow her whole. Instead, she twisted over the wet earth, coming face to face with two piercing eyes.

Instead of gray…

They were green.

26

"**Y**ou're alive!" The figure lunged, throwing their arms around her as if they were long-lost friends and not virtual strangers. Still, a name came to mind.

"M-Micha?"

He didn't seem to hear her. "You're alive. I thought… Thank God you're okay!"

When he finally withdrew, Loren noticed that—besides his lack of a shirt—a nasty bruise snaked along his jaw. His clothes, what little he wore anyway, were ripped and stained with mud. She wouldn't have been shocked if he claimed to have run the whole way here.

"No one would tell me what happened," he rambled. "Kyle's M.I.A. All they kept saying was 'an attack, an attack,' and I thought—"

He broke off mid-sentence as a shadow fell from above. He didn't even have the time to cry out before he was thrown backward.

Crunch! Loren winced in sympathy as Micha landed hard on the ground, a good ten feet away.

The next second, Officer McGoven stood over her, yanking her to her feet. "Are you okay?"

Without waiting for a reply, he was across the field, standing toe to toe with Micha. The moment the boy found his balance, McGoven shoved him to his knees. "You're one of Lukka's," he growled amid an audible sniff. "You were with Kyle—"

"Wait!" Breathless, Loren stumbled forward. Her ankle throbbed like hell, but it held up as she staggered toward him. "He wasn't doing anything—"

"Stay back!" McGoven's upper lip pulled back from his teeth as he inclined his head her way. He looked…feral. Coldly, he raked his gaze over her muddy knees, where his shirt had bunched up around her legs. Then, he turned back to Micha—only there was a lethal sharpness to his movements that made her heart lurch. He aimed to do more than shove him.

"Wait!" Clumsily, Loren moved forward. She hesitated, fingers outstretched, before bracing a hand against the skin of his bared shoulder. He felt hot, like the surface of an oven. His heart was racing, pounding beneath her palm. Anger battered off him in waves, along with something else. Something that a part of her marveled at…

Fear?

"He didn't hurt me," she said in a low voice. "I swear."

He shrugged her off but reluctantly lowered his fist. "You have five minutes," he growled to Micha. "So, you better start talking. What the hell are you doing here?"

Instead of launching into another whirlwind explanation, Micha bowed his head and raised one knee. The position would have been comical—he almost looked like a man proposing—but the thick tension in the air displaced any desire to laugh. Loren wanted to pull her hair out instead.

"I failed you," he said mournfully. "You entrusted your mate to us, and I—"

"You left her," McGoven interjected. "Alone in enemy territory, to the mercy of *thugs*."

"W-what?" Wide-eyed, Micha gaped at Loren. "Are you okay?"

"Don't you *dare* talk to her," McGoven bellowed. "Don't you even *look* at her. You left her alone in enemy territory. Do you know what they were going to do to her? I could *smell* their intentions. They planned to violate her in every way you can imagine. They wanted her to suffer. Should I go into detail?"

Micha flinched, but so did Loren. The inside of her thigh ached as if remembering that harsh, groping touch. She didn't think she could bear to have him elaborate.

Thankfully, in the end, McGoven released a harsh breath and cocked his head. "Why the hell are you here?"

Micha warily met his stare. Then he placed his left hand over his heart and sucked in a steadying breath. "I came to pledge myself to you. You can kill me. Have mercy. It's up to you. I accept your judgment—" He lowered his head, as if awaiting the bite of an executioner's blade. "For failing to protect your mate, I deserve whatever punishment you see fit. Even death."

"What?" McGoven looked confused. A black eyebrow twitched, threatening to disappear beneath a wayward strand of hair. The odd display seemed to diminish some of his anger—for now.

"That's an old law," he said finally. "I doubt that even *Lukka* would force you to obey it. Integrity wasn't his forte, from what I remember." His voice held so much derision Loren was surprised he didn't spit on the ground afterward.

Micha shrugged. "Sometimes, old ways are the best. My father was a member of the Oleron pack. It was how things were done there."

McGoven nodded. "There, maybe. Not here. Get up. I don't want anything from you. I'm sure your buddy Kyle had no shred of remorse, and neither should you."

"But—" Micha glanced in Loren's direction. "Kyle's not always right," he said, fumbling over the words. "And if you want to kill me, it's within your right. I won't even fight back—"

"Enough." McGoven scoffed, lowering his hands to his sides. "I'm sure you were just following orders—" Rather than sympathetic, he sounded mocking. "Though, *where* is your friend Kyle? Did he come to 'submit himself for my judgment,' as well?"

He seemed to eagerly scan the horizon.

The corner of Micha's mouth twitched. "Kyle isn't… Let's just say that I decided to face you alone after my own questions led me nowhere."

He gingerly fingered the bruise on his jaw. "Even Lukka doesn't know I left—but I just couldn't do *nothing*. You entrusted your mate to us, and we failed."

Mate, Loren shivered as he said the word, and so did Officer McGoven. She couldn't name the emotion in his expression. Whatever it was, made something inside her twist into knots.

"Get up," McGoven said to Micha. "Get back to your pack. You don't owe me a damn thing, and I don't want to see you around here again."

Micha seemed to hesitate. "But—"

"Go." Without another word, McGoven turned toward the house, and Loren followed him without him having to say a word. It just seemed natural—when he moved, so did she.

He didn't acknowledge her, but when he deliberately headed toward the path instead of cutting through the uneven field, she had a feeling that it had something to do with the way that she limped. Her ankle throbbed, and she practically hopped by the time they reached the front porch—but when she turned to stare over the darkening fields, a lone figure remained there, watching them from a distance.

27

*L*oren staggered to the couch the moment they entered the house. She could sense McGoven watching her, but all he did was crouch and prop her foot on his knee.

"It's not broken," he declared, though a purplish bruise discolored the skin. "But it's probably best if you don't walk on it for a while."

He reached for the med kit Sonia had left almost three days ago and withdrew a length of bandage. Carefully, he wrapped the foot from heel to toe. When he finished, she expected him to release her. Instead, he stared at her filthy toes, still cupping her heel in his palm.

She observed him in return, allowing her gaze to travel from that messy tangle of dark hair, down his chest, to the legs hidden beneath the bulky sweatpants.

And the blood pooling beneath him on the floor.

"You're bleeding!"

Freeing her foot, she sank down beside him and reached for the hem of his pant leg before he could stop her. His hand fell over her arm anyway, but not as a restraint. His fingers settled against her skin with a softness that made her pulse race. Focusing beyond him felt like wading through quicksand. The smell of his blood helped put her priorities in order, though. Gingerly, she pulled back the damp material to reveal a gash in his calf several inches long.

"You were hurt." She vaguely remembered him bleeding last night, but up close, the wound looked nasty. Way more debilitating than her ankle, but he hadn't even limped.

"You'll need to take care of this," she blurted, reaching automatically for the med kit and a bottle of antiseptic. "You don't want it to get infected. Or leave a scar."

"You know your stuff," he said. To tease?

Her cheeks flamed as she remained silent. Years of tending to her own injuries had taught her a thing or two. With a honed practice, she soaked a cotton ball in alcohol and cleaned the wound.

It had to hurt, but he didn't even flinch. His lips were quirked, seemingly with amusement. Her belly flipped with a sudden thought—he *had* been teasing her.

"It seems you didn't need my help after all," he said, presumably referring to his prior attempt at first aid.

"You may need s-stitches," she stammered while bandaging the width of his calf. "But I don't think that…"

His hand caught her wrist, and she broke off as a foreign emotion shot through her belly. Shock? Fear? Or *something else* that made her bare toes curl against the floor as he dragged the pad of his thumb carefully over the fragile bones?

At first, she wondered why, until she saw the way he stared, eyes dark with confusion, at a jagged section of skin that encircled each one. Scars, though far less pretty than the ones he sported. Hers were thinner, raised like bracelets formed of flesh.

His gaze found hers, silently questioning, but Loren just drew her hand away. The cause of those scars was one of the many secrets she'd shoved to the back of her mind—too dangerous to ever recall. Instead, she leaned back against the couch and sighed.

"Who is Lukka?" Her voice came out tired and strained.

Rather than deflect, McGoven copied her, sitting close enough that his shoulder brushed hers.

"He's the leader of a track of territory to the northeast of here." Loren sensed he deliberately avoided using another word—*Alpha*. "It's a place called Black Mountain, where a small community of sorts lives in relative isolation. Not a town like New Walsh. We have another name for it."

"You mean a pack," Loren said, utilizing that strange word Micha had.

Like wolves.

He nodded, gazing through the window as a flicker of lightning sparked over the horizon. "One of the largest in this region. At least five hundred strong the last I checked. Maybe more now. It doesn't sound like much compared to any town you're used to, but as far as our kind is concerned, it's massive." The words came hesitantly as if he expected her to argue. When she said nothing, he soldiered on. "Lukka controls hundreds of miles of territory. That's almost unheard of. Those born on Black Mountain can trace their bloodlines back generations. Centuries. The elders on his council have a wealth of knowledge between them. As far as packs go, his is the best around, especially for a young wolf. At least on paper."

The genuine admiration in his voice softened some of the sting of his reluctance to let her stay. He truly seemed to believe she would be better off at this place. One word, however, stuck out to her. "Controls?"

That definitely didn't sound like the political makeup of new Walsh.

McGoven nodded. "It might sound blunt, but that is how we live —under one set of laws, enforced by one person, the Alpha. Lukka has only been in power for a few years, but already things have…changed under his leadership."

He didn't elaborate on how. Sonia alluded to some of the changes, though. Lukka alone could decide if Loren would be welcome there or not—and that seemed to annoy them both.

"We have different ways of doing things," McGoven admitted. "But we don't turn our backs on our own. Never. The second I sensed the change in you, Lukka should have come to assess you himself that very night. Nothing could be more important than that. No fucking red tape."

It was like he'd read her mind. The intensity in his voice diminished more of her doubt. Crazy or not, he seemed to care about her. More than a stranger should, in her experience.

"If you think I'm…" She couldn't bring herself to say it, so she tried a different route. "Was my mother from there? My father?"

McGoven frowned. "Your mother could have been. Humans are sometimes allowed to live on the outskirts, but Fred Connors was one of Lukka's."

She didn't miss how he avoided calling him her father—though that wasn't the strangest revelation he let slip.

"You mean he was like you?" she asked.

"No." McGoven flinched as if the comparison were an insult. "Not like me at all. He was a made wolf—someone bitten by a full-blooded lycan. The Alpha accepted him into the pack out of duty years ago, but the bastard broke the rules and was exiled."

That sounded like him. No wonder he seemed to loathe New Walsh.

"It's the worst punishment among our kind," McGoven explained, his tone grim. "We are social creatures, more so than humans. Pack bonds are stronger than any other connection you can think of. We need it. We need to be surrounded by our own kind. Being excommunicated is a fate worse than death. In fact, most would *prefer* death over it."

"Why aren't you there?" Loren asked.

He grimaced and ran a hand through his tangled hair. "My job was to watch Connors. I knew that he took in a daughter, but I never thought that you would be—"

"Why?" she asked weakly. "How can you tell?"

He cocked his head in her direction. "What color are my eyes?"

"G-gray," she answered automatically. Though, now they glinted more like silver.

"That's how. It's as obvious to me as the color of your hair or eyes." He returned to his vigil at the window, and a flash of lightning reflected off his gaze. Rain had picked up again, running in rivulets down the glass. "I can look at you and see the instinct there. It's faint—but it's there."

Loren questioned that. When she looked in the mirror, all she saw was emptiness. Just what did this "lupine instinct" look like?

"How?" she gathered up the nerve to prod.

"Fred Connors was *made*," he continued as if she'd never spoken. "There is no way you could have inherited the blood from him. I'm sorry, but it is biologically impossible that he could be your father, Loren. He had to be someone else."

He sounded so sure, and strangely enough—if he *were* telling the truth—Loren didn't feel too much emotion at that. Was it strange to think that the man she'd been calling "dad" for the past ten months wasn't really her father? Yeah.

But when she thought of just how those ten months had been spent.

She felt relieved. *I didn't come from that,* a part of her sighed. *His nasty hatred isn't a part of my genes.* But then, what was?

"Was my mother a—"

McGoven shook his head before she even finished. "She was human, Loren. I'm positive about that. A full-blooded female would never give birth outside of her territory. Sometimes the Alpha offered protection to those without the blood. Victims of 'accidents' who weren't turned. That could be how she fell across Connors. I'll call Sonia and have her do some digging. What was her name?"

"Eveline," Loren said softly. "Eveline Connors."

"She might not have known what you were. If Connors made her leave the territory, she would have no choice but to follow him." He made it sound as if their relationship had been more of hunter and hunted than anything romantic.

"You, however, have lupine blood," he insisted. "In fact, your father must be a pureblood, most likely someone belonging to a nearby pack."

"Is that why you wanted me to go to Lukka?" She found the strength to ask. "So that I could be with a pack?"

He nodded, but kept his gaze on the window rather than look at her. "Isolation is *unnatural for* us. The need to belong to a pack is too strong—some go insane from it. Connors should have taken you to them the moment he sensed the blood in you. To keep you out here was unnecessarily cruel. Some might say criminal."

"What makes you think he knew?" She thought of the way her father treated her—cold and distant. Had he known all along that she might not have been his daughter? Was that why he hated her so much?

"It's obvious," McGoven said, facing her directly. "Maybe not right away, but…" He reached out, snagging a lock of hair. Before she could even flinch, he tucked it behind her ear.

"Anyone looking at you could tell that you are different."

He didn't make it sound like a compliment. Just fact.

"You belong with people *like* you, who can understand you. It sounds dramatic, I know, but once you feel for yourself what it's like to be in a pack… You will understand. You don't belong here."

Slowly, he pulled his hand away, but Loren couldn't ignore the trail of heat that lingered over her skin. Something lurched inside of her, making her chase the contact. Demand it. His fingertips brushed her shoulder as she inched closer.

He frowned. "Lukka could have given you that. Safety. Security. Everything you've never had."

Could have. She didn't miss his choice of words, but hope was a painful emotion to feel. It stabbed through her heart. Her eyes burned. "If it's so important, then why aren't you—"

He lurched to his feet gracefully, despite his injured leg.

"You asked why I left. I'll tell you. When you belong to a pack, loyalty is everything," he said in a low, gruff tone. "You should be ready to lay your life down for your Alpha at a moment's notice —I wasn't."

He entered the kitchen, swiping the remains of her sandwich into the trash before disappearing into another section of the house.

All Loren could do was sit there, watching the rain come down, and suffer the chill that replaced his heat.

It doesn't make sense. Bill seethed as he marched through the rain. He could smell the scent of fresh blood beneath the moisture and grudgingly acknowledged the source—him. His leg throbbed—one of those bastards had gotten him good with a knife hidden up his sleeve last night—but the pain barely even fazed him at this point.

Not when there were more important things to worry about. Kyle. Loren. The Eislanders. The whole thing didn't make any damn sense.

Eislander wolves were known to be ruthless, and fiercely protective of their territory—but it wasn't like them to attack strays on their land without provocation. Not without alerting their Alpha, at least.

Loreck Eislander may have been an overly aggressive prick, but he was honorable and fair—two words that could never apply to Lukka. Such a man wouldn't condone the murder of a young girl on his land. Not without his say so and certainly not without good reason.

Though, to be honest, that was the least of his worries.

The pack kept calling. They rang constantly, buzzing through the cell phone at his hip, a different number almost every time. He could guess the source without having to check the I.D. One of Lukka's many sycophants, or perhaps the bastard himself?

All to give him a half-hearted explanation as to how this had all been just some big misunderstanding. *Whoops!* They'd spew some shit apology and swear to come the next day to take the girl off his hands.

All nice and clean-like.

And all utter bullshit.

While he may not have been a brainiac like Lukka, Bill liked to believe that he wasn't stupid. Kyle hadn't taken a detour through enemy territory just to view the damn scenery. No—and the bastard wouldn't dare do *anything* without the go-ahead from his Alpha.

Only one conclusion fit the puzzle—they had abandoned her there on *purpose,* knowing full well what would happen.

It was a dangerous suspicion, borderline treason without any proof. Not to mention that he was breaking about fifty pack rules *alone* by ignoring the calls. In his mind, it was better not to answer at all, than cuss out the one man who held the keys to his freedom.

He loathed to admit it. The truth didn't matter in the face of his feelings. Lukka required just one excuse to revoke his exiled status and summon him for judgment.

One damn reason.

Though he would give them a hell of a lot more than that if Kyle had the nerve to step on his property after this. A showdown between the two of them had been a long time coming, anyway. Some might say it was fucking destiny.

Respect for Emma's memory was the sole reason he hadn't torn out his throat by now. As her brother, he deserved that much grace. But no more. Kyle could hate him all he wanted, but to use a young female as a pawn in his twisted revenge?

It was beyond cruel. Loren had no choice in becoming tethered to him. The thought of her made him pick up the pace, feeling the rain lash violently at his skin. He could still picture her, cornered and bruised in the center of that clearing. Her eyes had been wide with fear, and her heart pounded so hard he could practically taste her damn pulse in his throat.

The girl had lost so much already, only to be used as a pawn in some sick ploy—and to what end?

Bill had no idea.

At least now, he figured he wouldn't have to call her by that bastard's name anymore; wolves took the surnames of their father. If Connors wasn't a viable candidate, then…

Maybe *that* was the reason he'd been so damn eager to ship her off to Lukka? Wolves could sense family in a way humans couldn't. They wouldn't need a paternity test for the girl's sire to recognize her. Maybe he had hoped that if she'd gone to Lukka's pack, her real father would catch her scent.

And then what?

Claim the fully-grown daughter he'd never known? Accept her baggage with open arms? Like the fact that she had unintentionally mated a rogue?

Why don't you throw in sparkles, sunshine, and a happy ending, while you're at it? he thought sarcastically.

The point was that Loren was in pretty much the same boat he was—abandoned. Alone. Lukka had already failed her. Bill shuddered to think about what could have happened if he hadn't had the sense to follow her. Hell, it made him shudder to think what *he* might have done if—

He shook his head firmly, breaking off the thought, and headed for the trees. It was over and done with anyway. Only *he* could help Loren now. She needed a pack; she needed help. She needed…

Way more than he could give her. He might be able to help with the first two, not that it would matter much in the long run. There were things she should have learned almost a decade ago. Milestones she should have already reached.

And urges a female would need her mate to satisfy. He could feel it already. She was so damn innocent. Her arousal was so fresh. Sweet. Fragile. He doubted she even recognized the feeling for what it was—desire. Lust. Some sick part of him…*liked* that. His abdomen tightened, and he grunted, hating the physical reaction her nearness inspired within him. Sooner or later, she'd recognize the signs. His lingering touch. The way he couldn't keep his eyes off her. The erection straining the front of his pants.

No. Gritting his teeth, he shook his head. Loren wasn't his in that way. She couldn't be. Sooner or later, he would break their bond for her own good—once she became strong enough to hold her own, whatever path she decided. *First things first…*

With one hand, he yanked off his sweatpants, balled them in a fist, and tossed them in the direction of the house, cell phone and all. At the same time, he picked up speed, feeling his bare feet sink into the damp earth. Fresh blood dribbled harmlessly down his leg, not that the wound would plague him for much longer.

He inhaled the damp air, feeling his entire body thrum with the urge that preceded the shift. He had only a split-second's warning to throw his hands out in front of him before his body compacted, twisted, and transformed into the sleek form of a wolf.

He hit the ground running, barely losing momentum, and headed straight for the perimeter of his property. His land, while minuscule compared to Lukka's territory, was all he had. If that young pup had managed to walk right onto it without fear, then what was stopping someone like Kyle?

Or worse.

Justified or not, he had *killed* on another Alpha's territory. Offenses like that weren't just ignored—they couldn't be. Sooner or later, *they* would come knocking, demanding answers.

That makes two of us, Bill thought, as he began to scout, hunting for so much as a leaf out of place. Then, he pushed further into New Walsh, ensuring that Kyle and his cohorts hadn't infiltrated the town as well. He didn't like it. It was risky to venture beyond his property, especially with Loren there alone.

But therein lay the power of the mating bond. He could feel her despite the distance, always. Even if he hadn't followed her to Black Mountain, he would have known the instant she was in danger. If he were being honest with himself, he'd admit that from the second Kyle had arrived, she'd been afraid. That fear drew him like a moth to a flame, arguing with the logical part of him that knew she'd be better off with the pack. She was *his. His.* Even if he couldn't keep her here for long.

Regardless, if anyone dared to harm her, he'd come.

And ensure they never could again.

Thump!

Loren jolted awake with a wince. Her head was throbbing, her bottom lip stung, and the inside of her mouth tasted like copper. With one hand, she cradled her temple and tried to get her bearings.

For the first time since finding herself at Officer McGoven's, she wasn't in that large bed upstairs. She was on the couch instead, with a pile of schoolbooks on her lap and a pencil clutched in her fist.

Huh?

The last thing she remembered was attempting to tackle the work Naomi left. If she were going to stay in New Walsh a little longer, she might as well keep her academics on track. Plus, it gave her an excuse to stay up and wait for McGoven to come back—all while, trying *not* to be driven insane by the million thoughts crashing through her brain.

Dangerous thoughts. The main one being that the man who'd taken her in claimed to be able to shift into a wolf at will. Not to mention the bombshell that her father wasn't really her father after all.

She needed answers, and despite being obviously mentally unbalanced, Officer McGoven was the only person around. When he wasn't staying out all night, of course.

She guessed it to be a little after dawn, though not by much. A glance out the window revealed it had stopped raining, leaving the ground coated in a thick, silvery mist. Inside, the house was toasty warm and, despite wearing only a mud-splattered T-shirt, she felt comfortable. At least her ankle wasn't hurting anymore.

Yawning, she pulled herself upright, leaning against the couch for balance. It was only then that she realized that she hadn't woken up by coincidence. McGoven was back—she knew that as surely as her own name. And…he was angry. The emotion seeped into her in waves. It wasn't her rage. Her disgust. But his…

She could hear him. "Fuck!"

The sound sent her scrambling to her feet, and she raced through the house, stumbling onto the front porch. Icy daylight painted the landscape in muted shades of gray, creating a deceptively beautiful backdrop to the chaos awaiting her.

Blood flooded her nostrils first. Sharp. Pungent. But… It smelled different than hers or McGoven's. A heartbeat later, she spotted the source. Milky, large eyes stared up at her from the welcome mat, but they weren't human. They belonged to what once was a deer. Its head leaked a puddle of fresh blood that pooled over the wood.

A few paces away, propped against the steps, was its body.

"Get back!" She looked up to find McGoven racing down the path, his sweatpants caked in mud. "Get inside," he commanded.

She didn't even think to argue. Bile crawled up her throat as she turned away from the grisly sight. The smell haunted her, and the potential explanations weighed on her mind. Had the poor thing gotten lost? Had someone dropped off roadkill as a joke?

You know it wasn't a joke, that inner voice warned. *This is dangerous. Listen to him.*

She could hear him grunting, and curiosity made her peek out of the kitchen window. Already, he was halfway to the trees, the deer slung over his shoulder effortlessly. He moved with a grace that took her breath away—but his anger was glaringly apparent.

She tried to distract herself. She retreated into the shower and got dressed in the only clothing she could find—his shirt and a ragged pair of sweats. The second she entered the hall, her heart skipped a beat. Someone was in the house with her—in the kitchen, to be exact. Without bothering to be quiet, they rummaged through the cupboards, slamming several heavy objects down hard on the counter.

Thump! Bang! Slam!

The moment she crept to the doorway, the sounds stopped.

"Morning," Officer McGoven rasped. He stood frozen near the center island, holding a jar of mayonnaise in one hand and a slice of bread in the other. Slowly, he smeared the condiment onto the bread and slapped it on top of another already piled high with tuna.

"Are you okay?" His eyes scanned her face intently. He was hunting for something. Something that he didn't seem to find— and that relieved him. "Don't worry about... What happened earlier," he grumbled by way of apology. "Sometimes, the hunters around here choose to be generous with their bounty. I'm sorry you saw that."

He still wore that pair of sweatpants, which were damp and covered in mud. That dark hair was tangled in a way that made Loren wonder if he'd spent the night rolling around in the fields. Or *running* through them.

Suddenly, he closed the fridge with his hip and brought the sandwich to his mouth for a bite.

"Get washed up," he told her, before heading for the stairs. "I'll find you something to wear."

He took the steps two at a time, uncaringly tracking footprints across the floor. Had he really spent the night out in the wind and rain?

It sure smelled like it. His usual scent of pine was diluted by the earthy, musky scent of the woods. Rather than offensive, on him, the aroma seemed...wild. Untamed.

Feral.

Her heart pounded beneath his borrowed shirt, and suddenly the room felt way too small. Rather than mention that she had already showered, she stumbled into the bathroom and climbed into the shower for a second time without giving herself the chance to think about why.

The hot water pounded down—but, this time, every droplet felt...raw. Her skin was oversensitive, aware of every fluctuating temperature. His nearness. His smell. When she finally stepped into a towel, she shuddered at the feel of the terrycloth. Every fiber seemed to irritate her skin as if to tease her about a lack of something else. Something she craved, but couldn't name. Only images came to mind. Deep, golden skin. Calloused fingertips. Heat.

No! Terrified, she shook her head to clear it and saw that someone had placed a pile of folded clothes on the toilet seat for her, so quietly that she hadn't even heard them come in.

The thick flannel shirt and black sweatpants were about ten sizes too big, and she had to roll up the hems of both just to see her hands and feet. But they were warm and offered far more coverage than what she had on.

When she finally returned to the main room, McGoven wasn't there. From the sounds of rushing water coming from above, she guessed he too decided to shower. She had lived with her father for months, but the thought of a grown man showering—naked —in the same house *still* felt strange.

Especially when she could clearly picture his body—every taut, coiled bit of muscle. *No.* She bit her lip hard enough to sting and raced for the door. It wasn't the urge to escape driving her barefoot onto the porch.

No, it was something else.

Something that coiled in the base of her stomach like a snake waiting to strike. It taunted her, betraying just *how* much she remembered from earlier—dark skin and chiseled abs.

Not to mention the blood dripping from his mouth.

The thought made her shiver as she descended the porch steps. McGoven had worked fast. All traces of the deer were gone, and the landscape seemed as idyllic as usual as she crossed the field and headed straight for the barn.

Bunny greeted her as she slipped inside. Esther whinnied hello, and even Xavier seemed less shy. It could have been just another day, sneaking there to avoid her father—but it wasn't long before reality intruded.

The horses sensed him first. Esther shifted uneasily in her stall, while Xavier's dark head appeared over the mouth of his, nostrils flaring. Loren turned, unsurprised to find Officer McGoven in the doorway.

He held something—a dark shape that had her flinching back out of habit. There were two things, actually. Her pair of tan boots and his windbreaker tucked under his arm.

"It's freezing out." His tone was cautious, as if he expected her to bolt at any second.

Instead, she crept forward to take the clothes before darting back inside the safety of the barn. Thankfully, he kept his distance.

She wasn't *afraid* of him, she told herself. But, dressed in a thick polo, and a pair of jeans, he didn't look any less intimidating than he had in a pelt of fur. Even *more so*.

A shower had done him good. His hair was slicked back, his face cleaned of mud. The cleanliness made his gaze all the more piercing. He watched her as she pulled on her boots while leaning against Bunny's stall for balance. They were slightly damp and smelled like…

She sniffed and frowned. *Bleach?* They weren't the only odd-smelling item. This jacket seemed slightly older than the one he'd given her previously. Rather than pine, it reeked of laundry detergent. She zipped it up and waited for Officer McGoven to say something.

Order her back to the house?

All he *did*, was lean carefully against the doorway, arms crossed over his chest. Then, after a moment, he inclined his head toward the nearest stall, where she'd unconsciously gone back to stroking Bunny.

"You named them." It wasn't a question.

"I…I needed something to call them," Loren stammered, feeling her cheeks flame. "I couldn't find any names on their stalls."

"That one's Xavier?" He nodded toward the stallion.

"Yes."

"What about that one?"

"Bunny," she admitted.

"And the brown mare?"

"Esther."

The corner of McGoven's mouth twitched—barely perceptible, but still technically a smile. Though it only lasted a heartbeat.

Loren was mortified. "I'm probably not even close to their real names, am I?"

"Well…" McGoven's mouth returned to its usual frown. "They don't have any. When I…the person I acquired them from didn't tell me if they did or not."

"Oh," Loren said softly. She remembered the man Sonia mentioned. "Josiah Baker?"

He raised an eyebrow, surprised. "Yes. He was a good man. Cared for these animals himself for years, but let's just say talking wasn't his forte."

"He was a wolf, too? I mean a l-lycan."

"How do you… *Sonia*," he declared with a heavy sigh. Then he nodded. "A made. One of the few, if not the only, who I've ever known to leave the pack willingly. Not because he shunned our laws. I think he just preferred his solitude, and I couldn't blame him for that. He died not long after I was… After I left the pack.

He'd just gotten the black one, in fact. And if I *had* named these horses, I don't think I'd have picked those names. The old swayback I probably would have called Whitey. The mare, Brownie, and the stallion…"

"Let me guess?" Loren asked before she could help herself. "Blackie?"

He nodded, but his expression was so serious she couldn't smother a laugh. Just a soft, trickling *ha, ha,* at first, but pretty soon, she was doubled over, gasping for air.

God, she couldn't remember the last time she'd laughed this hard —if ever. Once she started, she couldn't stop. It just kept coming, until she blinked to realize that tears were streaming down her face.

"I was never really creative," McGoven said softly, still watching her. "Feel free to call them whatever you want."

Loren felt the corner of her mouth twitch. Was that a smile? He seemed adept at drawing emotions from her, one after the other. "I don't know…" She turned back to the stall and dragged a hand through the mare's long mane. "Bunny just doesn't have quite the same ring to it as *Whitey.*"

Had she just made a joke? She puzzled it over, still petting the horse. Suddenly, Bunny stiffened, shying back within her stall, her ears flat against her head. Esther reacted the same way, and Xavier shifted, prancing anxiously in his stall.

It wasn't until she felt a prickle over the back of her neck that she saw why. McGoven stood closer, fully inside the barn. His eyes flashed with confusion, as if he hadn't realized he'd moved at all. Awkwardly, he stumbled back until his toes toyed with the threshold once again.

Just like that, the horses quieted down.

"Is that…is that ah…" Loren trailed off. Hell, what did she mean to say? *Is that a wolf thing?*

He got the gist anyway.

"They can sense a predator nearby," he admitted, tucking his hands into his pockets. "It's instinct."

"But…*I* can touch them," she pointed out, trying not to let a note of "I told you so" slip into her voice. It did anyway.

"I know." His voice was that deep rumble again. "I've been thinking as to why…"

He never mentioned just what theories he'd come up with. He just watched her, until Loren felt the need to turn around. Her heart picked up speed, though she figured that it had already been pounding the moment he'd appeared in the doorway.

He felt too close—but not close *enough*. Everything running through her mind was conflicting. Her fingers shook as she dragged them through Bunny's mane over and over again.

What is wrong with me?

"I was going to clean out the barn," McGoven said.

"I can help," she offered. It was the least she could do after sneaking onto his property for nearly a year.

She turned to find him already holding two shovels, one of which he tossed to her. She caught it by the handle and had just a split-second's notice to set it aside before he grabbed a lead rope from the wall and tossed it to her as well.

"You can take them out to pasture if you want."

"S-Sure." Jerkily, Loren moved back to Bunny's stall and led the animal out.

McGoven wasn't anywhere in sight as she turned the nag loose in one of the paddocks. Confused, she went back in for Esther, who was almost too eager to get out into the fresh air, and finally Xavier, who nervously followed her out to join the others.

Afterward, she drifted back into the barn, only to find Officer McGoven standing casually in Bunny's open stall like he'd been there all along. He held a shovel, hefting soiled hay into a nearby wheelbarrow.

Without a word, Loren grabbed the other shovel and moved to help him.

They worked in silence for a long while, until Loren just lost herself in the busywork. She almost didn't notice the pair of eyes on the back of her neck. Not until she happened to turn and caught him staring.

Rather than look away, he held her gaze and cocked his head, demanding an answer to his next question. "What are you thinking? You seem distracted."

She would never understand how he could do that. Be so calm one minute. So authoritative the next.

"You knew my father?" The question slipped out before she could help it.

McGoven set the shovel aside and crossed his arms. "I knew Fred Connors."

Loren sucked in a deep breath, tipping her shovel to dump the last bit of soiled hay into the wheelbarrow. "What was he like? I mean…before…you said he broke the rules of the pack?"

Her heart swelled with a longing that caught her off guard. She just needed something…good? That he was kind once. Nice once. Life had ruined him—not her.

"I didn't know him well, but he did break the rules—at least from the outside looking in. Among us, any little infraction takes more effort than you might think. You must *willingly* go against the wishes of the Alpha. Such disobedience is never tolerated."

He said it the same, definitive way that someone might "You have to willingly go against the laws of gravity."

"What did he do?"

Again, McGoven shrugged, but his gaze turned to the wall behind her. "Nothing bad enough to die for, though, again, there are some who think that exile is worse."

The way he clenched his jaw told her that she wouldn't be getting anything else out of him on that subject.

"You said you were watching him? Why?"

The line of his jaw became tauter. "The pack sometimes sends rogues to watch other rogues. It keeps them... *Us* in line. Stray wolves can band together otherwise. Make trouble, by terrorizing humans or encroaching onto the territory of other packs. The presence of a stronger lycan helps them rethink those transgressions and adhere to the law."

"So you were like a parole officer?" At least that explained his role on the police force.

McGoven's mouth twisted into what could have been a grimace. "Something like that. More like an insurance policy. Unaffiliated rogues are dangerous, and exiles who wish to redeem themselves, or remain in good standing with the pack may sometimes watch another and report—" He broke off, frowning.

"Was that why?" Loren asked without thinking. "You stayed here."

She could read between the lines. Obviously, he wasn't "in good standing" with the pack either. Rather than answer, he took the handles of the wheelbarrow, and began carting the waste out into the field. A sharp jerk of his head was her only clue to follow.

She crept after him, sensing that his focus had shifted well beyond barnyard chores. Sure enough, he left the wheelbarrow near the front of the barn and just kept walking. When he reached the field opposite of the horse paddock, he turned, bent down...and twisted to throw something in her direction so swiftly she barely had time to catch it.

Dazed, she stared down to find a medium-sized rock clutched in her fist. Her palm smarted with the momentum of the blow, and she dropped it out of shock.

"You have good reflexes," he said, but his voice was devoid of any anger that might explain the unwarranted assault.

In one smooth motion, he advanced, capturing her chin before Loren even knew what was happening. "Your vision seems sharp," he commented, releasing her just as quickly. "Can you run?"

Loren glanced down at her still tender ankle before realizing that he probably meant in general.

"Kind of..." They ran laps in gym at the high school, and she kept up okay.

"What about endurance? Can you lift?"

She gave him what she hoped passed for a non-verbal answer by lifting her flabby arms, swallowed by the fabric of his clothes.

"These are skills you would have mastered, had you grown up in the pack," he explained. "Women and men are subjected to the same training. To master the change, one must hone both their body and mind."

Loren thought of Micha and Kyle, who all seemed to share his lean, muscular build. Even Sonia didn't have an ounce of fat on her.

"You don't seem *out* of shape," he said, eyeing her critically, but the words didn't seem like much of a compliment. "Unlike the myths surrounding 'werewolves'—" His voice held so much disdain that Loren half-expected him to put sarcastic air quotes around the word. "Our strength may be enhanced by our natural forms, but it doesn't come like magic. It is honed. Your body is a tool you must become accustomed to wielding."

Loren felt like she should nod, a student in the middle of an impromptu lecture.

"What about the full moon?" She found herself asking. "Does it—"

"We don't need it to shift if that's what you mean," he said, his tone mildly amused. "Think of it like this. You see better in the daylight, but that doesn't mean you have no vision at night. The full moon enhances our abilities, but we can shift without it."

Like right now.

He didn't say it, but he didn't have to. Primal energy practically radiated from every inch of him. His eyes told it all. He could shift at a moment's notice. Just rip off that dark shirt, sprout jet black fur all over and—

"But not on a whim."

"Oh." Loren looked away, fixating on the horses over in the muddy field. Her heart was still pounding, but not exactly because of the thought of him turning into a four-legged beast.

"The need to shift is instinctive," he said in a quieter tone that she barely heard over the wind. "Primal. Sacred. It's not something undertaken on a whim. It requires preparation. Respect. We embrace our other form with only the purest of intentions. Otherwise, it can be painful. You can cause injury to yourself or anyone who happens to get in the way."

He sounded uneasy about that, and she wondered just how much it had taken out of him to attack those men in the clearing. Though, he'd made it seem pretty easy in the moment.

"Why can't I?" She faced him, brushing the hair from her face, and sucked in a breath.

He had never looked more serious. His eyes practically glowed, his lips pursed in a hard line. "It's not that simple. It's like a muscle—the urge needs to be honed. Controlled. Exercised." He seemed to hesitate before adding, "Most learn those basics as children. You're older. You've grown up without learning the ways. You need—"

He broke off, jaw clenching shut.

Oh, no, you don't. He had taken her in and, so far, called all the shots with little explanation. It was about damn time she demanded some answers. "I need what? If I am what you say I am, why can't I shift?"

"It's not that simple," he grumbled.

"How?"

Too late did she realize her tone sounded challenging. Abruptly, he closed the distance between them and gently tapped the center of her chest with an outstretched finger.

"The instinct needs to be called forth," he murmured. "By an Alpha."

30

*A*lpha. The word sounded different when uttered by him. Powerful.

But Loren couldn't understand how that factored into what he claimed was instinct. "What do you mean?"

"You've been on your own for too long," he went on. "The urge has remained dormant within you. It's not like in the movies. We aren't born with a mastery of the change. Our skill must be nurtured by the needs of the pack, the same way you learned your native language as a child. That constant interaction. That *pull*."

Suddenly, he towered over her, his heat battering her in waves, easily cutting through the fabric of her borrowed windbreaker. The nearness conjured the strange sensation she'd felt earlier— that creeping, tingling warmth that pooled inexplicably in certain areas of her body. She was painfully aware of the fabric of his shirt, grazing her chest—her breasts. Her lips felt dry, and she desperately dragged her tongue along them, fighting to stay focused. It took twice the normal effort to breathe. Think.

His voice, however, was an anchor, too stern to overlook. "Proximity to an Alpha provides guidance. An example. Since Lukka isn't—" He broke off and seemed to try a different tactic. "You need a *pack*, Loren. I can help you, but I need you to trust me."

His earnest tone dislodged something at the back of her mind. A memory? Had he said something similar to her before? She couldn't remember. In fact, it was getting hard to remember a lot of things. Like the color of the grass or sky...

When he looked at her, all she could see was *silver*.

Until he turned and cut across the field, away from the barn. He didn't motion for her to follow. This time his body language seemed to convey less of a command and more of a question.

Trust me? Then come on.

Loren hesitated until he was halfway up the hill. Only then did she follow, and she wasn't surprised to find him waiting for her. Together, they neared the woods, with Loren only slightly behind.

Her mind raced as she struggled to keep pace with his long strides. Where on earth could he be taking her? The deeper within the forest they went, the taller the trees looming above became. The chilling wind didn't help calm her building anxiety.

Before any fear could truly set in, the underbrush thinned, and they stumbled into an open field where the tall grass had been mowed down.

There, Officer McGoven turned to face her. "You aren't like everyone else, Loren," he began, letting his voice carry on the wind. "That's your first lesson."

Lesson?

"You need to trust your instincts. Learn to rely on them."

Before she fully processed the advice, he lunged. The next second, she was lying on the ground, tasting dirt.

So much for instinct. Fear was a stronger impulse. *Don't move,* it told her. *Tuck. Curl into a ball—make yourself small. He'll get tired of hitting you eventually, as long as you don't move—*

"Loren."

Her hands were in front of her face. *Reflex,* she thought. Peeking through her fingers, she saw Officer McGoven standing over her. Not her father or any of the specters from her childhood. Rather than angry or aggressive, he looked…disappointed.

"Loren, get up. We can try again—" He paused with his hand outstretched, inches from her face. "I won't hurt you."

Shame flooded her cheeks. She could only imagine how pathetic she looked to trigger the concern in his voice. Warily, she took his hand, allowing him to pull her upright. The second she regained her balance, he let her go.

"You froze." His tone resonated with disapproval. "You didn't even see me coming, did you?"

She shook her head, wondering why he'd pushed her in the first place. He didn't even have the decency to look guilty.

"You hesitated." Confusing her further, his tone was softer, much like a teacher directing a student toward the right answer. "When I move, you watch me—don't think. Just react. Try again."

Though much slower, his arm swung out, giving her enough time to duck out of reach.

"Good." He watched her carefully, sizing her up with a single glance. "Watch where I am. Don't think. Let your body react."

Suddenly, he pivoted, aiming for her head. Loren obeyed his instruction and instinctively feinted to the left.

"Good," he praised. "You catch on quick. Maybe this isn't such a long shot after all—"

He broke off and let out a deep, heavy sigh.

"Look, we don't have the time for me to coddle you or hold your hand. This isn't a game. This is *real*, Loren. For whatever reason, there are people who want you dead, just to get to me. You have to be able to protect yourself, and I can only think of three ways for you to do that."

He held up his hand and began to tick off the options on his fingers one by one. "One, you get on a bus headed far from here and never look back. Two, you submit to your fate and don't put up a fight. Or three…" His voice deepened, almost into a growl.

"Three?" Loren pressed when he didn't speak.

He advanced step by step until it was way too late for her to run. "Three," he said finally when he was within arm's reach.

He was right; this wasn't a game. He caught her forearm in a bruising grip, forcing her to her knees. It hurt. Her free hand grasped at the muddy earth for leverage, and genuine fear ran down her spine. She tried to struggle, but he only tightened his hold. His strength was too much. She'd never overpower him. *No!* Her lips parted, readying for a scream.

But then another sound drowned out everything else. *Submit!* It was an order, echoing through her mind like a gunshot. His lips didn't even move, but it was his voice. Commanding her.

Submit. Give in. Obey. You are mine.

Confused, Loren could only stare up at him, her heart pounding so hard she could hear every beat. *Boom, boom, BOOM!*

"Give in, Loren," his voice commanded inside her head. He crouched suddenly, still gripping her arm. His eyes were pure silver holding her captive—she couldn't even turn away.

Couldn't think.

"Give in. Give up. I'm all you need. I can be your everything. Just give in to me."

Yes, a part of her whispered longingly. *He can take care of us. Help us. Protect us.*

Give in.

No! The fear came like a whip, cutting through the mindless drone. "No," she croaked out loud. "No, no, no, no—"

"Don't resist," he warned, raising his voice to combat hers. "Let me in. This is to help you—"

"No!"

She wrenched her gaze from his, and it was like an invisible chain tethering her to him snapped. With a sudden burst of strength, she was on her feet, running so fast she could barely feel the wind anymore. Just pure motion. Pushing her on, egging her forward.

Run, run, run!

Even still, there was a part of her that rebelled against the desire to flee. It sat, right *there* in the pit of her chest, and ached, no it *throbbed,* with the need to turn back. *Go back.*

Give in to him.

"No!" Slapping her hands over her ears, Loren kept moving.

She couldn't see, couldn't even think, to pick out a clear path. She just stumbled forward, feeling weeds and stray branches snag at her ankles, rip at her hair and slice into her cheek, drawing blood. The pain didn't even faze her.

He was coming. She could hear him on her trail. He was uncaringly loud, crashing over brambles and fallen leaves. Shouting…something.

Don't listen! Stupidly she squeezed her eyes shut, fighting the urge to scream just to block out the sound of his voice. It didn't work. She could hear him anyway, bellowing through her brain.

"Loren, watch out!"

Her eyes flew open just in time to catch sight of a rock-studded slope—but it was too late to change course. Her boot caught on a slick patch of mud, throwing her balance...

"Loren!"

Wham!

A solid force caught her from behind, knocking her down. She waited for the fall. Braced herself for the pain—but all she felt instead was heat and strength that encased her like a shell. A hand went around the back of her head, pulling her against a muscled chest that smelled like sweat and musk and pine…

She could sense motion around her—the thud and crunch of a body striking the ground. But the only thing she *felt* was sweltering heat and the breath being knocked from her chest as they finally came to a stop.

"Shhhh." The gentle murmur matched the concern her rescuer held her with. "It's okay. I've got you. You're alright—"

"Let me go." Loren didn't even recognize the sound of her own voice.

Stiffly, she pushed out with her hands—or at least as far as she could, considering they were restrained by an unmovable force. She still managed to glimpse their surroundings from over his shoulder—they were at the foot of the hill, with her body pinned against McGoven's. He held her so tightly that she could feel his breath ruffling her hair, basting her skin.

Even now, that overwhelming power radiated from him. *Give in.*

"Get off me!" She tried to kick him. Pinch him. Dig her fingers into the skin of his chest.

He resisted her easily and adjusted his weight to pin her to the ground. "Loren, wait. Breathe." His tone was insistent. Gentle. "Listen to me. You don't understand—"

"Get OFF me!" Was that her voice? Whoever it was sounded wild. Insane.

"Listen to me!" He held her tighter, growling each word against her throat. "Loren, please—"

She bit him.

She didn't know how. It was like a switch being flipped. Her mind went blank the second she lunged, teeth bared. Hard muscle gave beneath her teeth, and she tasted blood...

His blood.

Her vision flashed red. Everything congealed into scarlet as a dangerous voice picked up volume as if whispered in her ear. *Bite, tear, scratch. Fight!*

No one can hold you back.

"Loren!"

The pain in his voice startled her from the daze. She blinked to find McGoven hovering over her. For once—maybe for the first time, since she'd known him—he looked afraid. No, *terrified* in a way that he hadn't been, even when she'd gone off on Xavier or after fending off the men in the clearing.

"Are you okay?" he asked.

"Get off me," she whispered, horrified. This time her fear wasn't directed at *him* but the half-moon-shaped wound on his chest, right above the collar of his shirt. Scarlet liquid welled from it, dripping ceaselessly.

God, what had she done?

She was shaking. She couldn't catch her breath and panic had her teeth chattering together in a way that had nothing at all to do with the cold.

She had attacked a police officer. Not only that, but she'd *bitten* him like some wild animal. She'd be lucky to turn twenty-one after spending a long stint in jail.

Oh, God.

"Let me go, please!" She twisted, trying to crawl away from him, hands digging into the mud.

He dragged her back and wrenched her around to face him. "Listen to me," he commanded in a tone she couldn't ignore. "It's alright. Just listen—"

"No! I won't!" The moment the shout left her mouth, she knew it was a mistake. Fighting back against him would *always* be a mistake.

She would never win.

His gaze narrowed into slits of silver, piercing her down to the bone. He was angry. Her defiance annoyed him. Maybe, strangest of all, she'd surprised him.

She waited for him to yell. Hit her. Maybe *bite* her? Grow fangs, sprout fur, and…

She tensed as he leaned down, his teeth bared. Rather than go for her throat, he pressed his mouth against hers.

31

*I*t wasn't anything cute and romantic, like in the movies.

He kissed her *hard*, forcing her lips apart and stabbing his tongue deep before she even knew what was happening. Instantly, she realized that his previous actions had been child's play. This was a taste of his true power—his ability to turn physical contact into a weapon. Every motion was demanding. Taking. *Punishing.* Urging her to give in, *submit*, just like before.

Submit. The demand echoed inside her head, as loud as a shout. *Give in!* He didn't give her the chance to refuse. His weight pinned her in place against the wet earth as his free hand fisted in her hair. At the same time, he freed her mouth and pressed his lips to her throat.

Mine.

Sharp teeth nicked the column of skin, drawing blood. From far away, Loren heard herself gasp. He bit her. Really *bit* her.

She should have struggled. Screamed. Not… Tilt her throat to give him better access. She *shouldn't* have dug her fingers into the earth as his heat washed through her on a searing wave.

It was wrong. But, she couldn't ignore the part of her that insisted this was right. *This* was what she'd been unconsciously waiting for since the moment she faced him in the kitchen, wrapped in a blanket.

Contact. Acknowledgment. Claiming.

I'm his, some primal part of her purred—it was about damn time he proved it. As if sensing her thoughts, his touch turned possessive. One hand eased beneath her waist, crushing her against the hardness of his chest.

Her breaths feathered. This was…different. She could feel every inch of him, rippling with a strength that could easily tear her into pieces if he wanted. The thought made a part of her lurch, and suddenly she couldn't breathe at all. Her mind spun—dizzy. She couldn't think.

But maybe that was a good thing?

These days, it seemed like she thought way too much. This was so much better. Her body moved purely on instinct—ironically, just the way he taught her—and it wanted more. For all his strength, he wasn't doing enough. Touching her enough. Kissing her *enough*.

His mouth avoided hers on purpose, deliberately skirting the bruises on her throat and her swollen bottom lip. His fingers, flexing against her waist, never traveled any lower than that.

He was holding back.

Annoyed, Loren raked her fingers through his hair, forcing his head from the curve of her shoulder. His eyes locked onto hers, so damn molten they glowed.

Something unspoken passed between them, almost too quickly to track. A new challenge? This mattered more than her submission—his acknowledgment. Suddenly desperate for it, she arched her spine, seeking out his warmth.

He stiffened. A tortured grimace contorted his expression as if he were going to war within himself. In a second, something won out, and his posture shifted. He dropped the gallant act. His hips slammed into hers, driving the air from her lungs. That prickling heat returned, pulsing down her spine, between her legs... They parted to make room for him, and her eyes rolled at the sensation. His position applied pressure in dangerous ways. Too much to bear. Not enough...

This time, when she lurched up, forcing her lips against his, he didn't hesitate. He gave her what she wanted—needed.

Pain mingled with the harsh heat enveloping her like a blanket, so searing that it was a struggle to even remember what *cold* was. Her bruised lip ached, but his tongue was already there, caressing the wound before it really had the chance to smart. All before ramming his tongue between her lips and utterly stealing her breath away.

More.

Loren couldn't fight the violent urge that had her hands turning into claws, pressing against his back, forcing him against her, arching her hips to seek more contact.

Mine. More, more, more!

Suddenly, even kissing him, so harshly she could taste blood—his or hers?—wasn't enough. She needed him. All of him pressed against her so tightly it *hurt*.

He seemed to be thinking along those same lines. With a grunt, he rolled over, wrenching her upright, forcing her up to straddle his waist, mouth never losing contact.

His tongue battled hers, taking deep greedy pulls. Then, his fingers were dragging at the zipper to her windbreaker, tearing the whole thing from her shoulders, before tugging at her thermal. And then that was gone, too.

All that was left was her bra, which suddenly seemed irritating against her skin. She wanted it off—needed it off. *Now.*

Her hands flew up to the back-clasp, fumbling with the fastening, but a pair of thick fingers were there to impatiently bat her away. In seconds, he had the clasp undone, and Loren sighed in relief as the pale straps slid down her shoulders. She lifted her arms, expecting him to make the fabric disappear along with the rest of her clothes—

Wait.

She was so dazed that she wasn't sure if the word had been spoken out loud or inside her head. Suddenly, McGoven bucked his hips, knocking her aside.

"Shit!" He was on his feet in an instant.

Loren landed on her back. Before she could blink, a tanned hand was there, holding her bunched-up thermal before her. She reacted out of habit, sitting up to slip the shirt on over her head, only to become uncomfortably aware of her dangerously loose bra, threatening to slide from her arms.

She glanced down, almost in shock, at the bared flesh of her stomach as she wrestled the thermal on. Her windbreaker was a few paces away, crumpled on the grass, and Officer McGoven…

His eyes were so wide she half-expected them to fall out of his head.

"Shit," he hissed again, raking a hand through that wild hair. In two steps, he snatched up her jacket and tossed it in her direction. "Get dressed."

The next second, he took off, marching across the field at a pace that forced her to run to keep up. They were closer to the house than she realized. Within seconds, she caught sight of the barn and…a bright pink car currently zooming up the driveway.

Oh shit, Loren thought. Suddenly McGoven's haste made sense.

But how had he known?

She never got the chance to ask. They reached the base of the porch steps the exact moment Naomi Tanner stepped from her car.

"Hey." Her eyes were sharp, darting from her to Officer McGoven and back. "Am I interrupting something?"

Loren's cheeks flamed. Her hair was a ragged mess. Mud splattered her clothes, her hands. It was all she could do to wrestle her other arm through the sleeve of her windbreaker and zip it up.

But, if Naomi reached any conclusions, she didn't mention them aloud.

"I brought your work," she said. "So, um…"

She glanced at Officer McGoven and then down—namely to the thick tanned fingers Loren could still feel entwined with her own.

"I'll let you two get to it." McGoven let her hand fall and turned, taking the porch steps two at a time. "I have something to take care of," he muttered, before disappearing through the screen door so quickly it was left swinging on its hinges.

"Damn," Naomi stage whispered. "What the hell happened to you two?"

Cheeks flaming, Loren shoved her hands into her pockets. "Nothing."

Something had happened. Something that made her dizzy and dazed to think on. Made her clothes feel too tight—not tight *enough*.

It was confusing. Men were a taboo subject—as was sex. She'd never had a boyfriend, and any mention of the topic in school had been through gossip or clinical descriptions from teachers regarding the mating behaviors of animals. She had no frame of reference to draw upon. Nothing to contextualize the strange feelings rampaging through her.

Or him.

"Earth to Connors," Naomi snapped. "What is wrong with you?"

"Let's get this over with," Loren muttered, mounting the porch steps in a rush.

Inside, Officer McGoven wasn't anywhere in sight. As they entered the living room, a door slammed, and a quick glance out of the kitchen window revealed a dark figure marching across the field, heading straight for that battered pick-up truck. Seconds later, it took off so fast mud sprayed from the wheels.

"What the hell did *you* do to piss him off?" Naomi's snarky tones were grating on Loren's already frayed nerves.

Rather than answer, she snatched a cup from the sink and gulped from the rim. She nearly spit the water back out. The flavor was tainted—tinged with the tastes already on her tongue—mud and pine and a sharp metallic hint that made her belly twist into knots.

Images filled her mind before she could help it, each one more damning than the last. *Her. Officer McGoven. Heat. Her clothes being expertly torn off.*

Her throat went dry at the memory of the feel of his lips on her throat—his teeth. She reached up, fingering the flesh right beneath her collar. It burned, overly sensitive, painful to the touch.

"What the hell is wrong with you?" Naomi wondered.

Loren tried her hardest to ignore her.

"Whatever—" She blinked to find Naomi dragging a schoolbook from her bag. "When you're done being all psycho, I brought math, and social studies. Let's get this over with."

She couldn't agree more.

The latest "study session" with Naomi could be politely described as torturous. Not only due to the antics of the evil blond.

It was *him*—namely, his absence.

Where did he go?

She couldn't make sense of it. Aside from the weird moments of physical contact, Officer McGoven didn't seem interested in her more than to fulfill his heroic civic duty—and perform whatever he seemed to think he owed her as a lycan.

But when he kissed her…

There hadn't been any sense of "heroics" at all. Just a pure, raw hunger that couldn't be denied. *Lust,* Loren thought, blushing at the word choice. Not exactly the redeeming quality of a kindly, but much older, benefactor.

What about you? a part of her demanded. She hadn't exactly been so sweet and innocent, either. After all, she did bite him first.

"Lincoln."

"Huh?" Loren blinked in confusion, coming face to face with a scowling Naomi.

"*Lincoln* freed the slaves," the blond snapped before scribbling the answer down on a piece of notebook paper. That's right, Loren recalled. They were studying for a final, reviewing a study guide. "If I'm forced to come all the way out here every damn night, the least you could do is pay fucking attention."

Loren didn't waste her breath explaining that she hadn't asked for Naomi, in particular, to deliver her work in the first place. Instead, like they had every minute since the blond had shown up, her eyes darted to the kitchen window.

Night had already fallen, and it was raining again. There was no sign of that battered pick-up truck, or an impossibly tall man wearing mud-stained jeans, pulling into the driveway.

How long would he stay away, this time?

Until midnight?

Morning?

Would he even come back at all…

"Hey!"

Loren jumped as a pair of pink-tipped fingernails were snapped right in front of her face.

"I'm calling it quits tonight," Naomi declared, gathering her books. "I'll just come back tomorrow."

Mentally, Loren kicked herself for giving the blond another reason to stick around. Maybe she should have taken McGoven up on his offer to have the school replace her with someone else? Before she could latch onto the thought, Naomi was already marching through the front door without so much as a "ta-ta."

Loren shrugged and went back to staring from the window, watching as Naomi struggled to her car through the rain. The minutes passed by like seconds, until a furious Naomi reemerged, heading straight for the house.

Loren barely made it to the entryway before the blond barged inside.

"My car won't start," she hissed. "Is there a phone?"

"I don't know," Loren admitted. "This isn't my house."

"Fine," Naomi snarled, "I guess I'll just have to *walk* home, then. Let me borrow this—"

Before Loren could reply, she snatched a blue windbreaker from the coat hook by the door.

"Wait! That's mine."

"So?" Naomi tossed back, raising a blond eyebrow. "It's raining out. Unless you *want* me to get soaking wet and catch fucking pneumonia?"

Loren bit her lip. *It's mine,* a part of her hissed. Not just hers, but Officer McGoven's.

Still, she wasn't exactly inclined to invite Naomi in to wait out the storm, either. Heart heavy, she just watched the blond drag the zipper up beneath her chin and walk out into the rain.

"Wait," she called reluctantly. "Maybe you should wait?" It was a long way back into town.

"Not on your life," Naomi tossed back, letting the front door slam after her.

Loren stayed near the door, convinced the blond would return any minute, and demand McGoven gives her a ride. When a cry finally pierced the hum of the storm, she sighed and prepared to open the door.

"I told you, you should have—"

Naomi wasn't standing on the porch—or anywhere in sight, for that matter. Still, Loren could sense her nearby. Then her nostrils flared, picking up a scent through the rain. Something sharp. Familiar. Blood? Her brain identified it hesitantly. Maybe Naomi had fallen and hurt herself?

She was already racing onto the porch when she heard the scream.

$\mathcal{B}$ill drove mindlessly while rain lashed at the windshield. Each thud of moisture resonated like a million tiny punches—the imagery was poetic irony. He *needed* to be punched. In the face. Or, maybe somewhere else?

The bulge straining against the front of his jeans? At least then, he might be able to think of anything but her.

There were a million other issues to contend with—like what happened this morning. His heart panged as he recalled the present left on his doorstep. It served him right for venturing beyond his property. Though, he hadn't sensed another lycan in the area—whoever was behind the act must have used a human to deliver their message. Thankfully, Loren hadn't noticed. She'd even bought his lie, but sooner or later, she'd learn the truth. They—the bastards who sent that mangled deer—would come calling in person.

It was an old custom—the reckoning mark. To their kind, every animal's life was sacred. Killing a doe in such a brutal way was the biggest insult imaginable. A warning.

Someone wanted to pick a fight. The Eislanders? Lukka wasn't the sort to resort to such an archaic method of communication. No, he'd send one of his peons with a message instead. Obviously, the men from the woods had friends willing to avenge their cruelty.

But they could try. Loren was *his…*

He could still taste her. Sense her. Smell her. But the attraction went well beyond natural interest. It was one thing to have initiated the mating bond to *protect* Loren Connors—he didn't regret it—couldn't regret it.

But that didn't mean that he had to *maintain* it. Lukka or not, he should have broken the bond the moment she woke up and found some way to explain. Then he should have put her on a bus to a city far away, where she could live as a human and go on with her life.

She had no idea what was happening to her—what *had* happened to her. It made him sick just thinking of it. Or maybe that was just her memories crowding the back of his head? They were poison, though the girl seemed to have no idea what he'd taken from her that night in the woods—all the horror he'd just lifted off her mind like a telepathic vacuum.

The fear. The murder. The memories. *Especially* the memories. He never went through them, but they were dark—he could tell that much. Seeing the scars on her wrist confirmed that suspicion.

Her file, tucked away in some back corner of the precinct, didn't contain much. Just a general list of the places she used to live, some mention of a mother's suicide, and some vague annotations to a child abuse case.

Even her mother's name, Eveline Connors, didn't ring a bell— and names held more meaning to lycans than humans. If she had belonged on Black Mountain, he would remember her. Every packmate held a place in his mind, even Fred Connors.

Loren, however, was an enigma. The funny thing was, even after nearly a week, he still couldn't bring himself to type her name into the damn database and research her in detail. Her past, and whatever horrors it contained, should come from her—nowhere else. He would wait until she was able to do so without the mating bond driving her emotions.

A pang of guilt stabbed through him as he realized how different things might have been if he'd taken the time to interact with her before this whole mess. At the time, he'd told himself that it was better to keep her at arm's length. As recently as a few days ago, he still held the belief that distance between them would make it easier when Lukka came to integrate her into the pack. After all, once she left for Black Mountain, it wasn't like he'd ever see her again.

But now...

There was a part of him that craved to learn everything about her. Good and bad. What made her tick? What made those hazel eyes widen in fear if he came too close to her? What haunted her nightmares?

Oh, he could guess that Fred Connors had something to do with it—but there was more to it. *Way* more. And every day, it was getting harder to maintain that boundary between them. Though, hell, he'd pretty much smashed that "boundary" anyway.

What happened in the field had been a mistake.

He meant only to help her. Stir up her instincts and give her a temporary Alpha to follow until he could puzzle out what to do next. It was a good idea in theory. He could coax her to shift, diminish the mating bond somewhat, and maybe finally be able to *think* without her damn thoughts in his head.

It should have been easy to force submission from one little female. Until she fought back—fuck, she *more* than fought back.

Frowning, he took one hand off the steering wheel to brush the bleeding wound on his chest. She'd bitten him deeply, and his heart thundered as he remembered the wild little sound she'd made, right before she had.

He may not have been a genius, but he knew it wasn't normal—*she* wasn't normal.

He could sense her at odds with herself. The meek little girl she presented to the world was struggling to resist something deep inside that couldn't be controlled. Something wild he could sometimes glimpse behind those hazel eyes.

And despite his years of mastery over his lycan side, Bill still couldn't ignore the part of him that had risen up in challenge at that. It was like the urge of a predator to give chase when prey turned tail and ran. Instinct so ingrained it was damn near impossible to resist, not that he would fall back on that stupid excuse.

He still shouldn't have kissed her. The mating bond was driving her, confusing her. She didn't know what she wanted.

And it was his fault.

Would she hate him for what he'd done, when she eventually learned the truth?

Probably.

But he couldn't bring himself to feel an ounce of guilt— everything he'd done had been entirely to save her. From Fred Connors. From herself.

Or at least, that was what he'd believed. Until he started having pesky little thoughts that proclaimed the exact opposite. Thoughts that whispered things like *mine*, whenever he caught sight of her, small and pale, with that brown hair falling down her shoulders.

Mine.

The thought was in his head now—his mind—craving her, when he should have tried to push her away. She wasn't the only one susceptible to the mating bond. It was changing *him* as well, making him think very dangerous things. Like, maybe it wasn't *so bad* if she stayed?

Lukka didn't want her, and even if the bastard did, there was no way in *hell* he'd let her go—

Suddenly, he slammed his foot against the brakes, coming to a stop in the middle of a country road.

Something was wrong. He could sense it in the air. Taste it in his throat. Without thinking, he wrenched the truck into reverse and sped toward his farm, pushing the battered pick-up to the limit. 70. 80. 90...

Impatience pulled at his gut, urging him on.

Loren. At the thought of her, he parked the car on the side of the road, leaving the keys in the ignition, and took off on foot, ripping off clothing as he went. He was working on removing his pants when he heard the first scream.

It was faint—he was about a mile off from his property—but the sound pierced him down to the bone.

On the spot, he invoked the shift with his jeans still entangled around his legs.

Son of a bitch… It hurt like hell. Muscle tore. Bones shattered and reformed. His legs strained against the confining fabric as they compacted and stretched into long lines of sinewy muscle.

But he didn't care. He took off racing through the fields, hating himself for ever leaving her alone in the first place.

33

*L*oren raced onto the porch.

She couldn't see Naomi anywhere. Not by her car, or down the path leading to the road. *She probably just broke a heel,* a part of her scoffed. But unease had her inching forward, regardless.

Something is wrong. The ominous feeling unfurled in her gut as she leaped from the porch without thinking. A few more steps carried her down the driveway. She didn't have her boots, and icy rain lashed at her hair, but that sinking feeling drove her forward, past the front yard and across the field.

"Naomi?" Her voice barely rose above the howl of the wind and rain. "Naomi!"

It was so dark. She could barely see a few feet in front of her while her eyes adjusted. Out here, surrounded by wilderness, she realized how stupid it had been for anyone to venture this far alone.

"Naomi!"

Loren's heart started to pound with dread.

Even before she saw *them*.

Four men stood in a line beyond the trees that edged the clearing. They faced the direction of the house, bodies shrouded in shadow, but…

Beside them was a wolf. Huge and hulking, it hunched a few paces away from the others, its fur a deep brown.

And even *that* wasn't what made her gasp as she skidded to a stop, heels dragging in the earth.

A body lay on the ground before them, so limp and motionless, it could have been part of the environment. Minus the dark navy windbreaker and hot pink miniskirt covering a pair of tanned legs.

No. Loren froze, feeling the back of her throat clench. "Naomi!"

The blond wasn't moving. But that wasn't even the worst part. Someone stood in front of her. Someone lean and wiry, with a head crowned by wild dark hair.

They were bleeding. The smell rode on the air—way too strong to have been just from a minor injury. It didn't take much of a stretch to realize that they had gone up against that massive wolf, and were dangerously close to having lost.

No. Fear washed over Loren like ice. It couldn't be him.

He couldn't be hurt.

Her heart fluttered as she ran, ignoring the danger. The closer she came, the more she realized that the man wasn't tall enough to be McGoven.

But she recognized him.

"This isn't the way," Micha called, in a voice that carried across the field. "This isn't right—"

"Don't talk about things you don't understand, pup," one of the men tossed back, arms crossed casually over his chest, while the wolf crouched in wait.

He had to be the leader, judging from how the others were grouped around him. Even the wolf seemed to be awaiting orders, growling low in the back of its throat.

"This has nothing to do with the old laws," the man went on, taking a step forward to reveal an angular face crowned by blood-red hair. "This is about retribution, plain and simple."

Retribution?

Loren gaped at Naomi. What could she have done to warrant being attacked in the middle of the woods?

Not her, some part of her whispered. *She's not the one they wanted.*

"The rogue killed one of our own," another man pitched in, his mouth twisted in a snarl. "The laws give us the right to recoup the loss. We followed protocol. Gave clear warning. The bastard sent a woman to face us instead."

"Though," the first man said with a shrug, "it seems as though we've *miscalculated.*"

Loren could barely see him through the oppressive dark, but she could sense the exact moment his eyes locked onto *her.* His gaze was even colder than the icy breeze chilling her skin.

Glacial.

"L-leave her out of this," Micha stammered. He looked even worse the closer she came. His entire body was shaking, and his ragged sweatpants were filthy, and mud stained.

Or, bloodstained. Crimson liquid leaked from a gash in his left leg, and it seemed to take every ounce of strength he had just to stay on his feet. But he did. His gaze was steady, firmly fixed on all three men.

"This isn't about her," he said.

"It's not," the leader admitted with a shrug. "But *she* is the easiest way to get to *him*. Now stay back, pup. This has nothing to do with you." He moved to take a step, and everything seemed to happen at once.

Micha stumbled toward him. The wolf snarled, and Loren didn't think.

She reacted.

"No!" The cry was directed at Micha, who gaped as she shoved him back and positioned herself in front of him.

The four opposing figures were bulky, sporting varying degrees of muscle—and unlike the men from the clearing, she could tell that they weren't your average thugs.

They were organized. Dangerous. Should she have been afraid?

Probably—but, for some reason, she *wasn't*.

Not even when the wolf growled in warning, raising its haunches.

Silly little girl, she could picture them all thinking. *So damn naive.*

They don't matter, that inner voice warned, louder than ever. *This is about power. Focus on the leader, only him. He dictates their next move.*

For now, he seemed content to watch her. "This is nothing personal between you and me," he explained, sounding almost calm despite his previous threat. "Your mate killed one of our own—this is the law."

"This is stupid!" Micha snarled, appearing by her side. Loren could hear his ragged breathing, and she just hoped he wasn't stupid enough to try and fight. "She isn't a part of this! Those men were going to kill her!"

"Not correct," the leader said simply. "The man he killed was a trusted friend of Alpha Loreck—" His voice took on a lethal edge. "And he was *murdered* in cold blood."

"W-what?" Micha's confusion matched Loren's perfectly.

If this "trusted" friend was one of the men who'd attacked her in the clearing, there wasn't anything "innocent" about him. Still, these men didn't seem to be joking. Or lying. She could hear the honesty in their leader's voice.

"Alpha Loreck," he continued, "demands retribution. Which we are more than happy to act out on the rogue himself, if you desire. Where is he?"

"No." Loren didn't even realize that she'd spoken until the man's head swiveled in her direction.

Stupid girl! A part of her hissed. *What are you doing?*

What you should do, her inner voice murmured. *Assert your place. This is your land. Defend it!*

How? She had no clue. A cold sweat dripped down her spine. She couldn't breathe. The leader seemed aware of her weakness. He took her in with one skeptical gaze, raising a scarlet eyebrow.

"I'm guessing you're willing to suffer in his place?" He shrugged. "No matter—"

"Leave her out of this," Micha insisted, grappling for her shoulder. "She didn't do anything!"

As weak as he was, it was easy to shrug him off.

Completely devoid of emotion, Loren took a step, then another, crossing the short distance that separated her from the group of men. Her mind went blank. She didn't have time to process the fear.

"Leave," she told him in a voice she barely even recognized. It was cold. Hard. Icy. Nothing at all like the trademark Loren Connors' timid little whisper.

"I don't think so, pup," the red-haired man replied, with a shake of his head. "Your mate overstepped the boundaries. There must be consequences. Bill knows this."

Bill. Mate. The words bounced around the inside of her skull, but she pushed them away—*later.*

"*You* overstepped the boundaries," Loren insisted. Somehow, her voice didn't shake, easily rivaling his.

"Loren!" Micha sounded terrified in comparison. "Loren, get back—"

No. This time she didn't even waste her breath saying the word aloud. She just tilted her head back, ignoring the rain that slid down her forehead. With a confidence she couldn't explain, she met the red-haired man's mocking stare and held it.

Prove yourself, that voice in her head growled. *He is nothing to us. Nothing.*

He had brown eyes. Sharp and vibrant, they reflected the shadows and seemed to glow. *Animal eyes,* a part of her whispered.

But she didn't turn away—not that she could. Something deep inside forced her to keep the eye contact. *Don't back down now,* it warned. *Show no fear.*

"*You* are going to leave," she said, though her voice was even louder. A stranger's. "Now."

She heard Micha make a sound that could have been a groan. "Loren…"

The red-haired man didn't seem to mind the challenge. The corner of his mouth twitched like he wanted to laugh, but…

As time went on, his gaze narrowed, darkened, and as even more seconds passed, they widened again.

Then, he frowned.

The entire while, Loren never let her gaze slip. She kept it honed on him like a laser. This moment reminded her of middle school, where mental games of tug of war ran rampant. The strangest thing was that she wasn't the one struggling to stay upright in this little game.

He was.

It was like the reverse of her and McGoven. She could sense the fight in him. See his struggle in the way his mouth twitched almost imperceptibly. Then, slowly, but surely, a bead of sweat dripped down his forehead to mingle with the rain.

All of it added up to one conclusion that should have been *impossible*.

She was winning.

Of course, I am, some shadowy part of her insisted, almost bored. *He is no match*.

But the man didn't seem to accept the fact. He scowled, his upper lip pulling back from his teeth. It was like she could read his mind. She should have turned away, he assumed. Meekly submitted to die.

The hell I will. In a rush of determination, she took a step forward, not surprised a bit when the man took one step back.

He was close to breaking. She knew it. Relished in it.

Give in, she willed him, without ever saying it out loud.

She didn't have to.

The world around them faded away, leaving just the two of them locked in a battle for which he was no match. All at once, one word popped onto the tip of her tongue, and she found herself voicing it without any hesitation. "Submit—"

Grrrr…!

The sound cut through everything, as loud as the roar of a jet engine. Loren knew, even before the stocky body of a black wolf appeared over the crest of the hill, just who it belonged to.

34

McGoven growled again. Then, in a blur of shadow, he inserted himself between her and the intruders with one bounding leap.

Loren found herself pushed back by his bulk, and she stumbled, right into the hard chest of Micha, who maneuvered her behind him.

They waited.

The red-haired man watched them all—only he didn't look so smugly self-righteous anymore. He looked shaken. Loren didn't miss the way his eyes kept cutting to her. Partly confused. Partly…fearful?

Leave! In his current form, McGoven couldn't say the word aloud, so he just growled instead—but there was no missing what he meant.

"This isn't over," the red-haired man insisted. His tone kept it from seeming cliché. It was a promise. A statement of fact.

This isn't over.

"You killed a member on pack territory, rogue. Sooner or later, you will have to pay."

Like shadows, he and the three others turned and left.

But the ordeal was far from over.

It was like a switch had been flipped inside of her. In an instant, Loren deflated, sinking to the ground by Naomi's prone form.

"Naomi!"

There was blood. So much blood that she could smell it, thick and heavy and fresh.

"One of them bit her." The voice was Micha's, spoken from over her shoulder. "I tried to stop it…I—"

"She's not dead!" Somehow, Loren knew that even before she reached out for a pale throat and felt a pulse.

It wasn't very strong, though. While one side of her neck remained whole, the other side, hidden beneath a lank section of blond hair, was wet and dark…

"We need to get her to a hospital—"

Before she could even try to reason out *how*, a dark figure appeared beside her, gathering Naomi in his arms as easily as if she weighed nothing.

"Come on," Bill's voice was gruff. Loren didn't have to glance up to know that he was naked. All she did was lurch to her feet, too horrified by everything else to blush at the sight.

He took off, heading for the house, and Loren followed, croaking out to Micha, "Come on!"

He blinked and lurched into motion, heavily favoring his injured leg.

It seemed to take an eternity before they reached the house—though given the way McGoven moved, it could have only been minutes. He was already inside by the time she mounted the porch steps.

He had slung Naomi across the couch and began moving around the living room, flicking on the lights at random. With each one, Loren shuddered as the extent of the girl's injuries became apparent.

She'd been bitten in the neck. *More* than bitten—her throat seemed…

Torn.

Blood was everywhere. On him. On her. It even painted a scarlet trail out into the hall, staining the leather of the couch. Loren held her breath just to keep from gagging.

"Why?" she croaked. "Why would they do this?"

Of course, she already knew the answer. They had mistaken Naomi for *her*.

It was her fault.

"I tried to stop them—"

She turned to find Micha, hovering over the cusp of the living room, his eyes apologetically wide. At the sound of his voice, McGoven whipped around.

"What the hell are you doing here—"

"He tried to save her." Loren didn't even realize that she'd spoken out loud until McGoven cut his gaze in her direction. "He tried to save me."

The man didn't look convinced. "What the hell are you doing here?" he demanded of Micha, though his gaze never left her face.

"I told you," Micha insisted, "I'm not leaving until I've repaid my debt. And it's a good thing I was here, too. They weren't waiting for an invitation."

Bill's jaw tightened, and his eyes flashed with a mixture of rage and...guilt? When he spoke again, his tone was deeper. Cold. "They were Eislanders?"

Micha gave a sharp nod of his head. "I think so. They said you killed one of them—"

"I killed *four* of them," McGoven corrected without batting an eyelash. "But...they didn't seem like Loreck Eislander's type. What the hell did they want?"

"Revenge," Loren said, shuddering as the word left her mouth. "Either you or me, they didn't care."

"I wouldn't have let them touch her," Micha insisted heatedly. "I swear."

"Yeah," McGoven bellowed, "a lot of damn good you did. And you—" He turned to her again, his gaze demanding. "What the hell were you thinking? Do you know what he would have done to you? Ripped out your fucking throat!"

Loren faced his tirade without an explanation in mind. The truth "I mentally sparred with the man," didn't make sense.

Eventually, McGoven just sighed, raking his hand through his hair, as he glanced down at the motionless Naomi.

"Fuck."

Viewing the body in better lighting, Loren was sure a pulse had been entirely in her imagination.

"We need to call an ambulance," she said weakly. Deep down, she knew it wouldn't matter.

No one could survive a wound like that. The blank look McGoven gave her pretty much proved it.

"Loren…"

"No!" She backed away slowly, shaking her head. "We need to do something!"

It wasn't like she harbored any kind of love for Naomi, but no one deserved to die like this. In almost a week, Loren had already seen way too damn much of death.

No more.

"Do something." The words could have just been a pathetic form of denial—until she remembered… "You can save her, can't you?"

He could bite her.

"No!" McGoven's tone was firm, but that didn't keep Loren from stumbling across the room toward him.

"Please! You can save her! Do it! Please."

He looked away, his expression torn. "I can't."

"You know the rules," Micha said softly from the doorway, seeming to agree with him. "You turn a human without permission, and it's treason. Lukka won't like it."

"I know," McGoven hissed, but his gaze flashed as if that fact annoyed him. Then he sighed.

"If I do this… It won't be some simple good deed. Her life will be forever changed. There will be no going back."

A part of Loren stirred in acknowledgment, sensing exactly what he meant—and more. But… Her voice was small, "We can't just let her die."

"Turn around," McGoven snarled. "Close your eyes…don't look."

She scrambled to obey, eyeing the window and the storm raging outside. A second later, she heard a growl.

And then the snap of breaking bone and ripping flesh.

35

*L*oren woke up, frozen solid…except for the heat radiating from an arm slung across her waist. With a sigh, she relaxed into the embrace—until she realized her companion wasn't the man she'd become accustomed to waking up beside. They smelled wrong. Like smoke and rain instead of pine, along with a vague odor that reminded her of a wet dog.

Alarmed, she opened her eyes and rolled over—coming face to face with a boyish figure, their features half-hidden beneath a mop of curly hair. Micha. He was asleep, his chest rising and falling with gentle snores.

That's right, she remembered. They camped out in the living room to keep watch over Naomi. She and Micha had, anyway.

Bill left sometime before dawn. The dark glint in his eye warned against asking questions. Though, there were plenty that needed to be asked.

Enough secrecy. The need for answers loomed overhead like a storm cloud. She'd go insane without some kind of clarity. It had been hard enough keeping her mouth shut last night. All she'd done was watch.

And hear. Those horrific sounds still haunted her—the cracking of Naomi's bones being wrenched back into place—her neck had been broken during the attack, Bill explained afterward. He had to fix the fatal injury first…

Then, he bit her.

There wasn't any dramatic pause or fanfare. He merely hunched over that pale throat, teeth sinking deep. Then he cut himself, forcing his blood into Naomi's mouth with almost clinical precision.

A spoonful of sugar helps the medicine go down, a part of her snickered, though the situation wasn't funny in the least. After that, all they could do was wait. For what? Loren didn't know.

In the end, she and Micha must have passed out on the floor— though she distinctively remembered being on *opposite* sides of the room. *Not good,* a part of her whispered, cringing at the feel of him so close. *He shouldn't touch me.*

The fear itched at the back of her mind but, for now, she had bigger things to worry about. Sick with dread, she lifted her head and glanced over at Naomi. The blond still lay motionless on the couch.

In bits and pieces, the events of last night came flooding back. Naomi should have been dead—and the only reason she wasn't was because… Well, because a police officer, who just so happened to sprout four legs in his spare time, turned her into a werewolf.

How would she react? Even begin to understand? After all, it wasn't every day that you woke up in a stranger's house as something…

Else.

Tell me about it, Loren thought with a sigh, as she gingerly disentangled herself from Micha's grip and crawled to her feet. She just hoped that the blond's bitchy demeanor hadn't been just an act. After the events of last night, Naomi would need all the strength she could muster.

In the pale daylight streaming in from the bay window, she certainly didn't look any better. Dried blood splattered her designer ensemble. That expensively highlighted hair was a tangled mess. Her throat…

The wounds hadn't miraculously healed like in all the TV shows. They were still there. Still fresh. Still bleeding.

Loren's nostrils flared with the grisly stench, and she couldn't bear to look anymore. Eyeing the floor instead, she tried to rationalize her current reality. Relief and guilt went to war in the pit of her stomach. Within seconds, one emotion dominated. *My fault.*

This was all *her* fault.

What would happen to Naomi after this? She had no damn idea—

Thump. At the sudden noise, she realized that she hadn't woken up entirely by accident. Someone appeared in the entryway as she crept forward. Not an intruder. This man was painfully familiar, his shoulders hunched, his gray eyes glowing in the pale daylight.

Had he spent all night out in the fields again? It sure looked like it. He was barefoot, wearing another grungy pair of sweats. His gaze swept over her, then homed in on the still sleeping Micha.

His voice broke the silence barely louder than a whisper. "He touched you."

The low observation made her heart flutter. There was no point in denying it. Surprisingly enough, he grimaced, his nostrils flaring. There was a line he could have voiced but never did.

I'll break him. Destroy him. I'll kill him. With a hard swallow, he seemed to bite those threats back. Why? Because whatever happened between them in the fields was a mistake. He regretted it.

"You're starving." His voice fell flat as he changed the subject and headed into the kitchen before Loren's disappointment could fully resonate. "I'll make you something to eat."

Instead of fixing her a serving of tuna, he leaned against the center island, face in his hands. The sight pulled at something in her. Something that had her stumbling forward to the opposite side of the counter.

Once across from him, she couldn't bring herself to speak, let alone touch him.

He didn't acknowledge her, regardless. Didn't even move—but when he released a heavy sigh, she knew that his next words were directed at her.

"I'm not going to sugarcoat it," he began in a voice that rumbled with exhaustion. "This is *bad*, Loren." He withdrew his hand from his face, meeting her gaze. "You can't even *begin* to understand how serious. I've broken about fifty unspoken rules by doing what I did. I've put you in danger. Naomi…"

"You couldn't let her die," Loren whispered. "You couldn't just—"

"I *should* have." His tone was brutally frank. Honest. "You have *no idea* how hard life will be for her after this. She isn't like you—*mades* aren't entitled to the same status in a pack as a born lycan. They must earn their way in. Usually, their only chance is to be accepted by the pack of the wolf that originally bit them."

And it went without saying that wasn't an option in Naomi's case.

"Fuck… I should have let her die." His tone was cold, devoid of emotion.

"No!" Loren didn't know what possessed her to reach out, grabbing his free hand with her own. His fingers were cold and slightly damp—but they automatically tightened around hers with a strength that made something flutter deep inside.

"You couldn't just let her die," she insisted.

He didn't seem so sure, however. For a long minute, he watched her. Then he pulled himself to his full height. Loren didn't even have time to react before she found herself gently steered around the center island until she stood directly in front of him.

Her pulse raced. Up close, he looked even worse. Exhaustion dripped from him in waves, or maybe it was just rainwater? He was drenched, his hair plastered to his forehead. Still, he had never smelled more like pine. *Wild.*

She inhaled him deeply, drawing strength from his presence. Now more than ever, she felt convinced that he had done the right thing. Not for her, or even Naomi—but for *him.*

"You couldn't let her die," she insisted for the final time, voicing what she could sense through whatever invisible bond tethered them together. Like his anger, she was aware of something else lurking within him. An emotion he seemed determined to suppress.

Even if she hadn't begged him to intervene…he might have done so anyway.

"W-what's going to happen now?" she asked when he didn't speak. Her eyes darted over to the living room. "Will she—"

"It could happen slow." McGoven's hoarseness threw her off. He sounded drained. "It could take months—years. Her body and mind will change, but by the time the lycan blood takes full effect, she'll...be different. It could drive her insane. She'll be dangerous."

Loren winced. Naomi, sans claws, wasn't a pretty picture. The thought of her being capable of turning into a wolf, even *half* the size of McGoven was...

"There is another way," McGoven began carefully, but his tone had her stomach twisting into knots.

She glanced down to see that he still held her hand, and his grip tightened as if to make sure that—despite whatever he said next—she couldn't pull away.

"H-How?"

He sighed. "*Mades* need discipline; someone there to make sure they don't fall out of line."

He was dancing around the term, letting her fill in the blanks. *An Alpha*, she thought. As if reading her mind, McGoven nodded slowly, just once.

"But it isn't like I'm on good terms with too many of those. And...if *I* do this myself...I might as well jab a silver stake through my own chest right now—save someone else the trouble. There can be no turning back—" His eyes flickered a pale shade of gray. Again, Loren suspected he'd already made up his mind. "Out of everything I've done...this is the *one* thing that will serve as a direct challenge to Lukka. Something he won't be able to ignore."

"Why...why did those men—" She broke off. *You know the answer to that,* a part of her hissed. "Who were they?"

McGoven frowned. "Eislanders."

The name sounded familiar. Kyle had mentioned it, the night she'd been attacked.

"Loreck Eislander's pack has always rivaled ours," McGoven went on. "He's older, more inclined to fall back on the old laws. Lukka never really humored him; he's younger with less patience for the elders. But while their territory is roughly the same size, the Eislanders outnumber us two to one when it comes to fully grown males. Loreck doesn't tolerate any sign of aggression near his boundary."

Like four men being murdered on his doorstep. While she didn't know much about the "Lycan" way of life, she knew her father—and he'd gone ballistic at even the *thought* of having McGoven in his house. "What are we going to do?"

"We?" McGoven gave her an odd look. Suddenly, he released her hand and took a single step back. "*You* aren't going to do anything. This is *my* fight."

"No." Loren's cheeks flamed, but she didn't rush to apologize. Not even as he cocked his head, his gaze molten. Disobeying him felt more weighty than just mouthing off. A corner of his mouth twitched. His eyelids lowered. Restraint alone was what kept him from snapping back with a command—she knew it in her soul. *You will listen to me.*

"I told you to do it," she added in a rush. "I should be involved in the consequences."

He didn't say anything for a long time. He just stood there. Close enough that his heat leached through her, as blazing as a furnace. Then, all at once, he sighed and turned for the back door, motioning with a jerk of his head for her to follow.

It was chilly out. Loren found herself shifting closer to McGoven —*because of his heat*, she told herself. Nothing more. On bare feet, she was clumsy, stumbling into him. He stiffened at the contact, but to her shock, he didn't recoil. His focus remained on the fields, scanning each one for any hint of danger.

"I have to make her submit to me," he said finally.

"H-how?" Though, she figured she already knew the answer. He'd chase her down. Pin her to the ground. And kiss her?

McGoven shrugged. "I tell her to. The growing lycan inside of her should recognize my strength and give in. If not, I could always use force."

"F-Force?" A tremor sank into her voice.

McGoven's head swiveled in her direction as if the mere hint of her unease distracted him from anything else. Even his own safety.

"Nothing that would harm her," he clarified. "The more heightened her emotions, the more susceptible she'll be to my compulsion. My will. Anything I do would *only* be to help her gain control of her lycan side before it could overwhelm her. That is all."

"Is that what you tried to do to me?"

"Yes." He looked away from her, his jaw tight. "It's easier to invoke the shift under the compulsion of an Alpha. It's how children are brought into lycan form for the first time. After that, it's a matter of practice and honing the skill to master it on their own."

"But it didn't work," she blurted. "I didn't...submit."

And that's the problem, a part of her whispered—even before she saw the odd look he gave her. His strength was obvious—

undeniable. When he finally looked at her head-on, however, nothing in the world could have prepared her for the expression on his face.

He looked broken. A man at his wit's end. "Loren, I think you might be the exception in this equation. It might even be my fault. There... There is something you should know—"

"Sorry to interrupt!"

They both turned, springing apart, to find Micha in the doorway to the kitchen, leaning on his uninjured leg. The wound looked even worse than it had last night. For the moment, at least, his attention seemed to be somewhere else.

"Um...*she's* awake."

Sure enough, pained moans came from inside the house. Then a high-pitched curse promptly followed by a scream.

36

*E*ric Lanister had lived long enough—seen far enough— that few things surprised him. Sworn to the fiercest pack in the country, it took more than bloodshed to turn his head. So was the life of a lycan. Brutal. Predictable.

But… The sight of a little female—no bigger than his shoulder— demanding submission from one of his men…

He couldn't shake it. It was more than an anomaly. It was unheard of.

Her sex wasn't the sticking point—women were bred in the same den of violence as men. At least under Loreck. No. It was her youth that puzzled him. Her confidence. Rarely had he seen a pup so young with such potential to lead. Not since one man who belonged to a rival pack—and had since failed to live up to his potential.

To be fair, Michael—the man she targeted—was an idiot. An overconfident, egotistical, brain-dead *idiot*, but where he lacked in smarts, the fool more than made up for in brute strength. Loreck had tasked him with leading the expedition to confront the rogue purely on a technicality—the man had been a close friend of Jamal's. It was custom, after all, to let the loved ones of those slain seek retribution on their behalf. Hurting for said vengeance, Michael may have gotten a little carried away. They were only supposed to confront the man, after all.

The female and the other rogue had been casualties of war—though, Eric wasn't ashamed to admit that he would have easily killed them all. An eye for an eye, it was their way. But, then that little female had stared them down without flinching.

Without betraying one damn ounce of fear.

Who the hell was she? Puzzled, he pictured those haunting eyes —a shade not quite green, or brown, with a hint of gold sprinkled in. A gaze that even *Eric*—whose position was second only to the Alpha—had been uneasy to face head-on. He couldn't escape the feeling that it was *familiar,* somehow. He had seen eyes like that before. A gaze just as fierce and unfaltering.

But where?

"Tell me again why you *didn't* kill him?"

Eric flinched at the disapproving tone. With a sigh, he respectfully inclined his head toward the man sitting across from an oak desk in the center of the room.

Eislanders weren't concerned with pomp and circumstance like other packs—Black Mountain paramount among them. The Alpha held court in an office off the main communal building, in a large space with very little decoration. Aside from the desk, some bookshelves, and a bearskin rug thrown across the wooden floor.

As far as he was concerned, there didn't need to be. A true leader spent more time out of any dwelling than inside it. This study more than sufficed as the base of operations for the Eislander territory. The man sitting behind the desk made the place seem just as regal as any King's throne room.

Dark brown hair, speckled with gray, framed a face that could have been chiseled from stone. The cold expression was a hallmark of the man in question—one of many traits that made him a force to be reckoned with.

"It was one against four," Loreck Eislander went on, voice deceptively calm, as he shuffled a stack of paperwork over the desk's surface. "Tell me again how that ends up in a retreat?"

"Four against *three*," Eric corrected. He may have been the man's Beta, but that didn't make him any less intimidated. Called here like a naughty child, he resisted the urge to wring his hands and fidget. "There was another rogue, and the female there with him as well. Not to mention a *human*. Besides," he added quickly. "The rogue would be driven to protect his mate."

Making him stronger than about *ten* wolves, but he had enough sense not to say it out loud.

Loreck, however, wasn't impressed. The Alpha didn't look up from his paperwork, but Eric could sense his annoyance, buzzing from him in waves.

"Fine," he said simply. "Then *you* can explain to Janelle and Robin why justice for Jamal was denied."

Eric went cold at the mention of Jamal's mate and child. The man had been found a couple days ago, near the boundary of the territory, attacked before he even had the chance to shift.

It just didn't make sense. Out of all the bastards deserving of being murdered, why *Jamal?* The man had never picked a battle with anyone he couldn't handle. Not to mention, what the hell was a rogue doing on their territory anyway?

Something doesn't make sense...

"That's the thing," Eric blurted, thinking on his feet. "The other rogue kept mentioning an attack. Said the murder was justified."

Which, again, just didn't make any damn sense—Jamal wouldn't harm a fly. But, there were bruises all over the girl, and *someone* would have had to get her mate riled enough to kill...

"Justified?" Suddenly, Loreck glanced up, gaze sharp. "Did you check into it?"

"Of-of course," Eric said, shifting uneasily on his feet. "Trevor and Lyla reported some strange noises by the west border the night of the murder, but a scout of the area revealed nothing out of the ordinary."

Nothing besides a trampled field and some strange scents—but at the time, he'd just assumed that some idiots from that fool Lukka's pack had decided to push the boundary too far.

Again.

But, now...

"Something doesn't seem right—if you don't mind me saying," he added hastily as Loreck's gaze narrowed. But, it was too late to clam up now. Taking a deep breath, he decided to lay it all on the table. "Why would that rogue kill Jamal? If he has a grudge against *anyone*, don't you think it would be Lukka?"

The man had exiled him, after all. Not to mention, that the asshole had already made more than his fair share of enemies, despite being Alpha for a few short years.

The corner of Loreck's mouth twitched up into something that could have been a smile if the dark emotion in those hazel eyes wasn't all wrong.

Fierce.

"Well, it's a good thing he's *here* so that we can ask him, isn't it?" Before Eric could react, the man stood and raised his voice. "Let him in."

The wooden double doors to the study opened from the outside. Then, as if, out of some bad television show drama, Lukka strolled in through the doorway, head held high.

Eric struggled to smother his disgust—at least out of the guise of politeness. Lukka would smell his dislike, regardless.

The man was young. He had an almost pretty face, set by two blue eyes and a mop of curly blond hair. Eric figured that he'd seen Barbie Dolls with more spunk, though rumors claimed the man could hold his own, despite his looks.

But he was young. *Too* young for Eric's liking. Even worse, he was arrogant and seemed to think that his youth entitled him to exert his will outside of his pack. To turn his back on the old ways. To steal.

Upstart little tyke, Eric thought as the man walked past him. In his day, arrogance like that got rewarded with a beating. To submission.

"Loreck," Lukka called by way of greeting, moving to clasp the older Alpha on the shoulder.

Loreck didn't return the favor. He only stood back, keeping the desk between the two of them to create a distance that spoke of the tension between them more than any words could.

"We have a problem," Loreck began, in a firm tone. "Not *only* is it your constant encroachment onto my land, or the way that pack of yours has been using our resources without permission…"

He let the words hang for a second—judging the young pup's reaction. In the years of the old Alpha, one might say that the Eislanders and Black Mountain wolves had existed…peacefully.

They still had their squabbles back then, but more importantly, there had been respect. Respect based on the old laws—which plainly said to keep your people on the right side of boundary lines or suffer the damn consequences.

Lukka changed all that. He constantly tested Loreck's patience and allowed his people to slip onto their territory unchecked. He had too many mouths to feed and not enough supplies with which to do so. Everyone knew it. Even worse, there were rumors that the bastard had sold off parts of his *own* territory—farmed them out for humans to develop for *money.*

It was a disgusting thought, one Eric doubted. No lycan could be so damn selfish. So greedy. So undeserving of the mantle of a leader.

But actions spoke louder than words. Why else would Black Mountain wolves be forced to fish in *their* rivers or hunt beyond their own forests?

Eric knew that it was only reluctance on Loreck's part to start a real conflict that the man didn't respond to the trespassing with vicious retaliation. But there was only so much patience in the world, and Loreck's was quickly running out.

But, if being confronted with the evidence of his own arrogance fazed Lukka any, the man didn't show it.

"Hmm," he murmured thoughtfully. "I hadn't heard."

The man had balls. Eric could give him that much. Though, he had even more respect for the fact that Loreck didn't reach across the table to smack the young pup on the ass like he so painfully deserved.

"Oh," Loreck replied in an equally casual tone. "And I'm sure that you didn't hear of the murder of one of my men, either?"

Lukka visibly flinched, blue eyes narrowing.

"I did," he said, nodding his head. "That's why I'm here—to offer my…condolences."

"Condolences." Loreck scoffed, running a hand over the gray-tinged brown stubble on his chin. "Then maybe you can tell me why one of *your* rogues killed him?"

Another emotion flashed across Lukka's gaze, too quickly for Eric to get a good read on it. Excitement. Fear? Satisfaction? Whatever it was faded in a flash.

"A chilling accusation," the pup said. "Do you have proof?"

Loreck snapped his fingers, and on cue, one of the men by the door came forward to drop a single object onto the table. Eric hissed, his nostrils wrinkling with the stench. It was a knife, smeared with blood, days old.

The insult couldn't be understated. To kill another lycan while in wolf form was one thing—grisly, but honorable. Accepted. To utilize a crude weapon and stealth? Despicable. At least Jamal's killer identified himself by leaving the blade behind. From it drifted a faint, musky odor as characteristic to any wolf as fingerprints were to humans.

"We think Jamal tried to fight back," Loreck explained gruffly. "He ultimately failed… However—" He reached down to trail a finger along the edge of the blade. "He still managed to draw his attacker's blood…"

So he wanted evidence? This was it—a scent trail was just as damning as a signed confession.

But Lukka seemed ready for it. The man didn't even have the decency to look shocked.

"McGoven's dangerous," he replied, recognizing the scent. "He took a mate without permission—forced her against her will and kept her hostage on his territory. She's a *blood* lycan," he added, making the crime so much worse. "You know the law—"

"She belongs with the pack of her father," Loreck said with a frown.

"Yes," Lukka agreed. "Only…when I sent my man out there to bring her to us, McGoven tracked them down, ambushed them, and took the girl back. I'm guessing that your man must have seen them, tried to help her and…"

Gotten his throat slit with a silver knife. It made sense. Jamal was a kindhearted soul. Seeing a crazed man, dragging some girl off into the woods would have incited his need to help.

And he paid the cost.

But…

Something didn't fit. While filthy and bruised, that girl didn't exactly look like she was being kept against her will. Though, if McGoven *had* mated her, that wouldn't mean much. Her desires would be entwined with his by now.

If murder was the worst crime a lycan could commit, mating an unwilling female would be a close second. Both deserved only one punishment—death.

But, something itched at the back of Eric's skull, demanding acknowledgment. Doubt.

"Why let her go in the first place?" he wondered, speaking out loud. "If he took her by force, why would he let your man take her? Let alone, allow them to get all the way out here before coming for her?"

And, while he was at it…

"What the hell was a full-blooded, unmated female doing so far from your territory anyway? Isn't it *your* job to keep your own wolves in line? And why didn't you go to welcome her personally? To send a beta for such a task, it's… It's unheard of."

Too late, did Eric realize that his tone came across harsher than intended. So much for politeness.

Loreck glanced at him in warning. But he could tell from his thoughtful expression that the Alpha had been thinking along those exact same lines.

Lukka shrugged. "We knew of her. She was supposedly the daughter of another rogue—a *made*. We didn't think there was a possibility she'd inherited the blood. But now…" He sighed, running a hand through his yellow hair. "We think that McGoven may have murdered the man to get to his daughter once he sensed the blood in her. Then he kept her heritage a secret. It was only when she murdered someone that he came clean. I'm sure you can see why."

Eric felt his eyes widen, but Loreck nodded. Just once.

"With a mate of his own, he could evade his rogue status. Challenge another Alpha on equal footing. Even start his own pack," he murmured. But suddenly, he tilted his head, raising a dark eyebrow. "Though, you've always been worried about him, haven't you? That's what you've feared. The day he might return and demand you *earn* your position the way an Alpha is meant to."

The question seemed aimed at Lukka like a dart—and it struck the bullseye. For a split second, the young pup dropped the friendly-neighbor routine. Those boyish blue eyes narrowed, so damn icy that even Eric suppressed the urge to shiver. Perhaps the wolf wasn't all talk after all.

"I *am* the Alpha," Lukka hissed. "I fear no one." But in the blink of an eye, his casual demeanor returned in full force, mouth quirking up in a faint smile. "But I can understand your concern. After all, without an heir, who knows what will happen to your pack should you meet your end before your time. A threat like the one McGoven presents must weigh heavily on your mind."

Son of a bitch. Low growls of warning echoed throughout the room. Eric felt himself take a step forward before he could help it —though Loreck managed to keep his composure.

It was a low blow, though the lack of an heir wasn't exactly a secret. Normally, an Alpha named a successor outright. Though there was no guarantee they would become the leader, the designation ensured stability. Direction. While childless, Loreck had held off on even naming a successor. If he died before he did so…

Eric didn't even want to think about the chaos that might ensue. Violence. Bloodshed. Civil War.

Loreck did have one benefit to withholding the name of an heir, blood or otherwise. It meant their pack ran smoothly. There were no political games. Everyone stood on equal footing, and he didn't need to worry about a challenge. Yet.

Lukka, on the other hand, wasn't so lucky. Rumors had swirled mere seconds after he claimed the title of leader. Even outside packs weighed the risks of taking on Black Mountain and attempting a coup. He was on shaky ground, forced to defend his position at every turn. Paired with the obvious issues regarding feeding his enormous pack, you had a recipe for chaos.

"How ironic that you should mention heirs," Loreck replied, once the anger in the chamber died down somewhat, "when your own father named another man as his successor over *you*. It seems, an Alpha's will isn't always realized after death."

This time, Lukka couldn't have hidden the reaction if he tried. Pure, raw loathing crossed those handsome features—twisting them. It took way longer than a second for him to wrestle himself back under control.

"McGoven's *dangerous*," he insisted. "He's killed once, and he'll kill again. Do whatever you have to do to ensure justice for your own—"

"Wait," Eric said, ignoring the rival Alpha's glare. "What about the girl? I say we leave her out of this. She's full-blooded. If she's grown up in human territory…"

He didn't even want to think of what that meant. The mental damage that might be done, let alone physical, was horrifying. Especially if her first entry to lycan life was being mated against her will. Eric cringed as he thought of his own sister. That female deserved justice just as much as Jamal.

"She's an innocent," Loreck agreed. "If he mated her against her will, that just adds onto his crime."

"She's of no use to me. Just use her to get to him," Lukka suggested. "I never accepted her. She's not one of mine—"

Bang! At first, Eric thought someone had shot off a gun in the room, before he realized that the monstrous sound had come from Loreck slamming his fist onto the desk. A crack appeared within the wood, and Eric winced. It was an antique.

"You would *dare* leave one of your own? One of us? To fend for herself out there, pack-less? Have you no honor? No shame?"

His voice bellowed across the room. The territory, even. If the whole pack wasn't aware of this outburst, Eric would resign from his position on the spot. He doubted he had ever seen the Alpha so angry, without invoking the shift at least. Those hazel eyes flashed—emerald, brown…gold.

Wait a minute…

"No," Lukka admitted on a sigh. For the first time, he seemed to realize that he'd stepped too far. He shifted uneasily on his feet and cleared his throat. "But, I have a…liaison whose close to McGoven. I'll try to see if she can convince him to give up the girl."

"You do that. Or *we* will take her in. I will see to it personally," Loreck said.

Eric couldn't tell if he meant the threat, though he didn't feel the need to argue. A new female would be welcomed among them, as she should.

"There will be no need," Lukka said thickly. "She will be accepted into Black Mountain. Once she arrives."

"And after that," Loreck continued, his gaze electric, "we will have our justice."

Eric barely heard him. He was too busy trying his hardest to convince himself that it couldn't be—*she* couldn't be…

The girl's father was dead.

As he stared into his Alpha's hazel eyes, he knew that there was no damn way. Obviously, what he'd seen had been a trick of the light.

37

They entered the living room to find Naomi sitting upright, with one hand braced against the back of the couch, and the other clutching her throat. She looked entirely different from the confident, smirking figure Loren had become accustomed to avoiding. She was pale. That signature blond hair hung limply down her shoulders, dirty and clumped with mud.

"Where...where the hell am I?" she croaked, though Loren wasn't sure how she managed to speak at all.

Her throat...

Looking at her in the harsh light of morning, the futility of what they'd done hit Loren like a punch to the chest. All of it. Camping out, waiting for a miracle, had been foolish. A childish exercise. Forget McGoven's spiel on *lycans* and magic—Naomi needed a hospital.

Now.

She scanned the room, looking for a phone to do just that, but before she could so much as blink, McGoven moved...and every single shred of common sense just left her mind in an instant.

She could only watch him.

His exhaustion seemed to vanish. So did the guilt and hesitation she'd witnessed while on the porch. Now, only grim determination shined in those silver eyes.

Even covered in dirt and grime and streaks of blood, he looked one hundred percent... She couldn't seem to come up with a word *strong* enough, but one popped in her mind, unbidden—like an *Alpha*.

"Naomi." His voice was deep, silencing the blond's cries instantly. "Listen to me now. Get up." He didn't raise his voice, but he didn't have to.

Even Loren flinched, rocking on the balls of her toes. Despite her injuries, Naomi scrambled upright, leaning against the couch for balance. Those green eyes were wide, trailing from the bay window to the half-naked police officer facing her from across the coffee table.

"Wh...Where am I?"

"Follow me." McGoven turned, heading for the door without explaining.

And, for the first time, probably in her whole life, Naomi Tanner obeyed without so much as a snarky word in edgewise. Loren could only stare. It was strange—like watching every interaction she'd had with this same man, though from the outside looking in.

His knack for controlling people was...*eerie*, to say the least. *When he says jump, you don't even have the time to ask how high*, a part of her remarked in awe.

As if reading her mind, he cut his eyes to her. For a heartbeat, some of that icy strength softened. *Trust me*, he seemed to say. Just as quickly, his attention returned to Naomi. Her blood dripped onto the floor, leaving a trail of scarlet, as she struggled to follow.

"You—" McGoven eyed Micha, who stood near the doorway. "Help me."

Micha rushed forward, and together they took an arm on either side and manually steered Naomi outside. As they hastened out onto the porch, Loren's first thought was that they planned on getting her into the truck and taking her to the hospital after all. They should.

Instead...

They carried her down the steps and straight into the field beside the barn. There, in the grass, they released her.

Loren realized—as the wind pulled at her hair—that she had raced after them barefoot, with only her filthy flannel to protect her from the chill. Not that Naomi was any better off. Bleeding and dazed, the girl shivered, bracing her hands against the muddy earth. Panic filled her gaze as she eyed McGoven. Shockingly, she didn't scream or argue. She didn't seem able to.

"What now?" Micha stood back, serious for once. He had his arms crossed, his nostrils flared. Instantly, he looked older. Authoritative. "Are you sure about this? I've only seen one made successfully turned—with my dad's... The Alpha's guidance. It's not easy—"

"I know," McGoven said. Then he swallowed.

"And if it works," Micha added, "you know what that means, don't you?"

McGoven didn't reply, but his heavy sigh gave his answer away —*of course I do.*

"What are you doing?" Loren didn't know what made her step forward. After all, he'd already told her his plan. *Make Naomi submit.* But how?

"Stay back," Micha warned.

Both men didn't even look in her direction. McGoven, in particular, didn't seem willing to break eye contact with the blond curled up at his feet. Not even for a second. Suddenly, he squared his shoulders, and a low sound filled the air. A growl.

Loren felt it rumble through the earth. In her *bones.* The sensation was hair-raising, and she instantly pictured the black wolf who usually followed that sound. A wolf who could devour what remained of Naomi in one bite.

"No!" Blindly, Loren rushed forward, planting herself firmly in the middle of the fray. "Leave her alone!"

McGoven towered over her, and her heart sank. He wasn't like the man from the other day. There was no way on earth she could challenge him. But what was the alternative? Let Naomi die?

"She needs a hospital," she insisted, digging her toes into the wet earth as those silver eyes took on a darker shade. "Not...not *this!*"

"Loren—" She turned to find Micha at her side. Gingerly, he threw an arm over her shoulder and guided her a few paces away. "It's okay. Just wait. He's trying to help her. I know it looks scary, but it's not. She needs to trust him."

Loren couldn't imagine how bringing her out into the frigid cold air and dumping her on the ground was going to help anyone.

But then, she saw his eyes. He had turned to look at her, forsaking the blond for a painful second. *Trust me*, his gaze pleaded, before returning to Naomi.

Trust…

Loren wasn't sure if she even knew what that word meant. Could you trust someone when you didn't even know them? *Yes*, a part of her insisted without any hesitation. *You can. You will. You have to.*

Biting her lip, she waited… Though, nothing exciting seemed to be happening. McGoven just stared Naomi down and vice versa. On second thought, the eerie quiet settling in around them was an oddity. Despite the howling wind, the clearing was utterly silent. No animals. No birds. Nothing.

"She's weak," she heard Micha explain. He held her a little too close for her liking, but she was too engrossed by the unfolding scene to pull away. "I think he let her sleep to conserve her strength, though *I* wouldn't have. Changing sooner than later is her best bet. She needs to heal, and from a wound that bad, the only way to do so is to…"

"Shift," the word came from Officer McGoven as a growl, so damn compelling that Loren felt something deep inside of her shudder in response.

But the full brunt of the command was meant for Naomi. The blond trembled from head to toe, breaking the eye contact with a whimper.

See? The logical side of Loren whispered. *This is stupid.* But another part of her wasn't so sure. *Wait.*

Naomi didn't lurch up like she had, or turn tail and run. She didn't bite him. She didn't fight back.

She just…whimpered, pressing her body to the ground, and Loren knew instantly that this was what he'd wanted from her as well—*submission.* Triumphant, McGoven crouched and placed a hand on Naomi's shoulder, forcing her to face him again.

With Micha holding her back, Loren couldn't see what he did or hear what he said, but the next moment he bolted to his feet— dragging Naomi upright along with him. She whined, the cries harrowing.

"Stop!" Loren struggled against Micha's grip. "What are you doing—"

Before she could even get the words out, he turned, shoving Naomi in the direction of the trees so hard she went sailing to the ground.

Only when she landed…

The slender teenage girl disappeared.

And a wolf took her place.

38

It was the smallest one yet. Lithe and delicate. Not even half the size of the black wolf, though still larger than any version Loren figured you would find in the wild. If there were any question as to its identity, a coat of golden fur glinted in the daylight, as it rolled onto its feet and took off.

It was fast, darting between the trees and out of sight. Left behind were the scattered remains of Naomi's outfit—a tattered blouse, a broken heel, and the fabric of a mini skirt ruffling in the wind.

"I need to go after her," McGoven muttered, tugging down the waistband of his sweatpants. His voice was still that deep, commanding tone, but beneath it all, he sounded relieved. Satisfied.

He glanced back at Micha and nodded to his injured leg. "You should shift too. I might need the help. You can corral her away from the town—"

"Sure thing." Wincing, Micha released Loren and began to remove his clothing. "I'll cover you."

Loren gaped as both men stripped naked, before common decency made her turn away, cheeks flaming. Next came the soft hiss of clothing hitting the ground, and then the heavier thud of two bodies lumbering into motion.

When she finally gathered the nerve to peek over her shoulder, she only just managed to catch sight of two giant wolves—one brown, and the other black—bolting for the woods. She didn't know how long she stood there after that, just staring.

It could have been minutes. An hour.

By the time she finally forced herself to move, her only action was to stoop for a pair of ratty, mud-stained sweats, which she tossed over her shoulder. She did the same to another pair, and then the torn remains of a pink blouse and mini skirt.

How thoughtful of you, a part of her hissed sarcastically. *Three people just change into wolves right in front of you—what do you do?*

Gather up the laundry.

You should be there, that same voice insisted. *Out there, with him…*

Her eyes seemed pulled to the forest against their will, scanning the shadows beyond the branches. But it wasn't like she could just sprout claws and fur anytime soon.

Why was that? If she was what he claimed, then why couldn't she shift? He said the urge was like a muscle that needed honing. Or perhaps, a switch you could just flick inside yourself, and voila? *Presto chango.*

I think my switch is broken, she thought as a halfhearted mental search revealed nothing out of the ordinary. No magic lever marked "lycan button." It seemed like the only thing she *could* do was the one thing she seemed to be best at. Cleaning up the mess.

The dirty clothes she left in a pile by the front door. Then, she entered the kitchen and stood near the window. Rain picked up again, dampening everything beneath a heavy sheet.

In the end…she didn't really know what made her go upstairs and tiptoe into that large bedroom. Boredom? A need to do *something?*

After a few minutes of rummaging through the closet, she found several clean pairs of sweats and a few oversized shirts. She showered and claimed one of the sweatpants for herself. The rest, she brought downstairs and set neatly folded by the door.

How damn thoughtful. *Why not go all out?* a part of her hissed. *Corrupting teenagers has got to be exhausting—why not make him dinner, too?*

As evening neared, she found herself in the kitchen, throwing open the fridge to do just that. *Old habit?* she guessed. A hold out from the days of living with her father, who demanded his meals be waiting for him. Whatever the reason, she dragged a loaf of bread from the counter and rummaged in the fridge for a carton of tuna.

As Sonia had joked, he didn't seem to have much else. A quick peek revealed some steaks in the freezer, and there was a carton of apple juice and some eggs on the shelf in the fridge. Though, maybe he just supplemented his diet with fresh meat?

A flicker of movement drew her gaze to the window, just in time to catch two dark shapes crossing the west field. Her heart lurched. The sun had already set, and the resulting shadow revealed just enough of tanned skin and long limbs for her to realize that both figures were fully human…and naked.

A desperate impulse kept her from blushing. Modesty wasn't important. She needed to see him… Boldly, her eyes went to the first figure, who just so happened to be the tallest.

He moved easily, black hair ruffled by the wind. The chiseled lines of his chest stood out as if etched in stone. It was only when he made it to the porch—close enough to have been fully illuminated by the house lights—that she finally turned away.

Fingers shaking, she slammed a piece of bread down to create the last sandwich. At the same time, the front door opened to a flood of footsteps. She waited until they had an adequate amount of time to notice the clothes before she finally peeked into the foyer.

She noticed Micha first. He stood fully upright on two uninjured legs as he wrestled a pair of pants on. The skin of his calf was merely smooth and tanned. Awe robbed her of some of her frustration. No wonder they'd been gone so long—if this was what shifting could do to them. Heal.

With renewed interest, she turned to McGoven. He ignored the T-shirts in favor of another pair of sweatpants which he already had on. Mud streaked him from head to toe, and he looked exhausted, but oddly…satisfied at the same time. The exercise of running obviously agreed with him.

But…

"Where's Naomi?"

The two men shared a look.

"She's home," Micha blurted finally.

"Home?" The remnants of the girl's clothes were right in front of her, by the door. Loren suspected there wasn't a *mall* out in the woods, stocked with clothing suitable for Naomi Tanner.

Considering he *wasn't* arrested, she figured that it was unlikely McGoven had marched the girl up her front walkway, completely butt naked, either.

"Home," McGoven insisted, tightening the drawstring to his pants. "She's safe."

"She's pretty, too," Micha gushed around a crooked grin. "You think I have a shot? You know, once she gets used to the whole *Teen wolf* thing."

McGoven ignored him. As the thrill of his change wore off, his frown returned. Those gray eyes found hers, and for the first time, she sensed an emotion in them that wasn't stern, or determined. Just…exhausted.

"Loren—" He sighed and nodded to the back door. "We need to talk."

"Okay." She followed him without hesitation.

As she slipped onto the porch, she could hear Micha shuffling into the kitchen. "Wow!" he exclaimed. "Is all this food for us?"

Loren felt too uneasy to answer him. It was freezing out, though before she really had the chance to feel it in full force, a fierce heat was there to displace the chill. *Pine.* He stood behind her, not quite touching, but when he spoke, she could practically feel his voice traveling right down her spine in a low, deep rumble.

"Let me explain…"

"What?" She whirled to face him, not knowing what to expect. What she *found* in his expression completely threw her off.

He looked…*vulnerable.* There was an aching softness to that stern jaw that she had never seen before. Unlike earlier, those eyes were a soft, wistful shade of gray that seemed hesitant to meet hers full-on.

"Ask me whatever you want," he said seriously. "I'll try to explain. I know it wasn't easy for you to see that. It looked violent. Barbaric, even."

Loren bit her lower lip. In hindsight, barbaric wasn't the word she'd use. Perhaps just...primal. "Where is Naomi?" she asked.

"She's *home*. I wasn't lying about that—" He broke off to run a hand through his hair. Then, he gestured for her to follow him over to the steps, where he sat down on the top one.

Loren shuddered. The stair wasn't all that large, and she had to sit close enough for her shoulder to brush his. Not that it was exactly a bad feeling...

She felt warm for a change. The icy, evening air barely affected her at all.

"So, Naomi's home?" She risked sneaking a glance at him.

"Yes," he said emphatically. "I swear. Her parents were there, but I managed to come up with a...plausible story to explain why she didn't come home last night."

Loren glanced at him sharply. "Naked?" Even now, he wasn't wearing a shirt, and he was the type of person who could draw notice wearing a sweater.

"That didn't matter, trust me." Something that could have been a frown tugged at the corner of his mouth. "I can be very...*persuasive* when I want to be. I was able to tell the Tanners a plausible story to explain why Naomi didn't come home last night—*after* Micha snuck into her room to get her clothes."

Loren felt a flicker of amusement. Despite his "powers of persuasion," he wasn't stupid.

"If you're curious," he added, "I told them she didn't want to risk driving in the storm. So, you suggested that she stay the night."

"So, what happens next?"

"I don't know," McGoven admitted. He scanned the horizon, eyes narrowing as they passed over the trees in the distance. "But, it won't be good. In fact…"

He faced her fully, and she sucked in a breath. Gone was the doubt. His eyes glittered through the darkness. "If you ask me, I should put you on a bus right now—one way—heading straight to some destination on the other side of the continent. You'd thank me in the long run."

It was impossible to meet his gaze. Nervously, Loren inspected her hands instead. "I appreciate everything you've done, but you don't have to keep making decisions for me. I'm eighteen."

In her world, at least, that age counted for something.

"I know." His tone threw her off, and she looked over to find him staring at the fields again. "I know."

"Maybe you should come with me?" she suggested. Even she wasn't sure if she was serious or making a joke. "You know, once Naomi tells the whole town that you turned her into a wolf."

"She won't."

He sounded so damn confident. Loren couldn't even find the strength to doubt him. "Why not?"

"Because I told her not to. Listen… By submitting to me, Naomi has accepted me as her Alpha—" She didn't miss how he seemed to cringe at the word, but he soldiered on anyway. "Among our kind, the Alpha's word is the *law*. If I told her to stay home tonight and say nothing to her parents, then she'll stay home and say nothing to her parents. It shouldn't cross her mind to disobey."

Loren's first instinct was to be skeptical. Then, she nodded. She knew firsthand the type of effect his voice could have.

"I want to know what you're thinking," he demanded.

She blinked, thrown again. "I think it sounds…"

"Like what? You can tell me."

"Like a dictatorship." Creepy on top of that. Having your thoughts and emotions decided for you? What kind of life was that?

McGoven nodded as if he fully expected her reaction. "It would to someone like you, who has grown up on the outside. To those of us within the pack, it's the complete opposite. We look to the Alpha for everything from strength to protection, and in return, we accept their leadership. Not out of fear. Out of love. We function as a family, of sorts, where everyone has a role to play. There is mutual respect," he insisted. "It's a two-sided relationship, one based solely on trust. Not violence. Not aggression."

"So, Naomi trusts *you*?" Loren asked, skeptical of that.

McGoven grimaced. "She will. Eventually."

"And…you'll trust her?"

He made a sound in the back of his throat that could have been a laugh if it weren't so strained. "I'll have to. She'll be my packmate. My family."

Don't like that, a part of Loren hissed. She flinched as something hot and prickly darted down her spine. Was that anger? Rage? Jealousy?

You should be jealous, some nasty part of her taunted. *After all, they don't wear clothing when they shift…*

"You're uncomfortable with the thought of me being so close to her."

Loren jumped for several reasons. One was that he seemed to be reading her mind again. The second was that he had reached for her hand while she'd been distracted. In frustration, she must have dug her nails into her palms, because the pad of his thumb gently trailed across the width of it, causing her fingers to loosen their grip.

"I-It's nothing," she stammered.

"You don't have to lie to me," he replied, scolding. His gaze trailed her face with concern, while his thumb continued to caress her hand. "I know what you're feeling. I've felt it too. It's instinct, nothing to be ashamed of."

He'd felt irritation because of Micha, she thought, her face hot. Desperate, she hunted for a change in topic. "It's just that...why didn't it work on me? Why didn't I s-submit to you?"

You know why, that snarky, shadowy part of her huffed. *We don't submit to anyone. Even him.*

"I'm not sure," McGoven admitted, his thumb left her palm, and he just wound up holding her fingers instead, locked within his. "I think... That there is some part of you that doesn't like being told what to do."

Loren had to snicker at that—she couldn't help it. Did "Turtle Girl" have a backbone all of a sudden? But when she thought of what happened in the field and the man from last night...

Suddenly, the thought wasn't so funny.

"Is that normal?" she croaked.

"No," he admitted. "There aren't many wolves who can resist the pull of a superior. Not because of my sex, either. I'm bigger.

Stronger. Older. Your inner wolf should have sensed that and submitted within seconds. I've been questioning why you didn't, myself."

"Is it because I've been raised as a human?"

He shook his head. "I don't think so. But… One explanation is something we refer to as 'the calling.' When a young wolf resists the pull of an Alpha, not out of disobedience but instinct. It's rare, but it's happened."

Loren couldn't tell if he was merely trying to make her feel better. "Have you seen it happen?"

He seemed to tense. "Yes. It happened with me. I didn't submit to my Alpha the first time I was compelled to. I ran instead."

Shock rendered Loren silent. More questions buzzed her throat, aching to be asked, but she sensed it wasn't her place to rush this story. He needed to tell it in his own time.

"Such young wolves aren't seen as disobedient or flawed. They are nurtured and taken under their leader's wing. Lukas… He earned my trust, and then I submitted to him of my own free will."

There was something else. Something he wasn't saying.

"All this means is that I need to earn your trust. Your respect. I *also* think," McGoven added quietly before she had the chance to respond, "that we need to learn who your real father is. Soon."

"How?" Loren blurted, not understanding the urgency.

If Fred Connors really wasn't her father, she wasn't too heartbroken about that—but what did that say for her so-called "real" dad?

Was he any better? Considering that he had left her to be bounced from home to home after her mother's death, probably not.

"I need to know more about your mother," McGoven began warily.

"Like what?"

"Anything. Where she lived. Where she grew up. Her family, if any."

Loren squirmed. It shouldn't have been hard to respond. Children were supposed to know things about their parents, right? But, wracking her brain, all she could come up with were small details. Her smell. Her laugh. Her smile.

"I…I don't remember much of her," she admitted after a while.

"Tell me anything you can," McGoven urged. He didn't seem like the talkative, emotional type, so his encouragement shocked her enough into talking.

"She was p-pretty," she stammered, feeling like an idiot. "And funny, and that's all I really remember. Her name was Eveline, and we lived in Ridgerton. Before that? I don't know."

Her mother hadn't spoken much about her past life or where she'd come from. As to her real father, well, if Fred Connors wasn't it, she had no idea who it could be.

"Did she ever mention your father?" McGoven asked.

She shook her head. "Not to me, and I learned quickly that bringing up family around her wasn't a good idea."

She would get sad, Loren remembered. Clam up. Sometimes even crawl back into bed and stay there for the rest of the day.

"Does it hurt? To talk about her?"

Loren bit her bottom lip as she thought it over. "Yes. But in a way, it feels…good. She was a good person."

Unlike her father, the memories of her mother didn't sting and burn at the back of her mind.

"About my father…"

Beside her, she could feel McGoven stiffen as if knowing what she was going to say before the words even left her mouth.

"It's been almost a week, and I haven't been—" She broke off, trying to think of the right way to say it.

She hadn't been called for an interview. An autopsy report. To claim her father's body—legally, she was still his daughter after all. But some suspicious part of her couldn't help thinking that *he* had. He had done all of those things and didn't even think to include her in a single one.

Even weirder, he never mentioned the murder, or her father, or what she remembered from that night at all.

He's being polite, a part of her hissed. *Waiting for the right time.*

But would there ever *be* a right time to bring up something like this?

"I at least want to get some things from the house," she finished weakly.

That wasn't too much to ask, was it? But when she glanced at his face, it was carefully blank.

"I could arrange it with the station." He let go of her hand and stood. "If that's what you want."

Loren nodded. "I do."

He held out his hand, and she took it, allowing him to pull her to her feet. He was closer than she thought—she nearly ran right into him. But, seemingly out of reflex, his arm went around her waist before she had the chance to lose her balance.

Loren held her breath. Pressed against him, she could feel his heat. Her nostrils flared with his scent, and every cell in her body was tingly and alert.

She couldn't help but be flashed back to that incident in the field. The kiss…

At the thought, her throat went dry. She'd pushed the events from her mind out of concern for Naomi. But now…

She figured that she'd never really stopped thinking about it. It was always there at the back of her mind, far too dangerous to focus on.

"Did you… With Naomi? Did you…" She couldn't even form a coherent sentence.

Still, he knew exactly what she meant. "No. The bond between us —*our* situation is different."

"How?"

"I… Eventually, I will explain. I promise you that."

An awkward silence fell, and with every passing second her pulse raced, her cheeks warm. More than ever, she felt certain he was avoiding something. Something monumental. "Different" seemed to be an understatement when describing whatever lingered between them.

Intense, perhaps? Intimate. For instance, she could feel his uncertainty the same way she felt his anger—and more. He was worried. Restless. And… Something dangerous he seemed determined to smother. Hide, if not from her, then himself. It persisted regardless. Soon, he gave in with a low hiss that made her heart lurch.

A second later, he was smelling her, dragging her scent into his lungs with deep, greedy breaths.

She inhaled his scent in return, so rich it took her breath away. Suddenly, they were closer. Whether he had closed the distance, or she did, she didn't know. Only that she was the one who reached for him first.

Her hand landed flat against his bare chest, summoning a low sound that teased the air in response. His entire body vibrated with tension. No, this wasn't like the way he interacted with Naomi. Not even comparable.

But then, what was it?

Puzzled, she looked up, searching his expression. Any answer was elusive, hidden behind those gray eyes. They were darker than ever. Endless.

But she wanted to know more. For the first time since meeting him, she felt… Entitled to more. Entitled to touch him. Inch closer. Lower her gaze to his mouth and watch his lips twitch into a frown.

"Loren…" he was preparing to say something. Perhaps some variation of his usual request when it came to her. *Trust me. Listen to me. Obey.*

She wondered just what made him react to her in the woods. It hadn't been her nearness or even the heightened adrenaline from the chase. It had been this. Parting her lips, holding his stare and uttering just one word. "No."

His nostrils flared, his brows furrowing. Her skin tingled—she felt like someone on the verge of some great discovery. What made Bill McGoven tick? What could catch him off guard, make him react out of character?

It was more than disobedience, she sensed. *Oh yes,* that inner voice purred. It was whatever instinct had him lurching after her the second she started down the porch steps. She didn't dare go far—just beyond the circle of light cast by the porch lamp.

He was right on her heels. His hand caught her wrist, yanking her back. Her spine met the unyielding surface of his chest. And then…

They stood like that, breathing in tandem. His breath ruffled her hair, his pulse hammering through her skin. It should have been an awkward embrace. Instead, it felt…

Beyond natural. Right. He belonged here. He belonged with *her.*

But he didn't want to. He didn't want this. She could feel the second he wrestled his emotions under control.

"You should go eat," he murmured, pulling back.

"You should too," Loren countered breathlessly. If anyone needed food, it was him. But he shook his head, turning to face the trees.

"Need to scout," she thought she heard him murmur. "If those men really were Eislanders, they'll be back."

She could tell from the set to his shoulders that he intended to spend the night out in the fields again, patrolling for trouble.

"You should go inside," he added with his back facing her. "I'll keep watch."

His tone left no room for argument. *Go inside.* With a sigh, Loren turned, intending to head up the porch steps, when he called out behind her.

"Loren—" He was still turned away from her, but with every muscle in his body so tense, he could have been made from stone. "I'm sorry about what happened the other day. I...I got carried away. It...it won't happen again."

Before she could react, he lunged, taking off on foot beyond the shadows.

Carried away. Was that what they called it these days? Kissing someone so *hard* they could feel it all the way down to their toes? Absently, Loren reached up, trailing her fingers along her bottom lip.

"Hey!"

She spun around to find Micha leaning against the doorway to the kitchen, noisily chewing on a chunk of bread. He waved what she guessed to be the sole surviving sandwich through the air.

"Was I supposed to save some of these?"

She shook her head. "Knock yourself out."

Though, if it could help any at making sense of these past few days, maybe *she* was the one who needed a good tap on the head.

39

*B*ill scowled at the sky, hating himself for showing restraint almost as much as he was relieved to have lasted this long. Days with a warm, receptive female in his midst, and he hadn't gone further than a kiss—few men could say the same.

Not that he had a right to do a damn thing beyond that, of course. The logical arguments didn't matter. Biology and instinct didn't care about the morality of the situation. Add to it all that the female in question was his mate and…

There was no way they could go on like this for long. Already, he could sense her responding to the same urges plaguing him constantly. She craved his touch. His acceptance. More.

Breaking the bond now—with or without Lukka—could be the most humane decision in the long run. She would have to suffer her mental and emotional wounds alone, but she would have a sense of agency over her emotions again. Otherwise…

The longer the bond persisted, the more her unexamined memories weighed on his mind. Sooner or later, he wouldn't be able to keep himself from going through them and learning Loren Connors in and out. What haunted her at night when he could sense her fear and felt driven to comfort her?

A part of him didn't want to know. If he overstepped that boundary, there would be no turning back. He'd already lost one mate. He couldn't survive that pain again.

Not to mention, the threat of Lukka, Kyle, and now the Eislanders.

There were only a handful of ways both he and Loren could survive this mess unscathed—none of them appealing.

The first was to break the bond and prepare her to live as an unofficial rogue—at least until she could find a pack other than Black Mountain to take her in. It was a huge ask of an untrained lycan—assuming, of course, that she handled the revelation of their mating bond without…

Fireworks. Though she would have every right to be furious. Violated. Worse. Dropping that bomb on her and cutting her loose was cruelty he doubted he could go through with.

The second course of action was to try again to have her accepted into Black Mountain and go against every cell in his body, warning him not to trust Lukka farther than he could throw him.

But the third…

It was the option that lingered in his mind the most, feeding off every trace of Loren Connors he could still sense on the wind.

He could keep her here and accept the unofficial title thrust upon him as an Alpha. Going a step further, he could train her as a lycan. Educate her on their ways and prepare her fully for the dissolution of the mating bond. That, however, would require time—a luxury they didn't have.

Bill wasn't sure which decision he would be able to live with, let alone Loren.

But they would need to pick a course of action. Soon.

HOWL

THE BLACK MOUNTAIN PACK BOOK 2

Howl

Howl By Lana Sky

Copyright © 2022 by Lana Sky
All rights reserved.

No part of this publication may be reproduced, distributed, or transmitted in any form or by any means, including photocopying, recording, or other electronic or mechanical methods, without the prior written permission of the author.

This is a work of fiction. Names, characters, businesses, places, events and incidents are either the products of the author's imagination or used in a fictitious manner. Any resemblance to actual persons, living or dead, or actual events is purely coincidental.

Cover Design and Interior Formatting by Charity Chimni
Editing by Charity Chimni

ACKNOWLEDGMENTS

Thanks so much to everyone who supported this draft along the way, including the many beta readers who provided encouragement! Please keep in mind that this story includes dark, graphic, and explicit content matter that may not be suitable for readers under the age of 18—or for readers who are uncomfortable with the following subject matter: age-gap relationships, explicit sex, and graphic depictions of violence.

1

There was an old saying, "better to be safe than sorry." Whoever coined it had obviously never spent a week with William McGoven.

The man was anything but safe—and Loren found a strange peace in his wild nature. As far as the men in her life were concerned, he was a welcome anomaly. Violent and brutish, Fred Connors, her supposed father, had been ruthlessly predictable.

William McGoven, on the other hand, was an enigma. Frustratingly so. He single-handedly made decisions for her, only to claim, in the next breath, that she wasn't his responsibility. He could be moody and unreadable, and so damn closed-off she could count his few facial expressions on her fingers.

She should have resented him and how confidently he'd inserted himself into her life—but anger wasn't the feeling spreading through her chest whenever she saw him. Just confusion. Despite his gruffness, he was always there when she needed him the most.

And he hadn't held that fact over her head. Nor did he ever ask for anything in return, other than her trust. All in all, he made for the perfect hero after the hell her life had become.

Until he kissed her. Not a chaste peck, either, but a wild assault she could feel the aftermath of days later.

No one could blame her if she claimed he'd taken advantage. But when she went over her own emotions, things weren't so simple.

He kissed her, and there hadn't been anything "weak" and "meek" about her reaction. Even now, a part of her demanded... something. Craved it from him alone. The actual name for it eluded her, but the more she tried to puzzle out an answer...

Her throat went dry. The thin material of her shirt irritated the skin beneath. It felt...too tight. Especially when she recalled the feel of his lips on hers.

Get a grip, Loren. You need to forget, a part of her insisted. Obviously, he'd gotten carried away. Adrenaline could make people do crazy things—like kiss traumatized teenage girls on impulse, apparently.

But what's your excuse? she wondered. Looking back, she hadn't been confused or conflicted. Definitely not *sorry*, either. Being with him had felt *right*—and that was the scary part.

"I think you might be wearing a hole through the marble—" She flinched as a hand came down to gingerly grab the cloth she'd been scrubbing the countertop with. "I'll just put this over here," Micha added, tossing the rag in the sink before she could protest.

They were in McGoven's narrow kitchen. Wearing a mud-stained pair of sweatpants, Micha looked like he'd just come from outside and was in desperate need of a shower. Instead of rushing to change, he leaned against the fridge and crossed his arms. Despite the casual stance, his green eyes were unusually sharp, devoid of their playful gleam.

"You've been scrubbing the same spot for an hour." He nodded to her wet, pruned fingers. "Wanna talk about it?"

Loren turned away, feeling her cheeks flame. He was right. While she couldn't comment on the amount of time that had passed, she wouldn't have been surprised if it had been more than an hour.

"Ignoring your problems isn't healthy," Micha playfully scolded. "You can talk to me, you know."

With a sigh of defeat, Loren shrugged. True to his word, Micha didn't look judgmental—merely exhausted. Mulling over the complexities of a kiss with him wasn't very appealing, though. "Talk about what?"

"Everything."

That word wasn't vast enough to encompass the various dilemmas weighing on her mind, impromptu kiss aside. She still needed to reconcile what it meant to be lupine, not to mention her father's death, and the question of her paternity. Add to that what happened with Naomi—according to Bill, she was home resting, but it was only a matter of time before she would return. Then what?

Loren couldn't stop dwelling on the possibilities—and, so far, her usual method of distraction hadn't worked. It was only mid-afternoon, and she'd cleaned the kitchen twice. Done the dishes and mopped up the mud stains by the front door. Wiping down the counters had been a last-ditch diversion.

It hadn't worked. While she barely knew Micha, she was afraid she might explode if she didn't talk to *someone*.

Meeting his stare, she blurted out the first question to come to mind. "What do you know about him?" A pointed glance toward the window, in the direction of the trees, conveyed just who she referred to.

"Bill?" Micha wrinkled his nose. "That depends on what *you* know," he muttered under his breath. "But, back where I'm from—the pack, I mean—he's considered something of a legend."

"A legend?" Loren had a hard time picturing it. Sure, McGoven was brave, and maybe a little larger-than-life at times, but he seemed way too closed-up to inspire any legendary tales. In fact, when he wasn't sprouting black fur, he seemed boringly normal.

"Are you kidding?" Micha's eyes widened, and his usual exuberance returned in full. "Yeah. He's a *legend*. The young pup plucked from the crowd by the Alpha himself and groomed to lead. That's almost unheard of. Even more insane was what happened in the end. The guy had everything and just walked away from it all… I never met him in person before a few days ago, though. Just heard the rumors."

His cheerful grin fell flat. Going off his expression, those rumors weren't all positive. Loren felt a twitch of apprehension run down her spine—quickly followed by a stronger sense of greed. She needed to know.

"What kind of rumors?" As she spoke, her gaze returned to the window, once again hunting for a head of dark hair among the endless green. In a few more hours, it would be exactly a full day that he'd been gone. Presumably, he was patrolling for danger, though Loren suspected his real motivation was far more trivial— he was avoiding her.

"Just…stuff," Micha said, deliberately skirting the question. "Maybe, you should ask him?"

Ask him. Loren would have scoffed if she weren't so tired. Last night, she'd had the longest conversation with the man since meeting him, and she felt more clueless than before.

And even more confused.

"I wouldn't be asking you if I could ask him," she admitted in a small voice.

Her imploring stare seemed to tip Micha over the edge.

"Okay, I'll cave." He inched closer and cocked his head conspiratorially toward hers. "Rumor has it that he was set to take over when the old Alpha, Lukas, died—not Lukka, the guy's own son. Then there was an attack by hunters on the outskirts of the property. McGoven wasn't fast enough to respond, and as a result, his own mate was..." He grimaced and drew a finger across his throat. "McGoven stepped down after that and left the pack altogether. I'm not sure what exactly he did to become a rogue, but he's been on the outside ever since. I don't know if he could return to Black Mountain, even if he wanted to."

Mate. He said that word with the same reverence as another term Loren heard in reference to McGoven. A wife. Emma.

"He left behind a lot to move all the way out here," Micha added. "I don't think I can name anyone else who would willingly walk away from the position of leader in exchange for...this."

"Why are you here?" she asked, curious. "You haven't gone back to the pack either. Does that make you a rogue, too?"

Micha blinked as if the idea hadn't crossed his mind. "I don't know. Though, I will admit that it seems pretty interesting here so far. Things in the pack can be so boring. Safe, ya know. We don't have nightly ambushes, that's for damn sure."

In response to her blank expression, he flashed a sheepish grin. "Not funny?"

Loren shook her head, thinking of McGoven out pacing the fields. "Not funny."

"Well, I'll tell you what *is* funny," Micha began. He stood back and ran a hand through his thick hair while his eyes flashed wickedly. "You're right. I'm kind of a rogue myself. I never thought about it until now, I guess." Grinning, he puffed out his chest and placed his hands on his hips like a caricature of Superman. "I don't really belong to a pack either. Lukka hasn't accepted me fully yet, meaning I'm more or less a free agent."

"Why not?" Loren asked.

Given how McGoven stressed the importance of *her* joining a pack, she couldn't understand how Micha could be so nonchalant about not belonging to one.

His cheerful grin slipped. "It takes a while to integrate as an outsider. I came in on kind of a trial basis. I don't have a ranking yet—a place in the hierarchy. I'm more or less at the beck and call of everyone else."

He hid it well, but the sadness in his voice was evident. Loren recalled what little of his past he revealed during their ill-fated trip to Black Mountain. "You said that your dad was an Alpha?"

Micha nodded. "I'm a transplant. From Virginia, born and raised. My sister and I belonged to our father's pack, but he died."

His tortured expression gave her the feeling that he had fonder memories of his father than she did of Fred Connors. Considering how hazy her memories were, that wasn't much of a stretch.

"I'm sorry—"

"Don't be," he said tightly. "It's *life*. He ran the pack fairly. There's nothing to be ashamed of. Let's just say that after his death, the transition didn't go so smoothly. When he died, I got pushed out, but I was too young to put up much of a fight—" He made a "so what" gesture with his hands.

"My sister and I got separated. I came north, she stayed south—didn't want to leave our dad's territory—and I've been kind of bouncing around since then."

The whole time he spoke, he kept his smile, but as the minutes wore on, Loren figured it was more out of habit than anything else. His pain was obvious.

"I'm sorry," she repeated. As cruel as her life had been, she had no idea what that felt like—having a family member out there, lost.

"Don't be. Violet can take care of herself—" He chuckled. "I know I should probably say something along the lines of—*you remind me of her*—but you don't. You're the complete opposite. She's loud and bossy, and she would *never* in a million years let someone—"

He broke off abruptly and changed tack. "She's a firecracker, and you're not."

"So, what am I then?" Loren fully expected him to drop some lame, cheesy line to make her feel better.

"You're different," he said finally. He inclined his head, casting her a searching glance. "More like a brushfire, I think. Slow to start, but in the end just as bright as a firecracker." He winked, and Loren couldn't help the smile that tugged at the corner of her mouth.

"Ah! A smile!" He reached out to trail the length of her chin with the flat of his thumb. "I didn't think you had one in ya—"

Don't let him touch you like that! The thought tore through her mind, like a slap. She flinched, jerking on the balls of her feet.

"You okay?"

"F-Fine," she stammered. Inside, she felt anything *but* fine. Her heart was pounding, and her skin prickled where he touched her. But not in a good way. Not good at all.

"Maybe you should get some sleep? I know you didn't get much last night." Micha pursed his lips into a sheepish frown. "I heard you tossing and turning. It sounded like one hell of a nightmare."

A prickling heat crept over Loren's cheeks. "It's n-nothing," she stammered, turning to face the sink.

"You want to talk about it?" Micha asked. "I get bad dreams sometimes, myself."

Again, it was a tempting offer—only there was nothing to talk about. The nightmare had been the same one plaguing her since she first woke up in McGoven's house. It was hard to describe— endless darkness and a feeling of ruthless pursuit, though she never saw the culprit's face.

Her mind was probably just processing the residual shock of her father's death. That night was still hazy. Supposedly, he'd been killed by debtors, but…

Loren couldn't shake a shadowy whisper at the back of her mind that warned the explanation was a big fat lie.

"Hey! Earth to Loren." She glanced over to find Micha jerking his head toward the stairs. "I mean it. Go sleep. You've been up all morning. I heard you get up well before dawn. You must be exhausted. A nap won't kill you. I'll keep watch. And if you were worried about the…uh, mess from the other night, I took care of it while you were cleaning in here." His sheepish grin conveyed a sense of pride despite the grisly topic.

"Thanks." Loren took a step and hesitated. "I really should do the dishes…" Or maybe the chore was just another excuse to stay awake. At least until McGoven came back. Before she could finish the statement, a yawn ripped from her chest, and she found herself stumbling into the foyer anyway.

Rather than head up to that big empty bed, she entered the living room. She collapsed onto the armchair across from the couch—which repulsed her, even cleaned of Naomi's blood. As her eyes drifted shut, a part of her stubbornly remained alert.

Waiting for him to return.

*S*he *was running. Her chest heaved as if her heart might explode from it, but she couldn't stop. Not ever.*

He was coming, and there would be no escape…

The sensation of the world shifting beneath her jolted Loren awake, but one realization kept any fear at bay. Heat. Pleasant warmth engulfed her, radiating from the body of someone strong enough to hold her suspended in their arms. Those two details alone narrowed down the potential list of suspects, not that she had the energy to be alarmed.

"You two can get some sleep," someone called. "I'll keep watch." The chirpy voice sounded far enough away that she knew Micha couldn't be the owner of the heartbeat surging beneath her cheek. Intrigued, Loren stirred sleepily, peeling one eye open.

She couldn't see much—just a corner of the living room drenched in shadow.

"It will only be for an hour or so," a man replied in a voice rumbling through her skin. "Then, I'll go out again."

"Do you really think they'll come back?"

"Don't know. Eislanders are unpredictable. If they do return, I'll be ready."

"Me too! I'll shout if I see anything,"

"Fine," the speaker holding her replied. "But...I don't really have to threaten that if you go running off to the pack, it will be the last thing you ever do, do I?"

"Nope!" Loren could picture Micha emphatically shaking his head. "But murderous insinuation noted, regardless."

McGoven didn't reply—because who else's voice could affect her so viscerally? Instead, he just made a sound of agreement in the back of his throat. Then, heavy footsteps echoed in tandem as she turned—or rather, the person *holding* her turned—and headed for the stairs.

It seemed to take forever for her eyes to adjust to the faint, gray daylight creeping in through the windows. She could smell musk, sweat, and pine—a scent that seemed more familiar than her own these days.

Finally, the person holding her set her down, so gently that she barely felt the impact of her body hitting a familiar mattress. With a sigh, they dragged the top sheet over her, tucking it in, and Loren went still, squeezing her eyes shut. If the past was any indicator, he would leave next, probably to go camp out on the couch.

Suddenly, the mattress squealed beneath the weight of a heavier, muscular body that settled in, right beside her. Before she could adjust, an arm went around her waist, dragging her closer. While her heart raced in alarm, the halfhearted embrace seemed more comforting than anything else. The same way a dog might curl up against another for warmth.

Warily, she opened her eyes again, twisting around to face him directly.

He wasn't asleep. *Caught,* was the expression that flickered through those gray eyes.

"You're awake." He sounded so exhausted she had to resist the urge to yawn just looking at him. "Good. It's about time we talked."

2

He watched her from beneath that curtain of damp black hair but made no other move. He might not have been able to. Coming face to face with him drove in just how long he'd spent outside. Mud streaked him from head to toe. Beneath his usual scent, he reeked of sweat and musk—though Loren found herself breathing in the primal scent, anyway. It meant he was really here. She wasn't dreaming.

"Go back to sleep," he told her, moving to get up. "I'll sleep on the couch—"

"No." She beat him to it, lurching upright first. "If anyone needs the sleep, you do. I'll go downstairs."

She tugged the sheets from her legs and scrambled to the edge of the bed. The second her feet hit the floor, he was already dragging her back by the wrist. In one smooth motion, he maneuvered her onto her side, with her back facing him.

"If I left," he began, applying just enough pressure to keep her pinned, "would you stay?"

Loren didn't have to think it over. "This is *your* bed—"

"Thought so," he said, cutting her off. He held her down for so long her arm started to go numb. Then…with another sigh, he released her.

"Fine." The mattress groaned beneath his weight, and Loren turned, expecting to find him slipping through the door. Instead, he faced her with his head resting on the pillow. One eye was fully open while the other drifted shut.

"I don't have the energy to compel you," he said. Compel? It was a strange word. Did he mean order her? That made sense—he looked barely capable of carrying on a conversation without passing out.

"Though," he added, "I doubt that you would listen anyway."

Something in his tone made a part of her flare in agreement —*Damn right.*

He raised an eyebrow, appearing to read her mind. "Well, then, it seems we're at an impasse."

He lifted his arm and made a "do as you wish" motion with his hand. Then he closed his other eye—but Loren wasn't fooled. His posture was way too tense.

When she laid down with her back to him, she half-expected him to crash through the mattress like a lead weight. For a few seconds, he went silent, presumably asleep.

"You could have slept here last night," he said finally, dropping the charade. "You didn't have to stay downstairs."

She lifted one shoulder in a shrug. "I wanted to wait up. In case…"

"In case what?"

"In case those men came back."

He exhaled heavily. A heartbeat later, his voice dripped directly into her ear—he'd shuffled even closer. "You know that I would never let anyone hurt you. Don't you?"

The heat in his tone threw her off. Made her shudder, even as one question burned through her mind. *Why?*

The way he protected her seemed more than just out of duty. *More* than him being a concerned citizen aiming to get his good deed in for the day.

You don't track a stranger for five hours for the hell of it, she thought. Not only that… But, no one would kill for someone else on a whim.

He went silent for so long Loren figured he might have fallen asleep for real. But, no—his heartbeat pulsed so loudly she could hear it.

Thump…thump…thump.

"I'll make you a deal," he said, proving her right. "Give me three days. Three days with no questions. Three days where you *listen* to me—" He sighed again, so deeply that the warmth was like a blowtorch against her shoulder. "And then I'll tell you everything."

"There's more." It wasn't really a question.

There were a million subjects she wanted to ask about. Lycans. Questioned paternity. Having her entire world turned upside down, on its head. When stated plainly, it almost seemed doubtful he could adequately answer them all.

"There's more," he admitted. "But if you trust me, and give me those three days… There won't be anything else that I haven't told you. I promise you that much."

His grim tone didn't make it sound like such a prize—*I'll tell you —but it's bad, and you won't like it.* Still, it was better than nothing.

"Three days." She mulled it over, wondering what else she had to lose. "Okay. But you can't order me to leave—especially not there."

"Black Mountain," he surmised, naming the location he'd unceremoniously tried to have her shipped off to.

"Yes," she said. "You can't ship me away. Not now."

"Deal." His voice was softer, barely a whisper. "But, for three days, *you* trust me. No questions asked."

Haven't I already been doing that? Before she could voice the thought out loud, he was asleep—she knew without having to turn around. His breathing changed, tickling the back of her throat in a slow, steady rhythm. Something told her that it was the first time he'd drifted off in days.

If only it could be so easy for her.

3

She was running. Panting. Falling. With every stumble, he was gaining. Soon, there would be no escape.

He'd silence her forever…

Loren's eyes flew open. As harsh daylight stabbed at her vision, she groaned, more exhausted than when she first laid down. Blindly, she reached for another pillow—only, she felt *heat* instead of fabric. Panicked, she lurched upright, gaping at the figure lying beside her.

He looked tense even while asleep. There were some hints of softness, though. His jaw was more relaxed, and, for once, those black curls freely fell over his forehead, rather than be ruthlessly slicked back. That alone transformed him.

He looked so much younger, not that he seemed very old in the first place. Older than *her*, definitely—mid-twenties, maybe? Thirty at most. It was so hard to tell when he rarely deviated from a frown. In fact, Loren wondered—if she reached out right now and touched him—would he feel like stone, hard and cold to the touch?

Fingers shaking, she did. The pad of her thumb brushed the corner of his jaw, so gently that it barely counted as "touching" at all. Even so, she sucked in a breath. He was…soft. His skin had a gentle amount of give to it. Like silk.

In response, he made a wordless sound and turned, rolling onto his side—but his arm flew out, catching her across the waist. Loren froze. Her heart pounded as she waited for him to wake up, but he never did. If anything, he just shifted closer, burying his face into the pillow.

The touch reminded her of a little kid reaching out to snuggle a toy bear. But something told her that—though maybe not for a while—he was used to sharing this bed with something other than a toy. A woman—Emma.

Someone he didn't have to be guilted into sleeping beside.

At the sobering thought, she shifted, gingerly easing herself out of reach. Her feet hit the cold floor with a shudder, and she took off, tiptoeing into the hallway.

Downstairs was silent. Micha was gone, most likely out patrolling. Fortunately, she found plenty with which to distract herself—a pile of dirty clothes waited by the door, and someone had tracked mud across the foyer.

With a sigh of relief, Loren went searching for a mop. While living in Fred Connors' house, she'd fallen into the same defensive routine. As long as she cooked and cleaned, she didn't have to think, or listen to the little voice at the back of her head screaming at her to run.

Lost in the rhythm, she moped the entire first floor. The clothes, she tossed into an empty hamper she found inside what seemed to be a small laundry room near the back of the house.

Afterward, she drifted into the kitchen, desperate for a new distraction.

On impulse, she snatched the carton of eggs from the fridge. Just as she started to crack one, a knock rattled the front door. Several more followed, increasingly incessant. *Tap, tap!*

She froze. Was it Micha? Or someone else…coming back to finish what they'd started two nights ago? But why come knocking on the front door?

Besides, a quick glance out the window didn't reveal anything out of the ordinary. Naomi's pink car was still in the driveway, stuck in the same spot it had been since the night of the storm. There were no hordes of murderous men, or wolves, prowling hungrily on the front lawn.

And if they had come…Micha was still out there. Wouldn't he have warned them?

Heart pounding, Loren turned away from the sink and moved cautiously for the door. She opened it mid-rap, and came face to face with someone who, in another life, *could* have been Naomi Tanner.

She was pale, her face devoid of expensive makeup. Her highlighted blond hair was pulled back into a bun, and a gray tracksuit and mud-stained sneakers replaced her designer clothing and heels. If Loren had to guess, the girl had walked all the way here from New Walsh.

"Is…*he* here?" she asked, in a voice that wasn't laced with bitchy undertones.

Loren blinked. "W-who?"

Naomi fidgeted with the collar of her jacket while eyeing the floor. "*Him.*"

"He's sleeping," Loren blurted. But that was beside the point. She knew damn well that Naomi wasn't here bearing gifts of good fortune.

There was a scratch on her left cheek, opposite the scabbed-over marks Loren's nails had left. Beneath her tracksuit jacket, she wore a gray top with a high turtleneck to cover her throat.

The strangest change of all was in her *eyes*. That hazy green seemed brighter, greener, than before. They had the same, odd glow to them that Micha's did, or McGoven's for that matter.

"Well, can I come in and wait until he wakes up then?" Naomi's voice lost that tired edge, regaining the snappiness Loren was used to.

"Yes…" Warily, she stood back and allowed the blond inside. Before closing the door, she scanned the fields for Micha, but caught sight of no one, wolf or otherwise.

She shouldn't have felt so disappointed, but the lack of anyone else meant she had no choice but to face Naomi alone. The girl in question lingered awkwardly in the foyer. For a long time, they didn't speak.

"Are you one too?" Naomi asked suddenly. Her eyes darted around the room—anywhere but Loren's face.

"One of what?" It wouldn't score her any points to play dumb, but Loren couldn't resist the urge. Why make it easy? She wanted to hear her say it. Admit out loud that her happy teenage dream was over, and the real world had intruded.

Violently.

"A lycan." The blond peeked over her shoulder as if expecting McGoven to burst from the shadows. "Are you a lycan, too?"

Loren frowned. "Wolf" or "thing" she would have expected—but Lycan was *his* word.

"Yes," she said tightly. "I am."

Naomi bit her bottom lip. "He said you were. He said...that—" She broke off with a dry swallow, wringing her hands. When she glanced up again, those green eyes held an emotion that Loren figured the girl had never experienced in her life—fear. "So, can you?"

"Can I what?" Loren snapped. She felt guilty even before Naomi flinched back as if stung.

Why was she so defensive? Prickly? She had begged McGoven to turn Naomi, but now...

The sight of the girl irritated her. Or maybe it was just the knowledge that Naomi knew everything she did? Maybe even more. *Three-day rules don't seem to apply to her,* the shadowy part of her murmured.

"S-shift," the blond said weakly. "Can you shift too? He said I should ask you for advice on—"

A rush of emotion welled up in Loren so quickly, she rushed into the kitchen before she did something stupid—like scream. Approaching the counter, she grabbed a fresh egg with a vengeance, cracking it hard on the edge of a frying pan.

Despite the clamor, she still heard Naomi creep in after her.

"Well, *can* you?"

Crack! Went the sound of the butter sizzling in the heat, as Loren added a dollop to the pan and began to whisk the mixture with a fork. She was ruthless, scraping until the eggs resembled something more "whipped" than scrambled.

She made two more batches, utilizing the entire carton before starting on toast. As she reached for the loaf of bread on the counter, a pink-manicured hand snatched it away.

"I didn't ask for this!" Naomi's eyes were slits, her face mere inches from hers. "I'm not even sure what 'this' is! So don't you dare stick up your nose at me and act like this is my fault. You were always such a stuck-up little bitch, walking around with your nose in the air like you're too good for any of us."

Loren stumbled back. Not because she was intimidated by the tall blond but... Because her eyes darted automatically to the knife drawer, itching to grab something sharp.

Screw that, a part of her purred. *I don't need a weapon.*

"I'm going to wait in there," Naomi announced before flouncing into the living room. "The air's too bitchy in here. Pun intended."

Loren watched her go. Though, if she were being honest, she regretted wasting a whole carton of eggs more than snapping at the blond. At least until Micha stumbled through the back door an hour later and ate a majority of the food in one sitting, assuaging her guilt. His only reason for stopping was a grumbled realization that he should leave some for McGoven.

Then, he pulled up to the center island, spread his lanky body out over two stools, with his feet resting on one, and just watched her. Whatever he saw in her expression made him decide another talk was in order. "I saw you know who came back. How ya holding up?"

Loren darted for his plate before he had a chance to bring it to the sink himself.

"I'm fine," she lied, reaching for a washrag. "I just feel like... Like everyone is keeping something from me."

Shock nearly made her drop the plate on the floor. *Where the hell had that come from?*

She glanced back at Micha, but he just raised an eyebrow. "Like what?"

She didn't know the answer to that. "Something *big*," she settled on. Maybe why she couldn't "shift" like everyone else? Or why she couldn't remember a single thing about her father's murder?

Or why every single time she was around McGoven, a part of her wanted to...

Bite him? Kiss him? More? Hell, she didn't know.

She wasn't used to dealing with such a volatile range of emotions. Up until now, she had always excelled at keeping them locked up tight—but these days, it seemed as if everything was pouring out all at once. And she couldn't stop it.

"I just don't feel like myself anymore," she added half-heartedly.

In some ways, that was a good thing. Loren Connors wasn't the same meek little girl from a week ago. This new iteration wanted to punch something. Kick. Stomp her feet and screech for someone to tell her the truth.

Unfortunately for her, Naomi's presence was a lit match meeting dry tinder.

Three days, she tried to tell herself. He promised her that much. But since when did anyone keep their promises?

"Um." Micha cleared his throat. "I kind of meant...how are you holding up, with *that?*" He jerked his head toward the living room, where Naomi still sat, seething, on the couch. "New bloods can be a little prickly. It's their emotions, you know. They're all out of whack. Try not to take it personally. Their weird vibes can throw everything off. Especially if..." He flashed a sheepish grin. "There is already some unresolved tension going on."

Loren sighed and shook her head. *Don't even go there.* Naomi's presence irritated the hell out of her—only she didn't know why. Whenever she caught sight of that blond head peeking over the back of the couch, something in her *growled.*

"I need some air," she said finally, setting the plate down in the sink.

She slipped through the back door before Micha could react. In one long stride, she crossed the porch and headed straight toward the west field.

Her teeth chattered. The bitter cold made her instantly regret not grabbing her jacket and shoes. Ironically, the chill seemed to help her finally regain enough clarity to think—only it wasn't all happy, pretty thoughts.

She was frowning by the time she made it into the barn. Like always, Bunny, Esther, and Xavier greeted her the second she stumbled inside. They didn't seem too worse for wear, despite everything that had happened around them these past few days.

With a sigh, Loren worked the latch on the nearest stall, intending to slip inside and disappear, like she used to when seeking an escape from her father.

Before she could even get the door open, a shadow fell across the floor. The horses grunted their alarm, nearly drowning out the deep voice that echoed throughout the wide space.

"You okay?"

She looked back, unsurprised by the figure standing in the doorway, hands carefully at his sides. He had showered, swapping out the mud-stained clothing for a clean pair of jeans and a sweater. Her belly flipped at the sight. He didn't require fangs and fur to seem intimidating.

"I…I thought you were sleeping," she stammered.

Despite the freshened appearance, he still looked exhausted. His hair was a rumpled mess, and he yawned, even as he shifted to reveal something he held in one hand.

"It's kind of hard to sleep amid tension," he explained.

Loren flushed crimson. Obviously, he had heard everything that happened between her and Naomi. He didn't seem to hold a grudge, though.

"Here." He extended his arm, offering what she realized was another windbreaker, in black this time. "It might snow."

"Can you tell?" she wondered out loud. When she glanced through the doorway, the sky was the usual dreary shade of gray.

He shrugged and took a small step closer. "It's a combination of moisture in the air and the temperature. You'll be able to pick up on it eventually."

Loren doubted that. She couldn't smell anything but pine. Still, she took the windbreaker and slipped it on without comment. He wasn't wearing a jacket himself, though—not that the cold seemed to affect him. Standing there on bare feet, he didn't even have the decency to shiver.

"Come here—" He surprised her by jerking his head toward the front of the barn, but his voice lacked the urgency of an order. "I…I want to show you something."

Loren inched closer, but he only pointed to the tack supply hanging on the nearby shelves.

"Look under the crate over there."

She did and found something that made her gasp—a black riding helmet. Ignoring his effect on the horses, the helmet was way too small for someone of his size anyway. When she tried it on at his urging, it fit her well enough.

"Grab that saddle over there, the one in the middle—yeah." He nodded when she hefted the leather seat. "Put it on the rack. Now grab the tack and bridle…like that."

When she set everything aside like he told her, he inclined his head toward Esther's stall.

"Bring her out—clip on the lead. Be gentle…good."

He talked her through saddling the horse. Told her how to secure the straps and make sure they weren't too tight. Then when she finished, he turned and headed for the paddock. A wave of his hand was her only indication to follow.

Confused, she led Esther out after him and into the enclosed field.

It was small, with a patch of dirt in the center just big enough to ride circles in. The sight almost reminded her of the pony ride course at the fair, where ten dollars bought you a few laps.

"I know you can *mount* a horse," McGoven began, watching her from across the gate—far enough away that Esther didn't seem to be affected by his scent. "But let's see if you can start off in something a little steadier than a full gallop."

4

There was a time for primal instinct. For hunting and fighting and embracing the thrill of battle.

Unfortunately, a good leader also made time for politics—even if it meant parlaying with the leader of a greedy band of rivals hellbent on taking more than their fair share. Luckily for Eric Lannister, he wasn't Alpha and therefore not responsible for the nitty-gritty of said actions.

He merely had to stand and watch. Though, sometimes, he found it more infuriating than if he had to hammer out peace agreements himself.

"You are the one who advocated for action," Lukka Grehmaine snarled. With his arms crossed, blue eyes narrowed, he resembled a scowling pup more than a leader. "Yet you give McGoven even more time to surrender. How much longer are you going to cower to a rogue and his aggression?"

Eric knew he couldn't keep his disgust from showing.

Loreck, on the other hand, excelled at diplomacy almost as well as physical prowess. He sat behind the ornately carved desk in the central room of the main lodge. This wooden structure in the heart of their territory served as the root of all commerce and guidance for those in the Eislander pack.

From Lukka's haughty grimace, he wasn't impressed.

"You forget that presumably, I am the one with an actionable grievance against McGoven, not you," Loreck pointed out, his tone level. "Considering that you refused to accept the mated female initially, she was never integrated into your pack. Therefore, you have no claim over any crimes committed against her. I will lead an assault on McGoven when I decide to."

"Then you might be too late," Lukka countered. "He might kill again while you hesitate."

Eric couldn't silence a growl and surged forward, leaving his position in the corner of the room. One look from Loreck stopped him in his tracks.

"McGoven is the least of the concerns plaguing my pack," Loreck continued, addressing the upstart before him. "For instance… I am far more concerned about the increasing rate of perfusion between my border and yours. Our hunting lands are being depleted at a rate we have never experienced. It's almost as if the mouths our resources feed has doubled within the past year."

Eric had to give Lukka some shred of credit—the bastard didn't flinch, even while being presented with his own transgressions.

"It sounds like stray humans," he said dismissively. "Your pack has a history of tension with the nearby towns from what I hear."

"I doubt a few hundred farmers and laypeople could encroach onto my territory so stealthily," Loreck said coldly. "Your point stands. McGoven will be dealt with. In the meantime… I suggest you watch your borders carefully, pup. I won't tolerate an outright invasion for long."

Lukka said nothing before leaving, his entourage in tow.

Eric watched him go, more irritated than he figured he had the right to be. Even so, the unease persisted, nagging like an itch he couldn't scratch.

Something was off amid this entire mess with the Black Mountain wolves and their wayward rogue.

And he longed to get to the bottom of it.

5

Fuck, she made him reckless.

The Eislanders were at his throat. Lukka didn't seem to give a shit. He was still convinced Kyle had abandoned Loren in enemy territory on purpose—a capital offense. Not to mention that he had two young females and an unaffiliated rogue crashing on his property.

And yet, here he was…giving riding lessons. The strange part? Even as the cons mounted, he didn't feel remotely inclined to do anything else. This was a long time coming.

He'd bought that damn helmet at a thrift shop a few months back. *Not for her,* he told himself then. He had always thought about selling or renting out those horses—anything to get them exercise. It only made sense that he should toss in some supplies for the new owners…

But a helmet in *her* size, exactly? Bought only a few days after he first noticed her on his property?

Besides, he had been telling himself that lie about selling the horses for years and never acted on it. It was time to admit that those animals were stuck with him, whether they liked it or not, and that he had picked out the stupid helmet with only *her* in mind.

Seeing her finally wear it, he couldn't really bring himself to regret it. He had suspected she would love to ride, but witnessing that joy for himself was…

Indescribable. She couldn't hide her excitement. For once, her mouth wasn't wrinkled with worry, but flat in an expression of calm that made something in him ache to see her smile. Her body wasn't tense with anticipation or fear, but loose and languid as she easily adjusted to the rhythm of the saddle.

It was dangerous, letting her near those animals, considering what she was, but a part of him had to admit that they didn't seem to sense the predator lurking within her.

Oh, but *he* could.

The scent of her unease had jolted him out of a deep, dreamless sleep. Anger gave a dark edge to her already strange aroma—an animalistic, primal flavor that had a part of him humming in appreciation, even as his body throbbed with a need he couldn't ignore.

It was instinct—a male called by the strength of a female.

When she finally came into her own, she would be…

Not his. The thought had him gritting his teeth in irritation—but tough shit. He had already made up his mind. The night of the attack was the final straw. Seeing her in danger shattered any resolve he had left.

He couldn't protect her here for long. After sleeping on it, he'd made his choice. The best course of action was to train her to hold her own. Teach her as much of their ways as he could in three days. Then he would break the bond and deal with whatever fallout came after. It was better than the alternative, if not ideal—Loren needed the safety of a pack. She needed a *real* Alpha to tame the wolf she would become—not to mention, protect her, should the Eislanders return. Once her safety was no longer an issue, Bill was more than willing to face his judgment.

On his terms.

He felt his eyes narrow as he watched Loren circle the paddock. She had a willowy ease in the saddle that was almost unnatural. He had never seen anything like it. Like her…

The difference from the frightened, bruised girl he'd found huddled at the edge of his property was stark. She was stronger than she thought she was. Strong enough to handle the truth.

And strong enough to withstand the shattering of the mating bond—even if he wasn't. It affected him in ways he couldn't ignore. Made him do things…like curl up beside her merely because some greedy part of him craved her heat, her warmth.

Her scent.

He still had that damn dress she had been wearing that night in the woods. That nightgown. It was locked in his truck, hoarded like some pirate's treasure under the passenger seat. At the back of his mind, he knew it was creepy. Wrong. Sick. But that didn't help the urge to keep a part of her—any piece he could…even if it happened to be mud-stained, torn, and covered in blood.

She's mine, the possessive thought raced through his entire body like a pulse as he watched her circle the paddock for the hundredth time.

He tried to rationalize her youth, her innocence—all those delicate little details that humans liked to harp over. The beast in him just scoffed. "Rules" or "facts" or what was socially proper didn't matter to a lycan. They relied on instinct—fate.

And *fate* claimed that she was *his* the moment she unknowingly slipped onto his property. *His* the second he found her, traumatized and scared in the woods, desperate to take her own life. *His* when she marked him, sinking her teeth into his flesh, in a primal form of possession.

That kiss—despite how he might spin it—hadn't been a damn mistake. For that one, brief moment, he had *finally* been in control. The lycan instinct had broken free of its leash and claimed what it wanted. And her reaction had been unanticipated...

Don't go there, he told himself as she trotted past.

She was too busy concentrating on keeping her balance that she didn't see how he flinched, as her scent hit him like a punch in the gut. He leaned forward anyway, gripping the wooden fencing until his knuckles ached.

It wouldn't do him any good to wonder what she might feel for him, if anything at all. Her emotions were warped by the bond. Twisted. Besides, she wouldn't be here for much longer.

Like a grim herald of what was to come, he heard the distant sounds of gravel crunching under tires. His body tensed as he turned toward the main road, and a list of potential intruders marched through his mind. Lukka? The Eislanders? Someone else who wanted him dead? There were plenty of enemies to choose from these days.

When the black car zoomed into the driveway, he assumed it was the first of the three options. Thankfully, the slender figure exiting the driver's side was *not* Lukka.

"This is a surprise," he called while crossing the field in her direction. From the corner of his eye, he saw Loren remain mounted in her saddle.

"So nice to see you're still alive," Sonia called, slamming the door behind her.

Uh-oh. Her cheeks were flushed, blue eyes flashing as she marched toward him. In all the years they'd known each other, Bill had rarely seen her so angry. Despite the petite mortal frame, she was *all* wolf. And she was pissed.

"Do you have any idea how worried I've been?"

Smack! The flat of her hand connected hard with the side of his face, but Bill was already turning to confront another threat.

"Loren, no!"

Quicker than he knew how, she had dismounted, already bolting from the paddock. The second his shout reached her, she faltered, staring down at her hands as if she had no idea why they were balled into fists.

"Do you have any idea what you've done?" Oblivious to the sight, Sonia was still shouting in his ear. "Do you have any idea what will happen to you? BILL, ANSWER ME!"

A shadow flickered in his peripheral vision.

"Sonia—" Desperately, he scanned his surroundings for a way out—and found one.

Micha had scrambled out onto the porch, and Bill jerked his head in Loren's direction.

"Get her inside."

The kid lurched into action, bounding across the yard to intercept Loren before she could reach the road. In the distance, the abandoned horse shrieked and darted into a corner.

Bill just hoped that the animal wouldn't try to jump the fence, but he couldn't worry about it now. With a heavy sigh, he turned to Sonia, who glared at him, tears streaking down her cheeks.

"Ignoring repeated direct calls? Do you know how worried I've been? How hard it's been to talk Lukka out of sending an entire unit out to you?" she demanded, a hitch in her throat. "What happened? Why on earth would you attack an Eislander?"

Bill sighed. "It's a long story, but we can start with the fact that while I *did* kill—" He raised his hand as Sonia began to speak. "It wasn't an Eislander, that's for damn sure. I'm surprised Lukka sent you here to berate me for that. Considering that all this happened because he sent a minion to do his dirty work. What does he want now?"

"You got your wish," Sonia said coldly. "Loren's been accepted. I'm here to bring her back."

Bill figured he should have been relieved. Thankful? As it was, he only felt apathy. The events of the past few days had cemented the cold truth that his old life was far behind him.

"About that... I changed my mind."

Sonia blinked, raising an eyebrow. "What do you—"

"Loren's not going anywhere. *Yet*," he added through clenched teeth. "I owe a duty not just to her."

Sonia raised an eyebrow. "What do you mean?"

He took a breath. It was one thing to decide on a plan in his head, another entirely to voice it out loud. The second the words left his mouth, there would be no going back. "I'm going to petition Lukka to release me from all pack ties. Then I'm done. I'll head north, far beyond the territory. I'll push into Canada, even. He'll face no threat from me."

Sonia hid her shock, if any, well. Her only response was another question, "And Loren?"

Here came the tricky part, far more complicated than forsaking his entire life on a whim. "I'll break the bond and let her decide. After I teach her what she'll need to know to survive on her own. If she chooses to go to Lukka of her own accord, then so be it. But I won't force her."

He didn't even see the second slap coming.

"Have you lost your mind? Even I know that whatever is between you and Lukka goes beyond your standing as a rogue. He will never let you go. But you know that, don't you?" Horror dawned over her features, and Bill felt a pang of guilt. "Don't tell me… If he doesn't agree to sever ties completely, then… The only course of action would be to challenge him. Are you insane?"

It sounded so grim when put like that. "I plan to make him an offer he can't refuse," Bill said, eyeing the ground at his feet. "Win or lose, he can remain Alpha, but I get my freedom—no matter the cost."

"I know you can be stubborn, Bill, but I never thought of you as reckless! Do you even remember the terms that a challenge dictates? You need to face him first. Do you really think he'll risk meeting with you one on one? I'm sure you realized what I did— he sent Kyle for a reason."

"*Now* you admit that," he grumbled. "As for your insinuation, I may have been gone for a while, but I remember our customs well enough, thank you."

"Oh, do you? Then you won't mind if I refresh your memory," Sonia countered. "You meet him one on one. You issue the challenge—and he gets a full day to prepare. Let's not forget the witness, either—"

"I haven't," Bill snapped. Admittedly, his knowledge of pack law had gotten a little rusty. There were so many damn variables involved in issuing a rightful challenge.

"Do you think Lukka will honor that?" Sonia asked. "And who will serve as your witness? You know he would never allow me to do so, even if I wanted to—"

"Soni..." He looked up to find her watching him with an expression he couldn't decipher. "You've made your point."

But she wasn't done with him.

"Let's say it does come down to a challenge, and you win," she added. "To hell with the rest of us, right?"

"What I do shouldn't matter. Besides, I thought Lukka was a *good* leader?" He couldn't help the anger in his voice. "You sang his praises last time."

"Don't give me that! I knew that all it would take was the slightest hint of trouble for you to intervene. Despite all your talk, and your resentment toward us—"

"Not toward the pack," he clarified. "Never toward you."

Sonia flinched. "Well, I didn't tell you the whole truth. A part of me thinks I shouldn't. But before you take on Lukka you should have the whole picture."

"Tell me."

"It's a long story," she said tiredly. "He'll be waiting for me to call in. I'm meant to convince you to bring her back. I'll send word that it will take the rest of the day at least. Then we can talk. About everything."

"Before you head inside, there is something else you should know," Bill admitted. Gruffly, he reiterated the story of the Eislanders and Naomi's newfound status as a made.

Had he tried to predict Sonia's reaction beforehand, he wouldn't have come close.

She just sighed, utterly deflated. "Well, that kind of diminishes the chances that Lukka will just let you walk away," she said, but despair wasn't the emotion coloring her voice. No, Bill recognized that hard note, alright. "Good. Maybe that means I can convince you to seize this opportunity as more than a chance to run."

"I don't like the sound of that." Bill groaned. "Sonia... Don't tell me that you want to convince me to challenge Lukka for more than my freedom."

Sonia shrugged. "I'm going to try."

6

*L*oren said nothing as Micha all but dragged her into the house. Once inside, she headed straight for the bay window in the living room and…

Watched.

They were still by the car, yards from the house. Sonia was shouting, waving her arms through the air, while McGoven just stood there. They were practically toe-to-toe. Only a foot separated them but…when Sonia deflated, arms falling to her sides, he didn't hesitate to engulf her in his arms, holding her close.

No! A rage so intense it burned shot through Loren. She dug her nails into her palms just to keep from shouting. Screaming. It was the same impulse she felt when the woman had slapped him.

A need to fight. Defend. She couldn't recall ever *wanting* to get off the horse, but the next second, she'd been on the ground ready to—

What? she wondered helplessly. Hit her? *Attack* someone she didn't even know, just because the woman had the nerve to touch a grown man she had no hold over?

Yes, something inside of her growled, completely unashamed at the fact. *Mine—*

"Who is that?"

The sound of Naomi's voice was like pouring grease onto a smoldering fire. Utilizing her last shred of self-control, Loren moved as far from her as she could and bit her bottom lip so hard she tasted blood, just to keep from saying something nasty in return.

"That's Sonia Carlisle," Micha replied with admiration in his tone. "Her father was well-respected in the pack when he was alive, and she is a liaison for Lukka. That's probably why she's here—sending word from the pack. I wonder if they know about —" He seemed to stop himself from mentioning the attack or any of its relevant aftermath. "Actually, I think she grew up with McGoven. She's probably just here to see him. Rumor is, they're pretty close."

Only the relationship between them didn't seem so "close" now. Sonia broke away from his embrace, shouting, while McGoven frowned, replying to her intermittently with a nod or a shrug.

From his nonchalance, one might assume they were talking about something as trivial as the weather. But Sonia looked...

Terrified. Those blue eyes were wide, pleading with a desperation Loren could feel, even from inside the house. Whatever they were arguing about, it wasn't good. But that didn't give Sonia an excuse to lean against him, pressing her face into his shoulder.

"She his girlfriend or something?—"

The fact that Naomi spoke from halfway across the room was the only reason she didn't end up on the floor as Loren spun around. There wasn't a single thought in her head. Just the impulse to *hit* something.

"Hey! Whoa! Easy!" Micha darted in between them, quick as lightning. With both hands on her shoulders, he held her back. "Just take it easy."

His tone snapped something inside her. Heart pounding, she realized her nails were drawn—ready to do a whole lot more than scratch a pretty face this time. She wanted to kill.

The irrational anger surged through her veins unabated. She couldn't think. Couldn't breathe. The only logical thought she had left in her head was the knowledge that she was acting *insane.*

"What the hell?" Naomi had retreated to the corner of the living room, her eyes narrowed to slits.

Smart girl, something in Loren murmured darkly, relishing the fear in those green eyes.

"What the hell is your problem?"

Loren wanted to know the answer to that as well—what the hell *was* her problem? Why couldn't she even see straight? And why did the thought of Sonia, out there alone with McGoven, make her want to…

"I need air." She broke away from Micha, turned on her heel, and raced through the kitchen.

She wanted to run outside, fade beneath the trees, and hide until the strange emotions disappeared.

She barely made it past the foyer.

Slam! From the back of her mind, she knew that someone had barged through the front door, rushing straight in her direction. Before she could turn, a solid force dragged her back, spinning her around to pin her body against the side of the staircase.

Familiarity kept her from resisting. She just inhaled, breathing in pine. Just like that, all the anger…

Evaporated.

Though the newfound clarity might have had something to do with the man pressed against her so tightly she couldn't feel anything else?

He didn't say a word. He didn't have to.

He just stood there, with his hands braced against the wall on either side of her head. He wasn't close enough to completely block her in—not that she would move anyway.

"I leave you alone for five damn minutes…" His mouth was dangerously near her throat. Loren blinked as she remembered that he had been outside, yards from the house only a few seconds earlier.

He didn't look angry, though. That silver gaze just held her stare, as indecipherable as ever.

"Then, m-maybe you shouldn't leave me alone?" She didn't even have the strength left to feel embarrassed. A part of her relished challenging him, even in such a small way.

Until he eased back, enough for her to see Micha and Naomi watching from the living room.

Suddenly, that rebellious inner voice went silent in the face of shame. She turned to the stairs, desperate to hide.

"Wait—" His tone called her back before she could take a step. "We should talk. Get your shoes." He turned for the door, pausing only to swipe his keys from the hook, and grab a gray jacket and his boots. "I'll be out in the truck."

He wasn't asking.

She sighed, spotting her boots in the corner near the door. Aware of Micha and Naomi, she didn't even pause to put them on before slipping through the door after him.

She felt a hint of relief that Sonia wasn't anywhere in sight. Not in the field, not in that black car…and *not* in the passenger's seat of McGoven's truck.

Though why should I care if she were? she wondered. By the time she made it across the driveway, bare feet crunching over gravel, she hadn't come up with an answer. With a sense of dread, she opened the passenger-side door and climbed in, keeping her gaze lowered as she slipped her boots on one at a time.

McGoven drove without uttering a word and true to his prediction, fragile snowflakes began to speckle the windshield. Loren watched them fall as a tiny, apprehensive part of her wanted to ask where they were going. She kept her mouth shut, but she wasn't surprised when he parked in front of a crumbling, two-story ranch house at the end of a deserted block a moment later.

"Are you ready for this?" With a heavy sigh, he watched her from the driver's seat. Flurries drifted down from overhead, coating the hood of the truck. Eventually, he seemed to take her silence as an answer. "That's okay. I can—"

"I'm ready." Loren unsnapped her seatbelt, trying to ignore the fact that her fingers shook. Or the tiny little voice at the back of her mind screaming that she *wasn't* ready at all.

And that she never would be…

Still, it wasn't like she could turn tail and run now. It had been her idea to come here, after all.

"I'm ready," she repeated, slamming the door of the truck behind her—but she didn't know if she were speaking more to him…or herself.

"Okay." Face expressionless, McGoven led the way up the narrow concrete path, where a single ribbon of yellow caution tape dangled from the knob of the front door. Besides the splash of color, the place looked as dreary and cold as it had a week ago.

After fishing a set of keys from his pocket, McGoven unlocked the front door and looked back. "Are you coming?"

Loren realized that she was still on the curb. For once, something else held her attention other than him. The house looked the same. Empty, neglected, and cold. Had she really lived here?

"Loren?"

She could see him there, waving to get her attention. Out of habit, she lurched into motion. Then stopped. Every single time she tried to take a step, something held her back. A memory? The last thing she remembered was climbing up the stairs to go to bed…

"Loren—"

"I…"

She shook her head, turning on her heel, and…

Ran. The snow came down harder as she darted around the side of the house, into the backyard, as she skirted the porch, where the screen door swung on its hinges. If she were trying to get away, heading straight in the direction of *his* house wouldn't help her any. Before stepping on the path that cut through the woods, she turned, bracing herself against the trunk of a thick oak tree instead.

I can't do this. Whether it meant that she was weak, stupid, spineless—whatever. She couldn't step foot inside that house.

"Loren."

She wasn't exactly surprised when McGoven appeared, moving slowly as if expecting her to bolt at any minute.

"I'm sorry," she blurted. "I shouldn't have had you bring me all the way out here. I—"

"It's alright." He didn't even have to raise his voice for it to carry across the yard. "You're not ready yet."

Yet. At least he seemed optimistic. She wasn't. That house was like a dungeon, full of dark memories. Why unlock that gate?

"It's okay. I'll take you back."

"No." She shook her head. After spending the day cooped up with Naomi, Micha, and her confusing emotions, it felt good to be out in the open. Alone...

With him. She tried shaking her head to clear the thought, but it was still there clinging to the inside of her skull. *He belongs here,* a part of her insisted in a dark murmur. *With me. He's mine—*

"Do you want to wait in the truck?" He was closer now.

She could smell him. *More* than smell him—taste him, right there on the tip of her tongue. It was a scent that seemed way more natural than cologne and muskier than that crisp pine. Something sweet and wild and dangerous, all at the same time.

"No," she whispered, turning around to face him. "I..."

She trailed off as her eyes caught the jagged line of flesh right below his throat, partially hidden beneath the collar of his shirt. It looked grisly, more like the result of an animal attack.

But she knew the real cause—her. Horrified, she reached out. "I'm so sorry. I didn't mean—"

At her touch, he jerked out of reach, eyes flashing a shade so dark it was damn near black. *"Don't!"* The corner of his mouth twitched as if he wanted to say something else, but held himself back. Abruptly, he whirled on his heel, marching away. "I'll be in the truck."

"Wait…" In the end, Loren didn't really know what made her follow him—just a step. But he froze anyway.

Are you crazy? some rational part of her railed angrily at the back of her mind. She moved toward him regardless, cautiously slipping around that bulk to block his path.

She couldn't help it. Some sick, morbid curiosity infected her brain. Without hesitation, she fingered the fabric of his shirt, exposing the wound fully. It looked even worse up close. She could make out every individual tooth mark, etched into his flesh.

"It's nothing," he grunted, pulling back.

Liar, a part of her whispered. *It's everything…*

She let her hand fall, but she couldn't turn away. Because, even as she stared at the impression of her own teeth, cut into someone else's skin… She didn't feel one ounce of shame. Or guilt.

Mine.

The thought shocked her, and she took a hasty step back—but her foot never even touched the ground.

He moved so fast. His arm hooked around her waist, yanking her so close she had to brace her hands against his chest just to keep standing. Horror flashed in his gaze.

But he didn't pull away. Not even as her hands spread out tentatively over the hard, pure muscle of his chest.

What are you doing, Loren? the logical part of her demanded. *This is bad...*

But, it didn't *feel* bad. In fact, pressed against him, bathed in his heat, she felt better than ever. Warm, and so dizzy—like she could just give up right now and never even hit the ground.

Just float.

"I'm sorry," she repeated. She could only stare down at her fingers, pale against his tan skin. "I shouldn't have done that."

"Don't—"

"Does it hurt?" Without thinking, she let her fingers travel a fraction lower, amazed at the way he felt. Like stone, so damn solid. He barely seemed to breathe or move at all, even as delicate snowflakes melted against his skin...

At least, until he growled. The low sound broke from his throat, raising the hairs on the back of her neck.

She recoiled. Her hands had inched lower than she meant to, catching the two dark pink peaks that centered his pecks.

Uh-oh. Like a good girl who rarely interacted with the opposite sex, Loren knew that she should have turned and left him right then and there.

Hell, it seemed to be his way of handling things.

But she couldn't.

Mine. The thought was a fly buzzing around the inside of her skull, demanding acknowledgment. *Mine, mine, mine.*

"Loren…" As if from far away, she saw his hands gingerly encircle the fragile bones of her wrist—but he didn't brush her off. He just held her for so long that she finally forced herself to glance up at him through her lashes.

His eyes were *glowing,* as bright as moonlight. He looked confused. Torn. She could feel his hands twitching as if he wanted to let her go, but something deep inside wouldn't let him.

Loren figured it was the same, dark impulse that had her leaning up, pressing her mouth firmly against his.

Their lips met, and for that brief expanse of time, her entire world centered around *him* and nothing else.

Not the wind moving through the trees or the falling snow. Not his age. Not their situation, or the voices screaming at the back of her head that he was a grown man, and she was…

Stupid.

It didn't matter. Bold, her tongue slipped out, running along the seam of his, aiming to slip inside and—

"Stop!" He ripped his mouth from hers, shoving her back. "Loren, no. We can't."

Her heart sank as every argument against her attraction returned in full force. "I'm sor—"

He put a finger to her lips. "Will you *stop* saying that?" It was a plea, someone begging for torture to end. "You never have to apologize to me."

He just stared down at his outstretched finger, as if wondering why it was still there. She felt the pressure shift, slowly moving down from her mouth to cup her chin.

"If anyone should be sorry, it's me," he added, almost in a whisper.

She held her breath, feeling his hand move easily down her throat as if he'd memorized the slender curve.

"You have no idea—" Those fingers glided swiftly down her collarbone. "No idea…"

Yes, a part of her agreed whole-heartedly. He *should be sorry.* Sorry for stopping her. For holding her back. Especially because—despite all his insistence on stopping—he wasn't exactly slapping her on the wrist for being a naughty girl and dragging her back to the truck.

After eighteen years, Loren knew anger. She had spent months living in fear of that very emotion, glinting in her father's dark eyes.

She knew regret and pain.

And, in him, she didn't see a damn bit of either one.

Instead, he looked…

Hungry. His gaze centered on the column of her throat with an expression he couldn't hide. Like he wanted to bite. Tear. Lick. Mark her flesh the same way she'd marked him.

And she *wanted* him to.

The potential consequences didn't even cross her mind as she reached up, lacing a hand around the back of his head before he could stop her, dragging him down.

"Stop." He resisted, fighting to pull away. "Loren—"

No!

Impulsively, she seized his bottom lip between her teeth before he could, and tugged.

A sound like the roar of a jet engine broke from the back of his throat. He wrenched her closer, palming her waist, pressing her against his chest.

"Stop," she heard him whisper again—even as he brushed his lips over hers—but, considering how the next second his tongue plunged deep, it was kind of a moot point.

His mouth slanted against hers, but as his hands fanned out over her lower back, Loren sensed his true aim—not a kiss, but submission. He demanded it with every brush of his lips, and she couldn't find the strength to match his pace.

So, without an ounce of guilt, she bit down. Hard. The flavor of copper exploded over her tongue. Blood? His—and she relished the taste, greedily seeking out every single drop. Disgust didn't even cross her mind.

This felt right. Natural. The salty tang melded with the overall musk of him, creating a more visceral picture of who William McGoven was at his core. Someone dangerous. Virile. Wild.

A part of her recognized his strength and only wanted to prove her own in return. The bite wasn't a challenge but a warning. *Nobody will ever make me submit,* that shadowy voice at the back of her mind whispered—but he didn't have to.

She was already his. Body, mind, and soul. And he was hers.

He stiffened beneath the brutal assault, groaning in shock. She looked up to witness alarm flit through those silver eyes, right before a dark determination replaced it.

So you wanna play? That look warned her. *Let's play.*

The next second she was on the ground. He moved so quickly that her mind barely processed the motion of his leg sweeping out to rob her balance. Impossibly fast, he had her flat on top of a pile of damp leaves. Dead leaves. They smelled like rust, tangling in her hair the same way his fingers did. He fisted both hands within the thick strands to keep her pinned, uncaring as the weight of his body knocked the air from her lungs. His smell swamped her. She could feel his heart pounding in a steady rhythm that confounded her shock.

It wasn't the unsteady beat of someone experiencing regret or fear, or doubt. Nope. It was the steady thrum of a predator—one who knew *exactly* what it wanted. Her.

A blur of motion robbed her senses. All she knew was that her windbreaker was gone, tossed somewhere along the back of the house. She should have been freezing, but a raw heat displaced any chill. His mouth. Recklessly, he skimmed over her bare collar bone, finding her mouth again before he abruptly pulled back.

"No." Loren panted. "Don't—"

A deep, throaty growl ripped from his throat, silencing her instantly. Apparently, he wasn't the type to submit to anyone else, either.

That point, and more was proven as that silver gaze bore down on the tender skin of her throat. He moved slowly. So damn slowly, she felt about ready to scream when his lips finally feathered over a distended vein.

Her heart stopped beating. She stopped breathing. Every single nerve in her body seemed to hinge on the feel of the two warm lips spreading against her flesh, catching the thrum of her pulse.

Teeth next. Gingerly, he seized a bit of flesh, applying just enough pressure to sting. She gasped, throwing her head back to bare more of her throat to him.

But then he froze, wavering between the desire to pull back or…

Give in.

And, damn it, she was tired of him holding back. *Claim me.* The thought was so fierce Loren wondered if she'd said it out loud. Those silver eyes flashed as if she had, darkening to a shade identical to the sky overhead.

He needed to claim. Bite. Mark. Tear.

"Please." She slid her hand along the back of his neck, applying just enough pressure to let him know what she wanted. To make him…

Relent.

Suddenly, he surged, kissing her with the same ferocity she'd bitten him with. Her lips stung. Burned. It hurt. It felt… incredible. Adrenaline mixed with agony, feeding a giddy sense of triumph that she had pushed him to this. Driven him to this state.

Unhinged.

"Fuck." He hissed the curse against her open mouth, rearing back on his knees. Before disappointment could even settle in, his hands came down to settle over her hips. Higher, raking up the material of her shirt with every inch traveled, until…

Her chest became bared to him, heaving with the tumult of emotions washing through her. Excitement. Alarm. Some fear. The logical voice in her brain warned that he could see her bruises—the ones left by Fred Connors that had yet to heal.

Before she could think to shield herself, he noticed them. Heavy-lidded, his eyes skimmed over each and every one before settling over her face. His jaw tightened as another sound rumbled from his chest. Not quite a growl. More like an acknowledgment. *I see the damage done to you. You will explain.*

She nodded, feeling her entire body heat. It pooled in familiar places that only ever seemed sensitive around him. Her nipples she could feel hardening while exposed to the air. Inside her belly. Between her legs.

That ache was the most pressing. She had a sudden urge to rub her thighs together just to ease it. The second she tried to, he cocked his head, and she stilled. It was a warning. *Don't.*

Cautiously, one of his hands bridged the space between them, ghosting up her knee. As the contact registered, closing her legs became the furthest thing from her mind. She needed to spread them. Let him in. Let him…

"Bill!" The shout came from a distance, but sounded eerily familiar. A woman?

Loren froze. McGoven, however, was already on his feet, grabbing her wrist.

He barely managed to haul her upright before a breathless Sonia appeared through the gap in the trees. Judging from her frantic breathing, she'd run all the way here.

"Bill! Are you alright? I heard…" She trailed off, apparently realizing that McGoven—even as he swiped blood from his lip—wasn't exactly in mortal peril. "Growling," she finished awkwardly.

"It's fine, Sonia," McGoven grunted. "Go back. You too—" He didn't even look in Loren's direction. "I need to scout the perimeter."

Sonia frowned. "Bill, wait. We still need to talk—"

"Later." He darted into the woods without ever looking back.

"We'll talk tonight, then," Sonia called after him.

When the woman finally turned to her, Loren expected a barrage of questions. *What were you two doing out here? Why was he bleeding? Why is your jacket crumpled on the ground near the porch?*

But she didn't. Loren couldn't help feeling that Sonia knew damn well what she'd just interrupted. And she didn't like it.

"It's cold," she said softly, turning back along the path. "Let's get back."

Loren followed, but she couldn't stop herself from scanning the woods with every step, searching…

8

There weren't many things that Eric would classify as reaching a level of requiring discretion from even his own Alpha. The short of it was, he didn't trust Lukka. Not a fucking inch.

Loreck, being the leader of a pack bordering the bastard, needed to rely on a delicate balance of diplomacy and healthy skepticism. Eric, however, had no such limitations. He couldn't get the words of the rogue from his head. Or the girl…

Her presence made no sense, but he was beginning to suspect that some things about her weren't a coincidence. Her age. Her eye color. Her knack for demanding submission from wolves twice her size.

It was one thing to speculate. On the other hand, probing gossip was a step too far—and yet, Eric found himself leaving the pack borders under the guise of patrolling the perimeter anyway. An hour's drive, the town of Elkton lurked just outside the boundaries of Eislander territory.

Typically, there existed a strained peace. The lycans in the foothills kept to themselves, and the humans respected the large "nature reserve" nearby. No need for compulsion or bribes to go unnoticed.

Roughly nineteen or twenty years ago, things hadn't been so civil. Eric could remember the time vaguely—one of the few who'd ever entered the heart of the small town in person. His destination had been the same then as it was now.

The sheriff's office. The second he parked, someone was already exiting the building to greet him.

"This is a surprise," the man called. Balding, roughly sixty years old, he had been a patrol officer in those days. A gleaming badge affixed to his crisp shirt proclaimed that he'd been promoted since then. "I don't think I've seen you around these parts in over a decade. Eric, wasn't it?"

"Yes. And you are deputy—now Sheriff, it seems—Varl," Eric replied, impressed the man could recall his name. Some of the tension left his body as he continued to advance, sporting a strained smile that he hoped passed as genuine. "Morning. I wanted to know if you remembered an incident that occurred a few years ago involving a spate of murders in this area."

"Oh, the Dansforth killings. Of course, I do. Everyone around these parts does. Why would you want to bring up something like that?" The man raised an eyebrow, but Eric sensed no hostility.

Just curiosity. Apparently, that time had left its mark on the humans the same way it scarred his kind—though some details had been blurred throughout the years. What the mortals recalled as a serial killer had, in actuality, been a rogue belonging to a pack of vicious nomads.

"I wanted to know if I could look at those files," Eric said, still maintaining a smile.

It was a hunch, but it wouldn't stop niggling at his mind. The killings had brought unwanted attention to their territory. So much so they'd been forced to work with a band of outsiders to come to a resolution.

One of them had been a female, young, blond. He could barely remember her name.

But he could remember her attitude well enough.

"I could send them your way," the sheriff said. "You want anything in particular?"

"I do," Eric replied. "I would like all of it."

9

"*S*he marked you."

Bill wasn't surprised when, the second he tiredly mounted the back porch steps, Sonia appeared from the shadows.

It was just after sundown, but she looked as exhausted as if he'd been gone for days. Her hair hung loose and unbrushed, while she had arms crossed over her chest, lips pursed with an emotion he couldn't place.

"Where is she?" he asked, ignoring the question. *Close by.* His nostrils were already flaring, impregnated with her scent.

"Inside—" Sonia inclined her head toward the house. "I didn't answer any of her questions, if that's what you're worried about, but it's time that you do. She marked you," she repeated. "I saw it. Don't lie to me."

"I won't," Bill admitted. Hours of running and his head felt no clearer. If anything, the instinct Loren had unintentionally awoken was stronger than ever, howling for relief.

"How far did it go?" Sonia began tentatively. "Did you… Bill, please tell me you didn't give in to impulse. Please. Especially if you plan on cutting her loose! Have you stopped to consider how this will affect her? Have you?"

He grimaced. Three years his junior, and Sonia *still* had a way of making him feel like a kid about to get scolded.

"I wouldn't take advantage of her like that," he began.

Liar. The wound on his chest throbbed in disagreement—recalling the sting of her teeth, sinking deep. The primal beast within him still seethed at the challenge and craved to return the wound tit-for-tat. He'd come close. A groan escaped him at the memory of her skin, plush and pliable right between his own canines. If Sonia hadn't come when she had…

"Tell me," the woman prodded. "How far did it go?"

"She couldn't control it," he blurted, trying to rationalize it himself. "The bond is too strong. I should have never—"

"That isn't what I meant." Sonia advanced as he mounted the top step, barring his path. "I'm asking why did *you* let her?"

She could have punched him in the chest right then and there, and it wouldn't have hurt any less than that simple question. *Why?*

"I didn't," he insisted gruffly.

Liar, the wolf in him hissed. He could have compelled her to stop. Let her run off while her emotions were heightened. Bringing her to Connors' house in the first place was a risk—especially after her nerves were already frayed due to the presence of Naomi. He had pushed her too hard—she was bound to snap eventually. And, damn it, he had *wanted* her to. A sick, twisted part of him embraced her rage. Craved her mark.

And the sad part was…that even now, with Sonia staring at him horrified, he didn't feel one damn ounce of guilt. *Mine.*

"Do you know how much harder it will be for her now? For you?"

He frowned at her mournful tone. It was the same question he had avoided answering himself.

"It won't matter," he explained, shaking his head. "I'll tell her the truth. Teach her our ways. The more she learns, the easier it will be for her to understand why I did what I did."

Sonia didn't look convinced. She always wore her emotions on her sleeve. Currently, her frown was so pronounced it resembled a crescent moon. "You should get started, then. While you're at it, what exactly *do* you plan on teaching her?"

It was the million-dollar question.

"How to hunt," he said, choosing to list the safer topics first. "How to master her instincts. How to fight. Our customs, the most relevant ones, anyway. Our history."

"And the mating bond?"

After a pause, he nodded.

"And how will you explain abandoning her once you take on Lukka?"

He winced. "Low blow, Sonia."

"Is it?" She squared her chin, and he internally groaned, recognizing the stance. Like a dog with a bone, she wouldn't let this go. "Let's say you win and then decide to leave; she won't be welcome on Black Mountain. Especially if someone like Kyle takes over in the aftermath—"

"Don't even go there." The mere prospect irritated something inside of him, and he turned away, gritting his teeth. "I don't need that mental image."

"That's what could happen," Sonia countered. "Kyle or someone else just as ruthless and cunning. Can you imagine what state we'll be in after that?"

Bill grunted. It was a good question, recalling the truth she let slip earlier.

"I know you can only dance around the issue," he began. "But it's time to come clean. What's been really going on since I left?"

It was her turn to grimace. "Our territory has shrunk, for starters. No one will say why."

So much for her reluctance; he couldn't hide his shock. "Shrunk? What the hell do you mean?"

She shrugged helplessly. "What else? We used to find plenty of fish in our rivers. That's changed. Same with the deer. The bears. Even the birds seem fewer these days. It's gotten so scarce, in fact, that Lukka has all but given permission to push into Eislander territory to—"

"Encroachment," Bill snarled. The polite term for what was, in essence, stealing. It was unheard of. He wouldn't have believed the claim if Sonia didn't appear to be in physical pain. Breaking Lukka's trust to divulge this much must have taken monumental effort on her part. So, he softened his tone. "Seasonal shifts happen all the time. That doesn't necessarily mean mismanagement."

"I thought so, too," Sonia admitted. "But it's been three years, and it's getting worse. There's more—" Her eyes shifted toward the shadows as if she thought someone might be lurking within them, listening. "There was a forest fire a few years back. It was small, relatively contained. Only a few acres were damaged, and no one was injured. Afterward, the affected territory had been marked off as a forbidden zone, at least until the natural balance returned."

"That's protocol," Bill said. Out of tradition, they avoided wounded parts of the forest and allowed them to regrow with little disturbance.

"It's been years, but the ban hasn't been lifted. Rumors have run rampant, of course. Some of them claim that, in actuality, the land has been sold off. For development—"

"No." Bill couldn't believe it. Lukka was many things, but to sell off their ancestral lands? That was a step too far, even for him. "Do you have proof?"

Sonia shook her head. "Of course not. Can you imagine the uproar that would cause?"

He could, in fact. Even the threat of a sale would be enough to foment an outright rebellion, if not a direct challenge from any number of elder lycans within the pack. But while Lukka had never been much of a fighter, the bastard was smart. Smart enough to cover his tracks.

"What aren't you telling me?" he demanded of Sonia. Her eyes were darting again, avoiding his gaze. She wasn't merely nervous. She was being evasive. For her to play coy now, after everything else she'd revealed, there could only be one explanation. "You *can't* tell me. There is something he compelled you directly not to reveal."

Her lips twitched. Suddenly, she jerked her chin toward the house. "That boy you let stay here. I saw him around Black Mountain before."

He raised an eyebrow at the change in subject. "Micha. He was with Kyle when he came for her. He claimed that he wasn't a part of what happened. I believe him."

"Well, there are a lot of boys like him around lately," Sonia continued. "Young. Wild. Strong. Eager to fight. Loyal to Lukka. He's accepted them from all over. Dozens."

She said no more, but Bill could fill in the blanks. Despite his resources presumably strained to their breaking point, Lukka was welcoming in rogues with open arms. He'd heard the rumors, even out here, but he'd thought it was a sign of arrogance. A prideful young Alpha eager to show off the abundance in his territory.

Now, thanks to Sonia's obvious skepticism, another explanation seemed more plausible.

"He's building an army," he said. "If anyone speaks out, sale or no sale, he has a team of young pups ready to put them down. Does he even know how dangerous a game he's playing?"

But that was the point—of course, Lukka knew. He didn't care. To him, the position of Alpha was all about power and control. For his benefit, no one else's.

"There have been some good things," Sonia added bitterly. "There seems to be no end of money with which Lukka can expand his lodgings. To supplement the lack of fresh resources, he's been importing processed foods from the outside. You're angry hearing this…" She raised an eyebrow at his expression. "I'm surprised you care."

"Sonia! Of course, I do!" Bill hissed through clenched teeth. He may have left Black Mountain behind, but that didn't mean he didn't give a shit as to what happened to his old home. "And, despite all this shit, *you* remain loyal to him."

"I don't have a choice! I can't survive out here like you can. You put on a good show, but admit it—being a rogue feels no different to you than being under an Alpha. Pack life has always been a conscious choice for you. Some of us aren't so lucky. We need an Alpha for guidance. It isn't our place to question his intentions. Do you know how hard it is for me to even tell you this much?" Sonia's voice echoed, high pitched and broken. Unshed tears glistened in her eyes.

Bill winced. "Yes, I know. I'm sorry. Come here." He pulled her into an embrace that lasted barely a second before she pulled back, swiping any tears from her face.

"Don't worry about me. You told me before that Loren refused to submit to you," she said. "I wonder if it's because of your calling? Somehow, she's tapped into that part of you and it's shielding her."

"I don't know," Bill admitted.

It was a plausible explanation, but he outright scoffed at it. Loren wasn't utilizing his own instincts to resist him. That rebellious impulse came from her alone. Despite the "calling" being a rare gift, he had stumbled upon the one meek, brutalized girl who had the same instinct.

He wanted to write off the suspicion at first. Laugh at it, even. But he couldn't shake a part of him that warned it wasn't so farfetched. He had sensed her long before he even knew of her lycan side. She intrigued him in a way no other woman had. Not even Emma.

There had to be a reason for that.

Though, maybe the truth was that he was no better than Frank Connors, sensing easy prey and eager to take a bite.

"You'll learn soon enough," Sonia said tiredly. "Once you break the bond, she'll have only her own instincts to rely on. For better or for worse."

Bill grunted. This time, Sonia wasn't subtle in her attempts to sow guilt. "I've made up my mind, Sonia. It's the only way."

"No, it wasn't. You didn't have to intervene at all. You made that choice all on your own. I warned you what could happen."

Bill heard the creak of the floorboards as she shifted closer. Warm fingers gently ghosted the back of his neck before settling over his shoulder.

"And I don't know why you're fighting so hard to deny the obvious. You're attracted to her—"

"No, I'm *not!*" Scowling, he pulled away and stalked to the opposite end of the porch. "She's too young," he grunted, though he didn't know if it were to himself or Sonia. "She doesn't know what she wants. You're right. I shouldn't have intervened."

But the half-assed excuses just made the whole thing that much worse. She *was* young and naïve and so damn innocent he sometimes wondered if she were more *Bambi* than Lycan.

Though, she wasn't all innocent. He dragged a finger across his lower lip feeling the stinging marks left over from the assault of her teeth. Even Emma had never kissed him like that— but *Emma* had been fully in control of her own emotions. Loren wasn't. The various complications of the bond made his head ache. Still, there was no use dwelling on it now.

"She's young, maybe naïve, but she's not stupid," Sonia pointed out. "She might feel loyal to you because of the bond, yes, but it can't create love—"

"Don't go there, Sonia. Please. Besides, it's too late," he said, turning to face her. "I appreciate everything you've done for me so far, but you don't have to—"

"There's one thing you haven't factored in." Sonia crossed her arms, eyeing the sky. "You act as if going against Lukka would be some desperate last-ditch effort you have to undertake all on your own. You don't understand that plenty in the pack will rise up in support of you. What of them if you walk away after that, huh? To hell with us?"

"Us?"

He didn't even need to see the determined gleam in her eye to know that Sonia hadn't included herself by mistake.

"I never asked you before." She moved closer, forcing him to meet her probing gaze. "Why you left. I assumed it was because you couldn't bear being in a place that held so many memories of you and Emma. I thought you'd last a year at most before you came back. I don't care if that makes me childish," she added as he cocked an eyebrow in surprise. "I hoped you would come back. Every day, I hoped for that. But now that it's been several years, I have to wonder if it were always more than grief. So, I'm asking you outright. What drove you away?"

He gritted his teeth. There was no point in dredging up that part of his past. Some things were better left unspoken. "Sonia…"

"Tell me the truth. I know you never tolerated Lukka. You could have beaten him easily if you wanted to. The fact that you haven't… It's like you're *punishing* yourself. Staying away not out of apathy, but masochism. It hurts you more to be out here, alone. You *want* it to hurt—"

"Lukka may be a bastard, but if you don't hate me after all this time, then even that bastard has kept his word," Bill countered. "He never revealed the truth."

Sonia eyed him warily, her brows furrowing. "What are you talking about?"

"It's no mystery why Emma was killed. She died because I failed her. The same way I've failed you, the pack, and Loren."

"Is that why you were so desperate for her to be taken in?" Sonia said with an accusatory tone in her voice. "You think you're not worthy of helping her yourself."

"It would have been best for everyone," he muttered, ignoring the part of him that scoffed at that. "What's happened otherwise? I killed on enemy territory. I turned a human—"

Sonia flinched, but he could tell from the way she clenched her jaw that she knew he was right.

"I deserve my judgment. Always have."

"Emma was killed by hunters, wasn't she? How is that your fault?"

"I should have been there, and I wasn't."

There was more. More that Sonia wasn't ready to learn, and he wasn't willing to say.

Still, she wouldn't go down without a fight. "Running away hasn't helped solve anything, but you know what might? Facing your problems and demanding what is your right. You want time to train Loren? I can buy you some time, but in return, you promise me something."

"What?"

"You let me feel out support for you among the pack. If I can prove that it's there, that there are some of us who will stand by you, will you take that into consideration when you make your challenge?"

"*You* don't count."

"Enough to field a true challenge, then," Sonia said. "You take him on with the backing of others in the pack with the intention to become Alpha should you win. No running away. No more self-doubt. You lead us the way you were always meant to."

"And if I fail?" An outcome that even he could admit was a possibility. "You'll suffer the consequences. That would be treason. I can't let you take that on for me."

"And what do you think it's been like all this time? Not easy. Not one damn bit. Promise me that much, and I'll do whatever I can to help."

"And in the meantime, Lukka will just let me frolic in peace?"

"I can give you time at least," Sonia said. "Enough to train your ragtag pack to survive on their own, anyway. And to prepare Loren for whatever happens next. Plenty of time to transition her properly and avoid causing her any more trauma or pain."

"While you play politics," he countered. "Do you even understand the risk you'll be taking? Lukka probably has you under a microscope already."

"Don't worry about me. I can handle him."

"Fine. Do what you want, but I can assure you that nothing will come from it."

"I wouldn't be so sure," Sonia said, jutting her chin. "While you've been off playing rogue, I've come up with a few tricks of my own. You're not the only one who's had to learn to survive. You've always had your brawn, but I have some skills, too."

"I'm sorry." He nodded in deference. "You're right… You know, Lukas always said that leadership was mostly bravado—"

"But human nature was mostly politics," Sonia finished for him. "Wow. I don't think I've heard you talk about him since… Not for a very long time."

She was right. After his death, Lukas had been regulated to the same part of his mind where Emma dwelled—a cache of memories he rarely revisited, his strained relationship with Kyle included. What triggered him to do so now? Loren? Perhaps.

"He would know how to handle this," he admitted. A wave of guilt slammed into him and nearly took him off his feet.

Sonia reached out, placing her hand on his shoulder. "I don't know why you always seemed so determined to place yourself in his shadow. You are not him. Remember when we were kids? We would play for hours, all of us together. You and Kyle dominated any game requiring physical strength like wrestling or tag."

He nodded. "But anything requiring an ounce of brainpower and you would easily win."

She laughed. "I lost to Lukka a fair share, though. Emma too… That's my point. You have your strengths, and he has his. I know Lukka isn't your favorite person, but the way his father would pit you two against each other… I think you've grown accustomed to seeing yourself only as he did—as his prodigy, nothing else. But, you are *not* Lukas."

"I know," he rasped.

That was the point—Lukas would have never found himself in such a mess.

"He would have found a way to have Loren accepted, politics be damned."

"I wouldn't be so sure." Sonia turned away from him, but from the set of her shoulders, he could tell that something was on her mind. "I know you idolized the man, but I think you would have made for a very different Alpha."

"How so?"

She eyed him, biting her bottom lip. "You are fair and just, and you are willing to risk everything for what you see as right. The old laws deserve respect, but you won't let yourself be restrained by them."

"You think Lukas was restrained?"

Sonia shrugged. "I think he's gone. You're here now, and you shouldn't punish yourself because you didn't do things exactly the way he would. You want to know how I think you should handle this? Your way. No one else's. If you didn't kill that Eislander, you need to prove it. Find out who did. Contact their Alpha if you can. They're fond of the old ways. Use that to your advantage and think of some way to prove your innocence."

"How?"

Her eyes glittered with that cunning intelligence that made her a dangerous opponent in any game of wits. "I'm sure you can think of something."

"And what about you? Do you need to head back now and tell your Alpha to shove his summons up his ass?" He felt an irrational urge to find any excuse to make her stay. At least for a few more hours. A full-blooded female lycan was a much-needed buffer between a half-breed and a newly made wolf.

"I'll stay until tomorrow night to help you as best as I can," Sonia suggested. "Then the rest is up to you."

Bill didn't know how to interpret that comment. As a threat? Or encouragement?

"I need the help," he said, rather than question.

"That's an understatement," Sonia said with a playful grin. "You went from no women to two within the space of a week. You have no idea what you've just taken on, do you? I tried to keep them occupied as best as I could. I made dinner, too, if you want some. And I gave the boy some old clothing I could tell you haven't worn in a while."

"Thanks, Sonia. You have no idea how much I appreciate you."

"Then prove it. Go in there right now and talk to Loren."

He groaned. Anything but that. "Buy me a few more hours. I need to think, and whether I reach out to them or not, I'm sure the Eislanders will be back soon. I should scout some more, just to be on the safe side—"

"Then you tell her." From her tone, Sonia wouldn't drop this subject any time soon.

He hung his head in defeat. "Then I'll tell her."

"Good. The least I can do is hold down the fort. And I'm sorry to tell you that your fridge is practically empty by now. I'll head out and grab some groceries if you want."

"Thanks. And, I hate to use you as my middle man, but—"

"I'll tell the blond one to go home tonight. She should tell no one, blah, blah, blah. As for Loren, I'll handle her as well."

He felt like a coward for running. Maybe he was. A selfish part of him couldn't resist holding onto the lone rogue status for even a few hours longer, putting off the growing responsibility that had fallen onto his lap. A run would do him good, if only to give him time to convince himself that breaking the bond, and avoiding the pack were the only decent outcomes in the end.

Even if they went against every fiber of his being.

10

*L*oren lingered near the kitchen window, fighting for a glimpse of McGoven and Sonia between bouts of pretending to do the dishes.

It was wrong to eavesdrop, not that she could hear much from here. Her only consolation was that their conversation didn't seem to be intimate. They stood near the center of the porch, and Bill had his arms crossed while Sonia intermittently shook her head.

Eventually, they stopped speaking altogether and just stood there, gazing at the darkened tree line. Was there something out there? Loren craned her neck to see more and wound up dropping the plate in her hand.

It didn't break, but the clamor shattered the silence, loud enough to be heard outside.

Caught! Both figures turned toward the window, and Loren barely managed to duck out of view. It was too late. Footsteps approached the backdoor, and Loren raced into the living room, her cheeks flaming.

"It's about damn time he got back," Naomi sniped from the couch. "Does he expect me to just wait around like some homeless vagrant? No offense."

"None taken," Micha chirped. He sat on the floor across from her, a pile of clothing scattered around him. Sonia had fished them from the recesses of Bill's closet and invited him to take his pick. Under the guise of inspecting a sweatshirt with a faded logo, he looked up, meeting Loren's stare. "Hear anything interesting while you were eavesdropping?"

Loren blushed. In the end, she just shook her head and took up a post near the window.

It wasn't long before noise echoed in the kitchen, and someone warily poked their head through the doorway. Loren's heart sank as she saw Sonia's exhausted smile.

"Bill went out again," she said—a polite way of phrasing what Loren knew to be the truth—*he's out avoiding you.* "I thought I would get some groceries for you guys. At least, so you aren't living on tuna for the next few days."

"Thanks!" Micha chirped.

"Naomi, Bill fixed your car's battery while he was out, so you can go home tonight," the woman added, turning to the blond. "If you have any questions, he will talk to you tomorrow, I promise. Come on, I can follow you there just in case you have any more mechanical issues."

If she were disappointed, Naomi excelled at hiding it. Instead, she stood and headed for the door after Sonia.

The second both women were out of earshot, Loren turned to the window, hunting for any hint of a figure racing through the trees. It was too dark to make out more than shadow.

"Looks like I'll crash here, tonight," Micha declared, heading for the couch.

Rather than head upstairs into the empty bedroom, Loren remained by the window.

Just watching.

*L*oren woke up on the living room floor, curled into a ball. Her entire body ached in protest, and she sorely missed the comfort of the mattress.

At least she could get some sleep without the simmering tension of yesterday. After Naomi left, things felt strangely…normal. McGoven staying out all night was nothing new. In fact, the only change from the previous few days was that Micha was currently snoring on the couch with his folded pile of new clothing on the floor beside him. She assumed he planned on sticking around.

It was strange. Bill hinted that lycan bonds were different, and already she could sense that. In Bill McGoven's world, relationships were formed instantly based on subtle nuances. Strangers could become allies overnight. And friends could become lovers?

The image of him and Sonia wouldn't leave her mind, taunting her while she drifted in and out of restless sleep. The latter decided to sleep in her car, rather than take his bedroom. Still, Loren wasn't convinced their relationship was entirely platonic. Though, now might be the best time to ask.

She could sense his return before she even crept to the window. Sure enough, the sight of the dark figure picking his way through the trees made her heart beat faster. In relief? Or dread? He moved easily but Loren could sense the exhaustion his steady stride disguised.

A part of her wanted to lurk inside the house and wait for him to approach her first. Play coy. Pride wasn't her motive, but sympathy. So much unsaid lingered between them—too much to unload on him now. Still, those logical arguments didn't matter to that growing instinctive impulse that had her out on the front porch before she even realized it.

The cold air was a shock, and she regretted not grabbing a jacket. At least until a pair of gray eyes met hers from across the front yard and all fears of frostbite vanished. She was on fire. One look from him set her entire body alight with an emotion she couldn't name and didn't want to. It was unnerving and electric, flooding her veins with every breath.

He took his time, lumbering up the front walkway at a pace that conveyed more than anything else how reluctant he was. She could see the hesitation written clearly in his gaze. That didn't stop her lips from flying apart the second he came close enough.

"Can we talk?"

He flinched, raising a dark eyebrow. He seemed just as confused by her sudden bravery as she was.

"Later," he said in a neutral tone. "I promise. But first…"

He mounted the porch steps and palmed the space beside the front door. "There are some things we should discuss. All of us —" He slapped the wall repeatedly until a startled Micha darted to the screen door.

By then, McGoven was already bounding toward the west fields. "Get dressed," he called back. "Then meet me near the paddocks."

Micha didn't seem to think the first command applied to him, and he rushed after Bill barefoot in only a pair of sweatpants.

Loren scrambled to put on her boots and grab her borrowed windbreaker from the hook by the door. When she finally trudged toward the paddock, Micha and Bill stood facing each other. While tense, their posture wasn't hostile. Instead, they looked as though they were preparing for something.

Once she reached them, Bill acknowledged her with a curt nod. "It's time I let you both in on the risks you've unwittingly taken by staying here. What happened with the Eislanders was only the start. They'll come again, most likely with more reinforcements—"

"We can take them," Micha insisted with a confidence Bill didn't seem to match.

"We can't," he conceded. "Not alone. With that in mind, I've decided… My situation here is no longer tenable. If any of us are to have a shot at survival, regardless of what happens with the Eislanders, we can't remain here. If you're willing, I can teach you everything I know. After that… I've concluded it's time for me to leave the area. For good."

Leave? Loren didn't understand the word choice.

Micha did, though. His eyes widened. "You mean, you're going to challenge your status? Seriously?"

Bill nodded. "By creating a made lycan I've broken one cardinal rule too many. There won't be a choice. I either leave or surrender to punishment."

"Wow." Micha bowed his head as if overwhelmed by the severity of that possibility. "And then what?"

Bill shrugged. "I go north. Somewhere far from here, at least. Either way, if you attach yourself to me, you'll be signing up for the same fate."

"Wait?" Micha shook his head as if unsure he heard correctly. "You mean you won't challenge for Alpha status?"

"No. I only want the ability to cut all ties for good."

Cut ties. Whatever they were referring to, it sounded important. Desperation grappled with her long-honed need to remain silent. In the end, one impulse won out. "What does that mean?"

Loren flinched as both men turned to her.

"It means he's going to fight Lukka," Micha blurted in a rush. "That's a big deal! Huge! I mean, if he wins, he could take over. Become Alpha. But if he loses, it'll probably mean—"

"The point is," McGoven said over him, "you should know the danger you're in should you stay. If you don't agree with those choices, you are free to leave."

Micha squared his shoulders and appeared to dig his heels into the muddy earth. "I know you didn't kill anyone who didn't deserve it," he said in a tone an octave deeper than his usual cheerful chirp. "And if you fight for your freedom, then I will too. I don't think Lukka was ever a good fit for me anyway."

Bill winced. Obviously, he didn't expect this reaction. "You'll walk away from the security of Black Mountain for what? To follow a rogue you don't even know?"

"Not only that," Micha countered. "If what you say is the truth, then they used me. They used me to put a female in danger. Do you think I would stick around people like that?"

Bill frowned, but a new understanding flickered across those pensive gray eyes. "Fine. As for you..." He inclined his head in her direction, and Loren held her breath. "You have a choice in this, too," he said. "You can choose to go with the pack if you want. Leave with Sonia. Otherwise… You need to understand the danger you'll be in. If the Eislanders come again, I will protect you, but it is more important than ever that you grow into your lycan instincts. Learn to shift. Learn to fight. It's a monumental ask. You may have to push the limits of what you can handle. I can't deny that it will be hard. Dangerous. If you want to leave, I won't blame you."

And he did want her to leave. She could see the silent plea written clearly across his gaze. *Please go.*

Anger prickled inside of her, hot and irrational. Holding his stare, she lifted her chin and said, "I want to stay."

He visibly flinched, but disguised any disappointment behind a stern frown. "I won't go easy on you."

It was a warning. One that made her heart lurch at the sincerity. At the same time, something in her twitched as if eager to take him on. Prove her worth.

Fight.

Suddenly, Bill cocked his head as if picking up a far-off noise. Not even a second later, a pink car zoomed down the main road and parked in front of the house. As Naomi climbed out, dressed in a T-shirt and loose-fitting pink pants, McGoven nodded in approval.

"Now we can begin," he said.

Already, Naomi was advancing toward them, and Loren felt a flicker of what could have been jealousy flare in her chest. From the knowing glance McGoven sent her way, it was apparent he had communicated his intentions to her beforehand. Last night, even?

But then he'd avoided the house—and Loren altogether. She tried not to seethe over that fact as he moved to the center of their makeshift ring.

He took his time, inspecting each figure assembled before him with varying degrees of concern. He seemed reluctant while observing Micha and Naomi, but Loren noted that he seemed the most worried when he finally turned his gaze on her.

"Micha, you take Naomi to the northern boundary and help her practice shifting into her lycan form."

Both took off without argument, and Loren once again got the sense that this was primarily for her benefit. He was speaking in terms she would understand.

"As for Loren. You'll come with me."

He didn't explain his plan for her, and she couldn't suppress a shiver of apprehension as she followed him up to the hill that overlooked the property. This far out, she was grateful for his jacket as a barrier against the cold.

Not that the chill seemed to bother him. He stood tall, easily picking his way through the underbrush. Once they neared the crest of the hill, he stopped.

"I know you're frustrated."

His words seemed to penetrate beyond the surface tension, cutting to the irritation she could feel swirling within her.

"Loren, what happened the other day was my fault—"

"You keep saying that." She didn't know where the impulse to argue came from. She couldn't control the anger. The rage. It felt irrational, centering on the way he kept his gaze averted as if he were afraid to face her while isolated from the others.

"Loren, I need you to listen to me." His stern tone cut through her aggravation like a knife. She could think clearly for a split second and sense the sincerity in his voice. *Listen.* Whatever he intended to say, it was important to him.

"It's time I gave you a crash course on everything lycan. We won't have long, so we can start with the basics—pack structure. Every pack, big and small, consists of an Alpha at the head. Then a subordinate, usually called a beta, and finally several other members to fill the ranks. A lot of it is formal bullshit, rooted in tradition. In essence, you only need three to constitute a pack."

"Is that what you have now? You, Micha, and Naomi?"

He exhaled, not seeming to like that characterization. "Technically, yes."

"But then, what does that make me?"

He turned to face her, and the expression in his gaze smothered what little resentment she still felt. He looked so…torn. Conflicted.

"Whatever we are, you count as one of us."

But there was a reason why that was. A big one. Something he wasn't saying.

"What happens to me when you leave?" her voice caught at the prospect.

"That's up to you," he said evasively. "For now, I want you to only focus on what I tell you. These next few days will be hard. I'll have to push you to your limits. It's vital we get you to shift as soon as possible."

"Okay," she said, nodding. "I'm ready."

He didn't look convinced. In fact, Loren wondered if that were why he'd brought her out here alone. To warn her. From here on out, things would change. That talk about the pack wasn't mere information. It was a warning. In their unspoken hierarchy, she was at the bottom. No longer was he solely her protector but the Alpha of this ragtag pack. His job was to enforce order. Ensure survival.

By any means necessary.

"I want you to know that my main goal—my only goal from the start—has been to help you." He turned, catching her wrist before she could react.

Her heart lurched as she watched his larger fingers manipulate hers until they rested against his calloused palm.

"If you are to reach your full potential, then I need you to trust me. Without question. Can you do that?"

She didn't hesitate. "Yes."

"Good." He released her and took a step back. In that instant, something in his expression changed. His eyes? They were too bright. Molten silver.

"Then run."

11

"**Y**ou're dead." The cheerfully voiced statement came from Micha, who stood over her, his lips parted into a dazzling smile. "Try again?"

Loren groaned at the prospect. "Trying" seemed to be the only word capable of describing what exactly she'd spent most of the day doing. Trying to be patient. Obey. Learn. Put up with whatever McGoven threw her way without argument.

But she wasn't like him—or even Micha and, to an extent, Naomi. She was slower. Weaker. The equivalent of her "trying" to keep up turned out to be epic failure across the board.

She never knew it was possible to feel so sore. All over, she ached. Her hair was caked with mud, her body slick with a mixture of sweat and earth. Her legs trembled at the thought of taking another step.

But still…

Beneath the exhaustion was a thrill of excitement, she couldn't deny. It grew stronger with every second she spent out beneath the wavering branches and in the rolling fields. A hunger almost. For more. More freedom. More running. *More!*

Though, perhaps that excitement was nowhere near Micha's. He beamed as she extended her hand and allowed him to yank her to her feet.

"Again," she choked out. Then she ran.

Her eyes were on the white barn in the distance—her target destination for the past two hours of this "training."

This attempt, she barely made it two feet before she wound up on the ground again, coughing up dirt.

"That makes it ten deaths in a row. I think we should head back," Micha said tiredly.

Loren followed him without comment. Her mind was a whirl during the entire trek toward the house. McGoven seemed to think this would help her. But how?

After their talk, he led them to join Micha and Naomi—only to leave with the latter while she remained with Micha. Since then, the younger man had her run laps and try to evade him, only for her to fail each test miserably.

Beating herself up would change nothing—she knew that. Still, she couldn't resist seething over her lack of strength and speed. If McGoven had danced around the issue before, this brief training session had all but cemented his fear. Of the four of them, she was the weakest link. The one who wouldn't survive an attack should those men return.

The one holding him back.

No, a part of her growled. *We aren't weak. We held our own once. We can do it again.*

But whatever happened in the field that day with the intruders seemed to have been a fluke. She hadn't felt that same impulse around Micha. Not even McGoven. The only animalistic tendencies she'd shown so far today had been an uncanny ability to wallow in the mud.

But she was the outlier. Naomi apparently had already mastered whatever task Bill had given her, sans the dirt bath. Both figures stood on the back porch, watching them approach.

"We'll stop for today," Bill called as Loren mounted the porch steps after Micha. "Sonia made lunch. We can eat and then figure out the rooming situation for the next few days."

Apparently, he wasn't a fan of everyone sleeping on the floor of his living room.

When he entered the kitchen, Loren expected him to pull her aside and explain what went wrong. How to improve her instincts. Something.

Instead, he vanished, ceding the spotlight to Sonia, who greeted them with a mass of hot food waiting on the center island.

While Micha and Naomi didn't show their exhaustion as much, they ate ravenously. Even the normally chatty Micha was too busy shoving food into his mouth to spark any conversation. Between the three of them, they wolfed down their first helpings and were already onto seconds. With a nervous laugh, Sonia remarked that she would have to scrounge up something for Bill.

A pang of guilt struck Loren at the thought of him going without, though food seemed to be the furthest thing from his mind. Like a shadow, he appeared in the doorway to the living room, his arms crossed, his gaze thoughtful. He was sizing them up again, reassessing whatever judgment he had made earlier that morning. Micha and Naomi had apparently passed their tests.

But her… His gaze lingered in her direction, and she fidgeted beneath the scrutiny.

"Well then." Sonia seemed to pick up on the tension and seized the moment to change the subject. Despite spending the night in her car, she looked bright-eyed and well rested. Sometime during the day, she'd dressed in a blue sweater and jeans and smoothed her hair into a ponytail.

"We've tried to figure out a sleeping arrangement for the next few days," she went on. "The house is pretty small, but, Micha, there is a cot around here somewhere. You can take the living room."

"Cool!" he exclaimed around a mouthful of pasta.

"Loren, you can take the room upstairs, along with Naomi, should you decide to stay here."

Loren instantly felt her appetite wane. Not only at the thought of sharing a room with the prickly blond, but because of what that arrangement meant without stating it outright. Someone else wouldn't sleep beside her.

Her gaze was drawn to him, but he was no longer looking her way.

"I'll mostly keep watch," he explained grimly, "and find sleep when and where I can."

"So, is no one going to say it?" Naomi blurted. "Why we're all risking our lives like this is some war or something. We still have no idea what will happen when this is all over. Do you expect us to just do whatever you say without question?"

"I will," Micha declared before taking a bite of bread.

Naomi shot him a quizzical look before she squared her chin. "The point is I don't know anything about what's going on. I have school. A life. My friends."

"You agreed to come here," Bill pointed out. "But you're right. All you need to know is that you'll get your answers when you can better understand them. We'll stop for tonight. Tomorrow we'll pick up again. Micha, you should work on your stamina. Naomi, you need to hone your instincts."

Loren noted that he avoided her altogether as he headed for the door.

"I'm going to patrol—"

"Again?" Loren croaked. It was her turn to cause an outburst. "You haven't even slept."

And they hadn't talked the way he promised they would. *Three days.* She clung to that deadline like a mantra but still. She couldn't ignore the feeling that he was putting off being alone with her at all. Longer than to dish out his orders anyway.

"I'll be back tonight," he grumbled. By then, he was already bounding onto the front porch, taking off toward the west fields.

"Let's get everyone settled in," Sonia said cheerfully.

"And where do you fit into all of this?" Naomi demanded. Loren didn't know whether to be annoyed or relieved that someone else seemed just as disgruntled with this situation as she felt.

"I'm an old friend." Sonia's beaming smile never wavered. "I won't be here for much longer. Just visiting. But that doesn't mean that I can't tell you some things Bill hasn't." Suddenly, her blue eyes took on a serious gleam. "He probably glossed over it, but what he's done for you—all of you—has basically ruined any chance he has of ever returning to our pack. His pack. I know it doesn't make sense to all of you, but trusting him is the only course of action available."

Naomi scoffed. "What does that even mean?"

"It means we're a pack now," Micha declared. "Even if it's not for long. We need to have each other's backs and watch out for Bill."

"Exactly," Sonia agreed. "The time for doubt is over. Bill may not have admitted this outright, but I will—if he loses this challenge, Lukka won't let him go unscathed."

"What do you mean?" Loren asked, though a part of her already suspected the answer before Sonia voiced it.

"It means that if he fails, Lukka will decide his punishment. What that means, I can't say. Nothing good, I'm sure." That bothered her. Her blue eyes shone with a frantic desperation she couldn't disguise. Suddenly, she turned to Micha. "Can I speak to you for a moment?"

He shrugged. "Sure."

Sonia led him outside, out to the barn, and Loren could only watch from the window while Naomi grumbled beside her.

"She moves fast," Naomi said disapprovingly. "Looks like she wants all the men wrapped around her finger."

Loren didn't waste her breath replying. For what it was worth, Sonia and Micha's conservation didn't seem romantic in the slightest.

He looked tense, and Sonia…

She looked devastated.

12

Sonia's warning cast a grim pall over the rest of the evening. In a strained silence, Loren and Naomi showered and occupied the living room, while Micha prowled the kitchen for leftovers before eventually taking up vigil by the window, watching them both.

"I have to admit," he said once the sky darkened, and they turned on the lamps throughout the house. "This is the strangest pack I've ever been a part of. To be fair, I was born into the first one, and not really a member of the second. Still. This is really freaking weird."

Naomi looked up from the screen of her cell phone—the only fixture of the room she'd paid any attention to for the past few hours. "What is that supposed to mean?"

Micha shrugged. "My pack… My *dad's* pack was really old-fashioned. We did things by the book. Rogues weren't tied to the pack like they are here. They're driven out. As far away as possible." His grimace revealed that he had experienced that personally. "If I ever wanted to go back, I'd have to do what he's doing—" he jerked his chin toward the woods where McGoven prowled. "And make a challenge. To do that, you need to face the leader out in the open and get a witness to vouch for you. Someone who will oversee the fight, so to speak. It's a tall ask of anyone."

Naomi set her phone aside. Grudging interest flitted across her gaze before her lips pressed into a thin line. "If your dad was the leader or whatever, why didn't you take over?"

Micha winced. "I was too young. When the Alpha dies without naming an heir, the law dictates that those eligible fight for the right to lead. Otherwise, you grovel for acceptance or get driven out."

Loren recognized the tale. He'd told her this story before.

"You have a sister," she added, remembering as much.

He nodded. "Violet. I think she wanted to challenge Levi, but she wasn't strong enough. She stayed as close to the territory as she could. The last time I talked to her was maybe a year ago. It's hard communicating on the outside from this distance. When you're driven out, you aren't given money or a place to live. You have to make a living on your own any way you can. I came here because I'd heard rumors that Black Mountain was open to outsiders."

"So what about him? McGoven—" Naomi seemed to whisper the name as if fearful he'd overhear. "He has a house. A job. Whatever he is, it doesn't seem like he's had it as rough as you have."

"No." Micha shook his head sadly. "I'd say he's probably had it worse. I was never the strongest or the fastest, even around packmates my own age. But him? McGoven was poised to take over when the old Black Mountain Alpha died. Even though

Lukka was his son and all."

"What happened?" Loren asked, hoping he'd reveal more details than the last time he recounted this story.

Micha cast a wary glance toward the window. Then he shifted to face them. "I wasn't around then. I only heard rumors. They say Bill was a born Alpha. He had more promise than most, and even Lukka couldn't hold a candle to him. Lukas, the old Alpha, named him as his successor outright—which meant that when he died, there should have been no battle for supremacy. The pack should have been Bill's to lead with no dissent."

"But," Naomi prompted. "What? Was he too bossy even for a bunch of wolves?"

"No," Micha said. "I heard that after Lukas died, before Bill was accepted as Alpha, there was a breach on the territory's perimeter. Hunters." He shuddered as if the term referred to unspeakable horror. "They aren't common, but they roam the territories sometimes, and they don't care who they kill to make a point. I heard that they even kidnap people like us and torture them and run experiments."

"Great," Naomi said tightly. "Just great. I went from worrying about graduation, to worrying about creepy werewolf hunters. I'm sorry, *lycan*."

Loren felt her eyes narrow. Bill must have educated her on his preference of the latter term.

"Well, to be fair, I've never seen any," Micha admitted. "But in the attack that day, several people died. One of them was Bill's own mate. After that, I guess Lukka accused Bill of not heeding a warning and allowing the attack to happen out of fear. That gave him the premise to challenge him for the position of Alpha."

Naomi scoffed. "And Bill lost?"

No, a part of Loren growled even before Micha replied.

"No. That's the thing. He didn't contest it. He just declared himself a rogue and left. Whatever happened, he must have felt guilty enough to pledge himself to Lukka and remain on the outskirts. Around here, they use rogues to watch the wilder ones who can't be trusted among human society unsupervised."

Like Fred Connors, apparently.

"McGoven's been out here for years. He never even tried to reinstate himself or return to Black Mountain. And if he truly means to challenge Lukka, well, that's a big fucking deal. Pardon the language."

"Why?" Naomi demanded, though Loren was just as curious.

"If he wins, he can take over the pack. To go from a rogue to an Alpha… That's almost unheard of. He'd be welcomed back with open arms—if he could prove his standing fair and square, that is. Or he could earn the right to leave for good."

"And then what happens to the rest of us?" Naomi snapped, crossing her arms. "We just get left behind or dragged behind him like baggage? Some of us didn't sign up to howl at the moon for the rest of our lives. I need space."

She stormed from the room while Micha stared after her sheepishly. "I forgot that you two aren't exactly used to this," he said.

Loren didn't know what to say. In the end, she just shrugged. "We'll get used to it."

According to McGoven, they would have no choice. Sooner or later, danger would come for him again, and if they couldn't keep up…

You'll be killed, that inner voice said gruffly.

Micha seemed to pick up on the mood and said nothing else. Eventually, Loren spied him nodding off in the armchair by the window. While Naomi didn't return, she could sense her stewing somewhere close by. Was that by choice? Or because she didn't have permission to leave…

The thought made Loren's head ache. There were too many topics demanding her focus. Rather than face them, she put on her boots and retreated to the one place that remained her refuge despite all the upheaval in her life recently.

The horses nickered warmly as she slipped inside the barn. If she wasn't mistaken, she could sense that they missed her. Then she remembered how Bill had characterized their reactions to him— they saw him as a predator. With multiple creatures on the property who smelled the way he did, who knew how stressed they'd been?

Like always, they didn't react negatively as she approached. She had felt a stubborn pride at that fact before. But now? It bothered her. If she didn't smell like the others, did that mean she wasn't like them either? Lycan, perhaps, but different somehow. Broken. Corrupted.

That's why he's been avoiding you, that voice whispered, louder, more persistent. *You disgust him. You aren't good enough.*

It could have been paranoia…if it weren't for the many instances of his behavior that seemed to bolster the fear. He seemed pained every time he touched her. Their kiss or any similar embrace had been followed by abject horror after. There was no way around it —he seemed to be fighting something within himself whenever she was around.

And he's been lying to us, that voice hissed. Maybe not outright, but despite all his explanations of the lycan way of life, she couldn't escape the sense that he was avoiding something.

Whatever it was itched at the boundaries of their every interaction, but he deliberately ignored any mention of it.

Why?

Was it something about her true nature?

Did he know why she was so…broken?

The thought consumed her. She couldn't even bring herself to return to the house and pretend that nothing was wrong. Instead, she sought out a corner of the barn and curled up on a bale of hay. Out here, she would know when McGoven returned, and she could confront him in private, away from the others. Maybe if she asked him outright, he'd tell her whatever it was he was holding back?

It was the only tempting course of action.

Resigned, she waited, letting her eyes drift shut as the gentle murmurs of the horses lulled her into a fragile sleep. She wasn't sure how much time passed when a sound finally broke the quiet, startling her awake. Blinking, she stared through the darkness, trying to get her bearings—someone had turned out the lights in the barn without realizing she was inside.

That same someone sighed heavily, his pure exhaustion, so palpable Loren swayed, dizzy with the feeling. Apparently, his intention to nap had fallen by the wayside—he'd been out for hours. Securing the barn must have been his final act before retiring for the night.

Yet, here she was, waiting to pounce like a stalker.

Guilt and dread weighed her down as she mulled over how to make herself known without startling him. That was the strange part—he hadn't noticed her yet—he was *that* exhausted. Creeping to her feet, she prepared to approach the door to the barn when she stopped short as a light, feminine aroma reached her nostrils.

He wasn't alone.

"It's about time you came back," Sonia said disapprovingly. "I was worried sick that you'd pass out in the fields somewhere. You should be conserving your strength, you do realize?"

"You didn't have to wait up for me," McGoven replied gruffly.

"Don't look so surprised. Besides, I was already in my car. I'll have to leave soon, but I wanted to say goodbye first."

Loren clenched her teeth against another wave of irrational anger. She almost couldn't stop herself from barging through the doors. Then she heard Bill sigh, and her irritation instantly diminished.

"I'm sorry. I didn't intend to be gone this long, but I can sense it," he said. "Something's off. The Eislanders should have returned by now. The fact that they haven't doesn't bode well. Fuck, this is bad—"

"How do you mean?" Sonia's alarm matched Loren's.

"I thought about what you said, and you're right. It's time I approach them directly. Loreck, anyway. The only problem is…"

"You can't go near their territory without causing even more trouble," Sonia surmised. "I know you won't like it, but you could ask Lukka to vouch for you—"

"Bullshit. You don't think Loreck would go after one of Lukka's own rogues without his blessing? The men he sent here said something about one man I killed. A member of their pack—but he mentioned only one. Claimed he was innocent."

"I'll see what I can find out," Sonia said. "In fact, there's something else I wanted to talk to you about. I wasn't sure how to address it, but I'll just come out and say it. Remember when you asked me to look into Loren's mother?"

Loren held her breath. Did it bother her that he'd asked Sonia to delve into something so personal? Yes.

"You did? What did you find?" McGoven demanded.

His curiosity matched the desperate impulse Loren felt lance through her heart. She held her breath, paralyzed by anticipation.

"Nothing," Sonia said. "That's the thing. There was never any woman, lycan or otherwise, by the name of Eveline Connors on Black Mountain. Not only that, but all records indicate that Fred Connors was unmarried when he left the territory, and he never took the equivalent of a mate. I even talked to some of the men who were around back then. They said he was a recluse. Kept to himself and rarely got along with anyone else."

"That doesn't make any sense," McGoven replied. "He was listed on Loren's birth certificate. I saw it myself."

"I don't know," Sonia agreed. "He was exiled only a few years before you were. Maybe six, seven years ago? I dug into the reasoning, and it seems he lost control, strayed off territory, and attacked a human. They weren't seriously injured, but given his nature as a made, he was harshly punished."

"I'd heard that," McGoven admitted.

Loren frowned. She didn't know that tidbit of her so-called father's history.

"Things from that time are hazy at best," Sonia went on. "We were young, but I remember a little of it. The murders that went on in that human town nearby? You remember? I was five, I think. So you had to be eight or nine—"

"That was nearly twenty years ago, Sonia," McGoven grumbled. "But yeah, I remember."

"Fred Connors was made during that time. One of the victims. That just makes everything that happened with that poor girl far creepier."

"Yeah, but Loren's eighteen, almost nineteen. She was born long before the bastard was exiled, but after he would have been turned."

"It's quite the mystery," Sonia admitted. "But that isn't all. I never realized it until now, but given that Fred Connors was turned so long ago. Bill, that means that the Alpha who welcomed him into the pack was—"

"Lukas," Bill said tightly. Loren vaguely recognized the name. Micha had mentioned it. *Lukas, the old Alpha.*

"Yes," Sonia said softly. "If the man did father a daughter in that time, the Alpha would have known. There is no way he wouldn't have. I've tried to probe Lukka for what I can, but he hasn't exactly been welcoming of me as of late."

"I'm sorry, Sonia," he said. "I've gotten you into this mess. I didn't even stop to think how hard this must be for you."

"Don't apologize. If I didn't want to be here, I wouldn't be. But... I want you to think about what I said. Not because of me, or Loren, or anyone else. I want you to think about your future. What do *you* want? If it's to be on the outside for the rest of your life, fine. I won't like it, but it will be your choice. But if that *isn't* what you want... If you've been living this way out of some misplaced sense of punishment—"

"It's late," Bill said. "You should head back if you want to get there in time to put your plan into action."

"Don't sound so skeptical. You were always destined for more than life as a wayward rogue, and you know that. If it takes committing treason to prove it to you, well… I'll just have to do that, won't I?"

"Call me as soon as you get back, or when you have any updates," Bill said. "I mean it, or I'll go there myself to check on you. Promise me."

Sonia sighed. "I promise to call as soon as I can. But you make me a promise in return, huh? Talk to Loren. Tell her the truth. Can you do that?"

Loren heard the thud of a heavy set of footsteps. "Goodnight, Sonia."

Sonia's voice was barely audible. "Goodnight."

Loren sensed rather than saw her retreat. The same way she knew that Bill lingered behind. At first, she suspected that he'd caught her lurking in the shadows, but as the seconds ticked by, she realized that he might have been savoring the quiet.

Whatever was happening was taking a toll on him. He disguised it well while around Micha and Naomi but seemingly alone, he groaned, and Loren could picture him leaning against the barn door as the weight of the world bore down on his shoulders.

A part of her was tempted to lurk and savor his nearness. At the same time, something about it felt voyeuristic. Wrong.

Clearing her throat, she stood and crept toward the barn's entrance.

"Loren?"

He was there to meet her in the doorway. Even in the darkness, she could see how tightly his jaw was clenched. For perhaps the first time ever, she had caught him off guard.

"What are you doing out here?" Whatever he saw in her expression made him sigh. "Apparently, you've been here long enough to overhear that, huh?"

"You didn't tell me." She didn't mean to sound so accusatory. "About my dad—Fred Connors. I mean… You don't have to. I can understand. I just don't want to be in the dark, please."

His upper lip twitched in a way that might have betrayed guilt. She couldn't tell. Abruptly, he marched toward the paddocks, and a sharp tilt of his head was her only clue to follow.

He moved to where a lone lightbulb affixed to the side of the barn cast a puddle of illumination. There he faced her, an eyebrow raised.

His nostrils flared, sensing the air. At first, she wondered if he had picked up the scent of one of the intruders. He didn't stiffen in alarm, though. Slowly, his eyes widened as if he'd come to some startling revelation.

"I never noticed until now," he said softly. "I can pick up your scent from miles away. But here? I can't smell you at all among the horses."

She resisted the urge to sniff herself, unsure if his observation was a compliment or an insult. Yet another example as to how she was different, perhaps?

The longer he watched her, another puzzling detail seemed to creep to the forefront of his mind. "I'm sure you heard what Sonia said. About your mother?"

She nodded, suddenly overwhelmed by grief she didn't expect. It hurt. Not knowing more about the woman who gave birth to her. All she had left were a few scattered memories, none of them clear enough to cherish.

"What does that mean?" she asked.

He crossed his arms and eyed the sky. "I don't know. It just deepens the mystery surrounding you. I swung by the station earlier and dug up your file. I kept a printout. It's in the truck. We can look through it together, if you want. When you're ready."

Loren nodded, though she wasn't sure if she was ready at all. Not now, at least. Her heart pounded the same way it had when she stood at the threshold of her father's house. There was something lurking in her past she wasn't ready to face.

Though why was that? He had something to do with it. She could feel it. When she looked up at him, she swore he tensed, as if he knew the question that might leave her mouth next.

"I… I feel like you've been avoiding me."

Again, she didn't mean to sound so pathetic.

Bill, however, didn't shy from the accusation. "You're young," he said firmly. "You're scared. I don't want to overwhelm you. I know it seems like I'm being evasive. I'm being cautious."

Loren noted the subtle wrinkles etched into the skin around his mouth. They alone hinted that he was far older than she was. Just how old? She sensed that even if she asked, he would never tell her, using the information as a wedge to force even more distance between them.

And suddenly, she felt that irrational anger again. It wasn't his choice to make.

"I'm eighteen."

His eyes flickered, sensing the challenge conveyed in that statement. "You're young," he repeated. *Don't question me.*

The air between them shifted as a subtle dynamic came into play. Loren imagined it was something similar to a set of scales, swaying from one side to the other with the slightest provocation. They were weighted in his favor now.

But...

"You kissed me."

Just like that, the balance shifted, and she was on dangerous ground. Picking a fight with him was a battle she would never win. And yet, at the same time, a part of her insisted that she had to fight. Challenge him. Provoke.

It was the only way to make him listen. *No one controls me.*

"A mistake." The heat in his voice startled her. He meant it. Kissing her was a mistake.

Stung, she moved to run, but his hand latched onto her wrist before she could take a step.

"Wait—" The word seemed ripped from his chest. Against his will. He wanted to release her. But something deep within wouldn't let him. Wouldn't let her go.

She turned to face him, caught off guard by his expression. Pained was the only word for it. Her very presence was a knife stabbing through his chest. An agony he couldn't evade.

He *had* been avoiding her. It was all he could do to restrain himself...

Until he couldn't. One hard tug yanked her closer. Their lips met, and it was lightning. Shocking. Punishing. Even as he broke the kiss in the next breath and backed away.

"I don't want to fight with you, and you don't want to fight with me." His voice broke, reducing the threat to an outright plea.

Don't make me put you in your place. "You should go back. Get some sleep—"

"Is this a lycan thing?" Loren's chest heaved with the effort it took to breathe. "That I can feel your emotions. That I feel... Is this what it's like with everyone?"

"No." He looked pained again. "Your emotions are out of control. I can't imagine how confusing this is for you, but I need you to trust me—"

"Why? You're lying to me!" Where did that come from? She didn't know, but she felt it. The same way she could feel her pulse surging like mad through her veins. "There's something you aren't saying. I know it."

"You're right," he admitted. "You promised me three days, remember? Give me two more."

Her head swam as that impulse rose up, demanding she resist. Argue. He owed her respect, not coddling. She wasn't a child.

"I am not a child."

His eyes flashed. "You think I don't know that?"

Snap. She could almost hear one bastion of his self-control breaking. Another cracked as he shifted his weight to the balls of his feet.

"You have no fucking clue how hard this has been for me." Suddenly, he whirled on his heel, closing the distance between them in a heartbeat. "No clue. I can smell you every second. Your thoughts. They're driving me fucking insane."

"I can feel it," Loren admitted in a whisper. More than that. She could feel his anger then and there. All of it. His frustration. Pain. Confusion. Desire—

Wait. That emotion was the most foreign of the tangled mass, taking more effort to decipher. It was something she rarely felt for herself. The closest comparison she could make was when she desperately needed a new pair of shoes. She'd risk a beating just to get them. The thought of going without was…unthinkable.

And he felt that. Every waking minute, the feeling seemed to grow, transforming from mere desire into… Hunger. Craving. Desperation.

Then, all of a sudden, she felt nothing as if the tenuous, invisible link to him had been closed off.

"Go to bed." He stormed off, marching toward the forest. To hide, she realized. To run away and avoid her for another night. More hours. At least until he could get rid of her. Break ties. Cut her loose.

"No." The voice didn't even sound like her, but her ears rang with it. Her throat ached, her lips parted.

And he stopped short. She could count every ragged breath he drew in. Each one was a hallmark of how fiercely he grappled to regain control. He didn't want to shout. Argue.

He couldn't help himself. "Loren, I told you to—"

"You said it yourself," she stammered over him. It was like she was possessed. This wasn't just her saying this, but that inner voice finally making itself heard outside the confines of her mind. "You aren't my Alpha. You aren't my guardian. You didn't even want me here. So, what are you to me? Because you certainly aren't in charge."

Something dangerous flitted across his gaze, gone in an instant. Her breath stuttered regardless. If she had been on thin ice before, it just shattered, plunging her into a place from which there was no turning back.

"Who am I?" He advanced slowly, but the contrast in his posture —even the way he breathed—made her pulse race. She took a step back. Then another, retreating inside the barn, driven by an instinctive warning to run. Or fight.

At the thought, her feet stopped, bracing against the concrete flooring just as he reached the doorway.

She took a step, and he ruthlessly followed, matching her movement for movement. Only this time, when she retreated toward a corner of the barn, far from the horses' stalls, fear wasn't driving her. Just anticipation.

An electric foreboding so thick she couldn't stand it. The only cure was him. His heat as he lumbered closer, towering above her, blocking her in with sheer bulk. His breath fanned her throat as his hands palmed the wall on either side of her hips. But not close enough. He needed to touch her.

"Please," she croaked. What exactly she was begging him for? She didn't know.

But he did. His teeth gritted, a curse grated between them. "Fuck."

The muscles in his arms twitched with the effort he exerted to fight whatever impulse he felt. Until he couldn't. His fingers found her waist, feathering together over her lower back.

Loren's mind went blank. Nothing in the world could describe the feeling—none of their previous embraces came close. This wasn't a volatile reaction out of impulse. This was deliberate on his part, his way of answering her via the only method that mattered.

Touch.

Who are you? she'd demanded. The possessive brush of his calloused fingertips, easing beneath the hem of her shirt, satisfied that question more definitively than words ever could.

I belong to you. You belong to me. Don't question it—don't even fight it. Just trust me. Accept me. I know you. I need you.

That reassurance alone might have been enough for the scared little girl from over a week ago. But now? She needed more.

Unbidden, she reached up, lacing her fingers through his hair. It was wrong. She didn't know him.

That didn't matter. She continued to explore him, and the second her fingers made contact with the planes of his jaw, all doubt left her mind. *Yes,* a voice within her exclaimed, though it didn't feel entirely hers. *This is right.*

More than right. Vital. Only breathing felt more natural.

Yet, he still hesitated, his arms tensing. "I can't—"

"Please."

His mouth was on hers again before she knew it, prying her lips apart for his tongue to probe deep. This was different. He didn't test or goad her into fighting back. She relented to him, inching closer, inhaling as much of him as she could.

But it wasn't enough.

She needed more. Everywhere. She needed… Ownership. The greedy way he started to touch her next. His fingers curled around the waistband of her pants, grazing the flesh beneath, but fear didn't even enter her mind. She arched her hips to assist him, eager to get closer. Feel more.

Her eyelids fluttered as the roughness of his palm met the bare skin of her thigh, but the sound he made…

It ripped through her like a current, awakening nerves she never knew existed. Feelings came from nowhere and struck like lightning. She was only vaguely aware of his fingers inching higher along her thigh. Higher…

The first brush of his knuckles against the tender space between her legs made her head rear back against the wall so hard sparks exploded before her eyes. Almost instantly, his free hand was against her scalp, cradling the aching area—not that the pain was any match for the sensation of him.

A harsh voice, dripping into her ear, finally responded to her initial question. "You wanted to know who I am to you?"

Her heart panged—he'd never sounded like this before. This guttural. Primal.

"I am everything you'll ever need. Everything you could ever want. I am…"

There was a note in his voice some small, buried part of her didn't ignore.

He was *everything*.

Whether she wanted him to be or not.

13

S*low Down.* Bill felt like a bystander, screaming helplessly as a tragedy unfolded before his eyes. There was no stopping it. He could only witness the inevitable—and, in this case, he was both watcher and perpetrator.

You fucking monster. The moniker haunted him as he mouthed the pulse in Loren's throat while his fingers breached a part of her he had no right to take. Guilt didn't diminish his awe one damn bit. He groaned instead, his heart lurching at the feel of her.

If only he could stop his body's reaction there. Rebelliously, his cock swelled, straining against the thin cotton of his sweatpants. There was no ignoring the pure, biological response she inspired so innocently. She was molten, her body broadcasting in every way it knew how that she was ready for him. Aching for him.

No. The thought belonged to the one bastion of control he had left—like a drowning man, Bill clung to it.

Drawing back, he sucked in air and tried to refocus. His hand withdrew from her thigh, his teeth clamping down over any impulse to kiss her.

"No—" Her nails lashed at his chest so hard she drew blood.

He saw red. The next second, he had her slung over a bale of hay. She was so much smaller, but her body concealed its strength like a jackknife. One minute she seemed weak and ineffective. And then, as though with the press of a button, she transformed. Grew claws. Lashed out.

Her eyes blazed at him, her chest heaving as she clawed at his forearms, dragging him back.

"You don't want this." He tried to reason with her.

Her reply came in between harsh pants. "You don't know what I want."

But he did. He could feel her desire in every pore of his being. The tumult of emotions emanating from her felt poisonous in their intensity. Confusion. Desire. Greed. Lust. She wanted him so badly her entire body throbbed with the need.

He could smell it. Taste her arousal in the air. The scent had him crouching, nostrils flaring as he sought out the source. Something hampered him. Her pants—so he ripped them off, baring her legs to him as well as a pair of pink panties.

The thin strip of fabric irritated him. He needed to see her. Every inch. Take stock of her body in full. Like the pale, creamy skin of her inner thighs, marred with scrapes and bruises that drew a growl from his throat. There were other marks. Ones she'd wanted to hide from him. On her lower back. Her wrists. Her stomach.

Years of abuse and neglect scarred her like words on the pages of a book. Inspecting them made his heart ache. She was so strong. So frail.

But, as far as he was concerned, no one would ever hurt her again. Ever. He cemented the promise by nipping at the nape of her neck in an act only the most primal part of her would recognize as both a marking and a warning.

She was his…

But they weren't alone.

Noises scratched at the periphery of his consciousness. Shrieks. Cries. The horses? And something else. Voices, growing in intensity.

"…going on in there? I don't know… Going to see…"

"Fuck!" His common sense returned, allowing him to pick up two pairs of footsteps rushing in their direction. Probably because the horses were going haywire. The black one kicked at its stall while the two mares issued blood-chilling cries. He had no idea how he hadn't heard them until now.

"Shit." He lurched to his feet, scrambling to snatch an item of clothing from the floor. Her pants. Only they were torn.

He looked down to meet her gaze and went cold. The lust that consumed them both had faded. Now, Loren watched him horrified, and the guilt hit him so brutally he staggered with the force of it.

"Fuck… I… I'll hold them off," he told her. "When we're gone, get to the house."

He didn't give her the chance to argue. Already, he'd stepped from the barn, surging to meet Micha and Naomi. Just paces from the door, he barred their path and prayed they couldn't sense Loren within.

"What's going on?" Micha asked, an eyebrow raised.

The horses were still agitated, their cries drowning out any other noise.

"I think they smelled a predator," Bill said. "We should all take to the perimeter to be on the safe side. You two head south. I'll go north."

Micha and Naomi shared a look.

"What about Loren?" the blond asked, displaying an uncharacteristic but genuine concern. "She isn't in the house—"

"She's out doing a bit of training on her own," Bill lied. "I'll find her and tell her to head back. Now go!"

They both took off in the direction he indicated. Already, he was impressed with their skill. For a new made, Naomi had a decent grasp of her instincts. He just hoped both were far out of range when he finally took off, clearing the way for Loren to exit the barn. Despite every cell in his body warning him not to, he circled back and watched her leave while keeping his distance.

The darkness shielded her well, but his enhanced eyesight still caught the pale, milky limbs, bared to the elements. The sight made his jaw ache, his erection unbearable. Invoking the shift was the only method of relief—and even then, just barely.

He ached to follow her and finish what they'd started. Soon. Before…

Before he could even think of breaking the bond. If he cemented their joining for good, it would be too late. There would be no undoing it.

Enough! Groaning, he shed his clothes and took off for the north field. It was a good idea to patrol anyway. With Micha and Naomi, he could cover more territory in half the time.

Already, he could sense them both on the other end of the property, moving parallel to his position. Within minutes, they cleared most of the land, presumably finding no hint of a predator who could have spooked the animals so badly.

Because there wasn't one, of course. As he ran, Bill struggled to compose a more convincing explanation. He could always blame the weather. A rodent. Something other than the truth.

Though Naomi and Micha, to an extent, may have been naïve, they weren't stupid. Sooner or later, they would sense the bond between their Alpha and his mate. Already, Micha seemed to recognize it. For all their sakes, he needed to address the reality. And soon.

Though, there was always the possibility that he would fail in his challenge to Lukka, and everything afterward would be a moot point. Perhaps death wasn't a bad thing in that case...

No. He shied away from seriously considering that possibility. Turning his focus to the feel of the earth beneath him, he ran faster, clearing the full perimeter and gaining on Micha and Naomi. They were moving slower than he would have expected. Had they decided to wait for him?

Suddenly, his hackles raised as he picked up a scent that didn't belong. Not here and not now.

Shit.

He bounded through the trees in the direction of it, alarmed to find that Micha and Naomi were in the same location.

And they were in danger—there was no mistaking the animalistic musk that grew thicker with every yard he gained. *Fuck.* So much for training.

His ragtag pack was about to be tested for the first time—and he could only pray that this altercation went far differently than the last.

14

____

Chilled to the bone, Loren tore into the house and latched onto the first piece of clothing she could find—a pair of sweatpants in Micha's prized pile of hand-me-downs. With a mental note to replace the garment later, she pulled them on and struggled to regain control of her breathing.

The house was empty, but the loneliness resonated more intensely than even the days in her father's house. This felt…

Intentional. She had no doubt in her mind that Micha and Naomi would return first, but McGoven would stay out as long as humanely—or lycanly?—possible, if only to prolong facing the inevitable.

They kissed. They did far more than that…

Once again, he'd made a mistake.

No. The voice was so loud it was as if someone was growling into her ear rather than inside her head. *Not a mistake. He owes us more. So much more.*

Her skull ached as the thoughts swarmed into a chanting drone. They were painful. Almost as if something were fighting to claw its way out of her very soul. The dichotomy between Loren Connors and the creature strengthening inside her had never been stronger. They were two entities grappling to exist in the same body.

Or, as McGoven put it while referring to his lycan form, two halves of the same coin. For the first time in her life, she could feel the difference in mindset. A change. Something animalistic lurked within her.

And it was angry.

As awkward as the strange emotions felt, she didn't want to be alone with them. Alone with herself. She almost cried with relief when she heard the sound of footsteps bounding up the front porch.

At random, she snatched more clothing from Micha's pile and headed for the foyer, averting her eyes to the ground.

"Here—" Even before she realized that the muddy boots of the figure on the porch were too big to belong to Micha or Naomi, she knew something was wrong. She could…smell it. A scent like sulfur wormed into her lungs, proclaiming alarm. *Stranger!*

Though not exactly. One look and her eyes widened. She knew this man, with a haunting brown gaze that glimmered in the glow of the porch lamp.

The man from the day Naomi had been attacked.

"I'm not here as an enemy," he said as she drew back. His voice was harsh, and yet… Something in her could parse out the grudging truth in it. He wasn't here as an enemy.

Not that it mattered one damn bit.

"Go away!" She stood firm, possessed with a strength she never knew she had. Or perhaps she just hadn't felt often enough to recognize it. Whatever it was, resembled the confidence that took over that day in the clearing. When she bellowed a word that seemed ripped from her very core.

Admittedly, this time, the feeling was different. When it came to this man, that inner voice was more cautious. *He's too strong,* it warned. She would have to fight.

Her gaze darted to the kitchen, where a drawer near the stove held knives. Not that she could make it that far.

Already, the man had taken a step forward, blocking the doorway with his sheer bulk. That smell intensified, and she coughed. It was cloying. Suffocating.

"We intended to meet your rogue until I saw that he left you alone. I apologize for the crude measures—" He gestured to his body. The plain jeans and dark shirt he wore appeared more formal than what he sported in the clearing, but she wasn't put at ease. If anything, his approach seemed…bold.

Dangerous.

"All I want to know is the name of your sire," he said, advancing another step. "You're heritage. Family line. Legacy?" Her confusion seemed to confound him even more. He raised an eyebrow and swept his gaze throughout the empty hallway behind her.

Run!

She pivoted into the kitchen, and lunged through the back door. She wasn't anywhere near fast enough.

She didn't have to be.

A monstrous sound rattled the house to the very foundation. A growl. Several. Loren barely made it onto the porch before a large, black shape bounded from the darkness in her direction. She knew, before she registered the graceful outline of a familiar wolf, that she wasn't in danger from him at least.

"I meant no harm," the intruder said. He warily advanced through the back door, his hands held in front of him.

An answering growl revealed what McGoven thought of that assertion. He remained crouched, feet from the porch, and though she didn't know exactly how, Loren was sure she could sense his intentions. Hear them inside her head.

Come to me. Now!

She descended the steps and crossed the distance. Instantly, Bill moved to stand in front of her while two fellow wolves that she assumed were Naomi and Micha closed in on either side of her.

But there was another wolf, lurking just off in the shadows. Only a pair of glowing, yellow eyes revealed their position—but an overwhelming hostility came from that direction. They didn't belong here either.

"We aren't here on official business," the intruder in human form said, taking responsibility for the presence of the other wolf. "We merely wanted to talk. A parley of sorts. Between the rogue and me. No one else. This changes nothing regarding the justice you have yet to face, however. We merely want to discuss the topic at hand. Nothing more."

Silence hung for several seconds as both figures eyed each other, saying nothing. Despite the lack of words, Loren suspected that plenty of unspoken sentiments were being traded between them, too quickly to track. She couldn't tell which way the pendulum swung. Then, in a beautiful and violent shift of muscle, the black wolf seemed to distort and Bill McGoven appeared in its place, rising to his feet, starkly naked.

"You have some damn nerve coming here," he said, his voice bellowing. "You sneak onto my property. Attempt an ambush. Took efforts to cloak yourself in what? Deer piss? That isn't a very friendly gesture."

The intruder squared his jaw. "I wanted answers. I thought your mate would have them—"

He turned his gaze to her, and Loren flinched. *Mate.* That word had been uttered more than once—and each time, it seemed to hold more importance than a term of acquaintance. Way more importance.

"You wanted to talk. Then talk," Bill growled, sounding equally as ferocious as he had while in animal form. "Now."

"In private," the man specified. "I think it would be better for all involved if we did. My man will stand guard, as will your people. If I am to believe that you didn't attack Jamal in cold blood, those rules should be simple to abide by."

McGoven cocked his head, his posture unreadable. "And then you'll walk away without attacking another human on my property?"

The man laughed. "We will walk away. Tonight. I guess your Alpha didn't inform you as to the terms of our truce. Though, it looks like his liaison has left empty-handed."

Loren struggled to keep up with the conversation. Liaison. Sonia?

"Time is running out for you to do the right thing, rogue," the man added without explaining the reference.

Bill remained tense. For a second, Loren was sure he would transform again and go for the man's throat.

"Micha, Naomi, stay with Loren," he barked out eventually. "As for you—" he raised his voice so the other two figures could hear him clearly. "You want to talk? We do so out in the open. Afterward, you leave. Understood?"

The man descended the porch steps. "Lead the way."

Loren couldn't ignore a sense of aggravation as the two men headed for the west fields. Their conversation would involve her. She knew it. And yet they seemed more than content to leave her out of it as if she didn't matter. Had no say. No voice—

Something nudged her side, shocking her from the thought. The culprit felt cool against her hand. Wet—the snout of a large brown wolf, she realized. Its eyes glowed an electric green as they met hers with unmistakable energy only Micha could exude. *Don't worry,* he seemed to say. Then he nudged her again and inclined his head toward the house.

Her curiosity aside, Loren didn't need to be told twice.

The second they entered the back door, she moved to barricade and lock the front and close all the windows on the first level. The barriers wouldn't do much if the large wolf still lurking outside decided to attack, but it was something.

Because, if things did go south, she couldn't shift. She couldn't run. She couldn't even smell the danger until it was literally under her nose.

The pity party helped distract from her concern for McGoven—though not for long.

When she finally had the sense of mind to get her bearings, she noticed Naomi in the corner of the foyer, quietly scrambling into a set of clothes. Micha remained in the kitchen, and the confines of the relatively spacious room helped to illustrate just how massive he truly was while in lycan form. There was barely enough space for him to comfortably crouch between the center island and the wall.

"Are you okay?" she croaked. He couldn't be comfortable.

Comically, he snorted and shot her a glance that seemed to say, *I'll keep watch.*

Until what, exactly? An invisible pressure ratcheted up with every passing second, and she suddenly had an idea of exactly what Bill had been afraid of. Another confrontation with these men.

Another fight in which she was a liability.

Even if all went well and the intruders did leave tonight, it was only a matter of time before they returned.

And no matter how many days Bill had them running in the fields, they would never be a match.

She would never be able to hold her own.

And he would have no choice but to fight for her.

"Information wasn't the only reason I came out here, rogue. I wanted to see it for myself," Loreck Eislander's man called as Bill led the way from the house. "The bond between you and that girl. Your sick, twisted imitation of it."

Bill clenched his jaw so tightly he was surprised bones didn't crack. Respect wasn't his motivation but tact. Staying silent was his best bet. Indulging the bastard would do more harm than good in the long run. Still, he felt the urge to reply. "See what?"

"If our worst fears were true and you really are beyond help."

Bill scoffed. "And the verdict?"

The man didn't answer, not that Bill was particularly keen to hear one. Instead, he focused on testing the air, hunting for any sign of another player who might have ventured out to attend this little party. So far, beyond the two trespassers, he couldn't catch a trace of anyone else.

That meant nothing considering the man closest to him had cloaked himself in deer piss just to go unnoticed. It was an old trick. Something Loren had unintentionally taken advantage of by lurking within the barn. Similarly, the animals' scents had cloaked hers, obscuring her unique aroma.

Trick or not, he would need to learn how to combat the effect. Right after he dealt with the welcome wagon.

Walking in front of the bastard was a risk, but one he was more than willing to take. It meant he didn't have to school his expression, and for a few brief seconds, his true emotions could break through.

Fuck. This was bad. Sonia was gone, and with her went the slim chance of settling this diplomatically. Otherwise, he didn't have a real game plan should this visit turn out hostile.

The only course of action was to go on offense. "Well, you came here to talk," Bill began, turning to face the man directly. "So, talk."

He had to admit that he didn't resemble the bastards who attacked Loren. He was cleaner, for one. He didn't reek of booze or illicit substances. Just earth and the traces of his home pack beneath the piss.

Unexpected jealousy stabbed at him. He didn't miss life on Black Mountain—he couldn't. But there was something in the man's confidence he envied.

"The girl—"

Bill couldn't help the part of him that lurched at the unsaid insult. The man had deliberately avoided using the term "your mate."

"Who is her sire? I'm sure you learned that much, even if you did take her against her will."

"And why do you care?" Bill countered. "I don't remember you asking about her family tree when you tried to kill her. Neither did the *men* who attacked her on your land. I don't think you or your Alpha truly give a damn. What do you really want?"

He expected another threat. The man's raised eyebrow caught him off guard.

"Is that your way of saying you don't know?" Rather than hostile, the man sounded…concerned. "Your Alpha seemed to think her father was a previous rogue known to the area, but I made some inquiries. The man wasn't a born lycan. Either your Alpha wasn't aware of that fact—" the man scoffed, revealing that he didn't buy that belief. "Or he doesn't know her true heritage. He didn't seem too concerned to find out, either."

Bill frowned, curious despite himself. Was that disgust in the man's voice? "That doesn't answer my question," he countered. "Why are you here?"

"Frankly, this conversation isn't for your benefit, rogue. I came here as a courtesy but don't think for a second that anything you've done has been condoned by anyone in my pack. Your crimes are too numerous to list. If you want even a shred of mercy, you will relinquish the girl to me now."

Bill curled his hands into fists, hearing each knuckle crack. "And with that, I'm afraid you've worn out your welcome. As for my crimes? Humor me. What proof do you have?"

Besides four dead bodies, of course. Though again, Bill got the sense he was only seeing a small fraction of the actual picture here. *Jamal.* In his previous tirade, the man had only mentioned one murdered lycan he was supposedly responsible for. He doubted that kind of oversight was by accident.

"Evidence?" With a cold laugh, the man raised his hand. "A knife with your blood on it, drawn by the man you killed. That man's body, slain by a cowardly act. And your scent on our territory, far from your assigned post, rogue. Then we can touch on the fact that you took an unwilling, innocent female as your mate. You didn't try to have her integrated into a pack… Some might say that on the surface, your actions could be interpreted as an underhanded way to subvert your status in a desperate bid to regain power."

"It seems you've gotten everything you need from Lukka," Bill spat, shifting his stance in case of an attack. "So why come here? Unless…"

A sudden suspicion replaced some of his anger with pure confusion.

"Unless you don't believe him."

The man disguised his reaction to that statement well. Only a furtive glance toward the house gave him away. He was curious about Loren. Too curious for his own good.

"I'm assuming your Alpha doesn't know of this little visit?" he guessed.

The man's cold stare proved it. He had to be high ranking to speak with such authority. Perhaps even as powerful as Eislander's beta. Someone with that much to lose wouldn't make the trek out here on a whim.

Against his better judgment, Bill put off retreating a few seconds longer.

"The girl. Do you recognize her? Could she be a descendant of one of your men?"

Though, even as the words left his mouth, Bill doubted them.

The man's scoff proved he was thinking along the same lines. "We don't lose track of our females, and we certainly wouldn't let a full-blooded pup grow up on the outside." A growl edged his words. He wasn't lying. But...

Bill decided to take a chance and reveal what little he did know. "You were right. Fred Connors was a made from Black Mountain, and he's the one listed on her birth certificate. I thought her mother might have been a human, but there is no record of her ever living in our territory. Not even on the outskirts. Connors was only exiled seven years ago and turned over a decade before that. If he had sired a child, the woman couldn't have lived far away. We didn't allow outsiders unfettered access back then, and Connors wasn't high ranking enough to have traveled outside the territory unaccompanied. Though..."

Bill hadn't made the connection before, but something Sonia dredged up came back to him.

"Connors was supposedly attacked by a rogue who rampaged in your area twenty years ago. From what I know, the Eislanders dealt with that situation. Did you know the lycan responsible?"

He was rambling, but he couldn't help it. When said out loud, the mystery of Loren Connors was more perplexing than ever. It was as if the girl had come out of nowhere. In fact, that would make more sense than where the facts seemed to lead—in circles.

"I don't see how a rogue has anything to do with this. It seems as though you got your information wrong," the other man replied. "The mother could have changed her name to avoid drawing notice. Sometimes, humans who stray too close to our kind feel the need to take drastic measures if they decide our ways no longer appeal to them."

"I thought of that," Bill snapped. "But with every search in every goddamn database, Eveline Connors is the only name that turns up—"

"Eveline?" The man's entire demeanor shifted on a dime. His eyes flashed, his jaw clenched. "That was her name? Eveline?"

"You recognize it?" Bill asked. "Someone from your pack?"

He couldn't be sure. Already the man had schooled his expression into a blank mask.

"You mentioned Connors was turned by a rogue. You think it was connected to the attacks twenty years ago. Why?"

Bill felt his eyes narrow. "Connors might have been a victim. If your pack dealt with the rogue, then you know who it was. Could he have been Loren's father?"

A crazed murderer wasn't ideal, but it was better than the alternative. Loren needed answers, and Bill was willing to entertain any avenue to find them—even if he had to beg an enemy outright.

"Tell me."

"The girl should know her upbringing. Have you asked her?"

Bill couldn't silence an exasperated snarl. "She doesn't remember—"

"Or she doesn't trust you enough to tell you."

"You think I took her forcefully as a mate, but you don't think I'd take advantage of my access to her memories?" Bill laughed coldly. "That doesn't make very much sense, does it?"

The man hid his disappointment well—but not all of it. A hint of alarm flitted across his gaze before vanishing. "Either you're lying or…"

"Or someone hid her memories deliberately." The prospect sounded insane out loud. And yet… Fuck, it made sense. Too much sense.

"If that is the case, there are ways to recover those memories," the Eislander murmured, seemingly to himself.

Bill didn't bother to suppress his disgust. "You turn up your nose because I mated her, but now you casually suggest I break into her mind to satisfy your curiosity. That tells me you know more than you're saying."

The man turned away. "We're done here." He surged forward, continuing toward the property's boundary. Whatever he knew, he was choosing to keep it to himself. "If you care about that girl, you'll release her. Soon. Her presence here is the only reason we've shown you mercy until now, but we won't extend that grace for much longer. Sparing her the pain of your death would be ideal—but not a deciding factor. You can have two days to break the bond and send her to a pack. No more."

He sounded so damn smug. As if he were offering him a lifeline.

If anything, the bastard had just given him more of a reason to act on the very course of action he'd been trying to talk himself out of.

"In two days, I'll be on your doorstep. You can take up my punishment with Lukka right after I've dealt with him," Bill spat without parsing through the consequences of revealing that part of his plan.

It was too late.

The intruder stopped short, his head cocked as if he didn't trust what he'd heard. A slow, rich laugh echoed back, and Bill scoffed in return.

"I thought you were brazen, rogue—but this is outright foolish. You aim to challenge your Alpha? As if they will accept you now."

It stung to admit the bastard had a point. That was a hurdle he would overcome later.

"I don't intend to sit around waiting to be executed for a crime I didn't commit. I won't let Lukka spin the narrative, either. I killed no one who didn't deserve it."

The man hissed. "Maybe we will wait and let fate deal out your punishment in due time, rogue? If Lukka doesn't rip you apart, your own packmates will."

Bill didn't even waste his breath arguing. There was no point. Instead, he watched the man fade from view before he bounded toward the house—though a nagging voice at the back of his mind warned that the bastard had been right.

Loren would be better off without him.

Alive or dead.

16

*P*atrolling the boundary wasn't his excuse for staying out all night this time. Just reluctance. Oddly enough, rather than fade beneath the trees, he lurked outside the house in plain view without ever leaving the yard. Loren even caught a glimpse of him from the living room window, prowling in the form of a black wolf. Naomi and Micha must have sensed him as well, but they said nothing—and no one made any move to go outside and see for themselves.

He obviously wasn't in the mood to talk.

His irritation prickled the air like the scent of smoke mingled with his usual aroma of pine. He didn't want to be bothered. Not yet. For the first time, his presence wasn't a comfort, though. Loren barely slept, curled up by the window.

McGoven's vigilance contributed only partly to her unease. The nightmares were more intense than ever, descending the second she closed her eyes and haunting her until she wrenched them open again. No longer was her pursuer a distant shadow. He was closer, visible just beyond her peripheral vision.

Watching.

Waiting.

Ironically, much like McGoven.

Only when a tendril of pale daylight pierced the darkness did she find the nerve to creep into the kitchen. On the way there, she passed a snoring Micha who lay sprawled in the middle of the floor and Naomi, who slept soundly on the couch.

Before she reached the doorway, she could sense someone prowling in the room beyond. The scent of pine gave his identity away in a heartbeat. He must have entered the second she'd gotten up—though he managed to find a pair of sweatpants at least. For now, his back was to her as he rummaged through the food Sonia had stocked the fridge with. In the end, he resurfaced with a packet of tuna and moved to grab a loaf of bread resting on the counter. He silently assembled two sandwiches, but Loren didn't refuse when he abruptly offered her one.

"You have questions," he declared before taking a ravenous bite. "Ask them. I'll answer what I can."

Nothing regarding whatever happened in the barn. She knew without asking that topic was off-limits. Thankfully, there wasn't a lack of pressing issues needing to be addressed.

Squaring her jaw, she picked one issue at random. "Those men. What did they want?"

He frowned and took another bite. "I don't know." He admitted after swallowing.

"But they aren't going to leave you alone." She could sense the tension in the air. Even the way he moved screamed vigilance and hostility. He was on guard more so than before.

"No," he said gruffly. "You either. But believe it or not, they aren't the biggest threat facing us at the moment..."

Us. She swallowed at the word choice. Though, what did he think was the main threat they faced? He seemed unwilling to voice it out loud. Instead, he glowered at the window. The sky seemed perpetually gray these days—a stormy hue the same color as his eyes.

"That man," he began. "You didn't smell him before you entered the house, did you?"

Shame flooded her cheeks. "No," she admitted—but when she inspected his expression, she didn't find any blame or anger there.

"There was a reason for that," he said with a nod. "Can you explain why?"

It was a question dangerously close to the one her father always uttered, "Care to explain?" Only, his tone lacked any malice. She knew in her gut that he wouldn't strike her for a wrong answer, either. With that in mind, she took her time, parsing through every interaction. One glaring oddity stuck out.

"He smelled strange," she said, cringing at the memory. "Like sulfur. It was awful—"

"Or, to put it bluntly, it was deer urine," Bill said with a harsh scoff. "It's a dirty trick. Something young boys might do to sneak out of the territory unnoticed. The scent of prey overpowers anything nearby. It's instinctive, you might say. When we hunt, it allows for us to zone in only on our target and let nothing else distract from the pursuit. But it can also be used as a double-edged sword outside of a heightened environment. Especially in a place like this where prey animals live full-time. You've grown accustomed to the scent of horses, for example, and it allows other lycans to cloak themselves and mount a surprise attack.

Or," he added dryly, "it allows a lycan to hide in a barn and overhear a private conversation."

"I didn't know…" she trailed off as she recognized what he *didn't* say outright but merely alluded to—he knew her scent thoroughly. There was something primal in that knowledge that made her shirt feel tighter, and her throat constrict.

"There are other little nuances," he continued, oblivious to how her thoughts had wandered. "Interactions you wouldn't understand outside of our culture. Like, for instance, that deer you found on the porch the other day."

Loren stiffened. Apparently, the grisly carcass hadn't been left by a hunter after all. "They put that there?"

"They did," McGoven admitted. "But it's more complicated than that. Keep in mind that we don't kill for sport. Never. Only to feed. To leave a carcass like that is a warning. One of the most severe our kind know how to issue. Think of it as the equivalent of spitting in someone's face and rubbing their nose in it."

All in all, far more serious than he'd led her to believe.

"Why did you lie?" Her voice sounded calm enough but the anger she felt caught her off guard. He lied. He didn't trust her.

"I didn't want to worry you." From his tone, she couldn't discern any deception, but he was no longer looking her way. Instead, he once again inspected the horizon. "But it was wrong to lie to you. If I want you to trust me, then it must go both ways. I shouldn't hide anything from you. Starting with the truth of the full extent of the danger you're really in."

Loren swallowed. If she weren't mistaken, those words sounded like an invitation. One she'd be a fool to turn down.

"So, tell me the truth. What did those men really want?"

He sighed in defeat. "They asked about who your father might be. I don't know what Lukka told them, but they seem to think I… That you're here against your will. Finding your real father would go far in discovering how you grew up the way you did, though. Where you belong. I don't want you to take this the wrong way, but you present an aggravating puzzle. Nothing about you makes sense. Nothing."

Loren marveled at the characterization. She was used to feeling like a burden. But a puzzle?

She flexed her bare toes against the tile floor and awkwardly fidgeted with the hem of her shirt. McGoven had retreated inside himself, dwelling on whatever mystery he thought she presented. Unlike last night, she couldn't sense any emotion directly. Navigating this conversation felt very much like flying blind.

But getting the man to talk at all was such a rare occasion she didn't dare waste it. Clearing her throat, she tried a neutral question. "So, what now? Will they come back?"

He nodded. "They will. Not that I plan on us sticking around to greet them."

Because he still intended to fight for his freedom. Then what? He hadn't been exactly clear on that part. For whatever reason, that was a question she wasn't eager to ask.

Instead, she fixated on another aspect of what he'd revealed.

"You said you hunt. Do you mean you…"

"It's not a violent act," he said plainly. "Get the grisly images from horror movies out of your head. We are far more humane than human hunters with their guns. It is one of the most sacred acts a lycan partakes in. It might seem savage to you, but to us…"

He sighed again, wistfully this time.

"It's beautiful. Natural. I can't even describe what it feels like. But the hunt… Such a tradition is what has allowed our kind to survive for so long. Few wars. No famines to decimate our numbers. We could subsist during the harshest times, and everyone could feed in harmony."

It certainly sounded more wholesome than the cruelty she'd been exposed to in her short life outside of the pack and their laws. Hearing him describe even that small fraction of their customs made it sink in just how little she knew. About lycans. About him.

"You said you don't need the moon to change," she began, seizing upon his rare willingness to speak openly. "So then how? You said the Alpha calls it forward—"

"When we are children, around the ages of four and five—it differs depending on the pack and their traditions—we are gathered before the Alpha under a full moon right before that month's hunt. Around us, the others shift. For some, it might be the first time they ever see their mothers, brothers, fathers, and sisters in lycan form. Then, one by one, the Alpha approaches each child and presses his snout to their chest. That alone is enough to waken the instinct in most cases. Keep in mind that it's a bit more ceremonial than I'm making it seem."

He laughed, but not even a heartbeat later, his customary frown returned. "Afterward, the children are encouraged to submit. They join the fold and partake in their first hunt that very night."

"But you didn't," Loren said softly. "You resisted."

"For three years," he said thickly. "I'm sure you can imagine that made me a bit of an outcast in those days. I was well past the age of most when I finally accepted my Alpha and undertook the change. So believe that I, more than anyone, understand your struggle. It's easy to interpret the things that make you different as a sign of weakness. Don't."

A new emotion colored his voice, softening the rich baritone. Fondness? Pain? There were moments when he referred to the pack with such disdain. Then times like this where he recounted those memories almost reverently.

"But I am different," Loren said softly. "I can't shift…" Her voice broke. Only as she uttered the confession did she realize how much it actually stung. "Naomi can, but I can't, and I'm supposed to have inherited this. What does that mean?"

"It means that you are not Naomi," McGoven replied. There wasn't an ounce of judgment in his expression. "You will shift when you're ready. Sometimes being different isn't a bad thing. If you were in the pack, some would shun you. Others would support you."

"Like Sonia?"

He laughed. "Like Sonia. Though the most important thing to remember is that, at the end of the day, you can't always rely on anyone else. There comes a moment, when the only person you can rely on is yourself."

His eyes were downcast, his jaw clenched. That seemed to be a lesson he had learned the hard way.

"What is it like?" Loren asked. "Living with the pack?"

He shot her a questioning glance. Then he leaned against the counter and inclined his head. Just when she thought he might not answer, he sighed.

"It could be considered regimented by your standards, I suppose. Everyone has a place there. A role to play. Much like our lycan and human forms, we carry on the dichotomy in our daily lives. You might be surprised by how…normal our lives are for the most part. By day, some work in a communal kitchen or in private fields to grow vegetables. At night, we partake in various rituals to embrace our primal side. We develop very little of the land, to leave most of it untouched. Wild. The animals we hunt have been born and bred within our borders but roam freely."

"You miss it." She didn't know what possessed her to say as much. Still, his curt nod gave confirmation.

"It's hard not to. I grew up there. It wasn't perfect, but I can't say it was terrible, either."

The question of why he left in the first place was poised on her tongue. Just as she gathered up the nerve to ask it, a shrill sound pierced the quiet.

Bill stiffened, warily eyeing the landline phone attached to the wall near the fridge. He moved cautiously, reaching for the device as though it were a poisonous snake ready to strike.

"Hello?" Almost instantly, his expression softened, and his tone lost the hard edge. "Yes, sir. I'll make it in today. I may not be able to stay long… Yes, due to that family emergency I told you about."

She recognized that tone of voice—the one he used while in uniform. Apparently, a "family emergency" was the lie that had allowed him to miss work the past few days. When he hung up, he raked a hand through his hair.

"I need to go into the station today for a few hours. Just to tie up loose ends. But while I'm there… I would like your permission."

Her belly flipped at his serious expression. "For what?"

"When I reviewed your file, I did so intending to keep your privacy intact. But things have changed. We need to know anything I can glean from your past. Anything."

Deep down, Loren knew she should have been horrified by the prospect. Something bad lurked within those memories. Horrific. But when it came to recalling exactly what—or feeling the fear at full force... She couldn't.

So, she consented with a curt nod. In the same instance, she blurted out a question that seemed just as pressing as her murky past. "Do lycans feel emotions differently?"

He raised an eyebrow. "What do you mean?"

"Ever since my father... Fred Connors. Ever since he died, I haven't been able to feel... What I should feel. I can't even remember what happened."

She tried...

Nothing came to mind. Not even the night before his death.

"It's shock," Bill insisted. He stood fully upright and headed for the hall. "I'll get dressed and head out. In the meantime, I'll leave some exercises you and the others can work on. Basic training."

In other words, nothing requiring a lycan form.

"Is it time for breakfast?"

Loren turned to the living room as Micha appeared in the doorway, rubbing at his eyes. Without a word, she headed to the fridge and made him a few tuna sandwiches, along with one for Naomi.

By the time Bill returned downstairs, fully dressed in his uniform, all three house guests had eaten and were waiting awkwardly in the kitchen.

"I need to go out for a few hours," he said. "Naomi, you should go check in with your parents. While you're at it, see if you have any clothing you can spare for you and Loren. Then come back here. Micha, you and Loren run a few laps around the property. Stay away from the boundary. You can answer whatever questions she has, but try to stay on topic."

"Yes, sir," Micha replied with a mock salute.

On topic, Loren assumed, meant "no personal history" regarding McGoven or anyone else involved in this strange saga.

Not even ten minutes later, she and Micha were traipsing across the fields. Or, more accurately, Micha was traipsing while she struggled to catch up.

"Any questions?" he chirped. "Ask away! I'm an open book. We can talk about anything from moon cycles to pack dynamics—"

"What is a mate?"

Micha stopped short, so suddenly, Loren nearly ran into him. Instead, she tripped, landing on the dirt.

"Oh, I'm sorry!" Micha was by her side in an instant to help her to her feet. However, when she dusted the dirt from her knees, he wouldn't meet her gaze directly.

"Why do you want to know about a boring subject like that?" he asked. "I can think of ten topics off the top of my head that are way more interesting. Like scent marking and what it's like on the mountain, and—"

"Why won't anyone explain that to me?" Loren couldn't help the desperate frustration in her voice. She supposed it had been building since the very day she woke up to Sonia and Bill whispering about her, refusing to tell her outright what was going on. She hated it. Being treated like a child. An idiot.

A burden.

Something in her expression made Micha wince. "Okay! Okay! Don't make me the bad guy. I'll tell you."

He shot a wary glance over his shoulder as if hunting for McGoven. Then he conspiratorially lowered his mouth near her ear.

"A mate is like… Humans might compare it to marriage or something, but it's more than that. A connection. It outlasts any other bond—even between a lycan and his Alpha. A mate will always come first. But it's… complicated. You can't just walk up to someone and give them a ring like humans do." He laughed, only to trail off awkwardly once he realized she wasn't in on the joke. "It's a sacred bond," he said with a solemness Loren had only seen in him a handful of times—the day the intruders attacked Naomi in the fields and again when he pledged his life to Bill. "Lycans who are mated to each other… It's like they have two brains instead of one. Two sets of senses. Two strengths. They're one and the same, and not everyone can handle that kind of connection."

Butterflies came to life within Loren's stomach. "What do you mean?"

"There are downsides," Micha added. "A bond like that… If one mate dies, the other can go insane from the pain. It's like having their soul ripped in half."

The words felt way too eerie. Was that why she could feel McGoven's emotions? Sense his thoughts? Was he her…

"How?" she asked hoarsely. "How can you tell if someone is your mate?"

Micha fidgeted, suddenly fixated on the waistband of his pants. "You know what? Why don't we do one more lap before blondie gets back and brings down the mood with her pouting—"

"Please." Her voice lacked any true emotion, but Micha deflated as if she'd shouted.

"It's not random," he said thickly. "It's a choice. Two lycans meet, and they willingly share themselves with each other. Usually—" he cleared his throat. "With an intimate connection as well, but I've heard that's not necessary. It's a mutual acceptance."

Loren frowned. So much for that theory. She couldn't recall Bill McGoven ever asking her outright to be his mate.

"There is no other way?" she prodded. Was that disappointment fluttering in her stomach? She had no right to be.

Micha sputtered. "Well... I ah—"

"Tell me, please."

"I've heard stories of some really fucked-up lycans forcing a mating bond. It's... It's the worst violation you can ever think of. You force your way into someone's mind. Their soul. We are taught to never do something like that without consent. Ever. B-But," he added hastily. "Sometimes, in rare cases, it might be better for a female—a lycan—to have another lycan forge a mating bond to help them transition. Especially if they've been traumatized. The mating bond can offer relief from fear. Pain. Bad memories. If done with the right intentions."

He was dancing around something, but suddenly Loren didn't want to know. Whether with good intentions or not, the thought of someone else having control of her emotions and fears felt...

No better than Fred Connors using his fists to accomplish the same thing.

And yet. If her attraction to McGoven was just a fluke. Unrequited... That thought stung just as badly.

17

*I*n the five years Bill worked for the New Walsh PD, he had never received a less than stellar evaluation. Though, if a skilled investigator happened to dig into his past, they would discover that he had no university or academy training to speak of. In fact, he had no credentials other than the ones he left the pack with all those years ago—which, to say the least, weren't much.

Luckily, an unnatural sense of smell, reflexes, speed, and an ability to plant "suggestions" within human minds went a long way to fill any educational gaps. Besides, New Walsh was such a quiet town that most calls centered around silencing rowdy neighbors or finding lost pets.

Until Loren Connors. Tackling her case was the first time he'd ever felt out of his element.

In more ways than one.

Damn Fred Connors and the bastard's secrets. Bill had hoped that his death would end his hold over Loren, but that was turning out to be wishful thinking. The visit from the Eislander bastard cemented his gut feeling that something was off. More than questioned paternity. Loren's true origins had been…hidden somehow. Fred Connors had merely been a scapegoat.

But for who? And why?

Therein lay a wealth of suspicions that made Bill's stomach churn. Connors simply wasn't smart enough to plan such an elaborate ruse on his own. No… To have his name listed on Loren's birth certificate eighteen years ago, and though reluctantly, take her in without questioning her paternity, there weren't many explanations for that. Either Fred Connors grew a sliver of a heart in his time as a rogue, or he'd had no choice. Someone far stronger had compelled him to maintain the lie.

Bill didn't like where that possibility led. Not one damn bit.

Lukka was still the lead suspect—but he had already shown an inclination toward more violent routes to get his way. Beyond him, there were only a handful of other figures powerful enough to arrange such a scheme—but Bill cut off the thought then and there. Rampant speculation would help no one.

He needed real answers.

With that goal in mind, he left his truck and entered the modest station near the heart of the town. His first destination was the small room where they kept case files. Instantly, he realized why he'd been called in so abruptly.

"Hey, Bill," Mindy, the clerk, greeted from her desk posted near the door. A slight woman with curling blond hair, she'd been one of the few friendly faces to make his post here bearable. Usually, the only thing she kept on her desk was a mug of coffee. This morning, something sat beside it, glaringly out of place—a square package roughly the size of a textbook, bound in brown paper.

"Sorry to call you in from your vacation," Mindy went on innocently, "but this came over from Elkton with specific instructions to give to you ASAP. I don't even know what's inside it. They didn't say."

"Elkton?" Bill felt his brows furrow. "That's a town up north, isn't it?"

Fuck. Very north, in fact—not far from two large lycan territories nestled within the mountains.

"Yep!" He barely heard Mindy's reply. Jaw clenched, he fought to refocus. "A ways away," she went on. "Maybe five hours on a good day with light traffic. Do you have any idea why they might be consulting with you all the way down here in New Walsh?"

"No idea." Bill fought to school his expression. While the Elkton police had no business with him, he could think of someone who might. An entire pack, in fact, who happened to live just outside the town's boundaries.

Unease made him eye the package warily, suspicious of what might be inside it. Would Loreck Eislander really stoop to involve humans in whatever feud simmered between them? Considering the man's supposed beta had the balls to trespass onto his property the night before and issue demands, who knew what the bastards were capable of.

When he finally took the package and entered the case file room, he didn't feel confident it contained a harmless missive. It was heavy, with only his name written across the front. His nostrils flared, hunting for any trace of a nefarious substance the package might contain. Another carcass? Whether it was a good or bad omen, he couldn't smell anything.

When he ripped off the paper, all he found inside was a battered file that could have come from any one of the cabinets in this very room. Written on the front was one name. *Scolera.*

Bill frowned. He had heard the name before. It belonged to a pack somewhere out west. Nomads, to be more specific. They were less organized than Black Mountain or the Eislanders, preferring to roam their territory seasonally in makeshift caravans. That, however, wasn't what gave them their infamy.

Scolera wolves were wild and vicious. Rather than follow a single Alpha, they formed small, scattered clans with no real hierarchy. Due to that unorthodox nature, they weren't welcome in most spaces. In fact, he only knew of them through rumors—most notably, the belief they fed on humans.

Though, on second thought, they weren't entirely unknown to this area. If Sonia hadn't brought up the incident, he might have forgotten it completely—twenty years ago, a spate of human murders had been attributed to a rogue prowling the area. Things had gotten so bad that Lukas Grehmaine and Loreck Eislander had joined forces to tackle the threat before it brought unwelcome attention to both packs.

Bill barely remembered that time—he'd only been a child. All he could recall was the tension that had infected everyone for those tortured few weeks. Once the rogue had been caught, things went back to normal.

He'd said as much to the Eislander as a cruel joke, but maybe it was the truth. Could that monster have been Loren's father?

Puzzled, he flipped through the first few documents contained within the file, questioning the sender's motives. Was this some backhanded attempt at a warning?

Perhaps.

Though, when he skimmed over a particular line, his eyes nearly fell out of his head. It was buried within a list of names that seemed to document various Scolera family members known to the area.

One, in particular, stood out—Eveline Branshaw.

Loren's mother? Bill's first impulse was to doubt it. Scolera wolves, what little he knew about them, were rabidly fierce to their loosely connected clans.

Then again, nothing involving Loren had made sense up until this point.

He skimmed the rest of the file, finding nothing that stuck out. One mystery, however, was answered soon enough—at the very back of the assorted documents was a note. The ink smelled fresh, presumably written by whoever sent the package in the first place.

We need to meet, rogue, it said. *Wolfie's bar in Withead, outside of Elkton. Come alone. Bring any trouble, and you will regret it. This is about the girl, nothing else.*

Bill scowled, picturing the Eislander lycan from the night before. Apparently, the bastard had lied—he had recognized the name of Loren's mother after all. Enough to place her identity, at least. Did the bastard know who her real father might be?

All signs pointed to that farfetched scenario—a crazed rogue Scolera who fed on humans, Fred Connors presumably being one of them. It was a sick twisted bit of irony.

Sadly, it wasn't even the most tragic of turns in Loren's case.

Bill had spent all morning trying to ignore the inevitable—the Eislander bastard had a point. There was a way to enter her memories. A way to learn the truth without traipsing out to Elkton...

Though, he wouldn't have long to weigh the ethics of such a method. Sonia had to be back by now, but she hadn't called him. Putting Loren aside for a second, he tried her cell phone, but no one answered. To say her silence was bad news was a grievous understatement.

Either Sonia was in danger, or Lukka had tightened his leash. The bastard was planning something.

Bill groaned as the threats against him stacked up. His head ached. Would the visit from the Eislanders be capped by a direct assault from Lukka? Who the hell knew?

For the time being, he needed to focus on one dilemma.

Without letting himself overthink the act, Bill cleared a space on a table near the back of the room, fetched the file they had on Loren Connors, and prepared to read.

18

"Let's do one more lap," Micha insisted.

Loren groaned internally. He might as well have asked her to jump off a cliff for fun. They had been at it for hours, and he barely seemed winded, despite speaking almost constantly in addition to running.

"It's good to get some exercise," he chirped. "It can clear the head, you know. Put things into perspective. I used to run at least two hours every morning—"

To conserve her sanity, Loren tuned him out, though she couldn't deny feeling some guilt for his sudden chattiness. It seemed to be his desperate attempt at preventing her from asking him anything else. Like about mates and how that particular connection was forged.

But she needed to know. The craving for information burned beneath her skin, growing into an almost painful ache that plagued her every waking second. Contrary to Micha's insistence, running didn't distract her any. Neither did his steady stream of conversation. She was almost grateful when Naomi's sports car zoomed down the main road, and the blond stormed out, carrying a pink duffle bag slung over her shoulder.

"Who does he think he is?" she demanded as Micha and Loren approached. "Lie to your parents. Gather up some of your designer clothes to hand out to the paupers. Don't ask any fucking questions, and certainly don't waste time on preparing your college admission essays or community service projects. You know, the things that actually matter in my life? Though, hell, I guess I'm just lucky that school went on break this week, or he'd have me blow that off too just to squat in a house with a loser freak and wolf boy."

Micha whistled through his teeth. "Bad day?" he asked without a hint of mocking in his voice. Either Naomi's insults went right over his head, or he had way more patience for cruelty than Loren gave him credit for.

Naomi scoffed at him anyway. "Here—" she practically threw her duffle at Loren. "Make use of my charity. Though I suppose you're used to it by now. Living off the kindness of others. Crawling around like a sniveling little worm afraid of its shadow. You know, he told me you're lycan or whatever. I'm calling bullshit."

"Naomi…" Micha's voice suddenly dropped an octave, though Loren wasn't sure what caused his sudden alarm. She didn't smell any outsiders nearby. Just the cloying stench of Naomi's perfume.

"Oh, what is she going to do?" the blond demanded with a harsh laugh.

Only then did Loren realize she'd impulsively taken a step toward her.

Not that Naomi seemed cowed one bit. "She can't even change. As far as I'm concerned, she's totally fucking useless!"

Micha sprung toward her, sensing something Loren didn't. "Naomi, don't!"

Ignoring him, the blond lunged. Loren felt a pair of manicured hands collide with her shoulders. She went sprawling, nearly losing her balance. Then everything went black.

Her next coherent observation was watching her own fingers lash at a beautiful, tanned cheek. Again. Again.

The scent of blood tinged the air, beautiful and vibrant. It drowned out the sickening perfume—but barely. She needed more.

"Loren, stop!"

She couldn't. It was as if her body moved separately from her mind, wrestling on top of a squirming Naomi. The only action she consciously had control over was shouting. Screaming. The words echoed nonsensically, and only snippets actually registered.

"Kill you… I'll kill you!"

"Enough!"

Suddenly, a force hooked around Loren's waist, wrenching her back and off her feet entirely. *Micha.* He barely managed to insert himself between her and Naomi before the blond charged again.

Loren forgot her rage for a heartbeat, and genuine awe rendered her frozen. There was something undeniably beautiful about the way Naomi threw herself forward, and a golden wolf took her place.

It wasn't an instantaneous transformation when viewed up close. More…violent. The muscles in Naomi's slender jaw protruded and burst. Her green eyes widened while her body expanded three times its normal size, and her designer clothing shredded around the lupine form. Even so, it was a breathtaking thing to witness. So much so that Loren missed the moment Micha transformed as well.

He was the only figure large enough to inhabit the brown wolf that came from nowhere to pin Naomi's smaller form just beyond her reach.

Logically, Loren should have run. She was no match. One bite from those wiry jaws could rip out her throat. That logic couldn't penetrate the rage consuming her, though. She shifted her weight to the balls of her feet, ready to fight anyway.

Then...

Nothing. It was as if an unseen force smothered her emotions, rage, and all. She went still, surprised as Naomi whimpered, pressing herself to the earth.

Once her breathing slowed enough to register the scent in her lungs, Loren easily placed the culprit behind the sudden shift in the mood. *Pine.* Heart pounding, she scanned the fields wildly for the sight of a scowling Bill or snarling black wolf. Apart from Micha, there was no one else around.

But he was here. She could sense him as surely as she knew her own name.

And she wasn't the only one. Micha shifted back into human form, crouching—out of modesty for her, Loren suspected. He shot her an apologetic glance, but said nothing.

Not even a minute later, a patrol car turned the corner and parked halfway to the house. Bill emerged in a silent display of power, so effective Loren swallowed, rooted to the spot.

He didn't yell. He didn't storm across the fields in their direction. He merely stared for what felt like a solid minute. Then he silently reentered the patrol car and drove to the house.

"We should head back," Micha said with a weary sigh. As he turned to Naomi, the girl breezed past him, still in wolf form. In a graceful display of speed, she loped back to the house.

By the time Loren traipsed up the back porch steps, a hint of emotion tugged at her conscience, stopping her in her tracks. It wasn't the mixture of dread and guilt flooding her own mind, but... Something different. Not anger, but a darker and more brooding emotion.

Much like whatever lurked within Bill's gaze a moment ago.

"Get changed," he called from the kitchen the second they entered the foyer. "Then, we need to talk."

All four of them? Or just him and her? He didn't specify, and Micha herded Loren into the hallway before she could ask.

Already, the shower in the downstairs bathroom was running, and presumably, Naomi was inside it. Whether intentionally or by accident, the girl had left her duffle outside the bathroom door.

Loren hated the thought of wearing anything of hers, but she didn't exactly have a lot of options. Reluctantly, she fished a sweater and jeans from Naomi's bag and retreated upstairs to get dressed.

When she finally returned downstairs, at least one question became answered immediately.

This conversation was meant to happen only between her and Bill. He waited for her in the living room alone. Through the window, she could see Micha and Naomi in the field by the barn. Both were in human form, having a conversation of their own.

Loren couldn't tear her gaze away as a pang of jealousy stabbed at her. Would Micha's mindless chatter be preferable to this overwhelming tension? Maybe.

As if sensing her unease, McGoven sighed. As she turned to him, Loren noted that his expression was carefully blank.

"Sit," he commanded, nodding toward the couch.

She took a step, only to hesitate. It felt wrong to relax when he seemed so tense. Especially when his mood was very much her fault. Fighting with Naomi was such a stupid, childish diversion in the grand scheme. She deserved to face her scolding without cowering on the couch.

Oddly enough, Bill didn't question the disobedience.

Instead, he sighed and cut to the chase. "I found some new information regarding your mother. What do you know about a place called Hillmarrow?"

She blinked, shocked by his blunt tone. Taking his advice, after all, she sat down and tried to form a coherent response. "I don't think I've ever heard of that—"

Wait. Something itched at the back of her mind. A memory? It wasn't cohesive. Just a fragment.

Bill latched onto her discomfort. "What's wrong?"

"I think..." All at once, the truth dawned on her. She *had* heard of it. Once before, maybe years ago. She couldn't remember the context or what it meant. Only who said it. A voice like rich honey that made her heart ache to recall.

"I think my mother mentioned it one time," she croaked. "But I can't remember. I don't even... What is it?"

"Interesting." Bill leaned against the window and raked his hands through his hair. "It's the name of a territory out west," he explained. "Home to a clan of lycans known as the Scolera. I don't know much about them, but I have reason to believe your mother might have been from there."

Her mother. It was a drastic shift from teenage drama. Overwhelmed, Loren stared from the window and tried to process the new information. "How do you know? What does that even mean? If she was from that place, then..."

"It means she might have been a full-blooded lycan," Bill finished for her. She couldn't tell if that prospect relieved him, or unnerved him further. Probably both, judging from the taut line of his mouth. "Scoleras are reclusive. They don't tend to stray this far from their territory. I need to know more about her. Whatever you can remember."

The urgency in his voice made her breath catch. She wanted so badly to please him. Remember something. Anything. As the seconds passed, she could only lift her shoulder in a helpless shrug. "I'm sorry. I don't... I can barely remember what she looks like."

All that remained was just a heart-wrenching mixture of features. Blond hair. Blue eyes. Kind smile. The overall picture was blurry —as were any memories attached to her mother directly. All she could clearly recall was an overwhelming sense of peace. Love. Protection.

Sometimes, if she tried hard enough, she could still hear her laugh...

"I need you to remember," Bill commanded. "Try."

Loren flinched. Try. But how? She closed her eyes and attempted to fixate on those old memories and bring them into clearer focus. It worked…slightly. She could remember a small house on the outskirts of Ridgerton. The scent of spring flowers and fresh air. A beautiful laugh. A smile…

Then nothing.

"You can't."

Bill didn't sound angry as she opened her eyes to find him watching her. Instead, his lips were pursed, his head cocked thoughtfully to the side.

"I know you're trying," he said, easing some of her doubt. "One reason why those memories elude you could be that you were so young. Another reason…"

"What?" Loren prodded, desperate for any explanation. "Why? Because I can't shift. Is it my fault because—"

"No. It wouldn't be your fault at all." However, he seemed reluctant to voice this theory. For a few seconds, he said nothing. "The truth could be that you've been *told* not to remember. But that wouldn't make sense…" He started to pace, thinking out loud. "Only a powerful lycan could issue a command strong enough to last over a decade. It's a long shot, but at this point, I'm betting the answers we're looking for are obscure for a reason. They've been hidden."

"Hidden…" It was a strange way to refer to her own memories. "How? By my mother?"

"No." He shook his head. "Even if your mother was a Scolera, I don't think she had the experience to issue a compulsion this strong. It would need to be someone older. Stronger. An Alpha. But who?" He formed a fist that made every muscle in his forearm bulge. "This doesn't make sense."

"Maybe it's better if I don't remember." Loren couldn't believe the words came from her own mouth. As they resonated, however, she didn't feel the need to take them back.

Her mother's death was a blur on her psyche, but the pain was so fresh she could feel it now... It hurt—until suddenly, the discomfort vanished.

"I know this is hard for you," McGoven murmured, sitting beside her. Though they weren't touching, his breath tickled her neck. Awed, Loren watched as his thick fingers entwined with hers. He didn't seem to realize he even moved. The need to comfort her was instinctive. Irresistible.

As was her desire to respond to him.

She almost felt guilty. Nothing should have mattered in the face of discovering her true parentage, but one pressing issue broke loose anyway. *Mate.* Everything Micha described, she felt. All of it. All of him.

And yet, there had been no fancy, romantic ceremony. No willing acceptance. So, he couldn't be...

"I need you to focus."

Gingerly, Bill disentangled his fingers from hers and stood back up.

"There is a way to break through even a hold that strong. We can try it, but..."

Whatever this plan was, he didn't seem eager to put it into action. His entire body was angled away from her, his jaw clenched, eyes on the window.

"Tell me," she whispered.

"*But*, we would need to be careful," he said tightly. "I'll need your trust, and your…restraint. Patience. Fuck, I shouldn't even consider it. I shouldn't…"

"What?"

He pivoted and met her stare with a probing gaze that took her breath away.

"It's better if I don't explain it. Not yet. But… We'll do it tonight," he said. "But I want… I need you to remember what I said. Can you do that for me?"

Something in his expression made her bite her tongue against any questions—and she had plenty. She nodded instead.

"Good. But first… I can't take this tension. Whatever it is between you and Naomi, we squash it. Now."

He entered the kitchen and exited through the back door, leaving her to catch up. When she did, Micha was sitting on the bottom porch step. Almost comically, Naomi stood across from him, her eyes in their direction.

"What the hell is this?" she snapped. "The Spanish Inquisition?"

"Enough." Bill's tone was so sharp Naomi swallowed, her tan complexion a few shades paler. Even Micha flinched and jumped to his feet.

"You two," Bill went on. "Muck out the stables and come to an understanding. You are *not* to fight. You talk. All this hostility is giving me a splitting headache. I need to sleep. By the time I wake up, I expect some semblance of harmony. Understood?"

"Yes," Loren whispered. The thought of causing him pain, even unintentionally, smothered any irritation she felt toward the blond. For now.

To her credit, Naomi had the sense to look guilty as well.

"Good. Now go. Micha, you can patrol the perimeter if you don't mind."

"Sure thing!" The younger man shot off while Bill headed for the kitchen.

His voice reached back to them, slightly less stern. "Both of you aren't as different as you think and not to be a downer, but we have bigger things to worry about than teenage drama for the time being."

He was right.

But that didn't make facing this showdown any more appealing.

19

"I don't care what he says," Naomi snarled from her end of the barn. "Don't expect me to sing kumbaya and hold hands. As far as I'm concerned, our relationship doesn't have to extend beyond this stupid house. He's planning on ditching us, anyway, remember? No need to play happy family."

Loren let the vitriol fly unchallenged. Anger still simmered within her—though she could admit that mixed within Naomi's ranting was some small shred of truth. Either way, she lacked the energy to fight. Bill's plea might have been partly responsible, that and the overwhelming exhaustion she could feel lurking just beyond her own consciousness. It seemed crazy to even think as much, but… Could it be his? What *he* felt?

If so, he had minced his words. This tension wasn't merely exhausting him. It was draining him of everything he had left. Or, it was at least partly the reason.

While she wasn't sure if psychic abilities were part of the lupine power set, even the possibility distracted her from everything else. She was able to overlook her disgust for Naomi and purely focus on shoveling manure from the stables. Eventually, Naomi took the hint and pulled her weight, matching Loren wheel barrel for wheel barrel.

Finally, every stall was clean, but rather than guide the horses from the paddock where they nervously grazed, she and Naomi lingered in the pasture instead. Their unspoken directive loomed overhead, though neither party seemed eager to address it.

Finally, Loren sighed and faced the blond first. "I don't know what your problem with me is."

While not an apology, it seemed to be enough of a catalyst to garner a response.

"Problem?" Naomi threw back her head, her hands on her hips. "That would imply you were important enough to ever matter to someone like me. Newsflash—you don't."

"Fine." Teeth bared, Loren turned on her heel as fresh anger strained her sympathy for Bill. So much for a truce. "I won't bother. Be a selfish bitch then and hold onto your stupid grudge—"

"You have no idea, do you?"

Reluctantly, Loren turned back. "What do you mean?"

Naomi's scowl was still firmly in place. Her eyes, however, sported a hint of an emotion she wasn't used to seeing there. Pain?

"Innocent, princess Loren. Drawing sympathy and attention wherever she goes. With one look, you have the whole world eating out of the palm of your hand. I could respect that. But not the game you play. You scurry away as if everyone is out to get you, when hell! You bat your lashes, shed a few tears, and boom. Men like Officer McGoven are rushing into battle to defend you while those of us who aren't blessed with the damsel gene get treated like the enemy."

For once, the blond's voice boomed without the aggressive flair that made her such a cruel bully. In this instance, she was ranting, driven by pure emotion. Loren didn't even know how to counteract the tirade.

"I don't know what you're talking about."

"Oh really?" Naomi crossed her arms. "That's the point. I bust my ass to get good grades, make a decent impression, succeed where I can. Then little Miss Loren comes in and gets top marks within three months. Even with this whole teen wolf thing, I can't even have that. You want to know what he—" she jerked her chin toward the house. "Told me after he mutilated me and turned me into a monster? He said it might be hard for me to adjust, but I was lucky. Perfect Loren Connors was also a wolf freak, and we could bond over growling and shit."

Loren fought to keep up with the convoluted argument. "So, you hate me because you're jealous?" It sounded ridiculous.

Naomi, however, wasn't laughing.

"I hate you because some of us can't just play the victim and crawl through life knowing we'll be protected. We don't have that luxury."

Loren raised an eyebrow. "Playing the victim? You act like you know everything about me just because you heard about 'my case.' You have no damn idea what I've been through, so don't pretend to understand me."

So much for Bill's plea. Her anger flared hot, and it seemed impossible they would ever come to anything other than blows. Still, she fought to find some shred of a logical argument to respond with.

"You talk about me," she bit out, "but *you* have everything you could ever want." It stung to admit that. She used to pray for even a fraction of what someone like Naomi Tanner possessed. "How is your life any harder than mine?"

Naomi scoffed and stomped her foot in exasperation. "When will you learn, Connors? Open your eyes. You aren't the only person in the world with problems. Like him, for instance? Have you even noticed just how stressed he's been lately? Because of you. No? Or that weird guy, Micha? He's terrified of something, and I bet you don't even care. You're so caught up in the poor, sad girl narrative. Wake up!" She clapped her hands for emphasis. "There is more going on in the world than Loren Connors and her pathetic problems. Now, if you don't mind, I think that's enough friendship bonding for today. He wants us to come to some sort of truce? Fine. You stay out of my way, and I'll stay out of yours."

She stormed toward the house, but Loren watched her go, startled by a puzzling realization. Naomi…had a point, albeit an obvious one. Her issues with reconciling her lycan nature aside, Loren knew that she wasn't the only one struggling. Something was off, evident in Bill's recent moodiness and constant vigilance.

Her one shining bit of hope was that he promised to enlighten her. Hopefully soon. Curiosity alone was what finally drew her back to the house in Naomi's shadow. True to her word, the blond said nothing before storming to her car. She barely climbed inside the driver's seat when a voice boomed from the house.

"Get some rest," Bill said from the front porch. "Come back tomorrow morning. I suggest you pack enough clothing for a few days."

Naomi acknowledged him with a curt nod before driving off. As she finally disappeared from view, he turned his focus to where Loren stood.

She gritted her teeth in sympathy. He looked only *slightly* less tired. Despite his promise, she doubted he'd slept any. Dark circles lined his eyes, and he raked his hand repeatedly through his hair, tousling the strands into an increasing state of disarray. Like always, his own discomfort seemed an afterthought to him.

He fixated solely on her. She could feel it—like an invisible hand extending in her direction. A wave of comfort followed, though he never said a word. His only action was to beckon her closer with a tilt of his chin.

Loren swallowed hard and mounted the porch steps on trembling legs before following him inside. A quick glance through the kitchen doorway revealed that Micha wasn't in sight, presumably still outside patrolling.

They were alone.

Rather than remain in the neutral territory of the downstairs hallway, Loren was shocked when Bill approached the stairs and took them one at a time. Near the top, he hesitated.

"Undoing whatever block is on your memories is the most important task at the moment. Whatever it takes."

His tone made her stomach lurch. She still didn't understand exactly what he wanted from her. "How can a…" She scrambled to recall the word he used. "A compulsion from a lycan. How can that keep me from remembering?"

Frankly, it sounded too fantastical. Crazy. She intended to wait for him to answer, but despite herself, she was already mounting the stairs after him. Just as she came within reach, he continued ahead, entering the lone bedroom first.

"It's hard to explain." He sat on the edge of the mattress, smoothing a hand along the planes of his face. Behind him, a tendril of waning daylight pierced the bay window, casting shadows over his rigid features. Loren's belly flipped at the sight. Naomi had been right. Something was bothering him, far more than the tension with the hostile pack.

Her past? It seemed doubtful her problems could weigh on his mind so heavily—but something was. Speaking at all seemed to take an immense amount of effort on his part. Finally, he cocked his head to observe her.

"There is so much I haven't told you about our kind," he said, subtly changing the topic. "Our gift for 'persuasion,' for instance."

He paused as if gauging how she would react to that word.

A bubble of excitement fluttered through her belly. "Persuasion?"

He nodded and stretched out his legs while he leaned back, bracing his hands at his sides. Taking the stance as an invitation, she inched forward, leaning against the door frame.

"It's far more nuanced than the term suggests," he began. "Compulsion is the slang for it. A blunter way of saying that we can exert our will over others, even our own kind. It's how the Alpha maintains control. Order. There is a hierarchy as well, but it extends well beyond any physical constraints. It's internal. A lycan with a strong will can plant suggestions into the minds of others, as well as manipulate thoughts, feelings, even memories. If you're good enough, you can even see those exact recollections as if they were your own—though typically, only an Alpha can master that skill."

Loren went cold. An Alpha... Or a girl who felt a need out of nowhere to tell a much older, much stronger man to submit. Her mind kept replaying that day over and over again, but she couldn't bring herself to voice it. Besides, she had another example of this "compulsion" in action.

"Is that why I listened to you?" She was referring to their first few meetings in particular. Certain phrases from him had resonated like commands, compelling her to respond against her will. To refuse, she had to consciously resist him.

"How do you mean?" He raised an eyebrow, prompting her to explain.

"When you would say things, it was like I couldn't ignore it. I had to obey."

His lips contorted into something that might have been a smile on another man. "Yes. In retrospect, I apologize. It's not something regularly done among… Equals."

She squirmed, suddenly hot all over. He had deliberately substituted that word for another. Mate? Regardless her cheeks flamed at the thought of being on the same level with him in any context. Though, he was being generous. This close to his domineering bulk, they seemed the furthest thing from similar. He was all solid muscle, pure strength. And she…

"I could feel it, though," she croaked as a sudden thought took hold. "I remember what it felt like. I don't remember meeting anyone else who had that effect over me."

Because that was what he was suggesting. Wasn't it? Someone had told her to forget. As much as she respected him, she just didn't buy that explanation. A magical command gave her way too much credit. The truth was her mind was fragile, shying away from those dark memories out of cowardice. Nothing more.

"You wouldn't remember," he said tiredly. "Not if they didn't want you to. It's a tricky concept. Think of it as though your consciousness is a room. Inside it are various boxes where you've stored your memories and experiences. At a glance, it seems neat and orderly—but the reality is that some of the boxes have locks on them. You have no access to what's inside. You may not even be able to pick them out among your normal recollections. Time doesn't erode those locks, either. The only way to access whatever those boxes contain is for the person who originally stored them to grant you access. Or…"

"Or?" she asked as he trailed off.

"*Or* you break in." His grim expression sent a shiver down her spine—he didn't mean those words purely as a figure of speech. "You find a way to access those memories no matter what it takes. Even if you must shatter the box, lock, and all."

She winced. "That sounds painful."

"It is. More than you can imagine. Sometimes, agony is a necessary evil if the potential outcome is regaining control of your own life."

He was speaking more than just theoretically.

"Have you had that happen?" she asked. Though, it was hard to picture anyone having any semblance of control over him. "Did someone ever tell you not to remember something?"

"No," he said tightly. "Though I'll be honest. There are some things in my past I wouldn't mind having erased."

For a second, her thoughts drifted from her own dilemma to something he'd only hinted at. Never said. "Like what happened to make you leave the pack?"

His startled grunt answered her question before he even voiced a response. "Yes…"

From the way his eyes widened, he had surprised himself with that admission. How long had he suppressed a yearning for home? Loren wished she could empathize.

Her time with her mother was too hazy to yearn for completely. The horror that had come after… She didn't know what it was like to have a place to truly call home. Barring this exact farm, anyway.

"Maybe it's a good thing," she said softly. "Maybe it's better if I don't remember."

For a long moment, Bill said nothing else. The shadows around them grew and distorted, lengthening like fingers reaching from the corners of the room. Loren wasn't sure if unease or sympathy drew her closer, but before she knew it, she was standing beside him.

"Those memories aren't hidden from me like yours are," he went on, his voice hoarse. "I can access them and the pain they cause every single day. There are days that I wish I couldn't, but you should have that ability with your own memories."

He stood, facing her, his hands held open at his sides.

"I can help you access that locked box in your mind, but I need you to trust me. More than you ever have before."

This had to be the third time he used that exact phrasing. Loren wasn't sure if it were overkill, or his desperate attempt at a warning. Either way, he was giving her more than enough time to back out. Refuse.

And, even as her belly flipped with foreboding, she couldn't bring herself to do so.

Instead, she licked her lips, prepared to ask exactly what he planned, but he stepped forward before she could voice a single word.

"Those nightmares you've been having," he said, fixing her with a probing stare. "Tell me about them."

Loren blinked, caught off guard by the abrupt change in subject. "I'm running," she said haltingly. As she spoke, the images flashed across her mind in chilling clarity. "Someone's chasing me. I don't know what he wants, but… I just know he can't find me."

A cold sweat coated her skin. Even while awake, the fear was ever present, paralyzing in intensity.

"They're just bad dreams," she added in response to his frown. "It could be what happened with my father. I can't remember that night at all. I've tried to, but I can't."

She expected him to react with alarm, maybe pity. Anything but nod once as if he knew exactly why that was.

"You need to trust me," he insisted. "Because to break through that hold, you need…encouragement."

Her heart sank. "Will you chase me again? Push me down. Make me—"

"No." He snatched her waist, yanking her closer. Their chests met, her wide eyes finding his. The expression on his face wasn't the dangerous, predatory grin he'd sported during their chase. He looked somber, as if his next act would hurt him far more than it could ever affect her. "I need you to relax," he warned, securing her shoulders in an iron grip.

The next second, his mouth settled over hers. At the back of her mind, she recognized that this wasn't a kiss. It was a method of attack. His lips parted, easily prying hers apart. In the same instant, he utilized her shock to shove her back.

She fell and couldn't even cry out before a firm surface broke her fall. The mattress. Something heavy enough to support their combined weight as he settled over her without allowing her to regain her bearings.

"W-What are you doing?" Her heart hammered, trying to beat its way from her chest. She couldn't breathe. The oddest thing, though, was her overall lack of fear. All doubt vanished. Every trace of concern ceased to matter. His weight wasn't a restraint, but a welcome pressure she arched her hips to experience in full. As his heat seeped beneath her skin, a sigh ripped from her lips.

But, if anything, her acceptance seemed to irritate him. He lunged, utilizing his weight to pin her down and crush the remaining air from her lungs. His thighs, pressing into the mattress on either side of her, became a prison. All the while, he consumed her within another kiss—only one far deeper. Ravenous. One of his hands fisted through her hair, using the contact as an anchor.

But the physical touch was just one prong of his approach. She could feel him…inside her head. The sensation was akin to a battering ram slamming against her skull. The wielder's intentions weren't malicious, but that didn't negate the pain of his actions.

It hurt.

"Ow!" she whimpered, resisting the embrace. "W-Wait—"

"Loren, trust me." His lips met her forehead with a desperation she could feel, almost like a coherent thought. *Let me in. Please. Just let me in.* The plea echoed faintly at first, growing stronger and stronger. Clearer. Belatedly, she realized the pain was gone. All that remained was a fervent desire that consumed her from the inside out.

They needed to know. Needed to know. But he didn't want it to hurt. Couldn't let it hurt—

"Trust me," his voice, grated against her earlobe, was the catalyst needed to unlock something within her. She went limp. Panting and breathless, she could only obey his next command.

"I need… You need to be relaxed for this to work." His tone was gentle but with the slightest trace of commanding authority. Her body reacted instantly, and some of her alarm eased.

But not all of it.

The pain in her head quickly faded away in contrast to the growing realization as to how close he was. How heavy. His heat crept beneath the fabric of her borrowed clothes, but muffled. The material felt more like a nuisance than anything. She needed it off. Now.

His eyes seemed to darken with the same understanding. He reached for her sweater first, moving slowly as if to allow her plenty of time to recoil.

She didn't. When his fingers finally slipped beneath the thin wool to brush her skin, her eyelids fluttered at the sensation. *Right.* There was no other word to describe it other than perfect. Natural.

Her body was his to touch. Explore.

But, still, he hesitated.

Her thoughts swam as she struggled to look up. He stared down at her, fully clothed, his jaw tight, those eyes a stormy gray. Some moments, he seemed almost predatory in how he looked at her, like a hungry beast savoring a wounded bit of prey.

But others, he looked…guilty. Like he hated himself for giving in to the attraction she knew they both felt.

"It's okay." Her voice wavered, but resonated more strongly than she would have thought. "I'm… It's okay."

His eyes flashed as if to challenge that. Then he lunged. What happened next occurred so quickly she could barely track the progression. He kissed her first—*really* kissed her—so fiercely her lips stung in the aftermath. Then he pulled back. Snatched her sweater. Fabric tore. More kissing. Heat. Sensation. Skin on skin.

Wait. The little voice of reason spoke up from the back of her mind, only to be drowned out by the rush of warmth that replaced Naomi's designer clothing.

Her pants were gone. Panties too. A rugged, harsher surface replaced the thin fabric, running up her inner thigh before contacting the space between them.

Her breath caught. It was as if all her life she'd gone without something vital, never knowing what it was. Until now. His touch. His warmth. His possession. They cleared her mind of everything but the need for more. All of him.

Her nails raked over his forearm as she gripped it tight, still processing the foreign sensations wafting through her.

He went rigid, giving her that time, she realized. Then just as she relaxed again, he rocked his hand.

A sound she'd never heard tore from her throat, only to be swallowed by his mouth. He did it intentionally, smothering her gasp as a thick finger eased inside of her. She recognized the shape instantly, coated in warm, calloused skin.

Her cheeks flamed as her knees buckled—but there wasn't time to panic at the intrusion. As if from far away, she felt that probe against her mind again, but there was no pain. Just acceptance. He picked through her thoughts gently. Recalling that analogy he made, this room was his to explore as he wished. With single-minded focus, he fixated on only a handful of memories in particular. Her mother…

Suddenly, the agony returned tenfold. Wincing, Loren ripped her mouth from his, sucking in air. "W-Wait—"

"It's okay." He stroked her again, igniting a trail of fire that lanced up her spine. Her hips arched off the mattress, her mind adrift.

"Loren." Guttural and soft, his voice was her only anchor to the present. "Relax. I won't hurt you."

He wouldn't…

The discomfort was entirely her own. A part of her didn't like this. Those memories couldn't be unearthed. They were dangerous. Excruciating.

"Just a little more," he breathed against her parted lips. More gently than he had the right to be, he caught a sliver of skin between his teeth and nipped. It should have hurt, but it didn't. If anything, her body craved the sharp sting. Wanted him to bite down harder. "A little more, then it's over."

Memories flickered through her head in a torrent. They were old. From when she was six. Eight? As one image sharpened in clarity, she gasped. The woman was a stranger, but one so familiar, Loren questioned how she could have forgotten her in the first place. Her mother—so beautiful it hurt, with mournful blue eyes and pink lips contorted in a faint smile. Her heart swelled with an adoration she must have pushed to the back of her consciousness.

Then, without warning, someone else replaced her. A man? He was older. She'd never seen him before, or she couldn't remember.

Until now.

He was too close. She tried to run, but he pulled her back, gripping her arm. In the distance was a vaguely familiar living room with a simple couch and yellow walls. Her old house? She didn't know. Wherever they were, it was forever scarred with terrifying memories.

Panic rose up within her as her heart pounded, threatening to hammer its way from her chest. She couldn't remember! No! She couldn't!

But her will wasn't the force driving this recollection, and she could only watch in horror as it continued to unfold.

The unfamiliar man, wrenched her to face him as he crouched to her level. His eyes were so cold. A hue of blue like winter ice, devoid of all warmth. Humanity.

"You are never to access your lupine side." A harsh voice echoed throughout her skull, radiating so much power she cowered internally. *"Not even if your life is in danger. Not when you are afraid—"*

"Please," a woman cried. Her face appeared beyond the man's shoulder, contorted with pain. Agony, the likes of which Loren couldn't imagine. *"She's just a child. She doesn't know. I never even told him—"*

"Enough!"

It was only when she heard the scream resonate throughout the room that Loren realized it had come from her. She was crying. Sobbing openly and Bill stood paces from the bed, his expression horrified.

"I'm done," he insisted, his hands raised before him in a gesture of surrender. "It's over."

"I can't… I can't." She cradled her head, rocking back and forth, but already the pain was subsiding. All that remained was nauseating exhaustion. She couldn't keep her eyes open. Couldn't think.

We can't remember. Her mind seemed to conspire to suppress those memories again, burying them deep down to never be accessed.

We can't. Can't...

Overwhelmed, she slumped onto the mattress, squeezing her eyes shut. Even as the tiredness took over, she was aware of him. Bill.

Rather than relieved, he seemed...furious. His anger lashed through whatever tenuous link existed between them. The wrath wasn't directed at her—she knew that much.

It had flared the second he saw the face of the man from her memories. Her nightmares.

20

Well, his plan had backfired spectacularly.

If he had been confused about the origins of Loren Connors before, Bill was downright perplexed now. While he was no expert in recovering memories, they'd broken through, alright—and without fail, all the clues led to the same damn place. Black Mountain. Ironically, Lukka wasn't the man in the center of this chaos.

Damn. Bill loathed to even consider the alternative suspect. While there were many things he regretted about leaving the pack behind, they could be boiled down to recent events. Lukka. Emma. Kyle.

Never did he think he would ever question the one man whose presence had been a constant positive influence throughout his life. What he saw… It had to be a mistake. Someone else had starred in Loren's memory—not *him*.

But how many random men sported those features and happened to be an Alpha who spent decades honing his skill?

No… Only one could have been the figure who commanded Loren to forget.

Lukas Grehmaine, the former Alpha of Black Mountain.

Bill loathed to even consider it—the tooth fairy seemed a more likely culprit. There had to be an explanation, but there just wasn't time to think of one.

Her pain took precedence over all else. Though he tried to rationalize against it, he couldn't resist the primal urge that made him hold her afterward. Comfort her, even if it meant strengthening the bond. Enduring her heat. Savoring the feel of her arousal on his fingertips like the sick monster he truly was.

Only when she finally drifted off to sleep could he do anything else.

Even if it meant literally running in circles.

After an hour of patrolling the property boundary under the guise of hunting for Eislanders—or any other enemy—Bill felt no calmer than before. The physical exertion was merely a way to stall. Otherwise, there was nothing to distract from the reality of what he'd done.

And learned.

Predictably, once the shock wore off, doubt set in. Then guilt.

The quest for answers aside, the method he utilized to retrieve them was…

Beyond dangerous. He had played with her head, extending a game that no one would win in the end. Hell, he'd had no right to enter her mind in the first place, good intentions or not. Either way, it was too late for regrets.

He could only pray that she recovered quickly enough with no lasting side effects. At best, she would be exhausted and drained for a few days. At worst, she would be prone to irrational outbursts and mild paranoia—to say the least of any emotional damage he might have done just by touching her like that.

His fingers burned, unwashed, still drenched in her scent. *Damn.* It took everything he had to curl a fist and keep himself from bringing them to his nostrils and inhaling all traces of her.

Until he couldn't refrain any longer.

A strained hiss escaped him as guilt battled the arousal unfurling in his gut. Loren deserved so much better. Her first sexual encounter should have been with a man of her choosing—without the mating bond muddling her thoughts. His only consolation was that he hadn't gone any further than touching. Tasting.

But, *damn…* His entire body hummed for more. He couldn't get her scent out of his head, nor the memory of her writhing beneath him. If he could compel himself to forget, he would.

Nothing good would come out of this. The honorable man he claimed to be would go back now and break the bond, consequences be damned.

But how honorable could he be when he had based everything he knew on the example of the only figure in his life worth emulating?

Lukas had been his idol—and even that term was an understatement. That man gave him everything. His purpose. His place in the world. The knowledge he cherished and everything he admired about his lupine heritage. He wasn't related to the Grehmains by blood, but no one would have known by the way the Alpha treated him. Few men, lupine or otherwise, would have accepted him so easily.

Every interaction Bill could remember had been punctuated with nothing but the stern but kind man he'd known his whole life. That man wouldn't have compelled a child to silence. Not only that, but to deny her lupine side. It was…

Unheard of. Cruel wasn't a heinous enough word.

Monstrous came close.

Even if he had years to dwell on it, he doubted he could come up with a plausible explanation. *No.* Only one place held the answers, and they didn't have years to find them, but days. Maybe hours.

And if Lukka decided to preempt any move he might make… Well, that would certainly complicate things. Feeding his paranoia was the fact that Sonia hadn't called him yet. The anomaly buzzed at the back of his mind, only to grow into full-blown fear by the time he finally returned to the house. He entered the kitchen and reached for the phone, dialing the number she typically called from.

No one picked up. On its face, that alone wasn't enough to cause suspicion, but he knew Sonia. Either she was too busy to call him, or she physically couldn't. The thought of her facing punishment on his behalf was too damn much.

Besides, he had another dilemma to worry about. Someone had summoned him to Elkton for a reason. The Eislander beta?

Their actual identity didn't matter. Venturing so close to a rival territory—let alone Black Mountain—was risky at best. Though, hell, if he did plan on issuing a challenge, there was no better time than now to do so.

Lukka wouldn't sit around twiddling his thumbs, waiting for his next move. In fact, the bastard was probably goading the Eislanders into doing his dirty work. Should they falter, Bill didn't doubt the Alpha wouldn't hesitate to come after him directly.

Suddenly, a shrill sound pierced the quiet—the phone, a sign from the universe if there ever was one. Warily, he answered it, unsure of what to expect. Lukka, issuing a summons?

"Bill?"

His breath caught. The voice was high-pitched. Not Lukka. "Sonia?"

"You need to leave," she said in a rush. "Leave New Walsh. Now. Leave the state if you have to—"

"What's going on?" He'd rarely heard her this unnerved. Her voice shook, and he growled at the thought of what might have happened to have her so spooked. "Tell me."

Static interspersed her words. "Lukka isn't... I think he knows what you intend, and he won't ever let you face him to do so. If he sees you even attempt to approach the territory, he plans to head you off and have you killed."

Bill formed a fist and slammed it onto the nearest counter. "Predictable." He'd feared as much, though he'd hoped that even Lukka would respect the old laws enough to play fair, at least in this instance. No such luck.

But if Lukka was on the warpath, who knew what he might do to anyone he perceived as an enemy. "Sonia, get somewhere safe—"

"I'll be fine. He can't risk hurting me outright. Please, Bill. Just go."

She hung up. Hissing, Bill tried to call her back to no response. He wound up pacing in frustration, torn between his duty to Loren—and the others—and the need to rush to his packmate's aid. In the end, he decided on a grim compromise that ironically would kill multiple birds with one stone.

No more stalling.

He would return to Black Mountain.

Whether he liked it or not.

$\mathcal{L}$oren groaned as a loud thud shattered the quiet, snapping her awake. Her head throbbed, and every thought felt like jagged glass slicing through her skull. There wasn't time to wallow in the agony, though.

Something was off. Her heart started racing before she could pinpoint the reason why. Tension laced the air. She could practically taste it—a scent like pine, but bitter. Colder. Winter. Alarm displaced her discomfort, and she stirred, fighting to make sense of her surroundings.

She was on a bed. In McGoven's room? Before she could be sure, another sound reached her ears, providing more clarity.

"...my truck isn't large enough. ...need to use... Thank you, Naomi..." The voice came muffled from below. McGoven definitely, followed by someone with a higher cadence. Micha?

"This is so weird. All the stealth and stuff. I feel like we're going on a mission or something—"

"*We* aren't doing a damn thing," McGoven warned. His voice radiated quiet anger she suspected had been simmering within him since the two men from the rival pack visited. Only now it had seeped into the very atmosphere, tinging the air with that wintery chill. Whatever unease infected her—he was the source of it. "You pack up, stay close and stay out of trouble. That is all. Wait—"

Suddenly the voices went silent, and a pair of steady, quiet thumps echoed throughout the house, advancing in her direction. Footsteps.

Her cheeks flamed as she looked down, taking stock of her shivering frame crouched over the rumpled blankets. Throbbing headache aside, she was mostly naked apart from an oversized T-shirt she couldn't remember putting on. There wasn't even time to cover herself with the sheet. Not even a second later, a tall figure appeared in the doorway, and she felt her entire body resonate with relief instead of shame.

He wasn't…hiding this time. He faced her out in the open without the aid of nightfall or shadows to obscure his expression. The contrast was startling. Pale daylight bathed him in a soft, gray glow. It was morning—very early. Dawn? She must have slept right through the night, but judging from how her body ached, she could still use a few more hours. Every nerve and bit of muscle felt used and abused.

His nearness, however, soothed most of the uneasiness. She found herself shifting toward the end of the mattress, aching to get closer. It was all coming back to her now. What he'd done to help her remember.

His kiss. His touch…

She drew her knees together and swallowed at the memories. Looking at his face, however, made her blood run cold. He stood back, his arms crossed—the first sign that something was weighing on his mind. The second clue was that he was fully dressed for once, wearing a red and black plaid shirt that had to be the most colorful item she'd seen him in. A pair of dark jeans enhanced the look, and he resembled a lumberjack rather than an officer.

Or a lycan, for that matter.

Ironically, the hard gleam in his eye was reminiscent of a soldier ready to go to war more than anything else.

"Something's wrong," she croaked. "Tell me."

"How did you sleep?" he asked, skirting the question.

Loren tensed. She knew that tone—and that the harmless inquiry was merely to preface what he really wanted to say. Something unspoken loomed between them, suffocating her with every passing second.

"Fine. Now tell me what's going on." She drew her knees up to her chin and reached for the sheet, draping it over her front.

Whatever happened between them seemed over and done with. He was keeping his distance for a reason. Presumably, the same reason why his eyes never left her face, devoid of the hunger she could recall. By the second, the man who'd touched her so intimately felt more like a dream than reality.

"You should sleep for a few more hours. But..." He frowned imperceptibly. Then he sighed. "Tonight, we're leaving. There isn't time to pack much, but Naomi will bring some clothing for you."

"Where are we going?" she asked. Though deep down, a part of her already suspected the answer.

"To Black Mountain—"

"No!" She lurched to her feet, leaving the sheet behind. Her knees buckled, barely able to support her weight, but she gritted her teeth and fought to remain standing. This was a conversation she couldn't passively accept. "I'm not going anywhere. You promised!"

"You should rest," he suggested without so much as blinking—he'd been prepared for this reaction. "I forgot to warn you that there might be side effects from exploring those memories. You've been put through the wringer, physically and mentally. We won't leave until later tonight—"

"Why?" she demanded, horrified for cutting him off. But rebellious anger smothered the guilt. He deserved it for treating her like an afterthought once again.

"You're going to be emotionally raw for a few days," he explained, audibly straining for calm. It was the way he'd spoken when explaining why she needed to go off with a stranger like unwanted baggage.

Because he knew best.

"Stop treating me like a child. You said you'd let me stay. You said—"

"Will you listen to me?" He raised his voice by only a fraction, but she stiffened, her teeth slamming together. A familiar tingle raced down her spine—once again, she was experiencing firsthand his uncanny ability to manipulate and control.

But a part of her lurched, panicked. He wouldn't make her listen this time. The desire to move wasn't conscious. Her body took over, staggering past him before he could think to stop her.

"Loren, wait!"

Run! She tore down the stairs and ran through the front door before she did something stupid. Scream, punch, kick? Act like a spoiled child?

She just wanted to know *why…*

Why was he so intent on pushing her away? Eyes blurring, she made it out onto the porch, intending to run—disappear beneath the trees.

The second she took a step, someone appeared at the bottom of the steps, barring her path. McGoven. A twitching muscle in his jaw was the only sign of exertion. How in the world had he managed to move so quickly? She doubted she would ever understand.

"Loren," he said, still utilizing that firm tone. "Just let me explain—"

"Stop!" She slapped her hands over her ears, anything to keep that tone from penetrating deep. "I don't want to hear your rationale. I'm tired of you playing with my head. You've been planning this the whole time, haven't you? To throw me away again?"

He had the decency to look ashamed, at least. His lips moved, words distorted by the pulse rushing through her hands, but she didn't dare take them down.

She could guess his excuses. *It's for the best. You just need to understand…*

"Loren." He mounted the bottom step, and she scrambled back, throwing her hands out in front of her.

"Don't touch me!"

"Loren—"

"I'm eighteen," she shouted over him. "You can't make me go anywhere I don't want to."

His eyes flashed in a way that clearly said—*The hell I can't.*

"I'm not making you do anything," he insisted out loud, stressing every word. "We will go there together, so that I can contact the pack—"

"Screw the pack!" Loren didn't even recognize the sound of her own voice. It was loud, high pitched—the shriek of a crazy woman, but she felt too on edge to really care. All that mattered was the feeling ripping through her chest. Pain. Once again, she was being thrown away, pushed to the side like an unwanted toy.

"I don't want to go with *them*," she insisted. "I need to stay with you!"

He flinched as if she'd slapped him. The next second, those eyes narrowed, deepening to a dark shade of steel.

"No, you don't."

Nearby, a squirrel darted from the bushes and took off across the yard. Even Loren sensed the warning in his tone. Any other day, she might have backed down.

This wasn't one of those days.

"Yes, I do!" She raised her voice while his only got deeper.

"Loren—"

"I'm sick of you telling me what I want and what I need." The words seemed to just tumble out. She had no idea where they came from, but it was impossible to stop. "You don't know anything! I *know* what I want."

You.

He shook his head. "You don't have a fucking clue. And if you want to talk about this, then we're not going to have a screaming match at five in the damn morning."

Loren gritted her teeth, aware that her fingers were bunched into fists, nails biting into the flesh of her palms. The feeling pulsing through her veins wasn't *all* self-righteous anger—he smelled different. A low, prickly fury bristled off him in waves. It was in his voice. His scent.

I'm warning you.

The danger didn't frighten her. Not one damn bit. If anything, it was like a sick part of her fed off his rage. Her shirt felt tight. Whenever she breathed, all she could *taste* was fucking pine…

"Good." He seemed to take her silence as a sign that she was listening, giving in. "Loren, go back inside and—"

"No." The word seemed ripped right from the pit of her stomach. "I'm not going anywhere."

She turned, intending to march across the porch and jump off the other end, rather than pass him, but his voice yanked her back like a fish on a hook.

"You're not thinking straight. You need to sleep. Get back in the house."

"No."

"*Yes*—" his tone made her belly quake. "Whether I have to drag you up to bed myself, or—"

"Stop."

"Listen to me—"

"No!"

She remembered slamming the screen door and whirling to face him.

She remembered shouting…

But she didn't quite remember the moment she leaped from the porch and *lunged* at him. No logical thought ran through her mind, just action.

But the element of surprise gave her the edge to catch him off guard. Her hands slammed into his shoulders, and he fell back with a startled grunt. She saw him hit the ground hard.

But something more shocking distracted her from any concern— her hands, weren't really "hands," but paws topped by sharp nails that bit into his skin…and the words tearing from her throat, weren't "words" at all…

But growls.

22

oren Connors was gone, and Bill could only gape at the creature growling in that meek woman's place. It crouched over him, its body lithe, compact…

And purely lupine.

The wolf was barely half the size of his lycan form overall, but sleek and lean. A brown pelt covered her slender limbs, darkening to nearly black over a delicate snout. Her eyes were that same, unsettling shade of hazel—but both were wide with a horror he couldn't even begin to imagine.

"Loren…" He fought to keep his voice steady. "You need to listen to me. Wait—"

She took off, clearing his body in one long leap before darting for the woods.

Bill lunged to his feet, wincing as his shoulders stung, unintentionally scratched by her claws. Fear for her easily overrode any pain. "Loren!"

Already, she had disappeared beneath the trees with a quickness that took his breath away.

"What's going on?" Micha and Naomi rushed onto the porch behind him, but he only paused to shed his jeans before taking off.

He invoked the shift mid-step and hit the ground on all fours, growling in the back of his throat. Loren's scent pulled at him like a tether, leading him blindly through the woods, past the stream, and beyond.

Rather than chase her down, he kept his distance, giving her space to run freely. It was a risky decision. She could have gone anywhere—and a frightened, newly-shifted wolf was erratic at best and unpredictable at worst.

Either way, she didn't stay a beast for long.

He could sense the exact moment she shifted back into human form, near the boundary of his property. From yards away, he heard her startled gasp. After that, she just ran on foot, hurt, alone, and naked. His heart throbbed for her—at the same time, he increased his pace. If she made it into town, Bill knew that it would have taken all the skill of an Alpha to convince that many mortals to forget what they had seen.

In the end, her eventual destination didn't surprise him one bit.

With one last surge, he pulled free of the forest and entered the small, neglected backyard of a decrepit brown house. The location made for twisted, poetic irony—wolves were always drawn home.

Even if that place happened to be hell.

Heedless of any mortals who might have been strolling down the street a few yards away, he shifted and mounted the porch steps before his toes had even finished forming from paws.

"Loren?"

She said nothing, but he didn't need verbal confirmation of her presence. He could hear her heart pounding in a manic rhythm even from there. Regardless, he didn't relax until he finally caught sight of her crouched form through a gap in the back door.

She sat slumped against the base of a counter, face turned away from him. Her knees were drawn up to her chest, dark hair pooling on the floor. The sight triggered an unwelcome flash of *déjà vu*—he'd only seen her this upset once before.

The night Fred Connors attacked her and set everything after into motion.

"Loren." Cautiously, he entered the kitchen, but she didn't react as the rotted floorboards creaked beneath his weight. Even so, he kept his distance, hovering near the threshold.

"I should have warned you," he said gently. "What I did would leave you emotionally raw. You might be more prone to anger and fear. It's a normal reaction."

"Leave me alone."

Her toneless whisper affected him like nothing else. Her fear, confusion, and pain were like *knives*, driving deep into the pit of his stomach—drowning out that tiny voice in his head that proclaimed everything he'd done had been for her sake.

This was about way more than a misunderstanding. Still, for someone who had just phased for the first time, she seemed to be holding up well enough. At least she wasn't curled in a ball, cursing like Naomi had been.

"We need to talk," he went on softly. "I'm not sending you away, I swear."

"Oh, really?" Her voice came muffled. "Dropped the 'three days deadline,' have you?"

"You have the right to be upset," he admitted, gripping the screen door just to keep from reaching for her. "About a lot more than this misunderstanding. At least, let me explain."

Her head jerked up, and Bill sucked in a breath as those large hazel eyes stared from over the mountains of her knees.

"You want me gone. What more is there?"

Bill recognized her tone all too well. That wasn't the average talk of a scorned teenage girl. That was the lycan speaking. The lycan who valued trust and safety and loyalty above all else. The lycan who was inherently pissed at the deception of her mate.

Even if she didn't understand the depth of it.

"I'm not sending you anywhere," he said, stepping fully into the narrow kitchen. "I'm going *with* you. If you want something to be angry for, though, I can give you a few reasons."

A lot more than a few. But there was no need to traumatize her further by spilling the whole truth while they were both exhausted and naked.

"We should go back," he suggested. "You can shower, and we can get dressed. Then, once you're rested, I can explain just what I plan to do."

She stiffened, wrapping her arms tighter around her body. Her hair was long enough to shield most of her. Even so…he had to force himself to look away. To move at all.

The wolf in him yearned to bask in the glory of his mate without a shred of remorse. Instead, he pushed past her, into the living room, where he took the rickety stairs to the upper level.

Things like guilt or respect for the dead didn't stop him from rummaging through the tiny room that had belonged to Fred Connors. He grabbed a pair of sweats at random from a dresser and pulled them on for modesty's sake, suppressing his disgust at the thought of wearing the man's clothing.

Loren's room was different.

As he headed toward that tiny space, no bigger than a closet, he had to pause before he could step inside and held his breath.

Not that it helped.

The stench of her fear *still* tainted the air. It was everywhere, itching beneath his skin. Invoking a fierce desire to protect. To destroy anyone who'd ever hurt her.

Kill…

He shook his head to clear the thought before he barged in and managed to grab a sheet from the bed. He had removed any clothing the morning after the attack, but even a blanket would be better than nothing.

He returned downstairs to find her in the same spot. After leaving the sheet within her reach, he stood back. Seeing her so tense and fragile made him realize that taking her back to the house and putting off their inevitable conversation would be cruel. What better way than to just rip the Band-Aid off now? "Loren…"

Funnily enough, he didn't even know where to begin.

I found you? I mated you? I let you stay with Fred Connors even when I knew he was hurting you?

Those indiscretions barely cut the surface. His biggest crime against her sprung from his lips before he could hold it back.

"I lied to you, Loren. About more than you could ever know."

There was no way to easily explain—but he didn't have to.

"There's another side to the lycan way of life." He sank into a crouch just beyond the doorway. "Sometimes, it can be the only option for someone who has grown up without the shelter of the pack. A way to integrate them while minimizing the trauma. It—"

He broke off, grunting in annoyance. *No.* He wouldn't give her some bullshit explanation or try to pretty it up. With a guttural sigh, he tilted his head back to eye the ceiling. The truth, as repulsive as it was, needed to be said. No fluff. No excuses.

"We take mates, Loren."

She reacted to that word. A ragged gasp escaped her lips. For all his insistence on coming clean, he couldn't even look at her. *Coward,* the wolf in him, scolded as he focused on a light fixture. *You fucking coward.*

"It's the highest form of connection," he went on gravely. "Something deeper than any human concept of a relationship. Once a man and woman mate, it…" He grappled for the right words and could only find three. "It binds them."

He didn't even realize that he'd fallen silent until the sound of the screen door swinging into the side of the house broke the quiet. The wind had picked up, heralding yet another storm. The rain would help cover their tracks, at least. Sooner or later, someone would come looking for him. That fact only served to drive in how little time they had, but he didn't say a damn word to hurry things along. Loren deserved to process this in peace. It was the least he could give her.

Once a few minutes ticked by, he soldiered on. "Taking a mate without consent is a last resort. But that doesn't excuse the fact that it's wrong. It's a violation of the most intimate kind. When lycans mate, they become in sync. They can access each other's thoughts, feelings, memories."

On Black Mountain, it wasn't that unusual for a member to offer to mate an outsider to make the transition easier. But he doubted that anyone could dredge up an example of someone mating a naïve young girl to protect her from the horrors locked inside her own head.

"How?" Her voice came so softly he barely heard it. "How do you…mate?"

He made himself look up and reluctantly meet those watchful eyes.

"You enter someone's core. Their mind. It's a bond, more intimate than even sex," he said, cringing at the thought. The crimson spreading across her cheeks told him that she knew damn well what he meant. "But the two must be willing…to an extent, to prevent any difficulties adjusting."

Or, in her case, stunned, traumatized, and barely conscious. His skin *crawled* with the memory of her, lying there passively beneath him—but trying to forget wouldn't help him any.

What was done was done.

"It's not just that," he added, clenching his hands into fists. "The mating bond is strong—stronger than any other connection in the world. It shapes those under its influence. Drives them to protect and defend each other at all costs. It's…"

All in all, it had proven to be a pain in his ass.

He could feel it, even now, bristling at the fear and unease that wafted from her like a bad stench. He had to bite his lip just to keep from reaching for her. Holding her. Touching her. Fuck, he had to drill his own nails into his palms just to keep from…

"What aren't you telling me?" Her eyes were sharp, picking up on his hesitation.

Bill choked back a groan. "I *can't* tell you," he said finally.

Call it weak or stupid—whatever. He couldn't say it out loud and watch her reaction. He *couldn't.*

"But…I can show you."

He rose and moved toward her as cautiously as a soldier navigating an active minefield. To his surprise, she didn't flinch when he offered his hand.

It hung in the air for a long while before she finally took it, pulling herself upright. Bill had enough sense to turn away as she stooped for the sheet and wrapped it around her trembling frame.

"Tell me," she whispered, facing him from beneath that curtain of hair. "Please."

Bill couldn't help himself. Fingers shaking, he placed a hand on her shoulder.

Just this once. One last feel of her delicate muscles flexing beneath his palm before he lost her forever. Her scent teased the air, and his nostrils flared, desperate for one last whiff. Against every ounce of logic in his brain, he leaned in, allowing his mouth to brush the corner of her jaw before settling near her ear.

"I'm sorry," he rasped.

And then…

He just let go.

Finally, releasing her memories was easier than he ever would have thought. It was like a weight being lifted off his shoulders. A relief. He could finally *breathe* without that darkness at the back of his mind. Though, he would have gladly kept that pain for eternity to prevent the strangled sob that broke from her.

Her eyes widened, glistening as the memories returned faster than she could handle them all. Even now, Bill couldn't bring himself to go through the worst of them—but he could guess fair enough.

It was too late to change his mind, but as her expression fell, he would have given anything to do just that.

23

*L*oren swayed on her feet, knowing that his grip was the only thing holding her upright. But rather than comfort, his touch repelled her, confused her, irritated...

She recoiled as a tangled mass of memories overwhelmed her all at once. In a distorted slideshow, they ran through her brain, each one more painful than the last.

McGoven. Fred Connors. Uncle Bart.

Punctuating them at random intervals were the recovered instances of her mother, and the terrifying figure from her nightmares, now with a face.

It was like waking up from a hazy dream when she hadn't even been aware that she'd been sleeping. She could only stare into McGoven's silver eyes and attempt to process the various emotions rising within her.

Everything was...

Too clear.

Too sharp.

Too *much.*

Rage. Anger. Hate. Pain. Fear.

More pain.

Fear, fear, fear, fear, fear.

She'd forgotten so many twisted, horrible things—and wished never to remember them. Abruptly, the last night in her father's house came back to her in snatches. *He dragged her out of bed… shoved her down the stairs…beat her.*

She remembered running, falling, screaming for help.

The knife. The woods. Her nightgown was gone, torn around her like broken wings. She was curled up on the ground beside her father's dead body…

Only now she had a pretty damn good idea of who killed him.

"Oh…God." Her fingers shook as she braced them against the counter—anything to stay upright as the world started spinning. McGoven had danced around her father's murder for a reason, but one too horrifying to fathom.

Some nameless criminal hadn't killed him.

"I did it." She *had* to say it out loud. Admit what she figured some distant part of her had known all along. "I stabbed him. I killed my fath—"

"He wasn't your father," McGoven said gruffly. Throughout her violent recollections, he maintained a grip on her shoulder, keeping her upright. Though his fingers flexed, as if expecting her to pull away.

"You protected yourself," he insisted. "I'm pretty sure that if you hadn't, he would have killed *you*—"

"Don't." Loren wrenched out of his grasp and staggered for balance. "Don't try to pretty it up because you think I can't handle the truth."

She couldn't—but his concern didn't make it any easier.

"I killed him," she croaked. "I stabbed him with a knife. And you—"

More visions filled her head, chilling her to the bone. He had been there. *Standing over her. Watching. Dragging her back when she tried to...*

God, had she really tried to kill herself? The thought seemed so surreal, like it belonged to someone else. A whimper tore from her throat as more images flashed through her head. *He had pulled her back...confirmed that her father was dead, and...*

"Loren, just let me explain—"

"No!" She squeezed her eyes shut, fighting to remember. *Him. He was in her head. Her soul. Taking. Obscuring. Controlling.*

"I only wanted to protect you." He'd taken a step closer, towering above like a wall of muscle, eyes so bright they practically burned. She had never seen him this tormented, as if every breath he took was poisoned, killing him from the inside out.

"Loren, please. Listen to me." He reached out, and she flinched.

"Don't touch me!"

"Okay." He withdrew, displaying his hands passively in front of him. "I just need you to know that everything I did was to protect you."

"Protect me?" She would have laughed if the thought wasn't so horrifying. "From what? Why didn't I remember? Why now? Why? *What did you do to me?*"

Because he had done *something* alright. Something that had ripped away the mental veil keeping the dark thoughts at bay. Something to block out these memories in the first place.

Then, it hit her.

Mates. That damn word everyone kept flinging around. It was the real reason why he followed her the night he sent her with Kyle. Why he kept her near him at all. Probably the same reason why the very *thought* of him being around any other woman nearly drove her insane.

He entered her soul—but that wasn't the horrible part that had tears springing to her eyes.

After forging such an intimate bond between them, and seeing her memories and thoughts for himself, he then deemed she was a burden he didn't want any responsibility for.

And he threw her away.

"You made me feel like I was being crazy," she said in a rasping voice, spinning to meet his gaze. "But you knew why I was attracted to you. I felt like something was wrong with me, but… If you didn't want me, why do that in the first place?"

"Loren." Something she couldn't name flashed through those silver eyes. Was it pain? Guilt? "You have every right to be angry with me. Let me take you back—"

"No!" Suddenly, the room felt too small. Enclosed. Suffocating. Panting for air, she staggered for the door.

"Loren, wait—"

"Get away from me!"

She fled onto the porch, feeling the wind whip her hair back and enhance the fact that she had left the sheet behind. Ignoring the cold, she raced down the stairs and took off, choosing a direction at random.

But she would never be fast enough to escape him.

"Loren!" His voice resonated through her skull, rousing a sudden need to go back. *No!* She slapped her hands over her ears—anything to tune him out. Make him go away.

Her memories, her fear, her horror—all of it was too much. The specters of Fred Connors and Uncle Bart loomed large, but the men themselves were already dead. McGoven wasn't the source of her rage—not by a long shot—but he was the only target she had left to focus on. And in this moment…

She needed to fear someone. Hate someone. Blame *someone*. For her past and for the horrific things she had yet to face.

She needed him to just *go away!*

It was as if everything she'd ever felt boiled within her all at once. Until… She stumbled, tripping over her own feet, and her hand went to her chest. It *hurt.* Her initial fear was that something had hit her—a bullet? What else could explain this pain tearing through her? Ripping her apart?

But…he felt it too. His agonized grunt made her whirl around, frozen by the expression on his face. Her first thought was that he'd been mortally wounded. Stabbed.

But there was no blood. No one else was in view, either.

"You broke it," he said hoarsely in between pants. "On your own. How did you even… Fuck!"

He collapsed to his knees, gripping his skull with both hands as if he felt his brain might burst from it.

Despite everything—the pain and the rage—she couldn't stop herself from racing to his side. "What's wrong? What did… What did I break?"

Something vital—though she never even touched him. Horror ripped through her, and she wracked her brain for anything she could have done. Any touch. Any errant word.

Her tantrum alone couldn't cause this. As he struggled to regain control of his breathing, McGoven hunched over. His eyes were tight with pain before they suddenly widened, meeting her gaze.

"I'm sorry," he rasped. "I'm so sorry…"

It seemed surreal that he cared so much about her even though he was the one in agony. Sweat beaded over his brow, and she was convinced he'd been injured after all. "Do you need a doctor?"

"No." He shook his head and stood disjointedly, lacking his usual grace. As he towered over her, she realized that he was just wearing pants while she remained naked, in full view of anyone who happened to be gazing into the Connors' backyard.

That possibility seemed to matter to him more than his own discomfort. Grimacing, he headed for the woods. "I… I'll explain later. Right now, we need to get back."

"To leave?" Loren didn't move as her initial reason for running came back to her. Her cheeks flamed. It seemed so irrationally childish—freaking out because he had even hinted at leaving her again.

At the moment, the fear had felt monumental. Like a betrayal.

And now? It was harder to grasp that prior rationale. Her thoughts seemed to come all at once, from varying directions.

Fear. Shock. Alarm. Pain. Interspersed among them were images and fragments—memories.

Fred Connors. The night he attacked her. Her mother's death and the horror that followed.

She groaned, clutching her forehead. The mental assault was ruthless, unbearably painful. It took every ounce of control she possessed just to wrestle them aside and refocus on the present. McGoven—and one vital fact he himself had admitted. Looking up, she met his gaze, surprised as hot tears slipped down her cheeks unbidden.

"You're taking me back to Black Mountain."

"No… Not quite." He inclined his head in her direction, but she noticed that he winced as if moving at all hurt. "We're leaving *together*. All of us. That's what I've been trying to tell you. Lukka and the others… They'll come for me soon, and Sonia might be in danger if I don't act. Leaving now is the only way to stay ahead. Besides, Black Mountain holds the answers to your heritage, and we need to find them. Last night, the others and I loaded up my truck with whatever supplies we might need. All that's left is to hit the road before the pack comes calling."

"What if I don't want to know?" she asked in a whisper. "My past. What if… What if it's not important anymore?"

He squared his jaw, and she could see a bead of sweat drip down his forehead. "Well, I do. This isn't just about you anymore—I need to know. I have to."

Something in his tone warned that his motive was more than just curiosity. "Know what?"

"Why *my* Alpha compelled you to forget your lycan side and left you to be raised out here alone." His words registered in two distinct ways.

The first was that he was furious. So very angry. But, as she weighed his revelation, Loren couldn't process her shock. It was enough to diminish whatever mixture of confusion and horror she felt toward him.

"What? Do you mean..." The man from her memories. "You knew him."

Bill nodded, his expression darker than ever. "Yes. And the only way we are ever going to get real answers is to go and find them."

Loren didn't move, feeling her teeth chatter. Micha and Bill seemed rarely affected by the cold, but she was already shivering, and the prospect of walking the entire way to Baker farm made it sink in just how far she'd run in only a few minutes.

While a wolf.

"I just shifted," she blurted with a tattered laugh. That seemed to be an understatement. Amid that violent transformation of muscle and bone, she felt wild, untamed emotion she'd never experienced. Ever. Remnants of it lingered still, heightening her awareness of everything from her swaying stance, to the way her heartbeat surged beneath her skin.

Her nerves prickled, her knees buckling with unsteady energy. All over, her entire body hummed in a way that felt...

Primal.

Even his nearness resonated differently. His scent overwhelmed every ounce of air she drew in, and she could feel a shadow of his heat despite the distance between them. A part of her shuddered, drawn to him regardless of everything...

"Please," Bill called, snapping her back to the present moment— they were still in the middle of Fred Connors' backyard. "Come with me."

His tone alone coaxed her forward, and she followed him in a daze, still eyeing her thin, pale limbs. They looked the same, belonging to the frail Loren Connors, but within… It was as if her brain had expanded to twice its previous size. She was aware of so much more than her own fear, and discomfort. The sky seemed brighter, the wind far louder, rustling through the trees in a deafening clamor. Even her body seemed affected—her stumbling, unsteady movements were such a violent contrast to the way she'd moved while in wolf form. No wonder McGoven seemed to relish the change.

"Wait here," he said once they reached the boundary of the property. "I'll bring you some clothing. Then we'll load up."

"All of us?"

He nodded. "Micha and I will take my truck. You will ride with Naomi. It's safer for her to be with me than on her own. At least for now."

She couldn't bring herself to argue. "And then?"

"Then we get answers."

What he didn't say echoed in her mind, uttered by that shadowy inner voice—*By any means necessary.*

24

———————

"You drive," Bill told Micha before tossing him the keys. He didn't even know if the kid knew how. Still, if he took the wheel himself, he doubted they could reach Black Mountain in one piece.

From the corner of his eye, he saw Loren and Naomi entering the latter's pink sports car. Admittedly, the flashy model would stick out like a sore thumb anywhere near the relatively rural outskirts of Black Mountain. Oh well. He'd regret the oversight later—among other things.

While he'd kept it together enough, to grab Loren a fresh set of clothing, focusing was a struggle. Funnily enough, the shock was more startling than the unexpected pain.

How damn ironic. He had been prepared to play the hero and break the bond himself, when Loren did so easily without even understanding what it was. On her own. He hadn't expected that plot twist, and it… Unnerved the hell out of him.

Perhaps she had inherited "the calling" as he had, but even so— from the very start, he'd sensed something abnormal in her. A

629

duality of sorts, that allowed her to seem like a harmless human one minute, and a wild, feral lycan the next. Her unusual nature puzzled him, though maybe the horror inflicted on her as a child played a role in it all.

After being suppressed for nearly a decade, her lupine instincts had mutated, becoming just as unpredictable as the environment she'd grown up in. Hell, that might have been the only reason why she'd survived this long.

To protect her, the wolf within had learned to adapt and react however it saw fit.

Even against him.

The worst part hadn't been his own agony at the severance. No… It killed him to witness the pain on her face as she understood the truth. Being stabbed through the chest with a blunt knife would have hurt less. Only one other loss in his life overshadowed this mental anguish—Emma's. But while this pain was different in essence, it went just as deep.

And unlike Emma, Loren wasn't gone. Her scent lingered, taunting him even as they hit the highway, and all traces of her should have been diminished by the fresh air. He couldn't stop his gaze from straying to the rearview mirror, watching that pink car tailing them.

He pictured her inside it, but he couldn't even imagine what she might be thinking. Or feeling.

With the bond gone, he shouldn't have cared—not like this. Gritting his teeth and clenching his hands into fists couldn't suppress the urge itching through his veins. It didn't make sense. Damn it, he *still* wanted… To explain. Comfort her. Hold her.

Every damn thing he'd blamed the bond for.

It wasn't like he didn't have a frame of reference for how this *should* have gone. When Emma died, the pain had nearly hollowed him, but he had still been able to find shreds of himself within the wreckage. A hint of the person he'd been before.

This time…

A part of him still howled that the woman with the unusual scent belonged to him in a way that couldn't be erased—bond or no bond.

She was *his*, always. From that very first day she'd stepped onto his property, the wolf in him had craved her. Claimed her.

All along, he'd fed himself excuses and lies, but the grim truth was that he'd never had a choice. The moment he saw her desperate and in pain, there had been no stopping his instinctive reaction.

The worst part? He would do it all over again.

In a heartbeat.

"So, what's the game plan?" Micha demanded, sounding miles away. "Because, one would hope that, by us going up to Lukka's front door, you would have a strategy for how to announce yourself, and we wouldn't just barge in like lambs to the slaughter…" He laughed weakly. "You *do* have a plan, right?"

Bill gritted his teeth, fighting to refocus on the task at hand. His doubt, or whatever this feeling was, could wait. First things first.

"The 'game plan' is that we aren't going straight to Black Mountain. Not yet," he said. "First, we need to make a detour. I know a neutral piece of territory where we can camp for a night or two. Then we'll decide what to do next from there."

"That sounds…risky," Micha replied. He wasn't even trying to hide his nerves. He sat hunched over the wheel, his eyes bug wide. Every few seconds, he slammed on the brake as if afraid to touch the speed limit.

Bill's one consolation was that he might not have long to reconcile his feelings toward Loren if he died in a fiery car crash. Tentative driving aside, though, the kid had a point.

They couldn't just barge into Lukka's territory unannounced. Surprisingly, Bill had yet to think that far ahead. His gut told him that Lukka would be plotting a long, drawn-out plan to avoid confronting him directly. That's what the bastard excelled at —dirty tricks and underhanded lies. Not to mention Kyle. His thirst for misplaced revenge would play right into Lukka's hands. Bill had more than learned his lesson with Loren to never underestimate a lycan, especially one with nothing to lose.

Rather than dwell on the impending confrontation, he decided to change tack. "Tell me what *you* think we should do?" he asked.

"Well..." Micha cleared his throat. "I think your best option would be to meet with Loreck Eislander first. He's the main one gunning for your throat, and I can have your back. You didn't kill anyone who didn't deserve it. With him convinced, Lukka won't have a real reason to persecute you outright. Other than...well, Loren."

"At least that's one crime taken care of," Bill said tiredly. "Loren's broken the bond on her own, and I've already told her everything. There is nothing to punish me for."

"What?" Micha nearly drove off the road. Only his reflexes allowed him to regain control of the truck in time. "Sorry! I mean, wow. She broke it? Seriously? I've never heard of that before. That's..."

"Not important," Bill said. "What *is* important is keeping her out of my mess."

"Well, the no mate thing helps," Micha admitted. "Then it's Lukka and you on even footing. Though, I guess you don't really have a reason to fight him, if your mate isn't in question."

"Oh, I can think of a few reasons," Bill said quietly. "I've thought about it, and I've decided to challenge him outright. For my freedom…and for the pack."

"What?" This time, Micha slammed on the brake so hard they both almost went flying through the windshield.

"Maybe I should drive," Bill said with a wince. Still, he couldn't deny that Micha's shock was at least partly warranted. He scarcely believed it himself.

He was going home. Not to cut ties, but to reassert himself if possible and take control. Hearing it out loud only cemented how insane a plan it really was. Just twenty-four hours ago, he would have considered the possibility unthinkable. But here he was…

And there wasn't an ounce of doubt in his body. For years, he'd been so hellbent on running that he never stopped to ask himself why. Why had he spent so long on the outside, determined never to look back?

Emma was merely part of the reason. The whole truth was far more complicated. By failing her, he had failed Lukas and his teachings. In his mind, he'd lost the right to ever lead. Maybe taking up the role of a rogue had been his way of punishing himself?

But now…

The past was irrelevant. If his years on the outside had taught him one thing, it was that the world stopped for no one. By shirking the role of Alpha, he'd told himself that he was the only one who deserved to suffer—that he had been sparing the others. Only now could he admit the truth.

He'd been afraid. Afraid that Lukas had pegged him wrong. He was no Alpha. No leader. Just a flawed bastard who couldn't protect the one person he loved the most.

And here he was, letting history repeat itself. If he studied the reasons for his change of heart intently, Loren Connors was the main culprit. Watching her process her newfound lycan abilities made him realize how important community truly was. As Alpha, he could show her exactly what her life was meant to be.

From a platonic distance, of course—though something in his chest pulsed as if in argument. *Mine...*

Logic couldn't quell the possessive impulse. No matter how he tried to reason his way around it, his wolf rebelled at any thought of a future that didn't include her.

As more than just a packmate.

Whenever he envisioned keeping his distance, his mind would replay their every interaction. Every kiss. Every stolen, guilty bit of pleasure.

Every greedy gasp she'd uttered in response.

"I'll be honest," Micha said quietly, drawing his attention. "I don't know if this will work, but I've got your back."

Bill raised an eyebrow. "If you were smart, you would take off and try to rejoin the fold. Lukka won't show you any mercy."

"About that..." Micha squirmed in his seat, and Bill sighed. He knew that look. Today was the day for uncomfortable revelations, it seemed.

"What is it?"

"She made me promise not to tell you. Not until you made up your mind—"

"Sonia?"

Micha nodded.

"Tell me what?"

The young rogue exhaled. "That Lukka is planning on making a play for Eislander territory. Soon."

Bill was thankful he hadn't taken over driving, because now he would be the one running them off the road.

"That greedy son of a bitch. He wants to overthrow Loreck Eislander." Sure, he'd already suspected as much, but to hear it stated so plainly… What the hell was the bastard thinking?

"I had no solid proof," Micha admitted. "Just a gut feeling. That's one of the reasons I didn't want to go back. I got the sense that something bad was going to happen."

"Something so bad you would rather take your chances with a rogue who has an entire pack on his ass?"

Micha laughed. "Actually, yeah. I can't explain it. No one said anything, mind you, but there was something about the way we would ignore the boundaries between the Eislanders and us. It felt off."

"Like provocation," Bill said grimly. "Luckily for Lukka, I've given him all the reason he needs to tighten his borders even more under the guise of vigilance. He did something to Sonia. She told me to run before he came for me."

"So, what's your *real* plan?" Micha asked. This time, the question had a more pointed meaning. "Try to warn the Eislanders? Let's say they *don't* kill you on sight. What then?"

"It's too risky to count on them alone," Bill admitted. "And besides… If Lukka has gotten himself into this mess, it's because he's gotten too comfortable using pawns to fight his battles for him. If I'm to take him on, I do it my way. Alone. No distractions. No proxies."

And no mate. That was one detail Lukka would particularly enjoy —it made him far weaker, susceptible to the crushing doubt plaguing him for five damn years.

"No offense, but it sounds like you have a death wish," Micha pointed out.

"Maybe I do," Bill admitted. Regardless, in addition to the doubt, for the first time in five years, he felt some cruel, twisted semblance of peace having settled on a course of action.

He was done running.

But Black Mountain wasn't the only responsibility he'd abandoned. Sooner or later, he'd need to make up with Loren on *her* terms.

Though, he wouldn't be surprised if she never forgave him.

25

"You look like you're going to puke," Naomi snarled.

Loren had to agree. In the rearview mirror, she looked sweaty. She was wearing yet another of Naomi's old outfits—a pink sweatsuit that highlighted the alarming pallor of her skin. Her heart raced, her entire body jittery. Nausea wasn't the feeling churning her insides, though. Just confusion.

So much she felt she might explode from it.

McGoven had lied to her.

Hidden her memories.

Made her his mate…

And then pushed her away, dismissing everything she'd ever felt toward him.

It was such a strange, intimate concept that her mind couldn't fully process it. More puzzling was that he'd avoided telling her outright what he'd done all this time. A part of her wanted to seethe. Hate him. And why not? He made her feel so damn guilty for something that, for all intents and purposes, was *his* fault.

As she examined her emotions more closely, overall, she just felt… Lost. Buried beneath the recent trauma was a slew of emotions that remained intact. Her admiration toward him—and more. Her longing for his nearness, his reassurance, his touch…

While a mating bond explained her relationship with McGoven in many ways, in others, it fell short. Mainly his insistence that none of her attraction to him had been real. None of it.

That was what he wanted her to think, anyway. As she began to inspect the part of her mind that—ironically—he had helped open up, she wasn't so sure.

If her feelings had been artificial, then…why did they linger? She could still feel that crippling mixture of longing and desperation and need. A gasp ripped from her throat, and she had to bite down on her lower lip to silence it.

Overall, his loss hit her harder than she would have thought. Harder than the death of her father and the despair that had followed. All of it felt so real again, as if she were reliving every tortured minute.

Strangely enough, like always, even the memory of him could distract from the horror. She could smell him. Feel him. Recall his soothing presence, as reassuring as the very first day she woke up in his protection.

But the horror of her recent past wasn't all she had to contend with. McGoven had been right—that figurative box in her mind was now unlocked, allowing old, forgotten memories to seep out when she least expected them. One unfurled in startling clarity, and she sucked in a breath, transported from Naomi's convertible to a small, warm room bathed in sunlight.

It had been one of those lazy weekends she still cherished. Gentle fingers slipped through her hair, belonging to the beautiful woman nestled beside her. Faint remnants of emotion taunted her, just beyond her reach. She couldn't feel them fully—not yet—but she could recognize the sentiment well enough—love. So much so her heart threatened to explode from it.

Then guilt followed as she returned to the present. While he might have taken the bad memories away, McGoven had intentionally given her back a childhood she never realized she'd forgotten.

But he wasn't there to watch her relive it. If anything, he seemed determined to wipe her away for good. His excuse for returning to Black Mountain was supposedly to challenge Lukka, but she knew the truth. He wanted to get rid of her again. Run away. Hide.

Ironically, he'd swapped her for the pack, using her as a way to punish himself for some unspoken crime. That was it. She wasn't a burden to him as much as she was a tool.

A way for Bill McGoven to deny himself any ounce of pleasure or happiness.

He'd rather suffer.

Realizing the extent of his self-hate stung more than the fact that he'd penetrated her mind without permission.

If his motives had been selfish, she could understand that.

Not this.

"I swear to God if you puke on my leather seats… Here—" Naomi struck a button to lower the window on Loren's end. "Just stick your head out or something."

Loren was more than happy to oblige. The fresh air did some good, though mainly the beauty of the landscape whizzing by distracted her from her thoughts long enough to get her bearings.

This place was beautiful—she could admit that much. Rugged and wild, though they had to be hours away from Black Mountain. Still, the truck ahead of them pulled off the road, turning down a winding dirt path where a set of rickety signs led to various public campsites.

"Please don't tell me he plans on us staying out here," Naomi muttered under her breath.

As she turned her gaze to the windshield, Loren suspected that was exactly what he had in mind. This time of year, there was no one else in view, and they had their pick of the lot. Even so, she wasn't at all surprised by their final destination—the most remote area bordering a wild section of forest.

When the truck finally parked and Naomi pulled in after it, Loren stiffened as a wave of dread washed over her. So much lurked between her and McGoven that it almost seemed impossible they could coexist without addressing it.

And they couldn't. He wasn't in charge anymore, and she was done letting him dictate what she thought and felt.

It was her turn to decide what she wanted for herself.

And yet, when he stepped from the truck, head held high, he radiated confidence that rendered her silent. Once again, she'd underestimated his knack for suppressing emotion. It was easy for him to put personal matters aside in the face of the unofficial role he'd taken on as Alpha.

In fact, he excelled at it. Clothed in a black shirt, windbreaker, and jeans, he seemed every bit as breathtaking as he did while in wolf form.

"This location isn't ideal, but it's better than waiting at the farm to be slaughtered," he explained once she and Naomi exited the pink convertible.

They were on the outskirts of a small clearing speckled with wild grasses and a circle of beaten earth perfect for a campfire.

"We can stay here for the night and get the lay of the land before pushing further north," McGoven explained. "For now, we'll get some supplies and set up camp. Oh," he added. "If you were worried about the horses… I arranged for one of the local farmers to check in on them while we're gone—" He frowned at the word choice, even as it left his mouth. As if to betray him, his eyes darted in her direction, though she couldn't name the emotion flitting through them. "They'll be safe."

Loren released a breath she hadn't even been aware of holding. That last piece of information meant little to Micha and Naomi. It had been for her benefit alone.

More confused than ever, she watched him take off into the forest, presumably to scout on foot. Just like that, her hurt and anger diminished in the face of one grim realization. He had been right after all. The mating bond had been merely for her protection.

But, in that case, why did a part of her yearn for him now more than ever?

Maybe it was the same broken, lycan instincts to blame for her delayed ability to shift, and her knack for blending in with prey animals? Bill must have been an example of what a true lycan was capable of—someone able to shut off all emotion in the blink of an eye.

And pretend they never existed.

For three lycans—and Loren, who wasn't willing to classify herself in the same category—their camp turned out surprisingly…normal. Despite the earlier chaos, McGoven had come prepared. He withdrew a series of equipment from his truck, resulting in two tents, cooking supplies, and basic camping materials.

Already, he was in the process of building a small fire, utilizing dried logs he'd taken from the back bed of his truck. Loren could only watch, in awe.

He worked deftly. As his stern fingers glowed in the light of newborn flames, she nearly choked. Once, those very hands had explored her body with a precision that stole the air from her lungs whenever she dared to recall it.

Her salvation from the memories came, ironically, in the form of Naomi, who stepped forward, placing her hands on her slender hips.

"Do you camp a lot in your free time or something?" the blond asked, her tone devoid of some of its usual snark. She fidgeted awkwardly as he fed the embers with crumpled paper.

"No. This stuff is mostly old equipment that belonged to the man who owned the farm before me," McGoven said without looking up. "He loved the outdoors but wasn't keen on fleas and preferred to stay in human form."

"Weird," Micha said, eyeing one of the packaged tents skeptically. "It's gonna be hard to maintain a perimeter out here, though. I'm not familiar with this area, either. We could be stepping on the toes of a lone rogue or something."

McGoven shook his head. "I doubt it. This is municipal property, and most rogues wouldn't stray this close to such a heavily patrolled area. Luckily, with the storms passing through, the park rangers won't risk driving on these roads, and we shouldn't draw notice out this far from pack territory. I suspect we have a few hours at least before they notice we've moved. I aim to take advantage of that." The wicked gleam in his eye was enough to snap even Loren from her daze.

"How?" she demanded.

He frowned as if he'd forgotten her presence entirely. An awkward silence fell afterward, and only the crackle of the fire filled it.

Embarrassment prickled her cheeks. She hadn't spoken to him directly since what happened in the woods. It seemed he wasn't willing to bridge the gap looming between them, either. He just picked up a wayward stick and continued to stoke the fire.

"Ah, why don't you and I set this up, Naomi?" Micha grabbed one of the tents and set off with the grudging blond on his heels.

Bill watched them go, his jaw tight. Finally, he inclined his head in Loren's direction, though he kept his gaze fixed on the fire at their feet. "I have some business to attend to," he said cryptically. From his expression, she could tell he intended to say nothing more. Then he sighed again. "Part of it has to do with finding who your real father is."

"Why does it matter?" she asked. Her niggling paranoia supplied a few possibilities. So that he could have someone new to foist her onto? Someone else who could consider her a burden?

He furrowed his brows, mulling over his reply. "Because it matters. To me, anyway. You should know who your family is. And I want to know who tried to silence you and why."

"You knew him," she pointed out. It felt so surreal to finally put a face to the figure who stalked her nightmares for so long. A phantom more terrifying than even Fred Connors. "The man who took my memories."

His entire body went rigid, but the strangest thing was… She felt nothing—from him, anyway. She couldn't sense that invisible tendril of emotion that had allowed her to read him so easily before. Without it, they were back at square one—he was a stranger she had no idea how to predict.

Going off established precedent, she waited for him to close up again. To push her away. Instead, he met her gaze head-on, and she wasn't prepared for the intensity in his expression.

Gone was that perpetual doubt. Replacing it was a fierce determination. She couldn't suppress the shiver that wracked her spine at the sight. It was the expression he'd worn the day she goaded him into chasing her through the woods.

Right before he kissed her like mad.

"Tell me," she whispered. "Please—"

"His name was Lukas Grehmaine," he said in a low voice. "He was the previous Alpha of Black Mountain pack and a man I looked up to. I only ever knew him to be fair and honest. Though, hell… Maybe I never really knew him."

That bothered him—that he might have been fooled by someone he trusted. More than in an obvious way.

"I need to know why, Loren," he said so softly she found herself inching closer just to hear him above the crackling flames.

"I want to know why he would do something so fucking… Despicable." He stabbed his stick at the base of the fire, sending burning embers into the air.

"I want to know, too," she admitted, surprising herself. "Tell me about him. You shouldn't keep me in the dark."

"You're right." He lowered his head in a rare display of concession. "Even before we recovered your memories, I received intel that led to Black Mountain. Remember what I said about your mother? There was a small band of Scolera in this area roughly twenty years ago. One of them might have been her. She could have met your father then."

His openness emboldened her to ask, "Why do you think he did it? Suppressed my memories?"

"I don't know, but I think I have an idea of who might. They wanted to meet somewhere not far from here. I was planning on going alone. It would be safer for you to stay here with Micha and Naomi." She sensed that was his way of trying to convince her against the course of action she impulsively preferred.

"Or," she said carefully. "You can take me with you and let me find out the truth for myself. I'm not a child, and I'm not your responsibility, either."

"You have no idea—" He broke off sharply, only to sigh. "I want you to understand something. We don't need to talk about it now, but later. Still, you should know that the… Whatever linked us before, it's gone. You severed it."

His confirmation merely served to reinforce what she could already feel. The mating bond was gone. Shouldn't he have been celebrating? Dancing with joy?

Instead, he looked…exhausted.

"How?" she asked, grappling with the idea of it. She couldn't consciously remember choosing to break anything, bond or otherwise. She'd been too overwhelmed, as if every single emotion one person could feel had threatened to explode from her all at once. "I didn't mean to—"

"I don't know," he admitted, though he genuinely seemed as puzzled as she felt.

"You must be relieved," she said thickly. "I mean—"

"You want to come? Fine." He stood, wiping his hands on his jeans. "Be ready at sundown. We'll take my truck. But…"

His inflection dipped to a dangerous octave.

"I need your trust. If I say run, you run. Understood?"

He didn't give her the chance to argue. Already he was storming across the camp, his posture unreadable. Watching him go, Loren had no idea what to think.

Or how to feel knowing that his duty to her had come to an end.

And he didn't seem to care either way.

26

To say this situation was out of his element would have been an understatement.

Mating a stranger was one thing. Interacting with said stranger after said bond had been unceremoniously broken? Bill figured he should have been glad they were both in human form, at least. It made this confrontation marginally less awkward.

But no less tense.

"I'm not sure when we'll be back," he explained to Micha and Naomi once night fell. "Guard the camp. Call me if you sense so much as a leaf out of place."

"Will do," Micha said. "Take care, you two."

Bill took the request to heart. He couldn't even look at Loren as she entered his truck and settled beside him. Her scent flooded the narrow space, prompting him to lower the windows to counteract it. Blast the heat. Hold his breath.

It was either that or surrender to his body's primal reaction to her nearness.

Damn. He naïvely thought her aroma would cease to hold any appeal to him. Obviously, the mating bond had fueled his attraction. He should react no differently to her than he did to someone like Sonia.

Five seconds into the drive shot that theory to hell.

Her scent was driving him fucking insane. He could barely keep his eyes on the road, his thoughts on Lukka and the eventual challenge—or the fact that he was minutes from entering the territory of a rival pack that had made it very clear they wanted him dead.

Ironically enough, if whoever sent the information had planned to set him up, they picked one hell of a spot in which to do so. As it turned out, Wolfie's was a hole-in-the-wall just off the main highway. A swath of forest surrounded it, threatening to swallow it whole. Coincidentally, the dense underbrush made for the perfect cover for any lycan lurking in the shadows.

Under different circumstances, Bill might have liked the place. The location happened to be a quieter part of Elkton where everyone reacted to outsiders suspiciously and smoked indoors, ignoring the local ordinances. As it was—considering his tenuous relationship to the pack just an hour away—he regretted showing up the second he walked through the door with Loren at his side.

Should a fight break out, there wasn't a realistic way to minimize any collateral damage. The building was small and square, with a brick façade and few windows. Cigarette smoke flooded the interior, obscuring the wood-paneled walls and stained flooring. Despite it being just after nightfall, only a handful of patrons were inside.

Even so, Bill realized instantly that he had made one glaring misstep. He had spent too many days isolated, forgetting until now how a young woman with unbrushed hair wearing ill-fitting clothing might draw unwanted notice while in public. To her credit, she kept her head held high, her eyes observant.

And his gut tightened with every glance of her he stole while pretending to scan their surroundings.

"We should have a seat and wait," he suggested, warily eyeing the main bar where a man with a graying ponytail watched them while wiping down the counter. Had he come alone, he might have risked ordering a drink just to blend in. Instead, he picked the most inconspicuous seating arrangement and prayed their contact showed up soon.

Loren followed him to a booth and didn't speak. At first. He watched her eyes flick nervously around the barroom before darting toward his face.

Like a coward, he immediately eyed the battered surface of the wooden table rather than meet her gaze.

"Keep your guard up," he murmured. "I can't guarantee that this isn't an ambush."

In fact, this probably *was* an ambush. Why in the hell had he risked her life by bringing her here? As she quietly cleared her throat, some of his doubt eased up. She wasn't afraid.

She was determined.

"I want to be here."

He nodded, choking back a rebuttal. "How are you feeling? After everything... Breaking the bond can be a traumatizing experience, let alone reliving all those memories."

"I feel better," she insisted.

Skeptical, Bill snuck a glance at her face, surprised to find the statement seemed genuine enough. Her eyes were clear, her posture tense, but not unusually so. The only anomaly was that her cheeks were faintly pink.

He winced. If anyone should be embarrassed, it was him.

"I should have warned you of the risks," he rasped. "I'm sorry."

"Tell me more about him. The man I saw."

He groaned internally, conflicted between two brutal realizations. One, he had no right to deny her anything after what he'd done. Still, the second complication was…

He wasn't ready to talk about this. Though, considering he wasn't the one who'd submitted to having his mind torn open, he figured his emotions didn't matter one damn bit.

"He was the Alpha before Lukka." He swallowed hard, gathering the nerve to look up. When he finally probed those hazel eyes, he didn't find the anger in them he would have expected. Just a raw, naked need for answers.

"He was a good man. Strict but fair. I… I don't know why he would have done something like that to you. I truly don't."

"I believe you," she said, but Bill felt as though she'd stabbed him.

"I don't deserve your trust," he admitted. "Not after what I've done."

Rather than argue, Loren seemed to be in agreement. Her eyes were wide with alarm, and Bill feared he would never gain even a semblance of her respect again. Without thinking through the consequences, he reached for her hand.

"I'm so sorry—"

"I told you to come alone." A shadow appeared at his shoulder, and Bill realized he'd miscalculated the reason for Loren's unease.

Fuck. He fought to contain his hostility as a tall man stood from the booth beside theirs. He recognized him instantly as the Eislander spokesman—at a glance, at least, he seemed to have come alone.

While not cloaked in deer piss, his scent had been intentionally masked with cologne. As a glaring reminder of the human backdrop to this meeting, he'd opted for another inconspicuous sweater and a pair of jeans. Given how suddenly, every patron seemed to be averting their eyes from their table, Bill suspected the outfit was overkill.

"You compelled them to ignore us," he pointed out as the man pulled up a chair to sit at the mouth of their booth.

"And if I have?" the bastard countered. His eyes flickered from Bill to Loren. She stiffened beneath the scrutiny, her expression unreadable.

Bill couldn't silence a growl. Every nerve in his body lurched, ready to rush to her aid should the need arise. "I suggest you start talking."

"Unlike you, a reckless disregard for others isn't my style," the man continued. "I've taken every precaution necessary. But you haven't. Again, I remind you that I told you to come alone."

Bill couldn't muster up a shred of guilt. "Well—"

"If this is about me, I deserve to hear it."

Loren's voice rang out with a strength he'd rarely heard from her. Compared to the frail woman he'd rescued less than two weeks ago, drastic wasn't dramatic enough of a word to describe the change.

Apparently, he wasn't the only one impressed. The Eislander bastard couldn't seem to keep his eyes off her face.

"Well, we're all here now," Bill said coldly, palming the table inches from the man's position. Predictably, he pulled back, an eyebrow raised. "You might as well reveal whatever it is you dragged me all the way out here for, Eislander."

The man chuckled. "Out of respect for my Alpha, I must refuse that title. You can call me Eric, instead. As for what I am about to say… Well, to even suggest, is paramount to treason," he warned. "You really want to involve her in this?"

Bill hissed at his tone—but the bastard had a point, for a variety of reasons. One of which, Loren seemed willing to address, herself.

"I can decide what I want to do." Her voice was soft, devoid of the anger he would have expected. Curiosity was enough to make him face her directly, and he gritted his teeth at what he found in her expression.

Nothing like fear. Just a steely calm that made him regret ever underestimating her in the first place.

"She's right," he agreed. "She should hear this. So, what exactly do you have?"

The man, Eric, narrowed his gaze and scanned the nearly-empty room twice before speaking. "Did you follow up on the information I sent you?"

Bill could sense Loren's shock, but he didn't address it. That was one of the many conversations they would need to have later.

"I did," he said evasively. "Is this the part where you reveal it was all a trap to lure me here so you could execute me for a murder I didn't commit?"

"And if this were a trap, I think it would be easier than I would have thought to take you down. You think I can't sense the change in you? You're weaker," Eric declared. His upper lip curled back from his teeth, and he nodded dismissively. "You've broken the bond. I thought you might have been more shrewd than noble, rogue."

"And if I have?" Bill countered. "Shouldn't you be relieved?"

The man laughed harshly. "Then you're more foolish than I would have thought. Your Alpha is not known for his brute strength, but I'm sure he would prefer you weaker and unmated. A smart man would have waited until after he dealt with him before crippling himself."

Bill seethed at the insinuation. The worst part? He was right.

Not that any Eislander deserved to have any say in what he did or didn't do.

"Why does it matter to you whether I take on Lukka or not?"

"That's the thing..." The man leaned forward, bracing his hands against the table. "I've come across information that has led me to believe you might not have been responsible for Jamal's death. Which means that someone else is. Someone who might have a vested interest in shifting the blame."

Bill raised an eyebrow. "That sounds like a big fucking change of heart."

"Well, it's one that only I seem willing to accept," Eric said, frowning. "Loreck isn't a fool, but he's suspicious of anything dealing with your Alpha, even a rogue. He will require hard evidence to change his mind. Nothing less."

"He might have good reason to be suspicious," Bill said. "According to your intel, Loren's mother was a Scolera, and someone conspired to erase Loren's memory and compel her to suppress her lycan side. Do you have any idea why they might go through the trouble?"

The man went quiet for a long while. Finally, he cocked his head, but Bill couldn't tell what he was thinking. "Do you know how insane that sounds?"

Bill nodded. "Nowhere near as insane as the culprit's identity, but that is a detail I won't reveal until you come clean. No more fucking games. You suspect who Loren's father is, don't you? Who?"

From the corner of his eye, he saw her sit forward. Even without the mating bond tethering them, he could sense her interest. A tendril of protectiveness took root within him, spurring him onward to get her answers.

By any means necessary.

"I suggest you start talking, *Eric*."

"Now, it's my turn to play coy," the man replied. "First, I need to confirm your suspicions."

Bill didn't like the sound of that. "How?"

"I can't stay away from the pack for long, but I'll direct you to an address not far from here. Go. Meet with the person waiting there, and they will be able to confirm without a doubt if she truly is a Scolera."

"Why not bring them with you during your last little visit?" Bill demanded. "Or here now?"

He looked around, spotting no one out of place.

"They're a recluse," Eric said, his brow furrowed. "Paranoid. The fact that they're willing to meet you at all is due to no small effort on my part. Go there. Confirm it. Then we talk."

"No." Bill slammed his hands onto the table. As a testament to the Eislander's skill with compulsion, none of the nearby diners so much as flinched. "We start now. Why dredge up relics from the past in the first place? I want answers."

"You mentioned it yourself," the man replied cagily. "Twenty years ago, a spate of attacks forced the Eislander and Black Mountain lycans to work together. You might have been young, but I'm sure you can remember the time?"

"I do," Bill admitted. Though his recollections were hazy at best. He mainly remembered how tense Lukas had been during those volatile few weeks. Like the world weighed on his shoulders. "Tell me more."

"There was a rogue wolf, terrorizing nearby mortal towns. Their carnage brought unwanted interest to our region, and was directly responsible for multiple deaths and a slew of unintentionally made lycans."

"Like Fred Connors," Bill suspected. "May the bastard rot in hell."

"Yes," Eric said. "Our packs joined forces with the goal of tracking the rogue down."

"Why?" Bill felt his eyes narrow. Now that he thought about it critically, it sounded like overkill. "*Two* Alphas couldn't track one rogue wolf on their own?"

"Not in this instance." The man sat back, crossing his arms. "The problem was *this* rogue was a Scolera. Part of a wayward band roaming the East coast."

Now, things were beginning to fall into place. A band of Scolera with a member that coincidentally had the same name as Loren's mother. Two Alphas, tracking a dangerous rogue from the same clan.

"Go on," Bill spat. "This is getting interesting."

"Do you see now? Once that detail was made clear, it suddenly became apparent why the mad wolf was so hard to track and able to cause so much damage in the meantime. That breed is known for their cunning and stealth."

"Even while leaving a trail of bodies in their wake?" Bill countered.

Eric's lip twitched into the shadow of a smile. "Yes. Even then. You yourself have already been fooled by their tricks. They are notorious for masking their scents and blending in with their surroundings. Some call them 'ghosts,' a rather cliché nickname."

"I'm guessing they taught you a thing or two," Bill suspected. This man had managed to fool his senses not once, but twice. For that matter, so had Loren. If a bloodthirsty rogue was just as adept—or better—who knew what damage they could cause?

"The only way the wolf was found in the end," Eric went on, "was due to a tentative alliance between Loreck Eislander, your old Alpha Lukas, and the remaining members of the rogue's cell. It was a tricky endeavor, mind you. By that point, there were rumors of hunters in the area. We had to work quickly to contain the fallout."

None of his tale seemed like a lie. Bill decided to press for more.

"So, what happened?"

"This is a tale best left until you've proven her—" Eric jerked his chin toward Loren, "to be relevant. Until then, I'm not saying another damn thing. I've piqued your interest. Now go."

He withdrew a slip of paper from his pocket and placed it on the table. Then, he stood and headed for the door.

Rather than challenge him, Bill watched him go. The man had some damn nerve treating him like an errand boy—not that he was in any position to argue. "How do we contact you again?" he called out, snatching the folded note. All it contained was an address to a location north of Elkton.

"You won't," the man said without looking back. "If what you said is the truth, I will reach out to you first."

With that, he exited the bar. Even if he wanted to follow, Bill suspected that he wouldn't be able to. Scolera tricks or not, the man was good.

27

*L*oren sighed while gazing from the passenger window of the truck. McGoven must have broken something in her brain while retrieving her memories. She felt… Different. Her usual urge to cower and hide had been replaced by something else. Insanity? A need to speak up unprompted. Talk back. Even now, she longed to question McGoven more thoroughly, especially when it seemed like he wouldn't speak at all.

Once again, he had played coy, obscured information, and taken charge of her life—even though most of this new information pertained to her. Her mother. *Her* past.

She didn't even know what to think. After years of obscurity, her mother's memory was coming into clearer focus, robbing her of the tragic mystic Loren had always thought of her with. Now, Eveline Connors was more of an enigma—a lycan with a tormented past of her own.

Loren craved to know more. About Eveline. About who her father might be. About everything.

Confounding her irritation, McGoven remained stubbornly silent on the drive to the meeting place, his attention focused solely on the road. Barely a few hours since her blowup in the woods, and things between them felt so stilted, and yet so...

Unbalanced. It was hard to process her thoughts. Confusion, she would understand. After everything they'd been through, no one could expect her to completely reconcile her feelings toward him so quickly.

The guilt, however... It didn't seem fair that she was the one left stewing in that particular emotion. Especially when he seemed so unaffected by the million unspoken issues hanging overhead.

What better time than now to address them?

She cleared her throat. "You didn't tell me that he was the one who told you about my mother."

"I didn't," he acknowledged tersely. "I'm sorry. I shouldn't have kept that from you. I just..."

"Wanted to protect me," she finished, parroting his trademark line. Though, had that always been the full truth? If not, it no longer mattered. He'd said so himself. "You don't have to anymore. I can take care of myself."

"You're angry about more than that," McGoven suspected, easily seeing to the heart of her emotions. Apparently, he didn't need a mating bond to read her like a book. "You have every right to be. Don't hold back now. Let's address it all."

"Fine." She turned to him while he kept his gaze on the road.

A tendril of moonlight illuminated his features, highlighting just how stern the set of his mouth was. Her belly flipped in foreboding, but she took a breath and blurted the paramount realization weighing on her mind.

"You didn't tell me the truth. That you… About what you did. Why?"

He seemed to wince, though it could have been a trick of the light. Otherwise, his body remained tense, angled over the steering wheel. "I didn't think you would be able to understand."

The answer wasn't quite what she expected.

"I'm eighteen. I understand what mating is—"

"Not like that. I meant…it was too much to lay on you so soon after your father's death. You didn't deserve that kind of a burden." His voice hoarsened, and her heart lurched.

"It wasn't your job to protect me."

But he had anyway. The memories were so real now, clear, and distinct. Perusing them was terrifying, but she had no choice— though one image, in particular, made her palms slick with icy sweat.

"I'm the one who killed him. Fred Connors. You kept that from me?"

"Yes," he admitted, gripping the steering wheel tightly. "And more. Whatever might…upset you. I only ever intended it as a temporary measure. The mating bond allows that level of control between mates. Even mentally."

"But then you wanted to send me away after…"

"I didn't want the bond, Loren."

She swallowed at the unexpected pain slicing through her chest. Regardless, deep down, a part of her appreciated the honesty.

"I didn't," he went on. "I've spent years on my own for a reason. I never wanted you…anyone to get too close. Believe me, it wasn't a personal decision. I thought it would be best for everyone involved in the end."

"Why?"

"Because the last person who trusted me in that way wound up dead." His voice broke openly. He didn't even try to disguise his pain for once, and it bled into every single word. "I couldn't save her, and as a result of that, I realized that I didn't deserve to lead anyone. It might sound childish to you, but to us… Loyalty is everything. So is trust. To make a long story short, I took it hard."

"What happened?" He had avoided this very topic from the start, but she couldn't let guilt get in the way of her own curiosity. Not anymore. "Tell me. Please."

"Lukas, our previous Alpha, had died," he said softly. "It was unexpected. A heart attack. While we are lupine at heart, we are still human to our core. In his absence, I was poised to take over."

His voice fell into a tentative rhythm she didn't recognize. A halting, slower cadence that wormed beneath her defenses. This was the real Bill McGoven—a man who internalized everything.

But, for once, he willingly shared a fraction of himself with her.

"My focus was on securing the perimeter and guarding against any threats during the transition," he went on. "It's rare, but succession is a prime time for any outside enemies to mount an attack. I was more worried about the Eislanders, but I was caught off guard when Lukka approached me and warned of potential hunters spotted in the area."

Loren recognized the term. "Micha told me about them."

Even the Eislander, Eric, had mentioned that the threat of hunters was the driving force behind an unsteady alliance between the two packs.

"They're dangerous," he said. "But rare. I scouted the area myself and found nothing. If we were to take him at his word, that would have meant pushing back the ceremony by a few days. I didn't see the need. Stability seemed more important, but that night… They attacked the perimeter. We lost three packmates that day."

His grim tone alluded to a far more personal loss. One Loren hesitated to even mention. Still, there was no avoiding it.

"Your wife?"

He nodded. "I would give anything to do that day differently. Anything. Her death was my fault. I had been so focused on what I thought an Alpha *should* be that I didn't heed the real threat. I failed her. I failed myself."

"That's why you've been punishing yourself."

He barked a cold laugh. "You sound like Sonia. To hear her tell it, the past five years have been nothing more than an expert exercise in masochism."

"You're worried about her," Loren pointed out.

"She's like a sister to me. If Lukka hurt her—" he broke off, but she could easily fill in the blanks. "The sooner I can face him, the sooner I can end this."

"Tell me about it. The challenge."

He sighed. "There are old laws that govern it. What it boils down to is I face Lukka one on one, and issue the challenge in person. He shouldn't be able to refuse. After that, he has a full day to prepare, and then we fight in the center of the territory for the entire pack to witness."

"That sounds…simple," she said, preferring that word choice over *barbaric*.

"It's how things are done," he replied. "There are other formalities. Usually, the challenger offers up a witness who stays under the control of the opposing Alpha until the challenge is over. It's a way to ensure that both parties have something on the line. Tradition dictates that no harm comes to the witness, but I don't trust Lukka farther than I can throw him. Certainly not enough to offer up a sacrifice."

It sounded way more intense than he'd led her to believe. Yet, there was something he wasn't saying. "What happens if you lose?"

He adjusted his grip on the wheel, eyeing the road with renewed interest. When seconds passed in silence, she was sure he wouldn't answer. "If I lose… Lukka won't have to fear a challenge from me ever again."

"Why?" she prodded, though a part of her warned that she already knew the answer.

"Get ready." Suddenly, he inclined his head. "Looks like this is it."

Loren followed the line of his gaze despite the abrupt change in subject. "It" turned out to be a rundown road leading to a dwelling that resembled a shack more than anything else. Fred Connors' home looked regal in comparison. Weeds strangled most of the front lawn, nearly overrunning a decrepit porch covered with stacks of firewood.

"It doesn't look like anyone is here," Bill said. "Or we've stepped into a fucking trap. Either way, there's no point in running."

"So, what do we do?"

He sighed and cut off the truck. "We wait. And we listen."

"And talk?" When he didn't refuse, she soldiered on. This moment felt too precious to waste. For once, he spoke freely, and she was desperate enough to take advantage. "I want to know more about... About the bond."

He inclined his head her way. "Like what?"

"Was any of it real? My... It felt real—"

"It wasn't." He sighed, leaning back against the headrest. His eyes glowed in the darkness, reflecting the moon's light like mirrors. "I felt it too, but that is the way the bond works. The connection feeds off itself, strengthening the attraction between the two mates, exaggerating whatever concern might already exist. To put it bluntly, it wasn't real. None of it. Just instinct."

Loren tried to think objectively. His explanation sounded logical enough, but she knew what primal instinct felt like—mostly fear. She'd grown up in an environment that left little room for tender emotions. What happened between them had been...

Different.

"It was more than that," she whispered. The most horrifying part? She could still feel something tangled and painful lurking in her chest that belonged solely to him. It throbbed the more she focused on it, triggering snatches of memory.

But they weren't hers.

It was as if a part of her had stolen something from him. Recollections. Snippets... Of her? All of the observations had been from a distance, long before their first official interaction. They were more like hazy images. The many days she spent in the woods behind her father's house. Her smell.

The unexpectedly intimate nature of those insights made her pulse skip.

Were they real?

Yes, a part of her insisted. *They always were.*

"I could feel you," she said, struggling to put the concept into words. From his harsh intake of air, she knew he understood exactly what she meant. "Your emotions. Sometimes what you were thinking. Was that part of it, too?"

"Yes. And I could feel… You."

The tension in his voice made her heart race. She swallowed, her throat so tight it hurt to breathe. "Why did you do it? Why? If you didn't want me, then…"

"Because I couldn't bear to watch you suffer. I couldn't—but don't believe that makes me a hero." He shook his head, as self-deprecating as ever. "I was selfish. The motives for forcing a mating bond aren't always entirely noble."

She shuddered at the prospect. "How do you mean?"

"There are other benefits. I'm sure you can think of a few on your own." He inclined his head, meeting her stare. "Remember how I tracked you while you were with Kyle?"

She nodded.

"Our senses are heightened while mated. Expanded. One of the reasons Lukka was so opposed to what I did is that it could be seen as a direct challenge. A mated rogue is more dangerous than a lone wolf, so to speak."

"So why didn't you want one? A mate," she clarified.

He stared off into the distance as if stunned by the question. Perhaps, he hadn't really delved into the reasoning himself.

"You know about... That I lost someone close to me once," he finally said. "I think a part of me was unwilling to go through that pain again, but..."

He trailed off without stating the obvious.

Because, despite that supposed fear, in the end, that very thing had happened. Loss. Pain.

"Hurting you was the last thing in the world I wanted. I need you to understand that. Loren—" He reached out. She could see the regret dawn over his face the second his hand brushed hers— but it was too late. Their fingers entwined, and he didn't pull away.

Like always, his heat seeped through her skin, igniting a million conflicting sensations. Deep inside, she could feel that twisted mass of emotion unravel a little. One sentiment broke free, clearer than ever.

"It was real for me," she said. Hearing it out loud, didn't inspire the shame she would have thought. It felt more important to acknowledge those feelings. "I know myself."

"You don't know what love is," he replied, wrenching his hand away. "Don't think for a second that you felt it for me. You should move on. After this is over... I'll challenge Lukka," he reiterated. "Then decide from there."

"No." Loren blurted in a rush. "I know myself. I know what I felt —what I feel. I still do. I still—"

"Loren, please." She'd never heard his voice so guttural, on the verge of a growl. That alone made her bite her tongue.

"Let's stay focused on what matters," he insisted. "Please."

"The challenge," she croaked, submitting to the change in subject. "You plan to face Lukka..."

But then what? Would he leave as he suggested and expect her to join a pack of strangers? The idea wasn't anywhere near as appealing as he seemed to think it was.

"Can you fight him?" she asked finally. "Without the strength of the mating bond."

"I'll have to." His curtness warned her to let the subject drop.

But she couldn't. "Eric said it made you weaker. How? Just tell me that much."

"It was a dramatic choice of words," he said dryly. "The mating bond can help with doubt. Uncertainty. You felt for yourself, how I was able to help you?"

It was still hard for her to understand. Her gaps in memory. Her lack of fear and agony over the death of Fred Connors.

That was all because of him.

"You took it away," she said softly. "But after… You didn't feel anything for me at all?"

He *had*. The personal, foreign thoughts of her—long before they ever even met—proved it. His interest in her hadn't always been based on a noble, selfless need to help.

The very first day he ever caught her scent, he'd wanted to…

"Loren." The pain in his voice was palpable, contradicting her building hope. "Please don't do this. I trust you, and that's all that should matter. I trusted you enough to bring you here despite the risk. I'd lay down my life for you if I had to."

He meant it. Every word.

But even that promise wasn't enough to assuage the sting of what he didn't say.

I'd die for you—but I can't ever love you.

I won't.

Two hours into their wait, Bill left the truck and motioned for her to do the same. He withdrew a phone from his pocket and held a short, concise conversation with whoever answered on the other end.

"Naomi and Micha are okay," he said afterward, pocketing the device. "As for why we're here… I think we should scout around and then leave. This could have been a trick, but I'd rather not stick around to find out. Come on."

It was so dark she couldn't see much beyond the road, though Bill seemed to have no trouble with his footing. He moved assuredly, slowing only when she hesitated.

"It's too dark," she said, more aware of her limitations than ever. She might have been able to shift, but she couldn't control it. That part of her brain seemed sealed off, unable to be accessed.

"Close your eyes," he said. "Do you remember the feeling you felt when you shifted? Try to tap into that again. Not the anger, of course. Just that instinct."

"I don't understand." In some ways, she scarcely believed that she'd shifted at all. That creature hadn't felt entirely like her, but some primal extension. An animalistic impulse lurked within, whispering to her from the back of her mind.

At the moment, said voice was entirely silent.

"Trust me," Bill insisted. "Close your eyes."

She didn't understand why until she obeyed. It was as if a curtain had been withdrawn from a part of her mind, allowing in a million different stimuli she hadn't been aware of. Chirping insects. Rustling leaves. The hiss of the wind.

All of it felt magnified tenfold.

"Listen to the sound of my voice and follow it," Bill said next, sensing the second she relaxed. "This way."

She took a step and balked. "It's too dark—"

"Trust me," he insisted. "I won't lead you astray. Keep your eyes closed, and let me guide you. You'll get your bearings soon enough. Remember what I said about trusting yourself over all else? Let your instinct take over, just like before. Come on."

The confidence in his tone reassured her enough to push her unease aside.

With every passing second, her heartbeat threatened to overwhelm any noise he made, but it wasn't long before she realized… He was right. It was as if a disused muscle within her body was being stretched and tested. With every inch gained, a part of her awakened.

She could *see*, though her eyes were still closed. It was a newfound sense gathered from everything in the atmosphere down to the direction of the wind on her skin.

No wonder he could predict the weather so easily. This was…

Incredible.

"Good," Bill praised. "You're getting the hang of it. Now open your eyes."

When she did, the darkness was no less impenetrable. She could barely make out much of substance… At first. A glowing pair of gray eyes drew her notice, and the second she focused on them, the rest of the world sharpened in clarity.

"Wow," she breathed. "This is…"

"There is so much more for you to learn," he said with a hint of gloating in his voice. "So much more. When I…"

He trailed off, and she could sense his mood darken. He was speaking of the future—but one glaring reality stood in the way —whatever happened between him and Lukka was the deciding factor.

"Do you really want to do this? Challenge him?" Loren asked.

"I don't have a choice." He shrugged, eyeing the sky. "If he hurt Sonia… This has been a long time coming."

"And if you win?" Loren countered. "Can you really go back and leave New Walsh behind?"

He sighed wistfully, his eyes silver in the moonlight. "I think a part of me never truly left. But to answer your question, no. I wouldn't return without any regrets. There are a few things I wish I could have done differently, starting with you."

She sucked in a breath as he spun to face her, grabbing her hand. He always managed to feel scorching hot but comforting at the same time. The man was a walking contradiction.

Even now, the heat in his gaze took her breath away, but his voice was as stern and level as always. "I'm sorry for what I did. I had no right to insert myself into your life like that. To take control without your knowledge or consent—"

"Why did you then?" she asked.

"I could say that it was only out of a sense of duty. To protect you… But that would be a lie." He reached out, smoothing a strand of wayward hair behind her ear. Absently, as if he wasn't even aware of doing it. "The truth is, I wanted a connection to someone who seemed as lost as I felt. I think I believed that helping you would distract me from my own doubts. For that, I am sorry."

"But you would have broken the bond anyway?"

He hesitated. Then he sighed. "I… Wait—" Suddenly, he pulled her closer, bringing his mouth near her ear. She held her breath, panicked—until his voice returned to that gruff, cautious tone. "We're being watched. Follow my lead."

Alarm stiffened Loren's spine. She strained her ears, attempting to pick up on any odd sound. Nothing stuck out to her, but Bill had already released her, picking his way through the uneven landscape.

"Come out," he said, raising his voice to carry. "We don't want to harm you. Merely to talk."

As the wind picked up, Loren wondered if he had overreacted. The landscape seemed as empty and deserted as before. There was no one there.

At least…no one in plain sight. A flicker of movement drew her attention to a mass of gnarled trees just paces from their position.

"She can stay," a harsh voice replied from the shadows. "But *you* leave, Black Mountain wolf. Your kind aren't welcome here."

$\mathcal{B}$ill hissed through clenched teeth. Rarely had he felt this level of hostility directed his way. Kyle's hatred came close, but the nuances were different in this instance. This shadowy figure didn't just despise him. They were terrified.

Luckily, most—if not all—of their loathing seemed directed his way alone. Instinctively, he took a step back from Loren, drawing the stranger's attention to himself.

Damn the Eislanders and their tricks. What the hell had Eric led them to?

"Show yourself," he called. "I won't harm you—"

"Leave!" The voice came from north of their position, though he couldn't make out anything apart from a few swaying branches. Hell, he couldn't even smell anything out of the ordinary. Just wind, dirt, and Loren.

"I can't leave the area without knowing she'll be safe," he replied while keeping Loren within his view.

"Well then, leave now. I won't speak in the presence of your ilk."

Another cluster of branches swayed, and he homed in on a mass of trees yards away. Oddly enough, he couldn't catch a lycan's scent. Just fresh air. Straining his ears for any sound, he attempted to take a different tack.

"Who are you? Why did Eric from the Eislander pack send us here?"

"Eric?" the figure scoffed. Judging from their tone, he suspected they were a woman. "A pompous git. Ignored me for years, only to come crawling back when his precious pack is at risk. He gave no concern for us. Damn them all."

A flicker of suspicion as to the figure's identity flitted across his mind. They couldn't be…

"Who are you?" he tried again. "Are you alone?"

He sure hoped so—one shadowy figure was enough to contend with, though he couldn't sense anyone else. Eric wasn't the only one to employ tricks when it came to obscuring their presence. At least this figure wasn't into utilizing deer piss.

They were simply…invisible, blending into the landscape in a way he couldn't have replicated, with or without the aid of tricks.

"Someone who knows all about the cunning, twisted ways of your kind," they snarled.

"You are Scolera, aren't you?" Bill suspected out loud. A part of him doubted that. Why would a lone member of that clan remain out here, so far removed from their ancestral lands? Though hell, he was an expert on living apart from society.

Who was he to judge?

"You are from Black Mountain," the figure replied, skirting any confirmation of their own origins. "The fact that you would even dare to bring her here is merely an example of your hubris."

"Her?" He eyed Loren again, prepared to confront any threat that might come her way. "What do you mean?"

"You robbed her of her birthright, and then you parade her before me. Sickening."

"Birthright?" Loren spoke up before he could, and Bill smothered the urge to silence her. This was her heritage at stake. She had every right to steer the conversation.

Even if it killed him to watch her inch closer to the unknown by taking a single step forward.

"Her, I will speak to," the figure declared. "Only her."

Bill wavered between logic and a desperate need for answers. In the end, Loren made the decision herself.

She took another step, and—even though it took every ounce of control he possessed—he stood back, watching helplessly as the distance between them lengthened. A few paces. A few yards. Eventually, she paused right before the largest tree in the clearing —a rotting oak.

"Talk to her," he demanded, fisting his hands helplessly at his sides. "But if you so much as flinch in her direction, you won't get the chance to harm her."

"I remember you," the stranger said softly, uncowed by his threat. While they remained hidden in the shadows, their higher cadence confirmed his suspicion once and for all—they were a woman. "Such a sweet little pup. Such a shame what they did to you. A shame..."

Loren cleared her throat before responding. "What who did to me?"

"*Them.* They culled you from your family. All because of him."

Loren's voice barely reached him, distorted as the wind picked up. "Who?"

It was a second before the woman's reply reached him, a snarled hiss. "Lukas Grehmaine."

Bill gritted his teeth. This wasn't quite how he expected his old mentor's name to come up again. "What do you mean? Why would he want to hide a young girl?"

"Why else?" the figure replied, still lurking out of view. "Power. I warned her what would happen." A low wail pierced the quiet. "I did. But she never listened."

Loren took another step. "Who?"

"Eveline." Suddenly, a figure appeared from behind the oak. They were small and slight, with matted brown hair that obscured their delicate shape. Though barely larger than Loren, Bill could sense they were far older. Early forties, perhaps?

"Eveline?" Loren's voice broke. "What happened to her?"

The figure crouched as if desperate to hide within the scraggly underbrush. "She let herself be part of the trap, only it ensnared her in the end. She trusted them. They lied—"

"How?" Bill's voice mingled with Loren's as they voiced the same question at once.

Another wordless howl echoed in response. "We were outcasts, left behind by our own and driven further east," the figure recounted. "We wanted to join one of the local packs, but both were hostile because of our ways. They blamed us for the local human killings, but we knew who the true culprit was."

"Then what happened?"

"She got too close to the pack leader. I warned her to stay away, but she trusted he would protect her. He didn't. The other one made sure of that. He drove her away, but she didn't go far. When she knew her child was of age, she tried to bring the girl to her home pack. Then she wound up dead. You all will suffer the consequences of the same naivety. I've heard the rumors out here, boy. You think you can win on fair footing? Think twice. He'll rip your throat out while she watches, and you won't ever see the blow coming. I won't die like they did. I won't be a part of this anymore. Now go!"

The figure scurried behind the oak, but Bill sensed even if they tried to follow, they wouldn't find her again.

"Wait!" Loren started forward anyway. "Please. Just—"

"Let's go." Bill approached her. When he grabbed her forearm, she didn't resist, allowing him to guide her back. "I think we've overstayed our welcome."

Besides, they'd gotten more than enough answers. At least one mystery was solved. Loren's mother truly had been a Scolera— one who interacted with both Loreck Eislander and Lukas.

Fuck, what a mess.

"But I don't understand…" Her mouth fell into an anguished frown that tugged at his heart.

"I think I do," he said grimly. He didn't like this suspicion one damn bit, but it was the only one that made sense. "I think Lukas thought he was protecting his bloodline the only way he knew how. By denying his rival of an heir. You."

29

*B*ill drove them back toward the campsite, but he barely touched the speed limit. Urgency didn't seem to matter for the time being. Loren needed to digest what she'd learned. Even he didn't know how to process the slew of information. Instead of Fred Connors or some low-level wolf, Loreck Eislander might have been her father.

Talk about a plot twist.

That wasn't even the most stunning bit of information revealed. Not only had the Alpha of a rival pack taken pains to obscure her true identity—he'd left her under human jurisdiction to be abused. Neglected. The various implications churned his stomach, and he could barely keep his focus on the road. Though, his feelings didn't matter. Only Loren's did.

Without the mating bond, observing her was his only method of gauging her emotions—and it was proving more difficult than he would have thought. Her face was angled from his, her gaze on the window.

The building tension was too much, even for him. "Talk to me," he rasped.

Suddenly, she sat forward.

"Pull over."

Bill didn't question, parking immediately on a sliver of pavement that bordered a remote stretch of forest. The second he killed the engine, she exited the truck, and he followed, keeping his distance. For a few seconds, she just paced. He could hear her taking greedy, deep pulls of fresh air, and a part of him winced in sympathy. He ached to touch her. Provide comfort in a way he had no right to.

In the end, he settled on words of encouragement. "It's a lot to take in. Your real father… You deserve to meet him. He deserves to know who you are—"

"I don't care about that." She turned to face him, and he recoiled at the expression he saw straining those delicate features. Rage. "You could die tomorrow. You've been dancing around the issue, but that's what's at stake, isn't it? You could *die*."

For a long while, he said nothing. "There is a possibility. But what I do shouldn't matter to you. Your family and your life? That is what you should focus on."

Her eyes narrowed to slits. "And if you do die during the challenge?"

He answered her honestly. "It's a risk I'm willing to take."

He made it sound so trivial. As if death meant nothing to him, when the mere thought of it… Seemed to tear at something inside of her. Maybe it was the aftereffects of the mating bond? Or perhaps he just didn't know her as well as he seemed to think.

"Let me help you," she blurted in a rush. "I can do what you did for me. You said it was fear that stood in your way last time. I can take away your doubt. I *want* to. I know you think I should hate what you did for me… But I don't."

Good, because he hated himself enough for them both. Though, should he? Wincing, he thought back to the person she'd been the first time they met in person—a fearful creature living under a mantra of hiding in the face of danger. In her own way, she'd broken free of that shell and was able to face her life without flinching. That mattered more than any show of force, or protection he could have offered.

More than a bond.

"You helped me," she reiterated. "Let me help you. If you can look at this without the pain clouding your judgment, that could be all the difference."

"No." He shook his head. "I won't ask you to do that for me—"

"You aren't asking." She whipped around to face him. "I know you want to push me away, but I'm not a child. I want to help you because I care for you. I do… I always did."

A part of him lurched, aching to believe her, though he knew better. She cared for him. From the day he saved her from school bullies and gave her a spare bit of food out of kindness.

And he had always cared for her…

"Let me," she insisted. "*Please.* Let me do this."

"No." He moved away from her, turning his focus to the sky. "Let me be the noble one for once."

"I don't want noble. I just want… I want you."

His heart throbbed, even as the logical part of his brain listed a million reasons why she was misguided. He settled for voicing just one. "You don't know what you want."

"Stop telling me that! Stop talking at all." Her eyes flashed, and he stiffened in alarm. Uh-oh. Loren Connors alone wasn't speaking to him now. These words came from a part of her she couldn't control—not anymore. "It's my turn to be in charge."

He saw her lunge, but surprisingly, he wasn't fast enough to dodge the attack. Her hands collided with his chest, pushing him back a step. He couldn't silence the growl that broke loose.

"Loren, don't—"

"I don't want to be a burden to you. I want to be your equal. So let me set a rule for once. If I can't shift here and now, then you go into battle alone."

A lethal curiosity kept him from refusing outright. Damn her. Even now, he couldn't back down from a blatant challenge. "And if you can?"

He wouldn't humor her. No way in hell. Still…

A part of him craved to hear her answer.

She went silent for a heartbeat. Then she squared her chin, her gaze alight with the confidence of a new lycan. "Then I run, and you catch me."

He fought to smother a groan. *Fuck.* This was going too far. A good man would end it. Not ask, "And then what?"

"If you can't, then I win."

She licked her lips, and his abdomen pulsed. Bill, the man, immediately took a backseat to the wolf within him. She wanted to play?

Then, just this once, he'd humor her request.

"Is that your final offer?" he asked in a voice he didn't recognize.

Her nod just spurred on the dangerous impulse building within him.

Finally, he took a step and jerked his chin toward the wilderness surrounding them. "Then start running."

30

She knew she'd made a mistake the second the boast left her mouth. Still, she couldn't take it back.

And he didn't want her to. His eyes flashed dangerously—some primal part of him couldn't resist such a direct challenge.

Good.

He took a step and immediately backed away several more. "No." His tone lacked that unsteady rasp it had seconds earlier. "This isn't—"

Loren didn't think. Her hair flew out behind her as she pushed past him and lunged. Whatever he'd done back at her old house…

Maybe it was desperation—or a fluke—but she could access that shadowy part of herself again. Shifting this time was almost as easy as breathing, though not painless. Every muscle throbbed, suddenly hot, reminiscent of the shock of diving into water from a height.

She hit the ground unsteadily, struggling to regain her bearings on four legs instead of two—but that wasn't all she needed to quickly adjust to. A heavy thud echoed from nearby—dried leaves crunching and a low growl—the sound of another figure shifting. Every hair on her body stood on end.

As a man, Bill McGoven was intimidating enough, but in this form… His presence overwhelmed and dominated every nerve in her body. His smell was ten times stronger, slamming into her lungs with the force of a punch. A disarming musk mingled within the usual aroma of pine as if, in lieu of words, his very essence proclaimed his intentions.

Game on.

Run! Pure instinct took over as she sprinted between two trees. Instantly she saw that this area was nothing like the farmland near New Walsh. It was rugged and wild. Her heart pounded as moonlight drenched her from overhead, painting everything in an ethereal glow. Beautiful wasn't a strong enough word to describe it.

Towering evergreens loomed above, and rocky outcrops tore through the landscape, requiring her to adjust on the fly to dodge any obstacles. Micha's training ironically came in handy as she did her best to navigate the brutal terrain.

But she was nowhere near fast enough—McGoven gained on her easily. She could hear his ragged breaths. Smell him even more…

Defeat was inevitable, but she made him work for it, driving as fast as she could through the territory. With every inch gained, her body thrummed with the thrill of the chase.

Until, something in the atmosphere shifted without warning—it was as if an invisible pressure weighed her down, putting greater importance on every step. Every breath. This wasn't a game any longer. This was a test. A primal war.

And she was risking far more than losing an argument.

Increasingly, her pulse surged, goading her on. Faster. *Faster!* Up ahead, a small clearing came into view, but as the wind shifted direction, she inhaled a scent that proclaimed her defeat.

In a burst of fluid muscle, a black wolf flew from the shadows, barreling toward her.

And it was over.

Despair wasn't the emotion that had her roll onto her back the second he came near, however. Neither was fear. Her chest heaved as stray twigs crunched underfoot, and the wind blew a familiar scent directly into her lungs—during the tortured few seconds of his approach, she'd shifted back into human form.

Still a beast, he crouched over her, so massive he blotted out the sky. Viewed in this way, he was terrifying, capable of hurting her so easily if he wanted to. As his jaws parted, ivory teeth bared, that very outcome seemed inevitable.

So why was her skin prickling, her limbs so heavy she couldn't move? The wolf lowered his head, and hot breath fanned her exposed throat in warning. When he finally made contact, however, it was with lips so soft they felt like silk. Too quickly for her to even track the transformation, the body on top of her became all male with human limbs that trapped her beneath him. Gone was any hesitation. His hands palmed her waist, every finger trembling with possession.

With confidence that took her breath away, his lips feathered over her jaw, finding her mouth—but calling the resulting act a kiss would have been an insult. He tasted her, allowing her to become accustomed to the gentle, probing rhythm of his tongue.

And then, his teeth caught her lip without warning. Pain and copper exploded over her tongue, but there was no explaining the rush of desire she felt rip through her next. A craving for something… Anything he could give.

What that was, exactly? He seemed to have some idea.

At the urging of his touch, her entire body came to life—times a million. That aching, desperate warmth wormed beneath her thighs, driving her to clench them together just to ease it.

But he was in between them, far too heavy to dislodge—and she didn't want to. When he settled against her, all thoughts of discomfort left her mind. His touch was the cure. His fingers, his desire…

She exhaled, her eyes wide, as that emotion emanated from him in waves, evident in how he held her. Touched her. Pressed his lips frantically against her jawline. She moaned, tilting her head back to allow him better access.

Suddenly, he froze.

"We can't." With a groan like that of a man being tortured, he pulled back. "No—"

"I want this," she whispered, meeting his horrified stare. "This isn't just your choice to make anymore. I want this. I do."

Even if it didn't seem to make sense that she could feel so strongly for someone after a couple of weeks of knowing them.

Her voice echoed with a conviction she'd never heard before. Neither had he. Without giving him the chance to move, her hand found the planes of his cheek, and she smoothed back wayward strands of black hair until nothing obscured her view of those piercing gray eyes.

"I want you. I do."

To her shock, he didn't waste his breath arguing. Instead, he went limp, and his forehead collided with hers with a sigh of defeat. "You have no idea what you're asking for," he grated. "But I can show you."

Her thoughts quivered as a foreign pressure intruded against her conscience. It was like before, when he recovered her memories—but firmer. Persistent.

A part of her would always fear this level of intimacy—she couldn't help it. Though, for once, she wasn't afraid to go after what she wanted.

And she wanted him, no matter the price.

This was *her* choice.

And he was no match.

31

*B*ill groaned, partly in awe and partly in relief. Would Loren Connors ever cease to surprise him? He doubted that.

He naïvely thought he'd already known her mind inside and out, despite however short-lived their previous bond was. He'd been wrong. Entering her mind now was a stark contrast from the horrific aftermath of Fred Connors' assault. Her fear didn't threaten to drown him this time. Her thoughts enveloped him eagerly, with her body acting as his sole anchor to the rest of the world.

What had been meant as a show of force—to convince her to change her mind—became something else in an instant, more akin to an earnest probing of her thoughts and feelings. Greedily, he took whatever she was willing to let him see.

He couldn't stop. Even if he wanted to, the decision was no longer his—the lycan within him howled with the need to fulfill this one driving instinct.

Dominate.

And she gave herself to him in a way that astounded him. There wasn't an ounce of hesitation. No fear. When their eyes met, he barely recognized the woman gazing back, her eyes blazing with a naked acceptance that blew his mind.

And a challenge.

She shifted her balance, catching him off guard. The next thing he knew, she straddled him fearlessly, her hair streaming down her shoulders. Her eyes latched onto his chest, and he could see the intention in her gaze—feel it.

And yet he didn't even fight as she nuzzled at his throat.

And then bit.

"Fuck." He hissed through his teeth as his eyelids fluttered at the sensation of her biting deep, right through the ragged remains of her initial mark. Within, his wolf howled with acceptance, relishing the wound. Her claim.

And his canines throbbed in their gums as he fisted his fingers through her hair, pulled her close, and did the same. She whimpered as he seized a delicate strip of flesh along her collar bone. The wound bled. She would scar, but they would wear their marks in unison.

As they should.

Even as he finally released her, he remained there, his mouth against her neck, too overwhelmed to face her. Her genuine joy washed over him in an intoxicating rush. There was no comparison to the fragile bond linking them before. This connection was so much richer and deeper. Endless.

Soon, he lost track of what was purely mental and what was physical. He shifted his weight, desperate to get closer to her. As if watching a stranger, he saw his hand plunge between her legs, easing them further apart.

His cock throbbed, aching to fulfill this driving impulse that had been building since he forged the first bond—no, before that. When he caught her scent for the first time. He'd wanted her since then.

And now...

There was no holding back.

His body took over, driving him into her as deep as she could stand it. Not deep enough. Her heat was suffocating, every twitch of muscle gripping him like a fist. The fresh air and the moon above worked to enhance this moment despite the dying doubt at the back of his mind.

With a groan, he let go, sinking into her embrace.

The pleasure was a tidal wave, coming out of nowhere to drown them both.

As they finally resurfaced, the forest around them echoed with life, unconcerned by the act taking place beneath its swaying branches. Boneless, Bill groaned as he settled into the damp earth, pulling her close.

For what felt like an eternity, they lay there, catching their breath.

He recovered first, his gaze on the moon. "I should feel far guiltier than I do. You could still be affected by the previous bond. I... This might not be what you want when you grow into your own."

The strange part was, he didn't feel an ounce of regret. Not even a little.

And she could feel it. Her mixture of shock and awe thrilled him in a way he couldn't deny. This was what she deserved from the very beginning. An open, honest relationship in which she had equal footing.

And an equal say.

Her emotions and thoughts flowed into him easily, and there was no wall shielding his from hers. It was a level of openness he had only shared with one other person—and yet, there was no comparison, either good or bad.

Loren was Loren. Her mind was a new breed of animal, so alien to him and yet inherently unique.

"Maybe you're right," she murmured, resting her head on his chest. He craned his neck to watch her and couldn't resist smoothing his fingers through that thick mane of hair. "But I can think for myself," she added. "This feels…good. Right."

He had to agree. A corner of his lip quirked upward as he felt her contentment. Then a twinge of pain replaced it.

"I can see now," she said, grimacing. "Why you did what you did. If I could take your pain away, I would."

He didn't question her sincerity. Through clenched teeth, he replied, "I know. But I need to learn to live with it."

"But not punish yourself." She lifted her head, meeting his gaze head-on. "If I wanted to, how would I?"

He sighed, torn between his pride and… Was this relief? A part of him thrilled at her desire to help him. Craved it.

"You would reach out to me mentally and form a wall," he said. "More like…swallow the feelings you can sense bother me and draw them within yourself. But I don't want—"

He was too late. A grunt escaped him—he could feel her, creeping through their connection tentatively, eager to put his instruction into practice.

And yet, she seemed determined to distract him, continuing their conversation out loud, "So, what now? Will you still issue your challenge?"

"I could, but…"

Just like that, reality threatened to descend on their tiny sliver of peace.

"You're worried about something."

He couldn't hide the truth any longer, even if he wanted to. "Sonia called me. She thinks it's too dangerous. That Lukka will arrange an ambush the second I even think about approaching the boundary. She was supposed to feel out support for me among the others, but now… I have no way of knowing what the hell is going on. The smart thing to do might be to turn back. Forget the pack and take my chances by leaving without a formal release."

Even as the words left his mouth, he knew he could never bring himself to actually follow through.

Loren shifted, sitting upright, her gaze pensive. "That man we met with, he was from the other pack? The Eislanders. What if they helped you?"

He scoffed. "As if they would. You heard him. Loreck still doesn't buy my innocence, and there isn't enough time to convince him."

"What if you *could* get their help? And make sure that Lukka had no choice but to respect your challenge."

He raised an eyebrow. "How?"

"If you think I am…" She seemed unwilling to voice more, not that he could blame her. He couldn't imagine the upheaval she'd experienced over the past few weeks. First the mess with Fred Connors and now this—not only was she a full-blooded lycan, but the daughter of an Alpha.

"I believe that you *are* Loreck's daughter," he said, dropping that bomb for her. "Whether he knows about you or not is another matter."

"We could go to him," she continued. "Get him to back the challenge on your behalf."

"No." Bill couldn't disguise his frustration. "That won't work. If Lukka doesn't show his face, I can't honorably issue the challenge in the first place. Besides, if I show up on their doorstep with the Eislanders in tow, I might as well declare war. All of Black Mountain will react as if it's an invasion."

"Not if you *can* issue the challenge," Loren countered. "I could go to the pack, demand to see Lukka. If he came out to meet me himself…"

"You would do that?" He craned his neck, alarmed to find there wasn't an ounce of fear in her gaze. It was long past the point where her bravery should have surprised him.

Still, the sheer strength of her resolve took his breath away. Enough that he felt the need to humor her, despite the obvious risk.

"I would never let you. But yes. I could corner him then and there and issue the challenge in plain view." He chuckled coldly at the mental image. It was a plan so sneaky Kyle couldn't have come up with one better. "He'd have no choice but to adhere to the old laws. There would be too many eyes watching."

"Then I could find Sonia," Loren went on. "And help her gather support—"

"No." He slid his hand up her back, noting how her pulse surged beneath her skin. Physically, she was so delicate, but her eyes blazed in a way that conveyed anything but weakness. "Besides, they would never buy it. Lukka will make sure that I'm killed before I can even get within shouting distance. And let you go in there alone? Hell no."

"They won't expect any trouble from me," she pointed out.

He wasn't so sure. "They'd hurt you just to get to me."

"Not if they thought the bond was still broken."

Bill couldn't help himself—he played out the scenario in his mind. Forget Kyle. Lukka himself wouldn't see such an underhanded trick coming, not from him. It was a tempting prospect. Still, he sighed as logic prevailed. "No."

"I'm not asking for permission."

He recognized that hard tone in her voice. One suspicion was confirmed—any rebellious instinct in Loren Connors was entirely her own.

"Please… Look at me." He cupped the side of her face and silenced a groan. "I can't let you be hurt."

Even as he spoke, he sensed that her determination didn't waver. Not a damn bit. Chin in the air, she fixed him with a probing stare he recognized. A challenge was coming, and he stiffened in anticipation.

"Then fight for me," she said. "Because I can't let you keep holding yourself back just because of me."

Before he could argue against even entertaining her scheme, her conscience mingled with his, allowing him to see her thought process in detail. If she really were Loreck Eislander's daughter, and he shared even an ounce of her intellect, no wonder Lukas had been so threatened by him.

Few could match their level of cunning.

"It could work," he admitted grudgingly. "But it's risky. Reckless. It—"

"It has to work," Loren said over him. "At least let me try."

After everything she'd been through, her confidence took his breath away—as did one emotion he could feel resonating through her, entirely her own.

Trust.

The moon shone brightly by the time they returned to camp. After Bill stealthily grabbed fresh clothing for them both, they found Micha and Naomi waiting by the fire. One look, and Micha blushed, averting his gaze. Apparently, their changed relationship was glaringly obvious, even to him.

"It looks like you guys worked out your differences," he said. If Bill wasn't mistaken, he caught a hint of sadness in his voice. A thought that he promptly quashed.

Now wasn't the time for jealousy.

"It's time to make our move," he said. "But I realized that I can't go barging in alone. If this is going to work, I'll need backup, and… Help."

"You know I'm in." Micha sat forward and propped his chin on his fist. "So, what's the plan?"

"Well, it isn't *my* plan." Bill stood aside, letting Loren take his place. "It's hers."

She handled the spotlight well, her head high. Bill couldn't deny his admiration, even though a part of him railed against putting her in danger even for a second.

"It's risky," Loren said. "And dangerous, but if we all play our part, it could work."

Micha and Naomi shared a look.

"I'm in," the former declared.

The blond had her lips pursed but nodded in the end.

"That settles it," Bill said warily. "Now, we put the pieces into action."

Win or lose, there was no turning back now.

He was ready to fight for his home.

And let the cards fall where they may.

32

The sun had barely finished its descent toward the horizon as Loren left the campsite alone and hit the open forest.

She ran blindly. Not long into the sprint, her lungs heaved, her pulse surging through her eardrums. In contrast, the world around her became a muted, blurred backdrop. She didn't even see a figure lunge from the shadows until it was too late.

Wham! Strong arms caught her by the shoulders, holding her close to a body that seemed cut from stone. His touch was all wrong—too firm. Not McGoven. The scent flooding her lungs cemented that fear. This man was a stranger.

"Let go of me!" Panicked, she swung her arms, kicking her legs. Only when she paused to suck in air, did she hear the person holding her shout.

"It's okay! It's alright," they insisted. "Who are you?"

Heart pounding, she whirled around to face a tall man with dark hair. He watched her warily, flicking over her filthy, tangled hair before settling over her mud-splattered jeans and sweater. She couldn't discern what impression—if any—she made.

"Do you know where you are?" He inclined his head, calling attention to the two men behind him watching from a slight distance.

The landscape surrounding them was rugged, unfamiliar terrain—nothing like the gentle, rolling hills of New Walsh. It was frigid. Every intake of air stabbed through her chest with a mixture of foreign smells.

"Black Mountain," she said. "I'm here to see Lukka."

The man frowned, and she couldn't tell what he thought. As his eyes flickered toward the woods behind her, she felt a tendril of alarm gnaw at her confidence. He was suspicious. "Where is your pack? What are—"

"I came here for a reason," she said over him. "Bring Lukka to me. Please. I'll only speak to him. He should know who I am."

"The Alpha?" the man replied, frowning. "Who are you? I can't just—"

"Tell him that Loren Connors is here to beg for his acceptance," she said. "Please."

His eyes widened, but she couldn't tell if he recognized the name or not. From the corner of her eye, she saw that more men appeared, lurking in the shadows, watching. Luckily, confusion seemed more prevalent than hostility.

The one nearest her, cocked his head, speaking to someone behind him. "Send word to the main house," he said. "Let's see what they decide."

"They" being Lukka? For a heartbeat, she longed to have Bill's guidance—or at least his ability to explain what might be happening. Just as quickly, she smothered the weakness and just watched.

And waited.

Minutes seemed to crawl past as she and the men surrounding her remained at a quiet impasse.

Finally, two men parted, and one figure appeared between them, his hair golden, his eyes a haunting blue.

"I'm here." His voice rang out with unmistakable authority. Tall and thin, he appeared to be the total opposite of Bill McGoven. "And you must be Loren Connors."

She didn't know what to do. Bow? Instead, she nodded, clearing her throat. "Are you Lukka?"

"This is a long way from McGoven's territory," he replied, his voice dangerously soft.

Loren licked her lips. "He brought me in a truck. When he wasn't looking. I... I just needed to get away," she said weakly. "I just ran."

"Where?" Something flickered across those blue eyes Loren couldn't name. Fear? Either way, he inclined his head toward the woods, and two of his men stood at attention. "Which direction?"

Loren could only shrug. "I'm not sure."

"Well, you're safe now," the blond man said, sounding as noble as if he were her twisted knight in designer armor.

"But where is he?" Another figure stepped from the woods, his sharp brown eyes unsettlingly familiar. Kyle. "Where is William McGoven?"

Somewhere close by. Loren could feel him, railing against the thought of her being even near this man.

The trap had been baited.

Now it needed to be sprung.

$\mathcal{A}$*h, happy endings,* Kyle thought sarcastically.

Weren't they just the best?

He, for one, sure as hell felt all warm and fuzzy inside as he watched Lukka assure the Connors girl that everything would be "A-OK." She was safe now, and the big bad monsters were at bay.

Such the hero, that one.

It didn't matter that the girl looked traumatized and filthy. Or that she had come out of fucking nowhere—without her supposed captor in tow. Kyle figured he was the only one to second-guess this thrilling rescue.

Good ol' Lukka only cared that his entourage was there to witness every single action he made. With every halfhearted insistence of safety, the Alpha was all but screaming, "Look at me!" "I'm being an Alpha!" "I totally care."

Though Kyle figured that, for once, he and McGoven were of the same frame of mind—the rogue had been right to be skeptical.

Any concern Lukka showed the Connors girl was purely for show. The comforting words sounded hollow. His "reassuring" touch was more restraining than anything else.

"Where is the rogue?" he asked again.

Loren Connors blinked, turning toward a section of the woods.

Lukka stiffened, his nostrils flaring. "Fan out," he told his men—those who had been patrolling this boundary of the territory. "He's close. I can smell the bastard."

Showtime, Kyle thought coldly. After all, this was the main event he had been itching to see.

Not the rescue of some damsel in distress, but *this*—the big bad Bill McGoven about to be verbally spanked—all before being put down for the crime of being an "incorrigible rogue." He had some damn nerve venturing this close to their doorstep. At least there was no need to travel to that shithole human town. Kyle just wished they had brought cake and ice cream to celebrate this occasion.

At the girl's indication, Lukka started forward. "Stay back," he told them—not that Kyle listened.

Eyes narrowed, he brushed past Loren Connors and headed along a break in the tree cover. Sure enough, none other than McGoven himself was in the process of boldly advancing. Even now, he sported that infamous, stony expression, as cocky as ever.

Lukka seethed. "You have some damn nerve showing up here." He raised his voice so that it would carry to the crowd that had more than likely gathered, watching the chaos from the shadows. "You've broken a lot of rules, William McGoven. You took a mate without consent and trespassed on another Alpha's territory. You've committed murder—"

Kyle really had to hold in a snicker at this point—as if that pansy-assed bastard would ever *murder* someone without the instinctive urge of the mating bond. Only a real man, and a true lycan at that, could do what was needed to be done for the greater good and all that shit.

Kyle was pretty insistent that McGoven's eventual death would be for the good of *everyone.* He couldn't even bring himself to shed a tear at the fact that—technically speaking—the rogue had done nothing wrong.

It was all in the details anyway, like that random bastard he'd killed on Eislander territory.

Somebody had to do the dirty work.

"For all of these crimes," Lukka went on, in a tone that practically dripped satisfaction. "You will receive death. Do you understand?"

For someone who was facing the end of his road, McGoven looked pretty damn smug.

"You came yourself. It took you long enough…" His voice was soft, not out of fear—McGoven just didn't think Lukka was worth the effort. Of shouting. Of any anger at all. "You really didn't think I would make this easy, did you? You want me? Then face me. I challenge you here and now, before these witnesses. For the position of Alpha."

Kyle didn't believe his ears at first.

Not until he saw Lukka's reaction. He sputtered. "You can't—"

"I am," Bill said over him. "Tomorrow night. In the heart of the territory before the pack. We settle this the way it's been done for generations. One on one combat for the right to lead."

"And I'm supposed to be at the beck and call of a disgraced rogue?"

"If you want confirmation that I will return on good faith, you have the one person who will assure I will. I also want assurances that Sonia Carlisle is alive."

Kyle couldn't remain silent any longer. "You dare to make demands of us?"

"This isn't a demand. This is a promise." He nodded toward Loren, raising his voice for her benefit alone. "She will serve as my witness. I fight for her, and for the good of the pack."

Were they on that shithole farm, Kyle knew that Lukka would dispatch the bastard with little forethought. But here…

There were too many witnesses. Too many mouths to silence.

And that seemed to be exactly what the bastard McGoven wanted.

Kyle might have been impressed somewhere beneath the hate. Then he came to his senses—McGoven would never sink to such tricks.

He might break a nail or something.

Regardless of his intent, this little stunt would work in McGoven's favor. Word most likely was already traveling back to the heart of the territory. Any way they sliced it—there was no way in hell Lukka could avoid it now.

"And if anything happens to her between now and tomorrow," McGoven added. "I will kill you."

"Take her through the main entrance," Lukka snarled. "I'll join you later."

Kyle approached the girl, biting his tongue. He suspected Lukka would run for cover and plot a way out of this.

No way in hell would the bastard submit to a fair challenge, not that Kyle blamed him.

William McGoven didn't deserve an ounce of honor. He never had.

oren didn't know whether to celebrate or panic. Their plan had worked well enough to lure Lukka out into the open and convince him to accept the challenge. But now what?

As the adrenaline wore off, doubt crept in.

There was no going back. For McGoven's sake, she needed to ensure that nothing went wrong between now and tomorrow night.

A feat she was starting to realize was a very tall ask.

While she pushed for this plan, she wasn't foolish enough to suspect she would be safe behind the pack's boundaries. Not for a second. Even the overall landscape seemed to drive in the danger she was in. Gone was that rugged beauty that had captivated her earlier. This time of the day, very little light pierced the cover of trees overhead, rendering the landscape immeasurably more hostile.

She couldn't see much. Her only sense of reference was that they were on a road that winded through a thicker, inhospitable section of forest. Kyle stood ahead of her while another man took up the rear, radiating caution with every step.

The scene flashed her back to the night somewhere near these very woods, where the man guiding her now had left her alone to die.

"You're no longer needed," Kyle said abruptly, addressing the other man accompanying them. "Get back to your post."

The man acquiesced with a grunt, and Loren felt the hairs on the back of her neck stand on end as he retreated.

Was history about to repeat itself?

As they rounded a bend in the road, a massive wooden fence came into view, distracting her from her fear. Now she saw why Bill had been so worried about drawing Lukka into the open. This barrier was formidable, almost as tall as the nearby trees. Like some winding part of the landscape, it wove into the forest, blending in seamlessly with the shadows.

Just as daunting, was the metal gate presumably serving as the entrance to the territory beyond. Nailed to its front was a faded sign, barely visible through the dark, that read, "Black Mountain National Reserve."

That façade might have been easy to believe—especially to the average passerby—but two men stood on either side of the road, broadcasting alertness well beyond that of a typical park ranger. Tall, they cast long, lean shadows over the earth, bright eyes glowing.

"What's going on?" one of them demanded. "Where is Lukka?"

"Open the gate," Kyle commanded, avoiding the question. "Then go watch the border. Anyone approaches who isn't one of us, you attack. No questions asked."

Loren wondered if that were usual procedure before a challenge, though she tried not to let any doubt dissuade her.

"Yes, sir." The man and his partner rushed to open the gate, grunting with the effort it took to move the heavy sheets of metal. Once finished, they cleared the road, allowing unfettered access to the land beyond.

"Welcome to Black Mountain," Kyle said dryly.

As she peered over his shoulder, Loren was surprised to find only a gravel road stretching onward through a seemingly endless swath of trees. Already rushing to meet them, though, was a familiar figure whose appearance made her sigh in relief.

"Loren!" Sonia ran to them, panting with the effort. Her dark hair streamed behind her, her chest heaving as if she ran all this way for who knew how long. "What are you doing here?"

"Being rescued," Kyle snapped. "What a lucky coincidence that you show up for the welcome party. I'm taking her to the main house. This doesn't concern you, Carlisle—"

"Where is Bill? Is he—" Sonia seemed to stop herself from voicing the worst-case scenario. Her eyes couldn't disguise her fear, however, and they darted nervously to the yawning landscape beyond the still open gate. "Where is Lukka? What's going on?"

"You're impeding official business," Kyle replied. "Though I'm sure you and McGoven planned this down to the last detail. Ignorance doesn't suit you. Now move."

"No." Sonia placed a hand protectively on Loren's shoulder before Kyle could reach for her first. Thin and lithe, she easily slipped between them, a surprising match for the larger man's bulk. "No matter what's going on, there is no need to rile the entire pack and create a ruckus by parading a newcomer through the heart of the territory during supper. She can stay with me until Lukka can come for her himself. If he has a problem with it, he can tell me so in person."

Kyle raised a reddish eyebrow, and Loren was sure he'd refuse. Instead, he nodded, displaying his hands in a gesture of surrender. "Fine. Have it your way. Just to be on the safe side, I'll keep watch to make sure no one enters or leaves your cabin. Sleep tight. Tomorrow, we will make sure she's protected during the challenge."

"Challenge?" Sonia's eyes widened, and she swayed as if struck. "You mean… Bill?"

Kyle laughed, pushing past her. "I suggest you stay in tonight, Sonia. Because if you or your guest leave, I'll be watching. No need to cast doubt on tomorrow's proceedings, right?"

Without addressing him, Sonia took Loren by the arm. Behind them, the doors to the gate rattled as the two men rushed to close them again.

"Come on. There's no use worrying out here," Sonia whispered above the clamor. "We should head to my cabin. There, we can talk, and you can tell me exactly what the hell is going on."

Loren relented with a nod, allowing the older woman to guide her down the gravel road. The two men remained on the other side of the gate, and no one else was in view. Even so, she could sense countless pairs of eyes watching their every step.

If she'd been overly optimistic before, this moment reinforced that now was not the time to celebrate—and seeing this plan through would be nowhere near an easy feat to pull off.

She could only hope that Bill had evaded any tricks Lukka threw his way.

They would need all of his strength, and then some.

*L*etting her go was pure hell. Bill dug his heels into the earth to keep from following—right away, at least. Fear wasn't what held him back—not even respect for the old laws that supposedly dictated Lukka couldn't hurt her. It was respect for Loren alone that tempered him. After all, this was *her* plan.

He was merely along for the ride.

Though while he owed her his trust, he didn't dare underestimate Kyle or Lukka one damn bit. They wouldn't take this challenge lying down. As far as allies went, though, he didn't have many options—which was where phase two of Loren's plan came into play.

Providing he could enact it in time.

The obstacles were already mounting. If he knew Lukka, the bastard would have sent scouts on his trail—and he wouldn't put it past the Alpha to have him killed before the time came. Stripping his clothing, he shifted and took off in a full sprint that few short of the strongest scouts could match.

Fear pulsed through him anyway as Loren's fate weighed heavily on his mind, but the last thing he expected to feel, seeped into his veins in a slow but steady trickle—excitement? Joy, even? It had been so long since the last time he'd traversed these forests. Predictably, the earth hadn't changed much since then, but in a natural, gradual way. It was much like visiting an old friend who had matured in his absence. By the time he reached the very edge of the boundary, his heart swelled with painful nostalgia.

So much for honoring his role as a rogue. Fear was the real reason that kept him away. Fear of what might happen when he smelled the mountain air and neared his ancestral home again.

Being here, so close to the land he'd grown up on, he couldn't remember his reasons for leaving in the first place. For a second, he longed to breach the border, punishment be damned.

He was relieved when a figure finally broke the underbrush nearby, displaying familiar youthful energy. Micha. With one look, Bill drew his focus back to the task at hand, though it was harder than he would have thought to shift direction away from Black Mountain. Albeit, toward a far more dangerous strip of territory.

Even Micha's presence didn't lessen the insanity of what he planned.

If the Eislanders weren't already paying attention to their neighbor's borders, Bill would give them a good reason to. Together, he and Micha covered miles in minutes. As he neared the ragged plains the Eislanders called home, he boldly skirted their outer limits, putting every sentry on red alert.

Good.

He could only hope the provocation paid off as he finally stopped, just beyond the reach of both territories. Micha lurked nearby, acting as his lookout.

Though, an Eislander response was exactly what they wanted —needed.

Seconds ruthlessly ticked by. Minutes. As time stretched on, he strained his ears for any sign of trouble. True to her word, Loren kept a wall between them—but he could sense her beyond it as if peering through a sheet of frosted glass.

She had to be deep inside the territory by now. Would she be at Sonia's? Or would that bastard, Lukka, put her somewhere else?

A part of him bristled at waiting. He didn't trust Lukka further than he could throw him. Besides, he still knew all the old exits...the secret ways in. All he had to do was sneak in, seek out her scent, find her.

Forget his role in her plan. It was taking too damn long.

A rustle of motion was the only warning that someone approached, and he snapped into a fighting stance. They weren't a sentry. The intruder hadn't bothered to disguise their scent, and he recognized it easily. Within seconds, he was back in human form, lurching to his feet.

"Took you long enough," he rasped at the tree line.

"Well, you certainly have more balls than I gave you credit for." The Eislander, Eric, stepped from the shadows, his eyes glowing in the darkness. He had exchanged the nondescript clothing for a black tracksuit that seemed to suit him far better. At least this way, he resembled what he truly was—a dangerous threat, at home in the shadows.

"That was some stunt you just pulled," he said softly, jerking his chin in the general direction of Black Mountain.

"So, you've heard." Bill raised an eyebrow, though he didn't know whether to be impressed or alarmed that the Eislanders were so well versed in their neighbor's political drama.

"I've heard that you signed yourself up for what some might call a suicide mission." Eric inclined his head, and Bill couldn't tell what he thought. Not even a hint. "After what I'm sure you learned last night, I can't say I'm surprised by the route you've taken. But why come here now?" His tone dropped an octave. "Is this your way of declaring war on not just your own pack, but the Eislanders as well?"

"No." Bill forced some semblance of respect into his voice. "That was my way of getting your attention. You sent us to that Scolera for proof? Well, you got it, and if you intend to make amends to Loren for your Alpha leaving her in obscurity for eighteen fucking years, I have a few ideas of where to start."

"Oh?" The man scoffed. "And where do we come in? You think we would intervene in an official challenge? I hate to hide behind tradition in this instance, but some laws cannot be undone. Not even by you."

"Lukka isn't reckless enough to circumvent an honest challenge if it's made in view of the others," Bill pointed out. That was their hope, anyway. "He had no choice but to accept. That doesn't mean he has to oblige by it. In fact, I don't expect him to."

"So why come here? Without your mate, I see. I hope she's somewhere safe if you took on your Alpha directly."

Now came the tricky part.

"She's in Black Mountain as my witness," Bill said.

Eric chuckled, shaking his head in disbelief. "So, she's as good as dead, then. Have you lost your mind?"

"No," Bill countered, though a part of him hissed that same insult. "I trust that she can handle herself. But she has faith that your pack might owe her some shred of loyalty. What else can you do? Hide in your territory hoping that Lukka doesn't turn on you next?"

The man went silent just as the wind picked up, bringing a newer scent along with it. Bill tensed, picking up Micha's alarm. They had company.

"No," Eric finally said. He stepped forward, raising his voice to address whoever might be lurking behind him. "*We* don't plan on waiting at all."

Bill didn't even have time to react as the second intruder made himself known. They took their time approaching, partially hidden behind the trees.

This is it, he thought grimly. So much for Loren's plan—apparently, the Eislanders didn't want to cooperate. Oh well. He wouldn't go down without a fight.

Growling low in his throat, he crouched, intending to invoke the shift, while he observed his opponent from a distance. Their eyes were the first thing he saw clearly.

But their *hazel* hue caught his attention.

Abruptly, he stood upright and lowered his head with the minimal amount of respect he could muster. "Loreck Eislander."

Stepping into full view, the man didn't return the gesture, and Bill feared that Lukka was the least of his problems. He was dressed in a similar ensemble as his beta, his dark hair unbound, his steps firm with unmistakable strength.

"So, you are William McGoven," the Alpha said, his voice a guttural baritone. "Give me one reason why I shouldn't kill you."

It was a good thing, then, that Bill could think of several. Regardless, in the end, he decided to state just one.

"I am the mate of your heir. The daughter you abandoned."

36

Sonia lived among a lonely stretch of trees, along what appeared to be the edge of the territory. Her small cabin looked peaceful, nestled in a pool of growing moonlight. For all intents and purposes, it resembled McGoven's farm haven in New Walsh, isolated from any prominent structures.

"Let's get inside," Sonia suggested, unlocking the front door. "It looks like we have company."

Loren looked over her shoulder. Kyle had kept his word, it seemed. Farther down the road, three men remained at a distance, just watching.

Waiting.

As she followed Sonia inside, she was surprised to find that the interior was much smaller than even Fred Connors' house—though way more lived in, with delicate homey touches. With every new observation, it was harder to contain her surprise. Bill told her once that the pack territory was deceptively normal. He hadn't been lying. All in all, the cabin contained the same amenities any house in New Walsh might have. The only noticeable difference was that everything was made of wood, from the furniture to the floor.

Sonia flitted about the small living room and made a show of closing every window and drawing the curtains closed. Only then did she face Loren with a heavy sigh.

"What are you doing here, really? Goodness, we're just lucky I had the window open and caught your scent in time to intervene." Her voice sounded hoarse. "Is Bill… Is he?"

"He's okay," Loren said tactfully. "He's issued a challenge scheduled to take place tomorrow night. I am his…witness."

The term still felt strange on her tongue, but Sonia reacted to it instantly.

"You? Tomorrow?" She exhaled and sank onto a couch with a wooden frame. "My God. He's really going through with it." Her tone was a restrained mixture of hope and fear—but Loren didn't miss the way those blue eyes warily took her in. "I was praying he would go through with it. But still… Lukka won't take this lying down. I'm surprised Bill even let you go. He must be furious."

Loren bit her lip, unsure of how much to reveal. In the end, she settled on a vague explanation. "I ran from him. But he was worried about you. He was afraid Lukka might have hurt you."

Sonia scoffed. "I'd like to see him try. Though he has had my every move watched. I'm sure if you look carefully, you'll note a handful of his men lurking beyond the tree line."

She approached the nearest window and withdrew a sliver of the curtain. The road was now clear, and nothing of substance stood out from the swaths of emerald forest. Not at first. As if on cue, however, a man appeared in a gap between two trees without bothering to hide.

"You see? Though, if you're here… Bill is serious." Sonia's eyes widened, and she raked a trembling hand through her hair. "Well, then it looks like I can't let you out of my sight. Come on. I'll get you something clean to wear at least—" She darted down a hallway and reappeared with a pile of folded clothes. "Get dressed. Then I'll fix you something to eat, and we can try to figure out how the hell to get out of this mess."

"That's the thing," Loren said cautiously. "We already have a plan. Mine."

"Oh?" Sonia raised an eyebrow, but it wasn't obvious if she were skeptical or intrigued. "Well then, we definitely need to talk. The bathroom is down the hall. Take your time."

Loren followed her directions and entered the modest room. With trembling fingers, she gripped the edge of the sink, and for a second—just one—she let the mounting doubts creep in.

She was too weak. Without Bill, what could she do?

Even as she indulged the fear, she remembered his strength. His heat. His body against hers…

The weight of what happened between them felt more than any trivial biological term some might call it by. More than a kiss. More than sex.

He had entrusted himself to her, and she couldn't lose sight of that now. With a heavy sigh, she looked up, finally facing the mirror, and did a double take.

The girl staring back at her wasn't the beaten, broken Loren Connors she was used to seeing every day. She didn't even recognize herself. Her bruises were gone, the scratches faded. She had no idea why, until she remembered that McGoven and Micha had seemed to heal after they shifted.

On second glance, this new Loren wasn't completely flawless. The old scars were still there, telling a silent tale of too many beatings to count, and a hint of fear still haunted those hazel eyes. Still, it was easier than she would have thought to shrug off the unease and get dressed in Sonia's borrowed clothing.

As she reentered the hall, Sonia's voice rang out.

"Loren? I'm in the kitchen."

The cabin seemed to be one long level, with large windows looking out into a landscape that appeared bluish in the twilight glow. The kitchen looked clean, though lived in. Magnets covered the fridge, and appliances cluttered the counters.

Sonia watched her from over the rim of a steaming mug of coffee she held in her hands. Meat seemed to be frying behind her in a pan on the stove, but it sizzled unattended. For once, even cooking wasn't enough to soothe Sonia's emotions.

"What a mess." With a sigh, the woman set her mug down and crossed her arms. "I'm sure you and Bill have a plan of action, but I need to know. Ignore those spying bastards outside. It's just you and me here. What is his end game?"

Loren drew in a steadying breath. "He's challenging Lukka for the pack, but he's worried that he won't face him on an even playing field. So, he made sure to issue the challenge in front of witnesses."

Sonia's eyes widened. "And he used you as the bait to lure Lukka out into the open. Fuck!" With a sound of exasperation, she stood and marched from one end of the kitchen to the other. "I've been out of the loop. Lukka's kept me on a leash—I think he knows where my true loyalties lie. I've barely been able to take a walk without them watching me, but I know there is support out there for Bill. But if we're to capitalize on it, we need to move. Fast. There are people I need to talk to, but doing so now would be too suspicious."

Loren paced as well, picking up on her nervous energy. "How can I help?"

"You can't. No…" Sonia chewed on her lower lip. "He'd kill me if I even thought about letting you anywhere near a treason plot—"

"I'm here," Loren said bluntly. "It's a bit too late for that. Let me do something."

Something other than sitting in a cage like a damsel in distress awaiting her rescue.

"Fine." Sonia braced her hands against the nearest counter, her head bowed, knuckles white. "There is one thing you can do—stay safe," she said quietly. "Lukka or Kyle will come for you. I know it. If the challenge is tomorrow, they might try to lure you to the main house before then. In usual circumstances, that wouldn't be unheard of. As a witness, your duty is to serve as a neutral party. But where Kyle is involved, I wouldn't let my guard down for a second."

"What happened between him and Bill? It seems…personal," Loren said, though she suspected that was an understatement.

Sonia's sigh cemented that belief. "It's complicated. I'm sure Bill has told you about Emma?"

Loren nodded, though she couldn't suppress a painful mixture of guilt and envy. It felt wrong to be jealous of someone who was gone. Even a little.

"She was Kyle's twin," Sonia said. "I don't think he ever forgave Bill for what happened to her. It's a petty feud, but grief can make people do twisted things…"

Genuine pain echoed in her voice. Suddenly, she shook her head and stepped back from the counter. "It doesn't matter now. All that does is keeping you safe. God, I don't even know what to—"

"I can go with them." Loren's voice sounded so rough to her own ears that she swallowed as Sonia whirled to face her. "With their focus on me, they won't be watching you."

"And if they hurt you?" Sonia countered. "I can't promise you that they won't. In fact… It might be their plan. Goodness, Bill should have never let you come here—"

"I can handle myself," Loren said with a confidence she didn't feel. "You do what you need to do. Let me distract them."

Sonia didn't agree to the plan outright.

But she didn't challenge it, either.

yle was celebrating. Sure, he was alone, no decorations in sight. Even so, this was an occasion requiring commemoration. For that very reason, he'd taken up on the first floor of the main house, his feet propped against a desk in the study while he sipped liquor directly from the bottle.

Hurray.

It was important to cherish every victory, however short-lived and half-assed it might have been, right? And the fact of the matter was that they had *beaten* Bill McGoven.

By nightfall tomorrow, once and for all, the bastard would be put out of his misery in front of the entire pack. Though, why Lukka had chosen to waste said time on pretending to heed the rules of an official challenge?

Well…

Kyle tried not to include *brooding* in his celebratory plans.

After all, he wasn't an Alpha. Scheming and evil planning weren't his forte—his job was to put those plans into action, no questions asked.

"I hope you're enjoying yourself."

Kyle winced as his entire body prickled with the awareness of his Alpha. He looked up to find the man in question watching him from across the room. With a sigh, he wiped his lips with the back of his hand but wasn't inclined to stand to attention like a good little soldier.

Yet.

"Hphm." Lukka glanced around, blue eyes deceptively bright, demeanor relaxed—though Kyle wasn't fooled. "And here I was thinking that you would be upset. After all, McGoven issued a direct challenge, despite your clever little murder scheme. He wouldn't do so if he didn't have the Eislanders on his side already."

Mentally, Kyle rolled his eyes, preparing for some lecture on "loose ends" and shit. As if he didn't already know that. He hadn't been unable to sleep at night thinking of that bastard roaming free.

But hey, he was trying to "look on the bright side" and "be optimistic."

Which scenario would be more satisfying?

Tearing apart McGoven himself or watching the man be ripped to shreds by the very people he had once been hand-picked to lead?

Maybe if he drank enough, the latter option might sound more appealing…

"I'm sure you have nothing to fear," he grumbled, fighting to keep his tone under control. A flash of warning shot through his chest anyway. To distract from it, he snatched a bottle at random from the desk, tore off the cap, and downed it in three vicious gulps.

The low percentage of alcohol didn't affect him like heavy booze would. Maybe it had something to do with his metabolism that basically rendered the liquid into water before it ever had a chance to work its magic on his system?

Hmm, he thought, dropping the bottle to roll across the floor. *Lycan physiology...*

"I want him dead, Kyle." Lukka's tone bordered on the edge of a growl even while he maintained that nicey-nice posture. Anyone who walked in on them now might have thought that they were in the middle of a conversation about *sparkles* or something equally as asinine.

Not revenge, or subterfuge and...well, murder.

McGoven's would just be the beginning.

Kyle snatched another bottle from the desk, though this time, he cradled it in his palm, feeling the firm contours. *Easy,* he thought, frowning. It would have been damn easy to turn the delicate glass into glitter with the right amount of pressure, at the right spot, at the right time.

That was how most things in the world worked—so easily susceptible to damage by those who knew how to inflict it.

"Fuck a direct challenge. You force him to trespass. He will come after *her,*" Kyle said. "Either that or you let this charade go on so he can unman you in front of the entire pack. Before you panic and sick your minions on him, of course. Because that's what you're planning, isn't it?"

That stupid idea alone deserved another drink.

"Remember who you're speaking to, subordinate."

Alarm raced up and down his spine in response to the anger he could sense in the Alpha's tone—*dangerous ground.*

"I say we just kill her," Kyle grumbled, skirting an apology. "Frame it as the Eislanders. Use her body to goad McGoven into making a misstep. You kill two birds with one stone."

Mate or not, the murder would whip McGoven into a frenzy—making him about ten times the threat he already was—but the thought of seeing the bastard in that kind of pain was too tempting to resist. As far as Kyle was concerned, sticking Loren Connors' head on a pike was a damn good plan of action.

Of course, it wouldn't be so easy. Still, he couldn't risk adding, "But you'll adhere to the old laws…right?"

Lukka shrugged. "Of course. I am bound to them. But you? I'm letting you off your leash."

Kyle blinked. "Huh?"

"Provoke him," Lukka snarled, turning around to face the doorway. "By any means necessary."

As Lukka left the room, Kyle finally lunged from his chair and snatched the very last bottle from the desk, wrenching off the cap with his teeth.

Suddenly, it had turned into a *real* celebration after all.

38

oren felt like a medieval prisoner, right before the executioner came calling. Anxiously, she hovered near the living room window, peering through the curtains at the empty road winding through the trees.

As the darkness grew, so did the tension weighing down the atmosphere.

Behind her, Sonia puttered in the kitchen. Every now and again Loren heard the thud of the cupboards being opened and shut, but neither party spoke a single word. She tried not to relive what the woman had said to her—keyword being *tried*. Every time she shut her eyes, she'd see *his* face, engrained right there behind her eyelids.

Had she done the right thing by pushing him to this point?

Or had she only offered herself up on a silver platter and heralded McGoven's doom?

The sound of a knock on the door snapped her from the thought. From the window, she could see nothing out of the ordinary. Still, another stern knock rattled the door and Sonia rushed to answer it.

From behind her, Loren couldn't see who waited on the other end, but Sonia stiffened, her entire body rigid.

"I thought he would come for her himself?" she croaked. "That's what the tradition—"

"He was…" an oily voice replied, and Loren had no trouble at all conjuring a pair of soulless brown eyes to go along with it. "But, lo' and behold, he decided to send me instead. Alpha business. You know the drill, eh Carlisle?"

Sonia didn't answer, but when she stood back, finally revealing the man standing in the doorway, Loren wasn't surprised.

Kyle's blood-red hair clashed with an ebony sky and enhanced by the darkness, his eyes glowed, as sharp as a hawk's. When he smiled, it was a cruel expression—all teeth, zero warmth.

"Loren Connors. Do I have permission to escort the female from your premises, Carlisle?" he asked Sonia. Something in his tone reminded Loren of a cat, impatiently toying with a mouse.

"I…" Sonia glanced over her shoulder, biting her lower lip—the only hint of unease. "He didn't send word that *you* were coming."

"Didn't he?" Kyle raised an eyebrow. "I didn't know that the Alpha had to answer to a subordinate, silly me. According to the laws of the challenge, she must be prepared to oversee tomorrow's ceremony, no matter who comes for her. Or do you object?"

He smiled, but a fool could tell that he wasn't joking. All his weight was balanced on the tips of his toes as if he would have liked nothing more than to barge into the cabin—whether Sonia "allowed" him to, or not.

"Lukka's the only one who has any 'business' with her," Sonia snapped. "I know tradition was never your forte, but I'm sure you know that much."

"Well, Lukka wanted me to take her…sightseeing, first," Kyle said, eyes glowing. "It's time this pup learns her place, in the pack, of course. When the challenge is over, Lukka wants her to get a feel for her 'new home.'"

Sonia didn't respond to the concealed threat, though her face visibly paled. With her body angled toward the door, she blocked Kyle out *physically,* but Loren sensed that—even in her own home—she couldn't deny him for long. Authority was ingrained in the way he held himself, chin in the air.

Maybe not an Alpha, Loren thought, but he definitely wasn't someone to be ignored.

"Fine." Sonia shoved the door open wider. "But remember the code, Kyle. She's an innocent—a witness, nothing more. It won't do good for anyone to proclaim an early victory."

"Have faith, Carlisle." Kyle's mirthless grin widened. "I'm sure our Alpha will prevail, especially against a rogue. Now—" He cut those gleaming eyes to Loren and jerked his head. *Come.* "It's time for you to see the big, bad world of pack life for yourself."

No longer was he smiling. His expression had fallen flat, mouth in a cold, hard line.

And, as she stepped out onto the porch, Loren couldn't help feeling that she had jumped right from the proverbial frying pan…

And into an inferno.

As if reading her mind, Kyle chuckled and he headed down the front path, leaving her to follow—but his final words reached her in an ominous murmur.

"Carlisle turned into a bit of a hermit when her father died. As a witness to an official challenge, you belong in the heart of the pack. Right where Lukka can keep an eye on you."

Loren didn't say a word as she followed him down the trail leading from the cabin. Instead, she tried her hardest to take in every little detail of her surroundings—every potential route of escape.

Initially, she tried utilizing the tricks Bill taught her while meeting with the strange woman in the woods. Breathe. Close her eyes. Trust in her instinct.

But her instinct went to war with a growing sense of foreboding.

Run, a part of her whispered. After living around dangerous men for more than half her life, she liked to think that she was an expert at picking them out of a crowd—and Kyle displayed all the wrong signs.

How did that old saying go? *If it walked like a duck and quacked like a duck...*

Using that logic, Kyle's aggressive stance and Sonia's reaction to him all but proclaimed, *quack!*

You're being paranoid, she tried to tell herself—but the thought didn't make it any less apparent that she was alone with him in the middle of nowhere.

Massive trees loomed overhead, and a carpeting of thick foliage swallowed everything else. Endless green and a colorless sky were all she could see, stretching in every direction. Sonia's house must have had its own generator because there wasn't as much as a telephone pole around—nor any trace of modern technology. Nothing but the long road ahead that seemed to stretch on for miles.

Storm clouds gathered on the horizon, a darker shade of ebony against a slightly lighter sky. It was cold enough that snow was just as likely to fall from them as rain—not that Kyle seemed concerned by the threat of either. He wasn't even wearing a jacket, but a T-shirt that showed off thick, solid muscle and, when they reached the point where Sonia's thin, gravel road fed into a larger one, his strides took on a slow, almost leisurely pace.

"It's one of the largest territories for miles," he announced in a husky purr while eyeing every tall pine they passed. "Plenty of rogues would kill to get their hands on it."

His boasting tone made that almost sound like a *good* thing—as if the threat of conflict was somehow more important than the land itself. But there was that word again. One that seemed to have been tossed around almost as frequently as "Alpha" and "mate."

"What makes someone a rogue?" Loren didn't know what in the hell possessed her to speak up. Her voice was soft, rising barely above a whisper.

Good, a part of her murmured. *Be meek. Let him think you're not a threat.*

"Rogues turn their backs on the pack way of life," Kyle said without turning around. "They live in *exile*—what? McGoven didn't tell you all about his sordid little past?"

When she didn't answer, he whirled to face her and flashed a chilling smile that made the tiny hairs at the nape of her neck stand on end. "Then, by all means, allow *me* to do the honors."

He paused in what Loren cynically figured was his way of adding a dramatic effect. Only a second later did his lips part to add, "Believe it or not, the dear and honorable Bill McGoven *killed* someone."

Ice washed over Loren as though a bucket of freezing water had been dumped on her head. She faltered, nearly tripping over her own feet, but Kyle continued, unconcerned.

"Not *literally*, of course," he said, sounding disappointed about that fact. "But in our world, there's no such thing as an 'accident.' There is only failure—and when it came to protecting his own mate, McGoven *failed*. You didn't think you were his first attempt at a mated life, did you?" He chuckled, shaking his head. "No. *Her* name was Emma."

His voice was strained as if he were speaking through gritted teeth, and Loren didn't miss the flash of pain that shot through his eyes.

"She was beautiful. Of course, a boy scout like McGoven was drawn to her. But in the end, he killed her—I don't give a damn what anyone else says. He let her *die*."

Die! The word hit the air like a blow just as several snowflakes began to drift down, glinting silver in the darkness.

"Your hero has more skeletons in his closet than you give him credit for," Kyle added in a tone darker than the clouds up above. "Come on."

He kept walking, leaving her no choice but to follow or be stranded.

She was so wrapped up in her own thoughts that she couldn't name the point when the road ended, and civilization began. At least, as much "civilization" that one could find on a mountain in the middle of the wilderness.

Objectively, it looked like a logger's camp, illuminated by a few streetlights and external lamps. The buildings were mostly made of wood, with a few simple ones made of aluminum siding scattered here and there. The structures were spread like a children's toy set, haphazardly with no rhyme or reason—almost as if a new home or building sprung up whenever and wherever it was convenient.

The ones that weren't close to the road were all connected by a slender maze of paths that twisted as intricately as a spider's web. In the center, overlooking it all, was a grand building on a hill. It too, was made of wood, but nearly every inch of it sported elegant carvings. Four stories high, it dwarfed all other nearby buildings.

"The pack house," Kyle explained, as they passed. "I bet you've never seen anything like that, before?"

Despite the taunt at her expense, Loren had to shake her head. Even the courthouse—New Walsh's tallest building—didn't look half as grand. From this distance, she could make out snarling faces carved into the two, massive wooden columns that supported the roof on either end—howling wolves.

"Come on."

She struggled to keep up as Kyle led her right through the makeshift town. They didn't run into very many people, but the few they did see were dressed in warm jackets and hats against the cold. None of them spoke, choosing to eye them warily instead.

Despite the scrutiny, she didn't feel relieved when the road curved and the watchful eyes faded from view.

No witnesses, a part of her whispered.

Kyle hadn't been exaggerating when he claimed the territory was massive. The distance from Sonia's alone had to have been more than several miles. Yet, no matter where she looked, there seemed to be *more* stretching on in every direction—more forest. More trees. More impassive sky. More emptiness.

Despite the beauty of the landscape, she felt increasingly uneasy as Kyle led her deeper into the forest, and the warm glow of the town center faded. Soon, they left the road altogether and had to pick their way through the underbrush bit by bit in total darkness.

Something's wrong. The warning prickled down the back of her spine like an itch she couldn't scratch. Insistent.

When they finally reached a wide, open clearing, the sense of unease only grew, and Loren forced herself to speak up. "Where are we?"

Kyle didn't answer.

He kept moving forward until his boots seemed to toe an invisible line, just near the edge of the field. There, he finally stopped and scanned the horizon, as if hunting for someone who might have been lurking out of sight.

"I bet you're out there," Loren thought she heard him growl into the wind. "Watching. Well, watch *this* McGoven, and know that you've failed, once again."

Without warning, he turned to face her, and Loren knew his expression all too well.

"I suggest you run," he told her, sounding miles away, even as he advanced, step by menacing step. "That will make this all the sweeter."

"What are you talking about?" Loren wasn't even sure how she was able to talk—let alone breathe—fear seized her lungs, squeezing the air from them. That tired, old mantra ran through her mind on replay—*run, run, run!*

"Oh, I think you know what," Kyle murmured. "I think you know *exactly* what."

He kept coming, even as she staggered back just as quickly. Only too late did she realize, as her back hit the bark of a tree, that she was blocked in.

"Well?" he wondered, still creeping closer, as a predator would on a bleeding, hapless doe. "Aren't you going to kiss your new mate?"

RUN.

Loren lunged. Her boots skidded, sending mud flying in every direction as she tried to dart past Kyle for the woods behind him. He caught her before she could even go a step. Harsh hands snagged her hair, yanking her backward and down onto the ground.

Dazed, she struck a patch of damp, icy grass just as a heavy boot slammed into the small of her back.

"Scream," Kyle suggested from above her, as casually as if this were nothing more than a game. Loren gasped, choking on the damp earth, as he knelt down, pressing his knee against her spine. "Go on. Maybe he'll even hear you if he hasn't already turned tail and run like the coward he is. Hell, maybe..." The knee dug in, twisting as it did so. "Maybe he'll come running to the rescue, big, strong Bill McGoven? I'll even give him a head start."

Wham! A sudden kick to her side forced her onto her back. Dazed, Loren blinked up at the sky as Kyle moved to stand over her.

"Why don't you and I talk for a while?" he proposed, still speaking with that eerie sense of calm. "I wouldn't want to rush him—he must be pretty busy, being a hero and saving damsels in distress, and all. So, let's have a little chat. Don't look so terrified," the man admonished. He chuckled when she shied back, instinctively pressing her body into the earth.

"When you're mated to me, I'll make sure that you won't remember a single thing. You'll be the same, stupid little pup you were with McGoven—and seeing you like that will *break* him," a smug chuckle revealed just what he thought of that prospect. "He'll probably even surrender himself like a good little hero, though I hope he fights. That bastard's death by my hand has been long overdue. After all…he did kill my sister."

His expression clouded over, as if he were seeing years into the past. Seeing another face where hers was. "I knew he wanted her. Everyone knew. He was Mr. Golden boy and Emma… She was perfect. Good. Kind. All the shit someone like him couldn't wait to prey on—" He laughed coldly, clenching his hands into fists. "I should have seen that. Fuck! I should have known. But I was fooled like the rest of them. I… I was happy for her. I thought that if anyone could protect her, it would have been him. But I was wrong," he went on in a deadly soft whisper, crouching over her. "He failed her. So, I think it's only fair that I take someone from *him.* And when McGoven's dead, Lukka can have you—"

Dead. The word snapped something inside of Loren, and it was like a dam breaking apart.

"No!"

Kyle scoffed at the sound, apparently pleased that she was finally playing along in his sick game—at least until she sharply drew up her knee, ramming him right between the legs. He rolled off her with a groan, and she shot to her feet, instinctively balancing her weight on the tips of her toes. McGoven's voice echoed through her mind. *Don't think. Don't hesitate. React!* Real or imagined? It didn't matter. Lunging into action, she took off across the clearing.

"Bitch!" She could hear Kyle behind her, staggering to his feet.

Don't look back, that dark, shadowy voice in her mind, warned— this time not McGoven's, but her own. *Focus! Run! Run, run, run…*

It took him longer to catch up to her this time. She had nearly made it over the boundary of the field when a hand snagged her collar, and she went flying.

"You'll pay for that," Kyle swore as she landed hard on her knees. Using his hand on her jacket for leverage, he began to purposefully tug until the seams tore beneath the strain. *Rrrrrip!*

No, no, no, no! Panic welled before Loren could help it. Memories jarred through her thoughts like blows, threatening to drown her in fear. Fred Connors' harsh hands on her bare skin. Older, darker memories she could never relive without screaming.

No, no, no…

With a grunt, Kyle knocked her legs out from under her, and she went down hard, coughing on mud and snow. One final yank, and he succeeded in tearing the jacket from her shoulders. She could feel his fingers tugging at her thermal next.

Hide, that old, familiar part of her whispered. *Curl up. Disappear. This isn't happening…*

A tendril of recognition shocked her—it was the same voice that had lulled her the night she killed Fred Connors. That same desperate urge to just give up. *Give in.* Kyle was too big —too strong. There was no way in hell that she could fight him…

Bill had been right all along. She'd confused his strength for her own. Alone, without his presence, she couldn't drown out the doubt.

She was too weak. Useless.

Give in.

"I wonder what McGoven will think when he sees you with me?" She heard Kyle remark. His hands had left her shirt and had begun to work on her pants instead, thick fingers attempting to slide beneath her waist in search of the zipper. "I can just picture the look on his face."

Loren could, too—silver eyes burning with rage, perhaps glaring from the body of a black wolf. He'd hate himself for ever letting her do this in the first place. For trusting that she could handle herself.

Just like that, the suffocating fear went away. Suddenly everything was lethally sharp and as crystal clear as the thick snowflakes that had begun to fall. McGoven would come—a part of her just knew he would. The same way she knew without a doubt that he would protect her. Defend. Fight. Die…

If she were to prove herself, it had to be now.

Kyle never expected her to move so fast, which was probably the only reason she managed to catch him off guard as she reached out behind her, nails drawn, and swiped blindly at his arm. The moment she felt the give of flesh beneath her fingertips, she dug in, raking down until she felt the warmth of blood.

"Fuck!" Kyle drew back with a hiss of pain, and Loren lurched to her feet—but for the first time, her only impulse wasn't to run.

Instead, she turned, facing Kyle as he crouched, snarling at the sight of his arm. The deep ruts left by her nails bled freely, leaving a metallic scent in the air, but fear didn't deter her from taking a step toward him. And then another. The wind tore at her hair, whipping it out behind her as she lifted her foot, swaying with the effort, and delivered a strong enough kick that he fell back.

He stared up at her, dazed as she balanced the sole of her boot on the center of his chest and crouched down, much like he had. After a second, he started to struggle, cursing as he attempted to shrug her off. "What the hell—"

Loren didn't have to raise a single finger to stop him. All she did was stare into those eyes and finally release the anger she supposed had been building within her all this time. Building during those dark years living with Uncle Bart, and the months living with Fred Connors… It flared, like a smoldering inferno, blazing white-hot.

Like a puppet with its strings cut, Kyle fell back. His head hit the ground with barely a *thump!* Before he could regroup, Loren allowed herself to utter only one, single word that flew from her tongue as easily as if she'd been born to say it.

"Submit."

It wasn't like the previous instance in the woods.

This time, uttering the word was merely a formality. A part of her surged, just as violently as his previous assault. Instead of hurting him physically, this penetration went deeper.

Into his mind? Thoughts flooded her conscious, but they weren't her own—or even like McGoven's. They were prickly, wrought with so much rage and hatred nausea churned her stomach as they unfolded.

So much anger.

So much loathing.

But beneath it all was a pain that took her breath away. She winced at the force of it, feeling tears prickle her eyes.

"N-No," she heard Kyle rasp, though his voice seemed to come from miles away. "No."

He tried to resist—she could feel it—much in the same way she fought against McGoven's commands what felt like a lifetime ago. But as she stared into his horrified gaze, Loren realized that the fight was over before it even began.

"You don't hate Bill," she croaked, feeling a mixture of shame and disgust wash over her in response. "You hate *him*."

An image came to mind, growing in clarity—blue eyes, blond hair, mocking smile. She wondered if Kyle was even aware of the subconscious truth nestled within his own mind.

"You always knew," she went on, as the color drained from the face of the man before her. He looked hollow. Broken.

"You just couldn't face it," she said. "You know what he did. You don't hate Bill for Emma's death. You… You hate him for—"

"Stop!" Kyle threw her off, scrambling to his knees. "Just stop!" His throat corded with the force of the shout, but he didn't make a move toward her.

"No." As she found her balance, Loren shook her head. "It's the truth. You hate Bill for leaving," she continued, swaying with the effort it took to remain standing. Somehow, she did, though Kyle slumped, his face downcast, body trembling. "For leaving him alive. The man truly responsible for your sister's death."

He said nothing, but he didn't need to. A connection still lingered between them, weaker than what existed between her and Bill. It wasn't powerful enough for her to touch his emotions, or sense them clearly.

Though, she knew that she'd spoken the truth. And he knew it, too.

"If you still want to honor Emma, you know how you can," she told him. "Because he expects you to help him, doesn't he? Lukka?"

It was getting harder to grasp his thoughts clearly. She could only glean fragments of their plan—though it seemed as twisted as any Bill might have feared.

Kyle flinched and lifted his head. His eyes blazed, but with a different, colder intensity.

"Even if I don't, someone else will," he rasped.

"Not if you beat them to it," Loren countered. "And if you truly want to honor your sister's memory, you won't have a choice."

39

Of all the places he might find himself on the road to redemption within the pack, little did Bill think he'd wind up here—in a circular room in the heart of a building far less ornate than any found in Black Mountain. Still, his entire body prickled with awareness and a grudging sort of respect only an Alpha could inspire.

One with several decades to his tenure, at least.

Why he'd followed the Eislanders into their territory, he had no idea. Either way, it was too late for doubt.

Here he stood, facing down Loreck Eislander himself.

"You heard me," he began, his voice hoarse. "If you doubt anything that I've said, then let me know now so I won't waste my time asking for your help."

He took a step, fully prepared to leave. The funny thing was…

Loreck didn't look doubtful, smug, or even enraged by the convoluted tale involving him, a rival, and a daughter he'd never met. Instead, the man frowned, his gaze fixated somewhere in the distance where no one else could follow.

The other man, Eric, cleared his throat, stepping forward from the corner he'd stood in before now. For once, his probing stare lacked the hostility Bill had become accustomed to. He merely seemed curious.

Though if that was a good development or not remained to be seen.

"What exactly do you want us to do?" he demanded. "Send our men to the border? That could trigger an outright war, and I'm sure your Alpha would love to use a distraction from your challenge."

"He would," Bill admitted. "But I don't need an army. I just need protection. Yours—" he addressed Loreck, who finally inclined his head to face him. "I'm sure Lukka has a trick up his sleeve. Be there as a witness. Make sure this unfolds fairly."

The man's expression was unreadable, and Bill felt a pinch of recognition in his gut. If he still didn't believe in a connection between this figure and Loren, one similarity put all doubt to bed —their eyes. They shared the same piercing intensity, boring into him before he could even think to guard against the intrusion.

Where Loren gazed at him with only that haunting earnest hope, this man harbored anything but.

"And why should I?" he countered, raising his chin. "You forget rogue—if what you claim is true, I should have every right to go for your throat."

For mating his daughter, of course.

Bill gritted his teeth, uncomfortable with the thought. Rather than cower, he raised his head, holding the leader's stare.

"I thought I was protecting her," he explained. "But, as it turns out, she's more than capable of protecting herself."

He explained the events leading up to Fred Connors' death and selected snippets of what happened after—some things, however, such as his genuine attraction, he held back.

Still, by the end of his tale, Loreck looked conflicted between disbelief and confusion.

"So, you think your Alpha framed you in order to have me intervene?"

Bill nodded. "I didn't kill anyone from your pack. Just the outsiders who threatened Loren."

"It's true," Eric said softly. "Jamal was killed, but I have reason to believe he was ambushed by someone else. While the bodies of the men he claimed to have fought weren't found initially, my contacts in Elkton alerted me of several mutilated bodies found in the next town over."

"Which brings us back to Lukka," Bill said, empowered by the revelations. "He needs to be stopped."

Loreck grunted. "You really believe your Alpha would listen to me?" His voice boomed throughout the room, sending a shiver down Bill's spine that he couldn't deny. "If so, you've been gone far too long."

"I don't trust Lukka to play fair," Bill countered. "But if he knows that at least part of his ruse has been uncovered, it might drive him into a corner."

"And what do you intend to do when he does retreat to said corner?" Loreck stood from behind a massive desk and began to pace. At least four men in addition to Eric were in attendance, watching silently. Their lack of reaction didn't put Bill at ease.

Not at all.

As Loreck neared his position, the older man fixed him with a cold stare that penetrated down to his core. "Will you fall back like you did before and fail to uphold the duty placed before you?"

Bill winced. Maybe he deserved that. "What about you?" he tossed back. "Did you really not know? About her? Your own blood?"

Any anger he still harbored toward the man sputtered and died in the face of his answering frown. As if snuffed out, the fire left the man's gaze, rendering him hollow.

"I won't pretend that I understand why your Alpha would do such a thing."

"But..." Eric stepped forward, his head lowered in respect. "I'm beginning to have an idea as to *how* he did it."

"How?" Bill exhaled, caught off guard by the sheer panic that welled in his chest. Even now, some small, childish part of him might have held hope that he'd gotten everything wrong. Lukas wasn't behind this—someone else had been the true culprit all along.

As Eric met his gaze, however, he surrendered to the inevitable. "Tell me," he rasped.

The man looked to his Alpha, who nodded in approval. They must have discussed this information before deciding to share it with him.

"The hermit you met with is a lycan by the name of Eilene Branshaw, sister to Eveline," Eric explained. "They, along with a brother, formed a band of rogue Scolera who ventured east, eager to seek refuge with one of the established packs in the area."

"I think I can guess where this is heading," Bill said gruffly. Loren, it seemed, wouldn't be entirely spared of violent family members. "The brother was the dangerous rogue who wrought havoc."

"Yes," Loreck said, taking over the tale. "He cut off contact with his sisters and began to feed on humans. Casualties mounted, and we had no choice but to form an alliance with anyone able to track him down. While few in number, and disorganized, Scolera wolves can be formidable and stealthy opponents."

"So, you had to form an alliance with Lukas Grehmaine," Bill supplied. "I know that part. What happened between you and Eveline?"

Loreck had a mastery of his expressions that Bill had encountered in few men. Regardless, even he couldn't disguise his reaction to that name—he winced, and his eyes took on a faraway gleam.

"Yes. I knew her," he said tersely. "She wanted admission into a pack. I thought she had decided to join mine... Then she vanished, and I always thought she'd returned west." His jaw tightened, his eyes narrowed. "I never thought..."

"There is something else," Eric said, steering the reins of the conversation. "Something that was never made public knowledge about the demise of the lone rogue." He looked to Loreck, again seeking permission to continue.

The Alpha, however, said nothing. Eric sighed and soldiered on anyway.

"With the help of the two sisters, we were able to devise traps, and learn the ways of Scolera hunting methods. But it wasn't enough. If we went that route, it would have taken weeks, if not months, to corner the rogue."

"All of that for one wolf?" Bill questioned, his skepticism apparent.

Eric scoffed. "More than once, I've been able to catch you off guard by utilizing only a fraction of what I learned from the Scolera. Imagine that skill, but mastered by someone much faster, and afflicted with an insatiable taste for human blood."

"I see your point," Bill admitted, wincing. He hated to acknowledge just how easily Eric had been able to infiltrate his own territory. Such a wolf would be a danger not just to humans, but to any nearby lycans foolish enough to stop him. "So, how did you track the wolf?"

Loreck inclined his head, his eyes ablaze as he and Eric shared a look.

"Don't be shy now," Bill snapped. "Let me guess—by using your deer urine trick?"

"No," Loreck said. "By using hunters."

"You… What?" It sounded insane. Desperate. "No. There is no way that Lukas would have—"

"Who do you think put us in contact with them?" Loreck snarled. "Lukas was a man who valued survival of his pack and his bloodline above all else. Even if that meant making an alliance with a lone hunter. It didn't matter to him either way."

Bill couldn't process it. This was a trick. A way to undermine his resolve by attacking one of the few bastions of his past he still held dear.

"No," he insisted, shaking his head. "I don't believe that. Not for a second."

"Then don't," Loreck said, lifting his shoulder in a dismissive shrug. "And let your mate and everyone else you pretend to give a damn about die. The time for wallowing in uncertainty is over. State now exactly what you expect from me. I won't have my people go to war with yours."

"I'm not asking you to," Bill replied. "I'm asking for—"

A wave of emotion barreled into him with the force of a punch, nearly taking him off his feet. He staggered and braced his hands against a nearby wall just to stay standing. Something was wrong. He could feel it. An ache tore through his chest, and only one thing could be the source of it—Loren had dropped her wall.

She was in danger.

"I need to go."

He tore from the room, exiting the building. In the darkness, few landmarks caught his eye, not that he needed any guidance to find his way. He merely fixated in the direction of Black Mountain and took off, shifting in seconds. Minutes later, he cleared the border, and he didn't even see his pursuer until they collided with him, knocking him off his feet.

"What are you doing?" Micha's bones audibly popped with the force of his change. He still sprouted a pelt of brown fur even as he lurched upright on human legs. "Are you crazy? What about waiting until tomorrow? If you go in there now, he'll have you ripped apart."

Bill growled. Whatever fear he'd felt had already vanished. He expanded his consciousness, seeking out Loren's, but ran into a wall. Her mind was closed off and out of reach. *Damn it!* Logic warned him that giving Lukka any excuse to question the validity of his challenge would backfire.

When he felt another foreboding tug at his gut, it was already too late.

He took off, sensing Micha on his heels and Naomi right behind him. They weren't his only company—he picked up the approach of at least two others racing from the direction of the Eislander territory.

But diplomacy would have to wait.

Barging onto Black Mountain in a blind rage would do no good in the end. But neither had trusting in honor for the past five years.

The time for restraint was over.

It was time to play dirty.

oren wasn't sure how she found her way back to the center of the pack territory alone. Her chest heaved, her skin slicked with sweat as her eyes adjusted to the tendrils of moonlight filtering through the trees. Despite the time of night, the winding streets snaking through the sparse buildings weren't deserted.

People streamed from various directions, all of them staring.

At her.

The fact that she was a stranger seemed to be a moot point. Her hair was a mess, her steps disjointed. Sonia's borrowed clothing was caked in mud and rumpled, but she didn't give a damn as to how she might look.

Tension laced the air, prickling beneath her skin. Something was wrong.

Though she didn't have to look far to find the source of the unease. She barely managed to crest the hill overlooking the heart of the territory's center when she noticed a black streak cutting across the landscape. Mid-lunge, the creature shifted, transforming into a man, bathed in shadow and silver.

Her heart throbbed with recognition. Bill.

But, for once, she wasn't his focus.

"Lukka!" he bellowed, his voice easily riding the wind. With a start, Loren recognized that he was advancing on the large ornate building Kyle had pointed out to her. Ablaze in the orange glow of lamplight, it resembled a wooden palace.

And Bill was an errant warrior ready to burn it to the ground. Watching him, her hold on their bond snapped. A wave of emotion flooded into her—his fear, his relief as he sensed her nearby. His grudging realization as to who might have caused her terror.

And his resolve to punish those responsible.

"Show yourself," he bellowed, eyes affixed to the towering structure before him. "Lukka!"

The growing crowd gathered, flooding the narrow streets, but he seemed unaffected, his head held high. Despite his nakedness, he radiated confidence that took her breath away. Unlike any man she'd ever met, he embodied the term Alpha exactly as Micha had described it.

A true leader.

Her heart throbbed as she navigated the crowd, rushing toward him. She was barely paces away when he whirled in her direction. Their eyes met, and Loren could feel the relief that washed over him—but the sight of the two men accompanying him made her stop short.

They came from the same direction he had, but were in human form, their steps slow and cautious. They weren't here to hurt Bill, it seemed. But for what purpose? Her nostrils flared as the wind blew their scents in her direction. One she recognized instantly—the man who intruded onto Bill's property uninvited. But the other?

She didn't know him. Yet… The way he moved sparked an overwhelming sense of déjà vu that rooted her to the spot. A sudden recognition came to mind. Was he Loreck Eislander?

Any emotion she might have felt at the prospect was quickly replaced by loathing, only it wasn't her own.

"You dare to trespass onto our property?" Lukka's voice was a gnarled hiss as he descended the steps of the main house. He still wore the same clothing from earlier, his eyes an icy blue. Streaming behind him were at least four men, their postures tense —but Kyle, predictably, wasn't among them.

"This is treason," the Alpha went on. "This is—"

"I tried to do this nobly by the rules," Bill said over him in a rich baritone that put the leader's to shame. "That's what your father would have wanted, or so I used to believe." He raised his voice to carry through the assembled crowd. Loren swallowed hard at the sight of him, boldly facing the obstacle in his path. But she could still sense his pain.

His ever-lingering doubts.

"I admired Lukas more than anyone," he confessed. "I always believed him to be just and fair—but, as it turns out, you two were more alike than I could ever imagine. You always resented me because of the threat I presented to you, but the truth is, Lukas had little faith in your ability to lead before he ever chose me as his successor."

Lukka visibly flinched, and a murmur went through the crowd, growing in intensity. Loren couldn't sense which side the general sentiment was on. Just an increasing feeling of alarm.

And fear—especially as the two Eislanders drew near. Several men broke off from the crowd to stand menacingly in their path. None came to blows.

Yet.

"Like you, Lukas was willing to sacrifice anyone who might stand in his way for power," Bill continued, and Loren swiveled her head back to him. "Even an innocent. Your father decided to sabotage the heir of a rival leader, but you?"

He glowered at Lukka, his voice thick with disgust.

"You allow your own righthand man to attack a witness, merely to deter me."

Loren shivered at the rage she could hear in his voice as well as feel. It blew her mind that he had so easily discerned the truth merely from her haphazard thoughts.

Though, she could feel a mixture of emotions from him in return that her brain rushed to unravel. Anger, yes, but something else, mingled beneath. Determination?

"No more," Bill declared out loud, drawing her attention back to the present. "We fight here, and we fight now. I challenge you for the position of Alpha."

A shock went through every witness, rippling deeper than Loren figured was apparent to the naked eye. This was more than a simple statement.

It was a direct challenge to the way of life of every person living in this territory.

While she couldn't decipher much from the deafening din of voices, with every growing murmur, Lukka seemed to shrink. "Fine," he said. "You want to be released? I release you. You are no longer a rogue tied to the territory, free to resume your exile—"

"No." Bill shook his head, seeming more regal than his disgraced status would imply. Bathed in the glow of the full moon, only one word came to Loren's mind, worthy of describing him.

Lycan.

"My exile is over," he bellowed. "I am here to challenge you for the position of Alpha. Should I win, you step down."

Lukka's voice was a harsh shadow in comparison. "And if you lose?"

Bill met his gaze without flinching, forcing the other man to voice the outcome for him.

"If you lose, you die."

41

*L*ukka advanced on Bill's position as the crowd closed in, forming a circle around the pair. Loren noted women, men, and children among the watchers, their faces sporting varying degrees of fear and…

Excitement.

Tall and wiry, Lukka still managed to cut a striking figure as he stripped his shirt and faced Bill, his head lowered with determination.

Then, with seemingly no word spoken between them, both men shifted. A black wolf took the place of McGoven, growling low. Across from him was a leaner, more gracile creature with a golden pelt that blazed like sunlight.

From Bill's scattered recollections, Loren had no idea what to expect when it came to how a challenge might unfold. She sensed, however, that this one lacked any of the usual ceremony. All the better—the only thing that truly mattered was action over all else.

The first thing that struck her was the smell—musk tainted the air. Human sweat and a primal, animalistic undercurrent that made her nostrils itch. Then a growl drew her notice to the darker of the two wolves.

In a beautiful, chilling display, the creature threw back its head and howled.

The bloodcurdling lament echoed on the wind, and the sound seemed to trigger an avalanche of actions taking place simultaneously. The first was a swarm of people who seemed to come from nowhere, swelling the crowd three times its original size until Loren found herself fighting toward the center.

Someone larger muscled past her, knocking her off balance—only a stern grip on her arm saved her from falling.

"Careful!" That voice made her look up. Sure enough, a familiar figure appeared by her side seconds later as if drawn from thin air, his green eyes more serious than she'd ever seen them. Micha.

"Stay close," he warned, shouting to be heard over another howl —this one was shriller, as if answering the call of the black wolf. Lukka? As Loren struggled to keep up with the scene unfolding, she heard Micha mutter, "Get ready. This could get messy."

She hated to agree. With only a jacket slung over his waist, she suspected he'd shifted to arrive here in time. Not far behind him was a grim, fully clothed, Naomi followed by a panting Sonia who appeared in the distance, racing their way. Given that she wore only a thin sweater, Loren guessed she had been the source of Micha's makeshift ensemble.

How had they managed to get past the barriers?

Now wasn't the time to parse through the logistics. In the center of the chaos, the two beasts finally faced each other from either end of their makeshift ring. Displaying restless energy, they began to circle each other, fangs bared.

At a glance, the apparent mismatch of the two was painfully obvious. Lukka's form was smaller and compact, composed of solid muscle that rippled beneath a golden pelt. Visually, he seemed no match for McGoven's larger mass.

Without even an officiate or referee to signal the start of the combat, both wolves lunged.

Loren winced as they collided, her heart in her throat. It wasn't a fight as much as it was a beautiful dance of violence and muscle. Their bodies rippled in a grisly unison, as they grappled for control.

Loren bit her lip, wincing as McGoven growled, thrown back as Lukka collided with him. She had imagined what this moment would be like. None of her worst fears had come close. It was bloody. Almost instantly, scarlet speckled the road at their feet, and it became clear that, despite the size difference, both lycans seemed equally matched. Where McGoven was strong and domineering, Lukka was wiry and fast.

Lightning quick, his jaws latched over McGoven's side, and a howl ripped from him. Then, just as quickly, the black wolf turned the tables, putting the other on retreat. Snarling, he caught Lukka's leg between his jaws, biting so hard the latter yelped and threw him off.

But it wasn't over.

Suddenly, Lukka took off with McGoven nipping at his heels, disappearing beneath the trees.

"This is wrong," Sonia said fearfully. "This must be done in view of everyone. Lukka knows that. What the hell is he doing?"

Loren knew exactly the reason for the trick.

Ironically, she might have had her own plan in action—though it entirely depended on the one person other than Lukka who wanted Bill dead.

She could only pray that she'd reached him.

And that, beneath the hate, the love for his sister would prevail.

42

Bill ran blindly, despite every ounce of common sense he possessed warning him to go back. Pride wasn't the sole reason why he continued to give chase. Cynicism played a part—to back down now would be to admit defeat. Lukka would spin any ounce of hesitation to his benefit. Whether he liked it or not, he had no choice but to follow.

But he wasn't stupid.

This was a trap.

And, surprisingly, he suspected it wasn't the first time Lukka had employed such tricks against him. From the second he'd first learned that Lukas might have contacted a hunter, he hadn't been able to put it out of his mind. The man he knew and respected would have never stooped so low.

But his son would have. For five years, he never doubted the circumstances around Emma's death. Not once. But now?

The pieces were beginning to fall into place, and he didn't like the picture they formed. Not one damn bit. Even the prospect that

Lukka might have played a role in Emma's death made his blood boil.

And his heart constrict with guilt. How damn ironic. He'd left the pack out of shame, convinced that a true Alpha should have been able to lead without any regrets.

But as he gained on the creature bounding ahead of him, Bill felt none of the awe he'd always harbored for that sacred role. None of the respect a leader should command. He just felt hate.

From the direction of the compound, he could sense Loren's presence—her alarm, her fear, her aching need to help. But he didn't want her to take these emotions away.

He needed to feel them.

He needed to fight with every ounce of rage in his body. So, as Lukka slowed, still in lycan form, Bill skidded to a halt and shifted first, rising to his feet.

It was a risk. Lukka would be inherently faster, but he didn't care. He needed to hear the truth for himself, straight from the bastard's mouth.

"Did you do it?" he demanded. His voice echoed, betraying just how far on the outskirts of the territory Lukka had led him—Bill knew from memory that a steep cliff wasn't far away. Few from the compound would hear anything said from this distance.

The perfect spot for an ambush. Still, he pushed any concern from his mind, focusing only on Lukka.

"Did you call the hunters to our territory that day? I never even considered it. That was a step too far, even for you! But as I say it out loud…"

It sounded a lot more plausible than a random attack. A grunt of astonishment escaped him. How could he have been so damn naïve?

"You son of a bitch—"

Lukka growled, his eyes wild. Bill expected him to lunge then and there.

Instead, he shifted, his face contorted with rage. "You're insane," he hissed, rising to his feet. "And you accuse me of treachery, but what about yourself? You think I can't tell?" Suddenly, he cut his gaze beyond Bill's line of sight. "You're mated. This is no fair fight, and since you've forsaken the rules, so can I. Kyle!"

His gaze was fixed somewhere over Bill's shoulder, but he didn't even care enough to switch targets. *Mated.* The way he'd said that word made something click. It was as if a light switch had been flicked. Suddenly, he could see clearly into everything building to this moment. Everything.

"Was that why?" he croaked. "Why you wanted Emma dead? Because I would be less of a threat to you? You were so damn worried about facing me on an even footing that you killed her?"

It sounded so damn pathetic. So deranged.

And yet…

"Kyle!" Lukka's face reddened, the veins in his throat distended with exertion. "Help me, you son of a bitch!"

Bill scoffed, prepared for any assault that may approach from behind. Instead…nothing. If Lukka were bluffing, or if he truly expected his second-in-command to come to his aid, no one did.

The air was thin, devoid of any other scents. They were alone, far from the crowd a typical challenge should command.

Somehow, this felt more fitting.

Lukka didn't deserve a public death. Just this. Silence and darkness.

"We end this now." With a sigh, Bill faced his opponent and purged everything from his mind but the need to fight. To protect his mate at all costs.

In the end, he felt only a small shred of mercy before he lunged, shifting in mid-air while Lukka scrambled to do the same. Teeth parted, Bill put all doubts from his mind.

And he allowed instinct to take over completely before tearing into his prey.

It was strange. As he made his way through the trees in human form, his main concern was a growing list of all the rules he'd already broken.

All the traditions he'd desecrated.

How many things he would have to rebuild should he decide to truly take on the position of Alpha.

Triumph wasn't the feeling flooding his veins as he finally reached the outskirts of the main compound.

Just sheer exhaustion.

And relief, as Loren's mind melded with his once again.

43

The second Bill came into view, bloodied and naked, Loren ran to him. Before she could say a word, he caught her waist, holding her close. Pressed against him, she could sense just how exhausted he was. He favored his left side, and blood dripped freely down his arm.

Even so, the absence of Lukka betrayed who'd won their battle.

But the victor didn't look triumphant, in the slightest. For a moment, Loren rested her head against his shoulder, sensing the intensity of emotions that washed through him. Relief. Regret. Pain. She wished she could take them all away, every last agony. As if aware of the thought, he gently withdrew from her and moved to stand alone, drawing the focus of those nearby.

Already, most of the crowd had migrated toward them, their expressions wary in the moonlight.

Bill faced them all, seemingly to acknowledge every last person. Finally, he inclined his head, and spoke in a voice Loren could only remember him utilizing once before.

The day he wistfully reflected on what pack life meant to him.

"It isn't with arrogance that I accept the mantle of leading this pack," he said, letting his voice carry on the wind, "but humility. I once left these lands, believing it was for the greater good. But now, I see the folly and the sheer cowardice in that belief. I can't expect your loyalty after such a betrayal, but I am here, offering myself to all of you. An Alpha is not a ruthless leader, but a protector. A provider. I will do my best to understand the needs of Black Mountain and respond accordingly."

He looked beyond the growing circle of people to the few who lingered on the outskirts. Sonia. Micha and Naomi. Even the two men from the Eislander pack who lurked far beyond the rest.

"If you will have me. I will lead."

Utter silence fell, and Loren tensed. Could the pack still be loyal to Lukka?

The fear barely took root before several among the crowd sank into a crouch. Slowly, others followed in a silent display that said more than any verbal words of loyalty.

The display wasn't just for show. She could feel it—unwavering fealty being offered by everyone from the men down to the children.

Another pang of regret ripped through her, unlike anything she'd ever felt. Despite Bill's repeated insistence that she join a pack, it wasn't until that very moment that she understood exactly what she'd been missing.

This.

Luckily, there was plenty of hope she could experience it, still.

And that was only due to the man whose gaze locked with hers.

44

It was far easier than he would have thought—reintegrating into pack life despite years on the outside. Even the role of an Alpha felt as natural in some ways as breathing.

Which terrified the hell out of him.

There were, of course, old wounds that would be difficult to heal—the rift Lukka had forged between their pack and the Eislanders being one of them. For the time being, he would allow Loren to helm that front, letting her dictate how and when to initiate contact with Loreck.

Another bit of unfinished business was more internal, lingering in the memories he resisted even now. After five years, he could finally face the pain of Emma's death. She was still gone, but now he had grim closure that allowed him to recall those recollections of her without guilt.

Dwelling wasn't his aim—he only needed that last goodbye.

It was funny how the place looked the same as it had all those years ago—a meadow, just outside the reach of both the Eislander and Black Mountain territories, where he had spent pretty much his whole childhood. Back in those days, he'd come out here, into the fields, alone. Sometimes with Sonia. And then with her...

Before everything changed.

The tiny, simple grave, marked only by a round headstone, looked just the same. Worse even, it still *smelled* the same. Like the salty scent of the tears, he had shed for the first time in this very spot.

It was pathetic. But...if he tried hard enough, he could still smell her. That crisp, light scent of honey and rose—so different from Loren's.

Heart heavy, Bill sank down on the wet earth inches from the tombstone.

"Hey, Em," he called gruffly, reaching out to trail the worn name carved into the stone. "I... I'm sorry."

The pain didn't suddenly go away. He would always carry it.

But now, he could finally stop punishing himself for moving on. Emma was his past.

But the present?

It might hold just as much happiness for him.

No longer did he need to feel guilty. Just hopeful.

45

*J*ust a few days ago, killing Fred Connors had been the most traumatic experience of her life—in many ways, it still was. Loren knew she would have to deal with the long-term aftermath of that trauma later.

This moment, however, was a close second, though in a very different way.

Meeting Fred Connors had been a stilted, unpleasant experience wrought with disappointment. She could still remember the resigned way she'd accepted his cruelty without question. Already accustomed to violence, she had considered dodging blows a normal part of everyday life.

Loreck Eislander, however, didn't face her with a sneer or a brandished fist. He waited with his arms by his sides, on the other end of a small clearing on the outskirts of Black Mountain territory, far from any prying eyes.

Save for one—she could sense Bill nearby, lurking just out of sight—but she didn't feel the need to rely on him. Yet.

This moment felt too fragile. Too...delicate to risk even the presence of a third party.

As the minutes ticked by, Loren had no idea what to do or say. All she seemed capable of was staring at the man before her. Physically, Loreck looked so much older than Fred Connors. His brown hair was speckled with gray, his hazel eyes shrouded in wrinkles. Even so, he carried himself with confidence much like Bill's.

As if nothing in the world could defeat him.

Until they made eye contact. He swayed, his jaw tight, but Loren trembled with a similar unsteadiness. Bill had told her once that her father would recognize her on sight.

She didn't understand what he meant until she saw Loreck sigh, as though an invisible weight had been lifted off his shoulders.

"You look like her," he rasped, taking an unsteady step only to hesitate. One of his hands threatened to bridge the gap between them, his fingers trembling in the air.

Loren froze as tears prickled behind her eyes. Only recently had she been able to recall her mother more clearly, her round face, and gentle smile...

Whether they looked alike or not, she couldn't be sure, but Loreck seemed pained by the realization.

"I...." He shook his head as if fighting to find the right words. "He told me, but a part of me still doubted... I didn't know. I didn't know."

Her brain struggled to process his words. Was he relieved that it might have been true? Disappointed? Before she could fully comprehend, he moved.

And she followed. There wasn't any conscious thought to approach. Much like her interactions with Bill, instinct took over, and she had no choice but to give in.

She was in his arms without warning. An old, instinctive fear rose up before a sudden calm replaced it.

He won't hurt us, that inner voice murmured. *Family.* It was a new concept to her, but that primal instinct within her seemed to know exactly what it was supposed to feel like.

Not resigned terror, but a tentative sense of welcome.

Warily, she relented to the stiff embrace, settling against the unfamiliar contours of his larger, harder body.

"I didn't know," he said against her scalp. "But I'm here now... For what it's worth, I'm here."

She wasn't sure what to think of the offer. There would be time to mull over the details later. Either way, for the first time, fear wasn't the overriding emotion she felt toward the idea of having a father in her life again.

Just a strange sense of relief.

Maybe hope, too.

"How do you feel?" Bill asked as she rejoined him once Loreck retreated. Together, they lingered on the edge of the main compound, just as dawn was beginning to light the sky. In the short time since the challenge, he'd managed to change and shower away the dirt and grime, but one look at his face revealed the drastic shift in status he was struggling to adjust to.

Loren watched him through her lashes, struck by what a difference a few hours could make. Gone was the perpetual frown. His lips were in a softer line, not quite a smile. But close enough.

"I feel... Afraid," she admitted finally. Looking past him, she eyed a sliver of sky visible behind the canopy of branches overhead. "This is a lot to get used to."

An understatement if there ever were one. A part of her quivered at the many changes that were destined to come—forming a relationship with her newfound father being on that list.

"I know." Bill sighed and offered his hand, gripping hers gently. "I think we should get started with the introductions and go from there. Later, we can move onto the trickier subjects."

Like Kyle, and his eventual punishment for treason, should he return. Hours after Lukka's defeat, and no one had seen him anywhere within the territory. Loren felt a pinch of guilt that she might have been responsible for his escape.

Another dilemma to add to the growing pile.

For the time being, she pushed the stress aside, to focus on one of the few bright spots to look forward to.

"You plan on introducing me to everyone?" She wasn't sure if the sound trickling from her throat was a laugh or a groan.

Bill seemed to assume it was the former. "One step at a time," he said, guiding her to face him. "I think introductions would be a good place to start before we move onto diplomacy, at least."

There was so much requiring his input or judgment. Helming the pack and assessing the damage Lukka had done for one, let alone what would happen with Micha, or Naomi. Then there was the issue of where she truly belonged—on Black Mountain with Bill?

Or with Loreck Eislander…

Loren knew she would have dwelt on the milieu of problems for hours if it weren't for the strength seeping into her from an outside source.

It reassured her enough to push the worries aside for now.

Whatever awaited them, they would face it together.

As one. Eyeing the man across from her, she could think of several far worse positions to be in.

"I think I could use more lessons on the mating bond in the meantime," she suggested, feeling her cheeks ignite. Still, she felt a stubborn sense of pride as she met Bill's gaze and saw him swallow.

"That can be arranged…" He moved closer and released her hand in favor of palming her waist, groaning under his breath at the feel.

She inhaled in anticipation, lowering her gaze to his mouth. Their relationship still felt so strange, navigated on two planes at once—mental and physical. At the same time, nothing had ever seemed more natural. More right…

Until Bill frowned and cut his gaze to something behind her.

"One thing I miss about exile?" he said with a hint of amusement, "Privacy."

Loren whirled around to find what had his attention—namely, who.

Micha stood in between two trees, wearing an ill-fitting oversized shirt he must have borrowed and a pair of sweats. Sporting his sheepish grin, he appeared completely unaffected by any of the upheaval that had just taken place. At least, Loren would have thought so until she met his gaze and noted a hint of seriousness she wasn't used to finding there.

"I don't want to ruin the moment," he said, lowering his head in an unusual display of unease. "I just…"

"What is it?" Bill stood back from Loren and faced him, instantly embodying the leadership role he'd taken on. Even his voice changed, deepening an octave.

Micha shrugged. "Just that I won't stick around long, so there's no need to work me into your grand Alpha plans." He laughed, but Loren felt her eyes widen as the true meaning of his words sunk in.

"You're leaving?" she asked.

"You're more than welcome here," Bill said, inclining his head.

"I know," Micha said with a helpless shrug. "But… I think I need to take off for a while. Think things over."

Bill nodded as if he understood exactly what he meant. "Like returning to your pack?"

"Maybe…" Micha seemed to shrink beneath the question. After how he'd spoken of his old pack, Loren couldn't imagine him ever wanting to return. But when he finally looked up, his green eyes shone fiercely with determination. "I'm ready to think about it," he said.

"Good." Bill approached him, and for the first time, Loren realized that—despite the differences in their physical builds—they carried themselves the same way, heads held high, radiating steely confidence.

"If you ever need my help, you have it," Bill said. "In any way. I mean it."

Micha flashed his trademark smile. "I may have to take you up on that. One day. Don't worry, though. I'll stick around long enough to make sure Blondie doesn't get up to any trouble before you ship her back to high school." He cast a glance over his shoulder, in the direction of the main compound, presumably where Naomi happened to be.

Bill sighed. "She'll have a choice to make as well," he admitted. "So do you." His gaze shifted to Loren, and she held her breath, relishing his unusual brand of scrutiny.

In so many ways, helping him retake the pack had been just the beginning.

So much more lay ahead, but for once…

She wasn't afraid of what might come.

~ Want more from this world? Sign up for Lana's Mailing list to receive the latest updates on upcoming projects! ~

A WORD FROM THE AUTHOR

Hey there!

Thank you so much for reading! If you enjoyed the story, please leave a review and recommend the book to any friend you think would love this twisted world. You'd have my eternal gratitude. Even a short sentence goes a long way!

Then, come join the rest of us dark romance lovers in my Facebook Group where you can get snippets, sneak peeks of upcoming books and even help vote on aspects of future novels.

Come to the dark side:
https://www.facebook.com/groups/lanasbeautifulmonsters/

WANT MORE STUFF TO READ?
Join my newsletter and get a **free book**! Plus, you get to stay updated with any new releases, random giveaways and exclusive sneak peeks!
https://www.lanaskybooks.com/newsletter

Other Novels: https://lanaskybooks.com/

ABOUT THE AUTHOR

Lana Sky is a reclusive writer in the United States who spends most of her time daydreaming about complex male characters and parenting her Cockapoo Joey. She writes dark, twisted romance across several genres. Her titles include everything from mafia romance to vampires.

facebook.com/AuthorLanaSky

twitter.com/lanasky101

amazon.com/author/lanasky

pinterest.com/lanasky101

goodreads.com/lanasky

instagram.com/lanasky101

bookbub.com/authors/lana-sky

tiktok.com/@author_lana_sky

ALSO BY LANA SKY

For more titles by Lana Sky, please visit:

https://www.lanaskybooks.com